The Legend of
Mammy Jane

*An uneducated girl becomes
the lady of the manor in Appalachia*

Sibyl Jarvis
Pischke

Mountain Memories Books
Charleston, WV

©1995 Sybil Jean Jarvis Pischke

Originally published by the author.
Reprinted by Mountain Memories Books with permission.

ISBN-13: 978-0-938985-06-8
ISBN-10: 0-938985-06-X

Library of Congress Catalog Card Number: 81-82894

10 9 8 7 6 5 4 3 2

Printed in the United States of America

Distributed by:

West Virginia Book Company
1125 Central Avenue
Charleston, WV 25302
www.wvbookco.com

In memory of my grandmother
Labanna Jane Jarvis
and
my mother and father
Dock and Effie

In Appreciation

To my son Bill, who after reading my manuscript said: "Mother it's beautiful! Don't change a word."

To my brother Rex, after hearing it on eleven hours of tapes, told me—"It's too short."

To my cousin Anne, who cried after hearing HER chapter.

To my sister Irene for her courage in handling the throngs who have descended on Mammy Jane's house (now belonging to her), and for the many questions she answered after the first printing of *Mammy Jane*.

To the many friends who encouraged me when I became discouraged. And especially to all those who have read *Mammy Jane* and have written letters wanting to know more.

Thanks to all of you.

Sibyl

Hired Out

Labanna Jane was a bastard. There was no two ways about it, her pretty vivacious mother, Dolly, had lain with more than one. At times, she told Labanna Jane, that she was a Murphy, at other times a Mollahan. It was doubtful that pretty Dolly knew for sure, who her daughter's father was. Labanna Jane grew up nevertheless with a proud carriage and the instinct of a lady. The prettier she grew, the more haughty she carried herself.

The vivacious Dolly would look at her daughter and longingly wish for her the things she herself never had, and made a promise to guide her in her life toward a higher goal. Some handsome swain would give Dolly the eye, and off would go scatterbrained Dolly, all her good intentions forgotten. The good intentions came to a standstill, but for Labanna Jane the growing process continued. Dolly had given her a pretty name, a head of curly blond hair and blue eyes that caught the attention of most.

When Labanna Jane was ten, she took to the road, and got a job with a neighbor, not much better off than she was, for the "laying-in" of his wife. Helping the midwife with the delivery of the squiggly screaming baby, she took the wrinkled helpless thing to an out of the way corner and washed it. She dressed it in the flannel clothes the farmer's wife had ready and placed the baby at the mother's bosom.

While the midwife fussed over the mother, Labanna Jane took over the household and headed for the kitchen and the pile of dishes that had been there for several days.

Water was already boiling, it was needed for the "laying-in" and birthing. Hard work, even at ten years old, was no stranger to Labanna Jane. She soon had the dishes stacked neatly ready to cook vittles for the family. Looked as though they hadn't had a meal for a couple of days, she found a slab of fatback on a cluttered pantry shelf, quickly sliced it and rolled it in meal to fry. Grabbing a large brown bowl, she sifted the meal for corn bread,

1

added salt, baking powder and some thick buttermilk, a pinch of soda, an egg, poured bacon grease in a heavy cast-iron pan and had a corn pone in the oven in no time. She then turned her attention to the frying of the meat. She found butter and a big crock of apple butter which she added to the long family table. At a "laying-in," the midwife usually stayed for the evening supper and it was expected to be a little extra. Even though Labanna Jane was young she could put a tasty meal on the table better than some farmers' wives could. In this household, there was more than she had at home to work with and she made the most of it.

She looked out the window seeing the farmer coming in with a big bucket of milk and an old basket bulging with vegetables. At the door he handed in his load to Labanna Jane. Taking a head of cabbage, she chopped a big bowlful for cole slaw, mixed a vinegar dressing and added that to the meal. Good smells were coming from the kitchen with the corn pone in the oven and the fatback frying on the stove.

She could hear the younguns in the farmyard returning from a neighbor farm, where they had been sent while their mother was in labor. The farmer had finished his chores and she could hear him at the pump washing up. She knew from experience that a man wanted his supper as soon as he washed up.

Labanna Jane dropped a couple of eggs into the teakettle for the new mother. She meant to give her a little extra nice supper after what she had seen her go through that afternoon. Taking the prettiest plate and cup she could find, she started dishing up and put choice pieces of fatback on the plate, trying to make it look as neat and nice as possible. She added the eggs, some slaw and a big hunk of the steaming corn pone dripping in butter, a dab of apple butter for the sweet tooth, a steaming cup of coffee and she headed for the bedroom.

The new mother saw the attractive dinner plate carried by Labanna Jane and asked, "Law, child, did you make all these vittles?" "Yes, Mam," Labanna Jane replied. "Why that's as good as any cook could do and sure looks worth eating," remarked the receiver of the meal.

"What's your name, girl?" asked the midwife, eyeing her up and down. "Labanna Jane," she replied. "You were a lot of help with the Misses, but that's too fancy a name for a hired out girl; should be just plain Jane and that head of yeller hair will get you

2

in trouble one of these days." "Yes, mam," Jane answered. "Supper is on the table," she said as she started back to the kitchen where the farmer and three little boys were beginning to sit around the table. The midwife found a chair and looked with surprise at the plentiful vittles and attractive table.

"You sure are a surprising child," remarked the midwife, "You are not much more than a baby yourself." Labanna Jane bowed her head and said nothing. She knew she would have two weeks work here if she pleased the farmer. And that she intended to do. She had been promised two dollars at the end of the time. Labanna Jane had plans for all that money.

When everyone was seated and the vittles handed around, Labanna Jane made sure each of the little boys had a glass of milk and that the coffee cups were full.

She slipped out of the kitchen to check on the new mother and baby. Her patient hadn't finished eating. Picking up the chamber pot, she headed for a side door, going around back to the tool shed. She selected a shovel and went to a far corner of the garden, shoveled out a deep hole and dumped the contents of the chamber. The looks of the grisly thing made her stomach churn and hot water gushed into her mouth. She was learning young that being a woman had its shameful and demeaning moments. However, with a toss of her head, she got on with her chore; the afterbirth had to buried deep so that the farm dogs wouldn't dig it up. That done, she rinsed the chamber pot at the run and poked at the tub of bloody clothes she had put to soak from the birthing.

Entering the side door, she saw that she could now collect the dishes from the sickroom. "Anything else, Mam?" she inquired as she quietly deposited the pot under the bed.

"Nothing, dear," answered the mother. "And I must say you are a fine cook. You'll have me up in no time with all your care and good cooking." With a pleased and embarrassed "Yes, Mam," Labanna Jane collected the dishes and headed back to the kitchen, just in time to fill the coffee cups again.

3

The Dust Cap

Labanna Jane was up early and had a fire under the wash kettle. As soon as she had fed the family and gotten the farmer off to the fields she would get at the wash.

A rag tied around her head hid the beautiful "yeller" hair. The midwife had said it would get her into trouble and she had no intentions of letting that happen.

Jane had the wash on the line and dinner on the table by noon when the farmer came from the field where he was plowing.

She had time to straighten up the cluttered pantry somewhat. Her most important job was tending the new baby and mother. Other things could be "let go."

After dinner was over she cleared the kitchen and put the younguns in bed for a nap. Hurrying she swept the kitchen and sittin' room.

By the fifth day the new mother was sitting on the side of the bed, as she nursed the baby. Putting the baby down she asked Labanna Jane to bring her sewing basket to her. As Jane handed the basket to her she said, "Pull up a chair, child, I want to show you something."

Labanna Jane did as she was told, curious as to what was in the basket.

"This is a 'dust cap' I was making. This is the way you cut them out, then stitch along here. Add a drawstring, pull it through and tie it on top in a bow. The ruffle has to go on first like this.

"You are much too pretty, and young, to have a rag tied over your head. I'll help you finish this cap and its yours. You can learn to make them and have one to match each dress."

"Oh, thank you, mam. You just tell me how and I'll do the sewing." For the next few days every minute Labanna Jane could spare she spent in the bedroom sewing the long ruffle that went around the dust cap.

4

The new mother was up walking around. In another few days Labanna Jane's two weeks would be up. She had enjoyed the work here, the younguns were biddable, and she had learned to make a dust cap for her hair.

The days passed quickly, the farmer gave her the two shining silver dollars that had been promised. "You did good," he told her "the Misses liked you fine." His wife nodded as she told Labanna Jane good-bye.

Labanna Jane headed home, clutching the two silver dollars in one hand, her budget of clothes in the other, the dust cap still on her blond hair.

Labanna Jane decided to go to the store. She would get some things to take home. A new dress length for Dolly. It would be the sunniest yellow she could find, her mother's favorite color. She would get enough chambray to make her brother, little crippled Harn, a new shirt. The only one he had was patched in several places. She went over in her mind the things she would buy. Maybe enough material to make a dress for herself and a dust cap to match, in case she got another job. She had to be clean and neat if she wanted to work.

When she got home Dolly had gone off with a new beau, leaving the younguns alone. They were used to it and seemed to get along, no matter.

Labanna Jane, carefully measuring an old one, cut out the dress she would make for her mother. Dolly could never settle down long enough to sew and Jane was getting good at it.

Labanna Jane worked several places for the next few years. Stirring apple butter here, washing clothes there, whatever she could get to do. The money she earned kept clothes on her little brothers and sisters, and something for them to eat most of the time.

The year Labanna Jane was sixteen, Dolly married. They all moved into a house on the edge of the village where Dolly's husband worked. It was crowded, but a home of sorts for the younguns.

Labanna Jane didn't mind leaving them now to take work. She was usually in demand since she worked hard and caused no trouble.

That spring a Mr. Cook sent for her for the "laying-in" of his wife. Jane had dropped the Labanna and was now called just Jane. (Plain Jane, the midwife had said.)

5

The Cooks had a big farm and hired help to plant and harvest. Jane liked Mrs. Cook more than anyone she had worked for. She washed, cooked, and kept things going in the house till Mrs. Cook was up. It took both the women to keep food enough on the table for the work hands.

Jane noticed one man with the bluest eyes she had ever seen, and he had looked at her when he thought she wasn't looking.

Jane asked Mrs. Cook about him. "His name is Tom Jarvis, he has a farm about ten miles down Beech, and a houseful of younguns. He is a good worker. Mr. Cook hires him often to help."

Jane kept to herself, never raising her eyes toward him again. She wanted no "truck" with a married man.

Summer had gone and it was now fall. Harvest in full swing meant plenty of work to keep them all busy.

Mrs. Cook's oldest daughter, Ora, a few months younger than Jane, helped with the work. She taught Jane little tricks with the needle that Jane didn't know, and things about baking and cooking.

Jane caught on fast. She could cook as well as the next, however, it didn't hurt to learn new things.

Jane enjoyed washing, hanging freshly washed clothes to dry in the sun. She had just finished hanging the last batch in the middle of the afternoon, and decided to wash her hair while no one was about. She sat in the sun on a log idly combing her long hair, letting the sun and wind dry it.

Hearing the pulley on the well, she turned. Tom stood letting the bucket slowly down the deep well. He was watching her as he pulled water up and poured it into the jug they took to the field.

Jane turned her back quickly, her face as red as could be. It was almost as bad being caught naked as with your hair down in front of a man. She couldn't think what to do, only ignore him.

The jug filled, she heard him walk up behind her. She hunched her shoulders trying to look inviable, so weak she couldn't move.

"You are the prettiest little girl," the voice behind her said. "You look like an angel with a halo, your golden hair shining in the sunlight."

There was a moment of silence, then she heard him walking away back to the field.

By the time she dared to look, Tom was halfway across the

6

field, his back to her. Jane hurried into the house, braided her hair, and covered it with her dust cap.

When the harvesting came to an end, another job awaited Jane. Mrs. Cook told her she would like to have her back the next year to help. "I'll come," Jane promised. It was a job she liked. The house was big and airy and Mrs. Cook was so nice to work for. She would be there, that's for sure.

A Young Girl's Dream

Jane kept busy through the winter. By the time she finished one job, someone else wanted her to work for them.

She didn't get home for Christmas, not that it meant much anyway. She made things for her brothers and sisters, in her spare time, planning to go see them before going to the Cook's home in the spring.

At times, while she sewed, thoughts of blue eyes with the spark of the devil in them haunted her. Brushing her hand across her eyes, she made herself think of other things. As young girls do, she couldn't help thinking of being compared to an angel, and being told she was pretty. She knew Tom didn't mean no harm, she was like a child to him. He was older, but she didn't know how much.

Someday she would have a home of her own and a husband. She would not be a plaything to any man, that she had made up her mind to.

The winter seemed long. Once Jane went to prayer meeting with the people she worked for. A young man asked to walk her home. Thinking no harm would come, she said yes.

They walked along in the starlit night behind the older men and women.

The boy talked some to Jane, she answered as best she could. He was her age but to her seemed such a child. He asked to come to see her on Sunday. A quick "No!" discouraged any further talk, as he took off the way they had come.

The winter came to a slow end, or so it seemed to Jane. She was anxious for the time to go to work at the Cook's farm.

The day finally arrived, when her things were stacked neatly, all clean with starch and not a wrinkle in them, ready to be put into the carpetbag she had.

The people she worked for took her partway by horseback. She would walk the rest of the way to the Cook farm.

8

As she neared the farm she saw men and teams in the fields at the plowing. Her eyes traveled over and back searching for a familiar figure. "No!" he wasn't there, her heart had seemed to stand still as she looked. "Good," she said to herself. "I won't have to have him looking at me."

"Jane! how nice," Mrs. Cook said, coming to the door in answer to her knock. "We didn't expect you so soon, you are more than welcome. Come in, there is plenty to do and another two hands is a godsend. Put your things in your room. Then come sit for a spell. I want to hear all about your winter."

Jane took her things into a small room off the kitchen where she and some of the smaller younguns slept, then went back to Mrs. Cook.

"My! you've grown, and I do believe gotten 'prittier.' Do you have a beau? I'll just bet you do."

Jane blushed and dropped her eyes, "No, I don't have a beau. A young man walked me home from church, but I didn't like him much," she answered.

"As you see the plowing has started. Mr. Cook and our boy is all that is working now. All the other men will be coming soon to help. By the first of the week we should have a full crew." Mrs. Cook continued, "Tom Jarvis will be here as soon as he can get someone to take care of his children. He buried his wife this past winter."

At the mention of Tom's name, Jane reddened again.

"Poor Tom, left with five little ones. His wife had been poorly for some time now. She gave birth to another baby that died two days later, she died with 'childbed fever.' It's been four months now, I hear that Tom has been quite broken up over it." Mrs. Cook said sadly.

Jane listened, tears stinging her eyes. She couldn't bring herself to say anything.

"Tom's a fine man," Mrs. Cook continued. "He is left with a terrible burden to bear. The Lord works in mysterious ways! It will be hard for him to find comfort in that at this time, I'm afraid."

"That's a pretty dress you have on, if you want to change we will get right to work," Mrs. Cook said, changing the subject quickly.

"I'll be ready in a minute," Jane told her as she left the room.

9

As Jane changed clothes a tear ran down her cheek. Poor Tom, she thought.

There were soon no room for thoughts as Jane worked. She was sorting potatoes in the cellar, cleaning out the bins. When that was finished, the apple bins had to be gone over. Each shelf had to be cleaned down, scrubbed with soap and water. The old things moved to one corner to be used and the other shelves made ready for the new jars and crocks that would be put up through the summer.

It would take several days of work here. They had a sizable cellar, the cleaning had to be done between cooking, washing, and tending the house. Mrs. Cook kept a clean, well-run household, and it took plenty of work to keep it that way.

Several days passed, each one busier than the last. Tom had come back to work. Jane had watched him come through the gate with his team early that morning. He was sad looking, as though the weight of the world was on his shoulders.

Jane's heart went out to him, poor, poor man, she thought. So many troubles. Nothing downed a body as quickly as troubles. The sparkle was gone from his eyes.

Summer wore on, everyone was busy. Tom went home at night to his family.

The harvest crew would be there next week. Then the men slept in the hayloft, to be ready to work from daylight to good dark.

Jane did the milking during this time when all the men and boys were working at the harvesting.

Jane was carrying the big crocks of milk to the springhouse when Tom met her on the path going to get water to wash up. She suspected it wasn't by accident that he arranged to be there just then.

"Let me help you," he said. "I can manage, thank you," Jane answered prim and proper.

He held the springhouse door for her, nevertheless, as she went into the cool darkness. Tom stood waiting till she had to come out again.

"You are prettier than ever, little angel," he told her.

Jane's face turned scarlet as she hurried toward the kitchen door.

Each evening Tom managed to be at the springhouse to hold the door for Jane, saying a few lovely words to her that made her heart sing for hours afterwards.

A week went by, finally he asked, "Jane, will you go for a walk with me so we can talk?"

"Seems to me you do enough talking without going for a walk," she answered and hurried inside.

The household had started to notice Tom's attention.

"I do believe Tom has set his cap for you, Jane," Mrs. Cook said one afternoon as they sat stringing beans on the kitchen porch. "He comes from a fine family, his people own a big farm over on West Fork, acres and acres of bottomland with the biggest white house I ever saw. He's a good man, Jane, but whoever gets him takes on a heap of responsibilities and a ready-made family."

Jane took in every word, weighing each in her mind, not saying anything.

Mrs. Cook looked at her a long while. "Do you like him, Jane?" she finally asked.

"He has nice eyes and asked me to go walking with him," Jane answered, not ready to commit herself yet.

"There would be nothing wrong in that, Jane. It's been six months since his wife's death. He is a lonely man."

As they continued to work, nothing more was said about it that day.

Jane tidied herself and slipped into a clean dress, before the men came to supper.

Just at dark as she took the milk out, there stood Tom holding the door for her. "How long do I have to do this till you go for a walk?" he asked with the sparkle back in his blue eyes.

Jane placed the milk crocks in the water without answering. Coming outside, she said, "I'm ready," and started toward the road as Tom closed and latched the springhouse door.

They walked down the road, and sat on the rail fence and talked. That is, Tom talked. "How old are you, Jane?" he asked.

"I'm seventeen, was in May," she answered.

"I'm a lot older than you. And you know I have younguns, five to be exact. I suppose you know my wife died."

Jane nodded, "I'm sorry for that," she said.

Tom nodded, too. "She had been ailing for sometime, the baby was too much, she was a good wife, and mother, and much too young to die."

They sat in silence for sometime, each lost in their own thoughts.

11

Tom took Jane's hand in his, holding it tightly. Jane's heart beat so hard she thought for sure he could see it.

"Jane, you are so pretty and sweet, just like an angel. I love you with every inch of my being. I don't have much to offer you, a bunch of little younguns, hard work, and my heart. I want you to be my wife, Jane. I'll work the rest of my life to give you all you deserve, a beautiful home and grand things. I expect to have a nice farm one day. Will you think about it, Jane, and give me your answer tomorrow night?"

They sat in silence, watching the moon come up through the trees.

There was such sweetness going through Jane that it left her weak and shaking. She never knew there was wanting for a man like this before. "Best we go back to the house," she said as she slid down from the fence.

They walked the short distance, Tom holding her hand in his. "Will you think about it, Jane?" he asked again as they neared the kitchen door.

"Yes, I'll think on it," Jane answered as she went in to a restless night. She knew what her answer would be. That didn't keep her mind from going this way and that, as she tossed and turned through the night, dreaming of blue eyes full of love.

Betrothed and Wedded

The household was up and stirring before dawn. Jane was making biscuits while Mrs. Cook tended the meat and potatoes frying on the stove.

Everyone would be ready for the fields by daybreak. The men all stood, or sat in the woodyard after washing up. Mrs. Cook gave the rope tied to the big dinner bell a pull. As the sound echoed for miles, they all came in with a clatter of feet, and moving chairs to sit at the table. Big platters of biscuits, meat, and potatoes disappeared as if by magic, washed down with cups of steaming coffee.

There was little talk as they hurriedly ate, then headed toward the fields and the work that awaited them.

Tom caught Jane's eye as he left, and a smile lit his face. She blushed, thinking of the answer he wanted tonight.

Jane hoped to get a chance to talk to Mrs. Cook before then. The chance she had wanted came that afternoon as the two worked together.

Mrs. Cook asked, "How are you and Tom getting along?"

Jane turned her face away to hide the blush that covered it. "He asked me to marry him," Jane answered.

There was nothing said for a few minutes. "Did you give him an answer? I think you care for him, Jane. I've watched you two. I know he is in love with you, he couldn't help but be. He is older than you, Jane, and has all those younguns. I know Tom is a good man, and would make a good husband. He works hard and has a good name," Mrs. Cook said no more.

"I've gone over all that in my mind. I'll marry him," Jane said simply. Mrs. Cook went to Jane putting her arms around her. "I'm glad for you both. I hope you will finish out the harvest. I'll hate to lose your help."

"We will wait. Would it be alright if we marry here?" Jane asked.

13

"Oh, I would be so pleased, Jane. Ora can help you make a new dress and we will give a fine dinner, make an occasion of it."

"I'm beholden, I didn't want to go off somewhere, I want it proper. I'll tell Tom tonight."

"In two weeks most of the harvest will be finished. We can ask Reverend Cottrell to perform the wedding," with that Mrs. Cook left the room. She soon returned with a lovely piece of calico, a light blue with a "spriggly" darker blue pattern. "I want you to have this for your wedding dress, that is, if you like it." "Oh! It's pretty, you don't have to do that. I can buy some if someone goes to the store," Jane said in embarrassment.

"No, this will be your wedding dress, you can start work on it whenever you have time. Ora will help you."

"You've been so good to me, Mrs. Cook. It's been like home to me here," Jane said.

The afternoon work went well. Around three o'clock, Ora came in, "We can start your dress now, Jane. We have two hours we can work on it before starting supper."

The material was laid out on the bed and cut. Ora suggested "tiny tucks sewed down the front. The waistline tucked in and a full gathered skirt with a row of tucks above the hem. A tiny collar and cuffs on long fitted sleeves. There will be enough for a bonnet to match."

Mrs. Cook came with several yards of tiny white lace. "Why not put this around the cuffs and collar to dress it up?" she suggested.

"Just what we need," Ora said, "it will look real pretty." The girls worked their allotted time until Mrs. Cook called them back to the kitchen. The dress would be ready in plenty of time.

The men all trooped in for supper with the usual clatter and commotion of getting seated. Tom's eyes flew to Jane. Their eyes met. Blushing she gave him half a smile. That was enough to light his face and put a sparkle in his eyes.

When Jane took the full crocks of milk to the springhouse, her "door keeper" stood waiting, a big grin on his face.

"I'm waiting for an angel to give me a message," he said very low as she passed him.

When Jane came out she started in the direction of their usual walk. Nothing more was said till they reached the rail fence where they sat each evening.

Tom could wait no longer, placing his hands on her arms he

14

turned her face to his. "Tell me you will be my wife, Jane. I love you with all my heart."

She lifted her eyes to his. "I'll marry you, Tom, and try to be a good ma to your younguns."

His arms went around her squeezing her till she could hardly breathe. Tom's head bowed down, his lips found hers in a sweet first kiss that left them both breathless.

"When, Jane? When will you be mine?" Tom asked in boyishness, eagerness.

"Sunday a week. I started making my weddin' dress today." She went on to tell him about the material and Mrs. Cook's making the arrangements.

"That's mighty nice of the Cooks. Things are in pretty bad shape at home. I've had enough to get the younguns looked after while I work. I promise you, Jane, someday you won't want for anything. I want to give you the things you deserve, and I promise you I will."

They slowly walked back to the house. Jane didn't want to tarry for another kiss.

Each night they took their walk talking of their plans. Tom did most of the talking, Jane listening. Each night she refused to let him kiss her till they were outside her door. She didn't trust the sweetness of his kisses and wanted to be close to escape when the weakness took hold.

The threshing wasn't finished by the end of the two weeks. Mrs. Cook insisted on them going ahead with the wedding, knowing that Jane would go to Tom's home at that time.

The day arrived, the ceremony was to be at ten o'clock with dinner right after. Jane dressed in Ora's room with her help.

The preacher, his wife, the Cook's family and a nervous Tom waited in the big sitting room.

At ten o'clock sharp, Ora came down the stairs to stand by the fireplace to be a witness for Jane.

Jane came slowly down the stairs in the new dress. It looked lovely, fitting snug around her small waist and bosom.

She stood by Tom as the preacher read the vows and they answered in low solemn voices. With the command you may kiss your wife, Tom's head bowed, a quick touch of their lips, they were husband and wife.

Handshaking went around, Tom was urged to the back porch for a quick nip from a jug kept for occasions.

The wedding dinner was lively and everyone crowded around the table. It was a feast of fried chicken, fried apples, loads of mashed potatoes and gravy, slaw, jellies and jams, and fruit. A molasses layer cake was made by Ora, with cinnamon apple butter spread between each of the thin fourteen layers that made up the cake.

When dinner was over, Jane started to help do the dishes. "Not today you don't, Jane. You get your things together. I know Tom wants to get started home. It's best you have plenty of time before dark," Mrs. Cook told her.

Jane's things were all ready to be put into the old carpetbag she had that someone had given her. In minutes she was ready. Tom brought the team around, they were saddled for the trip.

Tom tied the carpetbag to his saddle and helped Jane mount the other horse. Everyone came out to wish them luck and tell them good-bye. They were off in a flurry of good wishes and waving of hands.

As they rode away, Tom said, "You are the prettiest thing I ever saw. That dress makes you look more like an angel than ever before, and you are my wife. I hope you will never be sorry 'little Jane.' "

Jane had "goose bumps" on her arms. Thank heavens she had long sleeves and they couldn't be seen. She was beginning to get scared, like when she took a job and didn't know the people.

Nearing the farm, Tom pointed out his boundaries. "It's not much yet. I hope someday to add on more land. And I'll build you a grand house, too."

It didn't look like much to Jane as they rode up. It's my home now and belongs to "my Tom," she thought to herself. No need to turn your nose up, my girl. You've never had this much to call your own before.

No one came to meet them as they brought the horses to a standstill in the "chipyard."

Tom dismounted and helped Jane down, untied her things, taking her arm he led her to the back door of the cabin. "We're home, Jane," he said as he held the door for her to enter.

16

The Home Coming

The cabin was dark and damp. The smell of pissy diapers and unwashed clothes hung over everything. A youngun was crying in a back room as Jane and Tom entered the kitchen. He threw her budget of belongings on a chair and turned toward the stove where an old woman rattled pots and pans, saying, "Sara, I've brought Jane home. You can name the younguns to her and show her where things are. I'll see to the horses." With that, he left them.

Jane looked around her, the shadows becoming clearer as her eyes adjusted to the gloom. What windows there were, hung with dirty dark rag-like curtains that closed out the air and light.

Tom had warned her that things were bad since he lost his wife with "childbed fever." She was beginning to see just how bad. Old Aunt Sara had done as much as she could, coming from her family to take care of the younguns while Tom was away at harvesting.

Jane took off her bonnet as she walked across the room, inspecting every corner, her eyes swept from one side to the other taking in the sparse furnishings and the dirt.

Well! she thought, so this is to be my home. I'm a wife and mother in one sweep. The first night with her Tom, he had promised her so many things. Looking at what was here, they now sounded like fairy tales. No matter, he now had someone at his side, someone with ambition and not afraid of hard work. She was learning to plan ahead, to get the most out of every day and every dollar. There would be plenty of work here and five little younguns to take care of besides. Thank God, she was strong, not like the first wife.

Turning to Aunt Sara, she asked, "Where does Tom sleep?" Sara dried her hands on her faded apron, and hobbled toward the other room to show her.

She soon discovered that the cabin which was made from poles,

17

you couldn't call them logs, had three rooms. The kitchen, where she had entered, had a door leading to the center room with another small one leading off that made the rooms seem strung out in a row. Tom's bed was standing in a corner of what she termed, in her mind, as the sittin' room. The bed was tumbled and unmade, with a youngun about two years old sitting, sobbing, and hiccuping, in the center of it. The other four peeked around the door from the small room at the back, their uncombed heads and big eyes all she could see.

Sara pointed to the baby on the bed, "That's Trude. Come in here younguns and meet your new mammy Jane."

They shyly sidled in and stood against the wall, standing like steps, one head taller than the other, judging about two years apart. My Tom sure has been busy, she thought to herself looking her new brood over. I've sure cut myself a handful this time. They were hungry looking and dirty and looked with big eyes at their new mother.

The oldest, judging about eight years old, was sullen looking, and stared her straight in the eye. That one would be William, if she remembered right and would be a handful from the start. The rest as Sara pointed them out, Elizabeth, Catherin, John, and the baby Trude. Jane looked at them and they at her, no one saying anything.

Turning to Sara, "Have they eaten?" she asked. "Such as it was," she replied. "All right, younguns, get outside and play while I set things to right. I'm your new maw, and you are to mind me. Your pa will be back directly." They slid along the wall and out the door like scared rabbits.

"I kept them in," Sara said, "I can't run after them, and I didn't want their pa to come home and find one hurt. You got a good man, one that has had a heap of bad luck. I wish you both good," and she hobbled back to her pots and pans.

Jane started to unbutton her dress; her wedding dress, the prettiest one she had ever had. A light blue "spriggly" calico that she had taken great pains in making. She folded it neatly and laid it on a high shelf in a corner cupboard. The way things looked, it would have to last a long time. She put on a faded, dark-checked gingham skirt gathered full to the floor with long sleeves.

It smelled clean after all the smells in this house. Putting her things on the top shelf with her dress, she turned and picked up the sobbing child. It was wet and smelly and dirty. Poking through the cupboard, she found some dry rags to use for a diaper and a small faded dress that looked like it would fit. Taking another smaller rag for a washcloth, she headed for the kitchen.

She took a wash pan and poured hot water into it, swished a tad of soft soap in it and started undoing the baby's clothes. She flinched when she saw the little raw bottom while washing its face and hands, and then used plenty of soapy water on the little behind. Drying it thoroughly, she reached over on the kitchen worktable and got a pinch of flour, dusted it on the baby's bottom and pinned the rag diaper in place. By the time she had the baby washed and diapered, the sobbing had stopped and the head had started to nod.

Holding the baby against her shoulder, she took it into the far room. Two shuck beds, one on each wall, were the only furniture in this room. Feeling one, she found it soaking wet. Finding a dry spot on the other, she gently put the child down. Poor little tyke, she thought, might as well start in this room.

She opened the half window by pushing on the bottom, then propped it open with a stick that laid on the sill. She was a firm believer in sunshine and fresh air, and plenty of soap and water.

She gathered up the wet bed and headed for the outside, laying it on a pile of wood in the sun. The quilts were dirty, but would have to do with just an airing.

Taking a broom made from cane heads, she swept the corners and overhead clean of cobwebs, sweeping the dirt through to the other room where it would be swept out the front door.

Sara, to her guess, had been sleeping in Tom's bed while he was gone. She gathered up all the quilts and the dirty sack sheet and took them outside, laying them on bushes to air. This bed had a flimsy feather tick, with a straw one beneath. She took both of them out and put them over a log in the yard.

With the broom, she dusted the wooden frame and slats. A hit and miss was all she could give the bed right now for it was fastly approaching evening. In a shower of dust, she finished sweeping the sittin' room. Tomorrow, if she had a minute, it would be scrubbed down.

Hurrying on into the kitchen, she could see that Sara had finished washing up the dishes. Going to the window, she pulled the curtain to the side and propped it open. Noticing the sun far down in the West, she judged it to be four o'clock or so.

She saw a dirty meal sack, about half full, and a flour sack, with

19

a little more than half full, and thought, at least there would be bread. The first thing she would do would be set some sourdough so as not to use the milk for bread making; the younguns needed it. The next thing she would do would be to get the younguns clean and healthy and keep them that way. Tom had said they had a cow and some chickens. That was good and would help.

As she had ridden up, she noticed a truck patch up the "holler." Sure hope there are some things left to put away for winter, she thought. It was late, already October, and nothing put up. They would have to manage somehow.

Sara took her apron off, turning to Jane, saying, "I recon you won't be needing me anymore? I won't mind staying a few days more, but you sure have made the dust fly, no longer than you've been here. If you work like that all the time, maybe Tom's luck has changed. He sure got him a looker, too," she chuckled.

Jane pretended not to hear the last remark. Her spirits rose with the compliment, nevertheless. "I'll ask Tom about your staying, but I don't think it's needed, he will know," she answered.

She walked out into the yard, as Tom came from putting the horses in the shed. They talked for a minute and he turned again to the shed to fetch a horse to ride Sara home. He hadn't unsaddled them figuring he would be taking her the couple of miles to where she lived with her daughter's family.

Helping Sara gather together her few belongings, they tied them in the apron that she had just taken off, and were waiting out by the chopping block, a big tree stump used for splitting wood and mounting horses. Together, they got poor Aunt Sara on the gentle old mare. "Be back directly," Tom said as they started out. The younguns were all sitting in a row astraddle a log in the yard.

Going back to the kitchen, Jane found an old sunbonnet on a peg behind the door. Putting it on, she picked up a willow basket she had seen beneath the worktable. Looking around for tools, she decided maybe they would be in the shed. Going there, she found a small hoe with a short handle. "Oh, Will, watch out for the baby. I'm going to the garden."

There was a picket fence, made from small hickory stakes, around the truck patch. It was a sizable patch, and she could see there were several things planted, and some going to waste. That would be the first thing to do, save what she could.

20

Several frying squash fluted around the edge and creamy white lay in a patch to her left. Picking two of the largest, she put them in the basket. She took the hoe to where the potato vines were dying and digging one hill had enough for a sizable meal. Thinking, as she looked around, fried squash rolled in meal, boiled taters with a creamy onion gravy, corn bread, and picking three large ripe tomatoes for sliced tomatoes. "I need an onion," she said to herself, "now where did they put them?" knowing full well there would be some. Looking around, she saw over by the fence several rows of Dutch onions, with their tops almost all brown. Picking one from the ground, she was surprised at the size, must weigh a pound. This was good soil and a fine place for a garden. She would have to get at it and clean out the onions and potatoes, and sow a bed of late turnips and some kale for greens. They would come along by wintertime and make good eating. She planned as she worked. Not having time to really look things over, she promised herself to be back as soon as she had Tom off tomorrow to the harvesting, he was helping the Cooks finish their threshing.

Still planning, she thought, I must ask Tom if we can get some straw for our beds. They sure do need it. I'll use the old straw to put in around the potatoes when I hole them up.

The sun was dropping fast now, with the shadows lengthening. She saw the chickens gathering by the little shack, where they were housed. Setting her basket inside the kitchen door, she went to look for eggs. Entering the little house, she saw someone had put a log nesting area with dry leaves in it for them to lay in, and a few small poles for a roost. It will do, she thought, for now. Shuffling her hand through the leaves, she found three eggs. Well, better than none, but they will have to do better than that, she thought.

Stepping back outside, she saw a brood hen with several half-grown chicks—three, six, ten, eleven, that will add to the flock, plus maybe a fat rooster for the pot. The chickens all looked fat and healthy. As best as she could count, there were nineteen hens and one big red combed rooster. Taking the eggs, she carefully held them till she got back to the kitchen and put them in a cracked bowl on the far side of the worktable by the stove.

Looking at the sun, she knew it was almost milking time. Calling out the kitchen door, "Oh, Will, has the cow come in yet? And where do you usually milk?"

21

"Over by the shed, Mammy Jane," he replied. "I see her coming down the holler now."

Hurrying to peel her potatoes and putting them in cool water to keep them from turning black, Jane saved every peeling. The cow would eat them all and she would be sure to come in for milking, for her treat.

Not knowing how much milk she gave, she rinsed out a gallon bucket and took a tin dipper to milk in; if she kicked, too much wouldn't be lost. With the younguns at her heels, she went over by the shed to milk.

"What's her name, Will?" asked Jane.

"Old Blossom," he answered. "She is a good old cow. She don't kick."

Looking her over, Jane could see she was part Jersey and should give some good rich milk. Her bag flapped back and forth, heavy with milk as she walked.

"I doubt I brought a big enough bucket," remarked Jane.

"We use the water bucket," Will said. "Go fetch it then while I start," said Jane, "soo, Blossom, stand still now. I'm here to do you a good turn." She had a good reach on her tits and milking was easy. Big streams of foamy milk soon filled the dipper and had to be poured into the bigger bucket that Will brought at a run. The cow didn't mind the younguns around, was gentle and quiet, licking up every scrap of peeling Jane gave her, and stood chewing her cud. The big water bucket had foam pouring over the top by the time they started back to the house with it.

"Aunt Sara didn't get much milk," Will volunteered.

"With them hands of hers, I don't see how she got any," Jane replied.

"They're sure bad, got big knots on them," Will said.

As they got back to the house, the sun slid behind the last hill. A whippoorwill called loud and clear down by the creek. "By the time I get supper ready, Tom will be back," she mumbled to herself as she strained the milk into a big stone crock, keeping out some for the younguns' supper.

"Will, you and the girls fill the woodbox, and bring in chips for kindling. We'll have to hurry. Night will soon be here."

"And the 'Booger-man' will be out," Will told the girls as they headed for the woodpile. Thank heavens, I don't have to cut wood, she thought as she grabbed up the bedding and hurried inside because the dew fell fast after the sunset. Throwing them on

22

the beds and spreading the covers didn't take long. She had to put the dirty sack sheet back on her's and Tom's bed. Tomorrow she would wash it.

The younguns were making a big "to-do" filling the big box by the stove. Slicing the squash to fry, she admired them again, thinking they sure are prime squash. She sifted meal and rolled each slice in it then poured lard from a can on the back of the stove into a big iron skillet, adding each slice carefully so as not to knock any meal off. The potatoes were on the back of the stove already bubbling. Soon a pan of corn bread was in the oven with an eye kept on the frying squash all the time.

Going through to pick up the baby, she noticed some of the smell was gone. Closing the windows so the damp didn't come in, she picked up Trude and sat her on the floor. Tomorrow, she intended to start training her from diapers. With my Tom, there will be another in diapers before long.

Will came to the door as she returned to the kitchen, Trude toddling along behind. "What else you want me to do, Mammy Jane," he asked. She had to smile for she had herself a new home, a new family, and two new names, Mrs. Thomas P. Jarvis and "Mammy Jane" all in one day.

Looking out, she saw Tom opening the fence at the road; supper would be ready as soon as he came in.

"Get the wash pan, I'll give you some warm water to wash every face in sight. Then your pa will be here," she said.

A dipper of cold water in the pan, she added hot from the tea-kettle on the back of the stove. They were splashing and giggling the first laugh she had heard since arriving. They took the sack towel to use for drying themselves. "Don't forget to comb your hair," she added. They all came in with clean faces and stood in a line. Will's and John's hair was plastered down wet, their clothes ragged and dirty. There was just so much one could do in one afternoon. A good supper would cheer them all. Tomorrow would be a busy day.

Adding the chopped onion, she creamed the potatoes and lifted the last piece of crisp fried squash to the big platter. The table had been set with seven tin plates with a fork at each. She put the vittles on the table; the big platter of golden brown squash, in front of Tom, the dish of sliced tomatoes, the bowl of creamed potatoes and the plate of corn bread sending mountains of steam up as it was set down. Tom gave her a look that told her he was sorry for the way she had found things.

"Alright, younguns, get on the settle in back," called Jane.

"Settle?" Will asked, "That's just an old table bench we sit on."

"Only poor people have benches. Rich people have settles. That's a settle."

"Is it, pa?" he asked.

"If Jane says so, it is," he answered, his eyes sparkling.

They all sat. Jane turned a chair, back to the table, for Trude to stand on by her. Tom took one look at the table and the clean faces. He looked at Jane with tears in his eyes, "You are a treasure," he said very low. Her heart leaped with pleasure.

Each tin plate got a good helping of potatoes and gravy, she crumbled corn bread and poured gravy on top. She saw that each youngun had a tin cup full of fresh warm milk by his plate.

There was little conversation as they all dived into their supper. "You're a good cook, Mammy Jane," Will said between mouthfuls.

Tom looked at her and smiled, "That sure is a fact," he said.

Looking at "her Tom" and his family, she knew things would fall in place. Already she felt at home here, and could hardly wait for the new day, to get so many things done. First, there would be the night and her Tom. She could feel the blood rush to her face with the thought.

cA Home at Last

The younguns were all bedded down in the back room content with full stomachs and a "mammy" to tuck them in.

Tom sat on the kitchen steps as Jane finished tidying the kitchen. She set the crock of milk in the dishpan when she was through and poured cool springwater around it. She didn't want it to get "blinky" before morning. She would skim the cream for churning, but needed the rest sweet for the younguns' breakfast.

Removing the old apron she had on that she had found on the peg behind the door, she went to sit by Tom.

The mist was rising up the "holler" along the run, and that old whippoorwill was still at it down by the creek.

Tom put his arm around her and pulled her close. "My little princess," he murmured, his hot breath against her ear. "You should have a big house and a matched team of fine bay mares, and a big buggy with bright yellow wheels to match your golden curls." With that remark he reached up and pulled her dust cap off and the few pins that held her hair, and it tumbled down around her shoulders. "We will have all that someday," she answered.

At that moment Jane finally understood the blood and pain, the ugliness women went through for a man. Her arms went up around his neck and she gave a breathless whisper "my Tom" as he picked her up and carried her to their marriage bed. The moon came up through the trees, shining on the cabin and the new-found happiness within.

"Cock-a-doodle-do! cock-a-doodle-dooo." On the second crow of the rooster Jane opened her eyes, all was dark and quiet around her and for a minute she didn't know where she was. Timidly reaching over she felt Tom beginning to stir.

There was no clock and she had no way of knowing the time. The moon had gone down. It was still dark in the cabin. Tom had a pocket watch, it would be too dark to see the time, and he had

25

probably forgot to wind it anyway last night. A smile touched her lips and a glow went through her as she thought, My Tom, I hope it didn't happen last night. Never, never do I want anyone to think we weren't married first. Let me wait a month, Lord, You know I was a good girl.

"Cock-a-doodle-doooo," there it was again, he must know that it's get up time, an old farm rooster can tell time without a clock.

Jane slid down to the foot of the bed and hurriedly found her clothing in the dark. Dressing quickly she went to start a fire in the cookstove.

The younguns had brought in an old wooden bucket full of chips, and they were bone dry so that a fire would catch easily. She had filled the teakettle the night before on the back of the stove. There were coffee grains in a sack that she measured and poured in the hopper to grind. When she started to grind she heard Tom's feet hit the floor. He would be in soon. She hadn't asked him about the straw yet. Jane made another mental note to scorch some meal today to add to the coffee. It stretched it further and made it more mellow at the same time. "A penny saved is a penny earned."

The coffee started to boil and a pan of biscuits were in the oven. She hadn't had time to look around to see what there was to fix in the kitchen, today she would "make do."

Breaking two of the eggs she had gotten last evening, she whipped them into a froth then added a spoon of cream from the top of the stone jar in the dishpan, some salt and a little pepper. It wouldn't be many eggs Tom would have for breakfast. They would have to be hoarded to buy stuff at the store. The last time she took any in as a hired girl, they had been eight cents a dozen.

Looking under every cloth-covered container she didn't find any butter, but then she didn't expect to. Will had said they hadn't been getting much milk. She did find about a pint of apple butter in a half gallon stone jar. That would have to do. Peeking in the oven she saw that the biscuits were raising nicely. Pouring a few drops of the melted lard into a skillet, she scrambled the eggs.

Tom had gone out to the back step to wash, she could hear him slushing the water around and making noises as most men did while washing their face. I wonder why, she thought. It was a good sound. The sack towel smelled sour but it was all there was now.

26

The scrambled eggs piled up on the tin plate looked good. Adding a dab of apple butter and three biscuits she sat them at the head of the table, poured two cups of coffee, added milk, and sat down as he did to drink her coffee while Tom ate.

"My! scrambled eggs! You even put the old hens to work when you came. Lord knows what you will do to me." His eyes sparkled and a smile played around his lips.

The pink flitted into Jane's face at the joshing. She was a serious girl by nature and joshing didn't come easy to her.

"I was pondering, Tom, if maybe the Cooks could spare us some new straw for the beds. They sure are flat and winter's coming on. Would it cost much? If we could have it right away, I could wash the ticks while the weather holds." Jane was all out of breath.

"Well now, already she is badgering me for new stuff. I knew it wouldn't be long till she started on me," Tom said as if to himself.

Jane looked at him very straight for a full minute not knowing how to take it.

Seeing she was confused and a little peeved he said, "Wash away, woman. I'll hitch up the wagon and bring some home tonight."

At the Cooks they took dinner to the harvestmen in the fields so Jane knew she didn't have to worry about that meal for Tom.

Jane left the table as he did, picking up the dirty dishes on her way to the stove. It was starting to lighten up outside, not quite daybreak. Tom would have to hurry now. They expected everyone in the field by sunup.

By the time Tom harnessed the horses and hooked them to the wagon, Jane had a smoke blackened tub across two logs, brought out a shovel full of coals from the kitchen stove, and had a fire going. With the water bucket she went from tub to the spring filling it with water.

Tom waved as she watched him go through the bars at the road. While the water heated she searched every shelf and nail for dirty clothes. They were a pitiful few. She had noticed a big wooden chest in the sittin' room and raising the lid she saw someone had folded his dead wife's clothes into it. Must be her wedding chest, she thought. Guess they missed the apron and bonnet behind the door. Lifting out some of the top things she could tell they were clean and some in good shape. Well not today but when

27

the weather got bad, she would make the younguns clothes from them.

On the bottom shelf of the corner cupboard was a stack of several salt and sugar sacks. They would do for towels and diapers.

One thing for sure she would wash the flour sack sheet on their bed and the quilts. Tonight they would have a clean bed and a soft one when Tom brought the straw.

Taking all the white things she could find she put them to soak in the other washtub in cold water, they could soak while the water heated.

The chickens had to be turned out and the cow milked before she could start the washing. Maybe she could get that done before the younguns got up.

Taking the water bucket and dipper—that water bucket sure had to do double duty, she thought as she started to the milk gap. Old Blossom was standing contentedly chewing her cud. She would want to be off to graze before the sun got hot and the flies came out. Milking as quickly as she could with another water bucket foaming over with milk, she slapped old Blossom on the rear. "Be off with you," she said, "and don't forget to come home on time." Blossom let out a moooo and slowly moseyed up the "holler."

As Jane stepped in the door with the milk, Will came in from the sittin' room, his hair standing on end, looking as though he didn't know where he was, or where he was going. "Morning, Will, the others up?" "Morning, Mammy Jane, they're coming."

"Take them all out to the privy and I'll make your breakfast," Jane told Will.

"Privy! What's a privy?" Will wanted to know.

"That's a backhouse. Nice people call it a privy," Jane answered.

"Oh, you mean like a settle and rich people? Are we rich? I sure don't feel rich," Will said as he tried to flatten his hair down.

"No, not yet, but we will be or at least well-to-do, that's almost as good. Now no back talk. Do as you are told. We have heaps of work to do today." Jane said as she stirred up the fire, set a pan of water to boil, adding some salt.

Will gathered the younguns together, Trude started to cry as he pulled her by one arm through the kitchen. "Do I have to take the baby?" he wanted to know.

28

"I guess not. I expect she will already be wet," Jane said.

"Yes, she is," he said, feeling her bottom.

"Hurry, all of you, soon as you wash I'll have breakfast for you." "What?" Will wanted to know. "Mush and milk," Jane answered him. Will made a face, "I don't like lumpy mush and milk. I'd rather have fried chicken myself." "We will all have mush and milk and it won't be lumpy. Scoot, before you get a lump on your behind." All through the conversation Jane had been busy straining the milk.

There were shelves in one corner of the kitchen where she had found some cooked cabbage in another gallon crock. She dumped it out in the slop bucket and since there was no hog this went to the chickens. Scalding it she strained the big bucket of milk leaving enough out for breakfast.

Cleaning off the wider middle shelf, she reserved it for a milk shelf. Too bad there wasn't a springhouse. You can bet by hot weather next year there would be at least a spring box in the spring tail to keep milk. It was a heap of trouble trying to keep it setting in cool water so it didn't spoil, and with only one pan it was needed for so many other things. Washing the shelf quickly with hot water she put a tin plate over each crock and tied one of the clean salt sacks over them to keep the flies out.

The water was boiling and slowly she sifted meal into it carefully stirring vigorously so as not to have lumps. It took only a few minutes to cook till it became clear looking and thick. One had to really stir to keep it from scorching on the bottom.

Taking the tin cups from the stack on the table she filled each half full of milk. Added a spoon at a time of the mush and set them around the table.

The younguns slid on the settle ready to eat. Jane sat down with them, standing Trude on the reversed chair.

"You gonna eat mush and milk?" Will wanted to know.

"We all eat mush and milk," Jane replied.

"Aunt Sara ate eggs. It was for her 'rumetism.' I recond she couldn't have got around without them," Will informed her.

So! that's what happened to the eggs, she thought. Poor old woman, she won't have many more eggs to eat in this life. So who could blame her.

The younguns all had a second helping and so did Jane. They would have to do on that most of the day.

"Will, punch up the fire under the washtub and let me know if

29

it's hot. I'll wash the dishes and be out." Jane emptied the half gallon stone jar of apple butter and adding warm water put the two unbaked biscuits she had saved in to start her sourdough, tied it up with a rag and sat it on top of the warming closet of the stove. Put the leftover biscuits in and pulled the hood down, they would keep away from the flies and be used for dinner at noon.

The flies were bad, she would have to find some fly weed and pound it, add a little milk and sugar to bait them. It would get rid of a passel of them in no time. Jane couldn't abide flies.

Finishing the dishes, she hurried into the bedroom to empty the ticks. "I don't know as I orta, maybe Tom won't get the straw." She stood a minute thinking—"I'll trust," she said to herself, taking the shuck ticks from the beds the younguns slept in. The frames were boards pegged together with legs, rope laced through holes in the frame and corn shucks for stuffin' in the ticks. About the poorest bed known, but comfortable when fresh and new.

"Oh, Will! go yonder to the shed and find me as many sacks as you can. Bring them and help me."

Old Blossom wouldn't know how old the shucks were, and a few at milk time would keep her in line. There would be enough to last quite a while, and the straw from Tom's and her bed would be the bedding for the "tater" hole. Nothing would go to waste around this house. They had so little.

Will held the sacks open while Jane poked the shucks and straw in. He had found six or seven sacks which were a windfall, and they got all the shucks and straw in them, stuffing them full. Will had fetched string to tie them so they would not spill. They piled them in a corner and took the white ticks out to shake all the pieces of straw out before putting them to soak with the white clothes. There was a tub full to the top. There wouldn't be much soaking time for them as the water was almost hot now.

The washboard was under the house where the tub had been. The pot of soft lye soap was brought from the kitchen. Jane rung the clothes out of the soaking water. She stacked them on a couple pieces of wood, dumped the water and was ready to fix the wash water. There had to be cold water mixed with the hot for the right temperature for washing. Jane dipped the water bucket into the kettle and then had Will fetch the cold from the spring. The white things had to be boiled and some of the lye soap went into the tub on the fire.

Jane added as many of the white things as she could manage in the tub, and looked around for a clothesline to use. There didn't seem to be one so to dry the clothes they would have to be hung on bushes and the fence or whatever would hold them for drying. There were so many things they needed. She had gotten used to having things to work with. If people could afford a "hired girl" they usually had plenty.

"Make-do, make-do," she mumbled as the soapsuds flew. Scrub, ring, shake out, and another piece went into the boiling tub.

The younguns were playing in the woodyard quieter than most would be. "Will, don't let Trude get close to the kittle. All of you keep back away from the fire," Jane called as she worked.

Picking up a long stick, she punched the straw ticks to the bottom. In an hour she had all the white things in boiling, and went into the cabin to get the colored things. The curtains didn't look like they would hold up through a washing, at least they would be clean rags so down they came, taking them to the door she shook them, and throwed them on the pile in the middle of the floor. Looked like there would be two tubs full. Tom's things would need ironing and maybe a touch of starch, if not this time then the next. There was so much for her to wash today. Jane went back to the tub stuffing in as many as she could of colored things, then punched the white things as they started to bubble. The clothes would all be put through another wash, the second wasn't as hard and wouldn't take as long. When all the colored things were washed, they were rung out and stacked in a pile on a log. The white things were ready for the last wash and rinse. They were lifted with the long stick from the boiling tub into the water bucket letting the hot water drain so she could lift them safely. They were let down into the big water bucket and carried to the tub. Jane's arms ached by the time that they were all in the tub ready for the cold water.

"Will, fetch me some water from the spring," she said as she sat down on the log in the yard. Will couldn't carry a full bucket for it splashed as he walked, while she rested he was able to get some in the tub to cool it enough for washing.

A few scrubs on each piece and they were ready for the rinse water. If she only had another tub she could rinse and hang them out as she went, not having one meant she had to finish them all and use the same tub for rinsing. It didn't take long to finish the

31

second wash. Soon there were clothes hung on all the bushes, the fence and the logs in the yard.

Pulling the unburnt sticks from under the boil tub she decided to use it to scrub the cabin. "Oh, Will, add some cold water to the kittle." Going into the cabin, she pulled the bed frames from the younguns' room into the sittin' room, slushed a bucket of hot sudsy water over the floors and scrubbed frantically with the broom, sending Will for another bucket. Two buckets of the sudsy water with plenty of scrubbing made the floors clean, then a cool clear bucket of water from the spring to rinse it. She propped the windows open to let it dry out. The same thing for the other two rooms stacking the sacks of flour and meal on the table the wood box and everything else that rested on the floor went on chairs out of the way. All windows and doors were opened to let the air and sun dry the rooms out.

The sun had climbed in the sky around eleven o'clock she judged as she glanced at the shadows, having learned the way of judging time by putting a stick in the ground knowing North-South-East-West, seeing the way the shadows fell would tell the time.

"Come, Will, help me carry the settle outside, then bring the chairs so I can scrub them down in the wash water that is left." Finishing quickly they left them in the sun to dry.

Jane sat down to rest for a minute on a log that was in the shade of the house, all the younguns came and straddled the log. Will, in front, and all the rest behind in a row.

"What are we going to do now, Mammy Jane?" he wanted to know.

"We're gonna sit a spell, then have our dinner. After that we will gather our work things, and we are going to dig taters. And if everyone works good, when we are finished we will all go down to the creek and wash ourselves," Jane answered.

"Oh! Boy! going swimming. I'll work good." "Me too, me too," each one echoed in turn. They were all bouncing up and down on the log. Soon they quieted down and sat still for several minutes. "Are you rested yet, Mammy Jane?" Will finally asked not being able to hold back any longer. "I know you are 'parfull' tired. I'll do most of the digging if you want me to. I'm strong and can work real hard."

"You're a fine boy, and a heap of help," Jane remarked. "What about school, you been?" she asked.

"No. My maw learned me a,b,c's. I forget some of them. And I can count to fifty sometimes," he hung his head shameful at this admission.

"Bring a bucket of fresh water from the spring and we'll eat our dinner now," she said as she went inside. Taking the biscuits from the warming closet that was leftover from breakfast, and the fried squash from supper she made each a sandwich. Skimmed back the cream from the crock of milk and dipped a tin cup for each. Without further ado they ate their dinner.

Tater Digging

Picking up the tin cups Jane deposited them in the dish pan on the stove, adding water and left them till later.

If they were to get the potatoes dug they would have to get at it. With a basket on her arm and all the younguns following, each carrying a tool for the work ahead. Taking a row at a time she started to dig. Being careful to sink her hoe well outside the potato hill so as not to cut the potatoes underground.

"Will, you and the girls fill the basket as I dig. Give me enough leeway so I don't hit you with the hoe," she said. "We will take them down to the end of the garden where we will 'hole them' for the winter. First they have to dry in the sun. So spread them out some. We will have to wait till tomorrow to 'hole them.' "

'I never holed taters afore," Will said. "Tell me about it, Mammy Jane."

"First you dig 'em," Jane said. "Get as much dirt off as you can. Sort the best for seed for next year, put those aside and keep them separated. The smallest ones we keep in the house to use and the bigger ones we let dry. Then dig a hole about a foot deep, put straw, shucks, or hay in the bottom and around the sides, then put the taters in a big pile in the center. Then you put more straw on top, stand boards or stovewood slats up around the mound, make sure you fix one in the front of the hole where you can remove it and put it back as you want to take out taters. Shovel plenty of dirt all over and tamp it down hard. They have to be covered good and tight so water don't seep in. They will keep plump and fresh till spring."

All these instructions were given as the hoe kept swinging up, down, up, down, and the potatoes lifted from the loosened soil.

"Make sure you don't miss any, Will," Jane called knowing some would be missed and come up as "volunteers" next spring as a pleasant surprise and with luck would produce their first mess of small sweet creamed potatoes. This treat was looked forward to with relish.

The digging went well, the soil was just dry enough to loosen easily around the potatoes. There were ten rows through the garden from one end to the other. The yield was good. Will couldn't keep ahead with his basket. Jane had started back on the fourth row. She would finish that one to the end and help pick up and carry the potatoes to where the hole was to be. They would spread them to dry and cover them with sacks for the night.

Maybe Tom could rive her some boards for cover for them if it wasn't too late when he got home. All this went over in her mind, by the time she reached the end of the fourth row her arms were so tired she could hardly lift the hoe.

The baby was crying, setting in the dirt by the pile of potatoes. There were welts on her little arms where the sweatbees had stung her.

"Will, keep picking, I'll take the baby and put her down for a nap." Jane took Trude on her hip and headed for the cabin. Washed some of the dirt off, gave her a drink of water and put her in the bed in the sittin' room for her nap. She seemed glad to be in the cool room, stuck a thumb in her mouth, and closed her eyes.

Jane got a drink from the spring and took both washtubs to help cover the potatoes till they were holed. They soon picked all they could find and piled them up. Two good-sized piles were covered by the tubs. They were drying fast in the sun and she didn't want them sunburned because they would turn green and bitter when that happened.

Will's face was streaked with sweat and dirt as he looked up at Jane, "Are we done for today?" he asked.

"I think so," Jane said, "take the tools to the shed. I'll find some things for supper and be there directly." Taking the basket she put in several of the small potatoes, picked six or eight ripe tomatoes and a head of cabbage. With that in her basket she closed the gate and went back to the cabin.

Taking the basket she put it on the worktable, went on into the sittin' room to check on the baby and found her fast asleep.

When she came back to the kitchen, Will and the other younguns were all standing in a bunch on the kitchen steps. They were all dirty and sweaty and looking at her.

To tease them she said, "Now, what do you want?"

35

Will was quick to answer, "Swimmin', you said we would go swimmin' when we got done."

Taking off her bonnet she hung it on the peg behind the door, took the soap bucket and a sack towel, came out of the cabin and closed the door.

"Come along," she said. The creek was only a short distance where she found a shallow hole of water, without willows and rocks. There were snakes in the trash piles that washed up in the willows. She didn't want to have the younguns close to anything that could hide a snake.

"In you go, clothes and all," she said, "I'll give you clean ones when we get back, the wash will be dry by then."

With a whoop and holler, Will was the first in the water hole. The water came to his waist. He turned and took his little sisters' hands to help them walk in without falling on their face in the water.

They were splashing and giggling, having more fun than they usually had and getting clean and cool at the same time.

"Can we get our hair wet?" Will asked.

"Sure! then come and get some soap to suds it with," Jane told him. Letting them play for an hour, Jane called, "It's time to go."

"Ah!"—said Will and the rest gave their moan of disappointment at the ending of their fun. "I don't think I've ever been so clean in my whole life," Will said. "Sure feels good and when we get clean clothes and our new straw bed, whoo—ee. It will be as good as Christmas."

Jane smiled. "I agree," she said, "cleanliness is next to godliness."

"What is godless?" Will wanted to know.

"Not godless, it's godliness, that's being very good and not doing anything wrong to anyone to hurt them," Jane explained.

They started back to the cabin, water dripping from their clothes. Jane dried the girls' hair and fluffed it so it would dry in the sun. Taking bloomers and dresses, overalls, and shirts from the bushes, she herded them toward the cabin.

"Girls first in the kitchen and take off your wet things, dry yourselves, and put on your clean things," Jane ordered.

"Boys next," she said as the girls came out. "Will, fetch me the comb from the comb case."

Piling the girls' wet things by the step she sat them down, combed and braided their hair, and taking a string from her apron

36

pocket she secured the ends of their braids. That won't have to be done for several days, she thought as she finished. Jane parted the boys' hair on the left side and combed it back from their shining faces.

"We had a good day, Mammy Jane," Will said as she finished his hair.

"The floor is dry. I'll make a pallet and you can all have a nap. You worked hard and deserve one." Folding one of the quilts several times she spread it in the sittin' room. The four laid down all in a row, tired and content. It wouldn't take them long to all be asleep, she knew. There was plenty to keep Jane busy while they slept.

First she skimmed the milk into the churn. She would have to save cream for about three days before she would be able to churn. Then they would have butter for their biscuits, and fresh buttermilk to drink and make bread with, although she made fine bread with sourdough.

That done she brought in the clothes from outdoors. Folded them and stacked them neatly in the cupboard. They smelled of soap and sunshine, in her mind, no better smell.

While the younguns slept she washed herself with soap and a rag from top to bottom and put on a clean skirt and waist. The day had been busy and all hard work, but after her bath she felt refreshed. Like Will had said, "It sure does feel good."

She had things ready for supper. Then laid a fire in the cookin' stove ready to light when she saw Tom coming home. By the time he had the horses taken care of and washed up she would have supper ready. The chickens and milking would be taken care of before then.

If we only had a pig, she said to herself, as she continued to work. She had saved thirteen dollars but hadn't mentioned having it. She intended to keep it for something special. She didn't know what yet. It had to be made to count. Something that could make more money.

Will came in from his nap and headed for the privy. "See if old Blossom is in yet," Jane said, "We will milk early if she is so we can fill the straw ticks when your pa comes."

"Old Blossom is up the holler," Will said when he returned. "Want me to go fetch her?" he said.

"No, we don't want her to get used to that. I have the tater peelings ready with a little salt, she will come for that no doubt.

37

I'll get the eggs and then we will milk," with that she went to the chicken house. This time there were six eggs. "That's better, but not good enough. You had better get busy," she told them, "if you don't want to be chicken and dumplin's. Soo, Blossom!" she called as she took the eggs to the kitchen.

Will had the water bucket ready with the dipper. Together they did the milking, as Jane had predicted old Blossom was ready for her treat, licking and lapping every morsel.

"Pa's comin'," Will said as they reached the cabin with the foamy bucket of milk. "Boy! you can't see old Madge and Maud for the straw." He ran toward the road to open the bars for his pa to drive through.

Jane stood with her hands on her hips looking with pleasure at the fine load of new straw. Her wish for new bedding, a certainty now.

Entering the cabin for the newly washed ticks and some safety pins, she went out to the shed to meet the wagon and Tom.

"Here you are, old woman, here's your beds," he called. "If this isn't enough, I'll bring more tomorrow. And didn't cost a cent. Old Will Cook said you take that new bride of yours all the straw she needs for beds."

"Oh! what a 'purty' sight, and it smells so good," Jane remarked, sinking her hands to her elbows. "Come, Will, and help hold the ticks. We will get them filled before it gets dark and the dew falls on them."

When they finished every bit of straw was stuffed into the snowy clean ticks except the few mouthfuls old Blossom had snatched from the end of the wagon.

Tom finished with the animals in time to help carry the first one in and put it on the bed.

Jane lit the fire in the stove to cook supper and let Tom and Will bring in the other two beds. She had pinned the ends with safety pins so the straw didn't fall out. Tomorrow she would sew the openings securely. They would have to last till another harvest and none of the straw must be lost.

That night supper was a lively meal. The pleasure of the new beds, and the telling by Will of the day's work and the wash in the creek. The younguns' clean clothes and hair gave evidence that a lot of water and soap had been used that day.

Tom looked at the pleased shining faces, his eyes sparkling. He

38

looked at Jane with a big smile. "Seems you had quite a day," he said.

Will, with importance, said, "We need some boards rived for the 'tater hole.' Mammy Jane and me will have all the taters dug and ready tomorrow."

Tom got up from the table and went outside. As Jane cleared the table, she could hear the squeak and snap as new boards let go from the bolt. Will hurried out to help and watch with the other younguns at his heels. Tom had a pile of chestnut cut into bolts ready. It didn't take long to rive the needed boards.

"That's a blessin'," Jane said to herself as she tidied the kitchen.

Holing Taters

The next day Jane had Will bring one of the tubs and fill it with water, put all the wet clothes from their swim to soak, including Tom's. He had washed and changed before getting into the big, clean bed that night.

Jane milked and did the house chores before going to the garden. Tom and Will had carried the new boards to the "truck patch" the night before. They stood bright and smelling of new wood against the fence.

Starting in their routine, Jane digging and the younguns picking up and lugging them to the pile to be dried and sorted. By getting an early start they had the rows all dug by late noon when they all trooped to the house for a well-deserved rest and dinner. Milk and corn bread was put on the table and no one had to be coaxed to eat, cup after cup of the crumbled corn bread with plenty of sweet milk over it.

Jane made a pallet in the sittin' room again and put the younguns all down for a nap, while she and Will went back to sort potatoes and start holing them. They each carried a bag of straw that had been saved for the potato bedding.

Digging a shallow hole about four feet wide and six feet long, Jane decided to put them all in one hole and open both ends. Placing the seed potatoes in the center for safekeeping. Now that she had plenty of boards she could put one between the eating "taters" and the seed ones.

Emptying a sack of straw, she firmed it in the bottom and around the sides good, so it would be ready for the potatoes, as they were sorted.

Starting to sort she turned the tub to put the choice seed ones in, showing Will how to pick the firm ones with plenty of eyes for seed. As they got into the swing of sorting, the three piles grew— one for seed, one for holing, and one for the kitchen use.

"Why do we use the little ones and not hole them?" Will wanted to know.

"Little ones tend to shrivel and besides we need some to use on, these will last well on to Christmas, then we will open the 'tater hole,' to use and have plenty till they grow again." I hope, she thought to herself. Seven people could eat a heap of taters.

"Can we hole anything else, Mammy Jane?" Will asked.

"Oh, my, yes. Apples, turnips, cabbage, parsnips, hanovers and some I don't even know about, I recon," Jane answered.

"There's some apple trees up the holler," Will said. "My maw never done so many things like you do. She felt poorly and was in bed a lot." Looking thoughtful, Will continued, "Mammy Jane, I like you most as much as I did my maw. She is up there on the hill in a burying hole and the little baby, too. Pa cried something fierce. I recon I did, too. I think he is glad you came to live with us, me and the other younguns are too."

That was a long speech for Will even as talkative as he was.

Jane looked at the hardworking little boy and her heart ached for him. "Will, I don't want you to ever forget your maw, or quit loving her. She was a fine woman. As soon as we have the money, we will have a tombstone put at her grave. A big one, tall and white, that can be seen for miles. Your maw would be proud of you, Will."

The "tater" sorting kept going, nimble fingers throwing potatoes in whichever pile they belonged in. The sun and air had dried them enough to start placing them in the hole. Jane had decided to sack the seed potatoes to be put in the middle of the hole, they would be easier to get out and not mix with the others.

The sun was starting well on its way to the West as they bagged and tied the sacks, and added them with the rest in the hole. The straw packed firmly on them and the boards stood overlapping to form a pyramid to turn the rain. One overlapping board at each end formed a handy opening to the hole.

They shoveled dirt, covering the hole a foot deep. They stood the other boards that were left around the outside to hold the dirt till it settled and crusted to turn the rain.

"That's a fine looking tater hole, Mammy Jane," Will said, standing leaning on the shovel to admire their work.

"They are safe for winter fare," Jane said. "Let's sack up the rest of the taters and carry them back to the kitchen. You take the tools to the shed, Will, while I sack and get them ready."

All the tools were cleared away and the sacks of "taters" carried to the cabin. Some was carried in buckets and poured into the sacks to finish filling them, they would weigh sixty or seventy pounds full and too much for Will or Jane to tote.

The onions would be next and the ground leveled where they and the potatoes were dug for her winter crops, and as fast as they could get it done. It would be frosting in another two or three weeks.

Over by the fence on the opposite side of the garden were several rows of ripe corn that needed to be cut and shocked. The pumpkins could be gathered and put in the corn shock for now. Dead bean vines clung to the stalks of corn, they would be searched for beans, seed had to be kept for next year. Any dry beans not needed for seed could be used for food. There was still time to get that done this afternoon. Tom could cut and bind the corn when he came home. It would be ready for him to begin right after supper.

"Fetch the basket, Will. We will strip the corn patch for cuttin', and see if you can find more sacks for the corn." Jane went through first looking for beans, tied one corner of her apron to her waist band, and started picking all she found no matter how small. There appeared to be more than she thought and soon had an apron full. Will came with the basket and they soon filled it, made a trip to the cabin putting the tub into the kitchen and emptied the beans into it and went back for more. Up and down each row careful not to miss any. They both admired the big pumpkins hidden between rows of corn. It took them the afternoon to pick the beans. Jane decided to leave the corn picking for Tom. There was just so much she and little Will could get done.

Jane's back ached and she felt dizzy from being in the sun all day. "Let's call it a day, Will," she said as they made the last trip and emptied the beans on the tub that overflowed.

"You go to the creek and wash if you want, but only where we were before and, mind you, watch for snakes. Take your clothes off this time, because you don't have any clean ones to change."

"All of them?" he wanted to know. "Yes, and don't tarry. The younguns will be getting up and I don't want them going to the creek. Hurry now," said Jane.

"Maw! Maw! Mammy Jane!" Will screamed as he ran for the house, jumping logs, yelling at every jump.

Rushing to the door and out into the woodyard to meet him,

Jane's heart jumped into her throat, her first thought, Lordy, he has been bitten by a snake.

Will rushed up to her out of breath and still trying to talk. "Calm down, calm down so you can talk," Jane told him.

"Deer! Deer! Lots of them. Five or six over by the deer lick. Boy! Oh, Boy!" he danced from one foot to the other trying to drag her by one arm to see them.

"Hush up, Will, you will scare them to kingdom come with all that hollerin'. When your pa comes we will have him decide what to do. We may have to wait awhile till it gets colder. All that meat would spoil as hot as it is now. Sure would taste good, though. We will see. Go finish your wash now. Hurry, then get at the chores."

The younguns were all up now coming out to see what was going on.

While Jane was out she went to gather the eggs, got ten this time. Oh, I do hope they lay good, we need so many things, she thought.

They would finish the chores early and have dinner on the table when Tom came. He could cut the corn in the garden if he wasn't too tired.

Telling of the Deer

Will told the younguns all about seeing the deer. They all wanted to see them, too, and were so excited they could hardly wait till their pa came home.

The wait seemed hours to them, but it wasn't long till they saw their pa coming through the bars at the road, riding old Madge. The team wore harnesses for he and the team were hired out for the harvest.

Jane had their supper on the table when he came. Will could wait no longer, talking so fast no one knew what he was saying.

Tom didn't know what to make of it. "Slow down, son. Now, what is this all about?"

When Will was finished telling all he could think of, Tom looked at Jane with dancing eyes and a smile. "Well, now," he said, "I'm surprised Mammy Jane didn't take the broom and kill a couple of them for supper." "I'll bet she could," Will answered. "She can do most anything."

"Don't you go putting fool notions in the youngun's head," Jane said.

Will had to tell all about the "tater hole," and what a good job they had done. "Nigh on twenty bushels they had put away. That will be enough till they grow again, Mammy Jane says." He then explained how to go about "holin' taters," and the corn patch was ready to cut anytime his pa had a mind to.

Tom looked at Jane and smiled, "Seems you have had another busy day."

"Without Will, I couldn't have done it. He is a heap of help, we make a good team."

"Just like Madge and Maud?" little John wanted to know. Will turned to John, "That's right, when you get a little older you will know what it is to do a good job."

"Don't forget, they all helped, every hand is needed to put the garden up for the winter," Jane told them.

44

As Jane cleaned up the kitchen she saw Tom start toward the garden with the corn cutter with Will and John at his heels. When Jane finished and came outside the girls were all astride their favorite log. "You younguns ride your log horse, and if you watch you may see the deer. I'll go help your pa. You can see us, mind you, stay in the chipyard." Taking the willow basket Jane crossed the creek to the garden.

Tom already had a shock started far enough from the fence so as not to tempt the cow and horses to try and reach it, breaking down the fence in the process.

The pumpkins would be gathered and put into the fodder shocks until it got cold enough for a hard freeze. Jane intended to dry a lot of them while the sun was still hot enough. Everything that could be saved must be. The winter would be long and food scarce.

It was good to know that meat was close-by, they could almost certainly count on a deer or two for the winter. Tom was a good shot and owned a good gun.

It would be better when they owned their own hogs and knew where their meat was coming from.

Tom stopped cutting as she came up, almost reading her mind, said, "the Cooks had a late litter of pigs. The old sow had eleven, and one is a runt, but, it's a sow. Do you recon you and Will could get it raised if I can figure out a way to get it cheap?"

"We have plenty of milk and I don't see how we could fail," Jane answered with a pleased smile.

"I was thinkin' if I could get a deer and give them half for the pig, we could both make out. I'll talk to Mr. Cook tomorrow. They could use the meat with the threshing crew they have been feeding. We could use up half of one, don't you think?"

"I can cook it up and put it down in grease for a while, or put it in brine, we have salt," Jane replied.

They went back to work, Tom cutting, binding and shocking. Jane and Will picking and carrying the pumpkins and rolling them into the shock. Some very large ones they couldn't lift they left to let them ripen as much as they would. The seed from them would be saved for next year. Jane would cut them up in the field for carrying and get them to the cabin that way. Watching Will carrying a big pumpkin Jane knew his arms must be aching. He would be such a help to his pa with a little more growth on him.

The whippoorwill had been calling by the creek a long while,

45

dusk was turning to dark as they finished and started back to the cabin.

Jane gathered her basket of tomatoes and took it back as the menfolk took the tools to the shed. She would give Tom creamed tomatoes and biscuits for breakfast. The eggs would be saved to take to the store to help purchase the long list of things in her mind that were needed; a couple of five-gallon stone jars, some smaller ones for curing and storing things, one for sauerkraut, and if they got apples the peel for vinegar. All these thoughts were running through her head as she washed the younguns and put them to bed. Jane gave Will a pat on the shoulder, "You done good," she told him. He needed no urging to go to bed.

Jane and Tom sat on the kitchen steps watching the moon come up through the trees, soon they would wash up and go to bed too. Jane's face grew warm with the thought. Her Tom never got so tired that he wasn't ready for their loving in the night.

Next morning Jane laid a fire under the washtub and filled it with water to heat. She would wash up the things soaking from the swimming and a couple of quilts. Today she could churn for the first time. She would get that done while the water heated.

As Tom left for work she went with him to the shed and milked old Blossom. Getting the dasher and lid hanging against the wall and fitted it on the churn, pulled a chair over by the door and started the churning. That was one job she didn't relish, and as soon as one of the girls got a little bigger it would be her job. They would all be taught to work as they grew up. The sun was coming up as she started to pat the dasher to gather the butter. Picking up the churn she sat it on the worktable and dipped the butter into a bowl, poured cold water into the bowl and washed the milk from the butter. There was a nice mound of it when she finished. Churning would be regular now, with plenty of butter for breakfast.

Hearing the younguns coming she got ready to dish up their breakfast which was still on the stove. Will saw that they all went to the privy and washed up without being told. While they ate she got started with the wash. Needing the tub, she spread the beans out in the corner of the kitchen floor to dry so they wouldn't mildew before they could be hulled.

One of the things she intended to buy as soon as possible would be another washtub, and a kettle to heat water in. The washing went well, since there wasn't so much to do today, and getting started while she was rested helped. The sun wasn't too hot which made things even easier.

Will and the younguns were soon out in the woodyard as usual. He was splitting some chestnut blocks of wood. They were easy to split and he didn't have much trouble with them. He had the girls stacking the split sticks between two stakes he had driven in the ground to brace the stack. He was busy explaining why it had to be done just that way while he worked. "You don't want to be out here stacking wood in your bare feet when there is a snow on the ground," he told them.

With some much needed education Will would amount to something. Jane knew from experience how much difference it made in life. He would never have a chance to learn. If she could teach him she would, but she could neither read or write herself. She never let on that she couldn't, keeping that knowledge to herself.

The wood splitting slowed down as Jane shook and hung the last piece of wet things on the woodpile.

The sun had climbed overhead as Will asked, "What's the next job, Mammy Jane?"

"We are going to peel and string pumpkins to dry," she answered. Everyone looked interested. Catherin wanted to know if they hung it on bushes like clothes? "You'll see," Jane told her, as they all went into the cabin. Jane noticed that they had gathered all the tin cups and plates and put them into the dishpan on the stove to soak.

Jane went to the big chest and lifted the lid where she had seen some needles stuck in a scrap of cloth and she felt sure there would be a darning needle. She had already found a ball of twine on the shelf saved from raveling out the stitching in the sacks. It would be used to string the pumpkin on. The strings would be hung behind the stove to dry since there was no clothesline where she could hang them outside in the sun.

They took the basket and a knife to the garden to fetch one of the big heavy pumpkins. Jane sank the knife in and pushed it toward the ground, and the big ripe pumpkin split open with a tearing sound. The center was bright orange and the seeds plump and black, these would be the seeds saved for next planting.

She split one half and put a quarter of it in the basket for Will to carry, and taking the other half on one hip they went back to the cabin. The seeds were carefully taken out and put in a bowl to be washed and the pulp all removed, then dried thoroughly, and

47

tied in a cloth to be hung from the ceiling where mice couldn't get to them. The field mice seemed to find ways into a house no matter how careful a body was. They could destroy all the seeds for the next planting in a matter of minutes. Seeds were guarded carefully either by hanging from the ceiling or put into tin containers with lids. More than were needed were saved in case a neighbor lost theirs and you could share.

After removing the seeds, Jane cut two-inch strips across the big pumpkin, peeling it and cutting in three-inch long pieces. The needle was run through and the piece slid to the end of the long string, and another added. Jane showed Catherin how this was done and let her do the stringing while she peeled and cut the yellow squares of pumpkin.

The seeds were laid on the table to dry. When each string of pumpkin was finished it was hung on a peg behind the stove after tying the ends of the string together.

Soon three big pumpkins were cut and strung making an orange curtain behind the kitchen stove. They would hang there for several days till Jane judged them cured enough to be taken down and put into cloth bags, then hung up in a corner and more fresh strings hung to dry till most of the pumpkins were done. A few would be kept to cook through the winter.

The Pig

Another day's shadow had fallen across the windows, the rays of the sun barely peeking from behind the last hill up the "holler."

The younguns were on their log horse in the chipyard watching for their pa.

Jane was at her usual chores, never finding a moment when she wasn't busy at some work or other.

"There's pa, there's pa!" rang out from five mouths, each one anxious to spot him first and let it be known.

Will came running in to tell Jane in case she hadn't heard. "I think he brought the pig." He dashed out again.

They all marched out to the shed to meet Tom. There was no doubt now they could hear the squeal of the confined pig wanting to be let out of the burlap sack. Tom had a grin on his face, pleased as he knew Jane would be. Coming to a stop he slid from the horse and placed the sack on the ground at her feet. "Two!" Will shouted in surprise.

"Sure thing," his pa said, as he explained. "I was going to buy the runt, but Mrs. Cook said to give it to you as a weddin' present and me buy a good male. I got it for two dollars. The sow pig is yours, if you can get it unstunted enough to make anything of it."

Jane, eyeing both pigs, pushed the male that had saddled up to her with her foot. "That's a fine male pig," she said. Looking at the other one, "It will do fine with old Blossom's good butter-milk. It will grow in no time."

"Where're we going to keep them?" Will wanted to know.

"For now we will fasten them in the shed at night and let them run in the day. I'll fix a pen soon as I get around to it," his pa said.

"It sure does please me seeing hogs on the place," Jane told Tom as they went back to the cabin for supper.

Tom gave her a pat on the arm and with the younguns at their heels that was as much affection as he would show.

Jane had been married just one week, and her days had already formed themselves, falling in place as she made progress being a wife and mother. Their poor home had already added wealth in a pair of pigs, and order out of the confusion she found a week ago. By spring the pigs would be big enough to breed and they would have a litter of their own.

She wouldn't let herself feel beholden to the Cooks about the runt, because she had worked hard there. Jane didn't forget to tell Tom to thank them for the gift. She surely was thankful for a pair when she was only wishing for one, preferably for a sow so they could get a start.

Tom had told her that he had "drove" the cow which meant old Blossom would "freshen" sometime in April. That also meant they would be out of milk for a couple of months before she dropped her calf. Hopefully, it would be a heifer and they would then be on their way to a farm herd. To build up from nothing was hard but could be done with hard work and careful planning. The planning could be done while the hard work accomplished it, Jane said to herself.

The days flew one after the other. The threshing of the oats and wheat at the Cook farm would be finished on Thursday. At supper Tom told Jane that he would be taking a load of wheat to the mill at Minnora. He would stop off at his father's place for dinner on the way. "How would you like to come along?" All the little ears at the table perked up to see if they were included, they knew better to ask or break in on the conversation of adults.

"We can go on to the store and get what you need for the winter. It won't be long till the snow flies and we can't get there," he told her.

Jane had seen the Jarvis mansion, big and white, sitting away from the road in a big green meadow, and had been to the store once, where they had everything, it was an adventure to go.

"Send Will and have Aunt Sara come stay with the younguns," Tom told Jane. "I'll be paid for work at the Cook farm. I get a dollar a day for me and the team, and worked twenty days. The pig comes out of that, I will take wheat for part of it for our winter supply of flour. I have a little put by, and there will be the corn cutting and shucking yet. We should have plenty for what

50

you need. Jane reminded herself of the big basket of hoarded eggs that she could trade also.

"When will you start?" she asked.

"Well before daybreak tomorrow. The wagon is loaded and they will bring the team in and meet me. I'll ride old Madge till I meet the wagon and take over from there, I'll leave old Madge at the gate on my way back. Will can turn her out."

"Alright, I'll get ready," Jane said. As bad as she hated going to meet Tom's mother and father, she was more curious about the big house, she had always wanted to look inside a house that size. It had to be done sooner or later. Tom had disagreed with his family on politics, something about the talk of war. Jane didn't rightly know what, but there was a rift and that didn't make for much close visiting, even if there had been time.

Saddling Madge they sent Will off for Aunt Sara. She would have to spend the night, possibly two. A pallet could be made on the floor of the sittin' room for the girls, Aunt Sara could have their bed. Will would be back by good dark with Aunt Sara, if she came.

Jane went ahead with supper and the chores. Thank heavens for her weddin' dress and bonnet, Tom wouldn't have to be ashamed of his wife before his family. She would wash her hair and bathe before going to bed and be ready for the morning trip.

The eggs would have to be wrapped in layers of cloth to keep from breaking on the way, a list of things kept running through her head, things she needed and those she could do without.

As they finished eating they heard the sound of the horse coming. Looking out, saw Will opening the bars at the road and leading the horse through with Aunt Sara.

The trip was a reality now, and a small thrill went through Jane at the anticipation of tomorrow.

51

The Trip

Before the first crow of the rooster sounded from the hen house Jane was up. Lighting the fire she had laid the night before she started breakfast. A big pan of biscuits with more in a skillet, she needed to make plenty for Sara to have for dinner that day for the younguns and herself.

Getting Tom up Jane made him a couple of scrambled eggs so he could be on his way to meet the wagon.

Looking out, Jane saw old Blossom lying by the shed. Hurriedly she readied the milk things to get the milking done and the chores finished before she dressed for the trip.

Everyone else still slept. The mist rising over the willows by the creek meant that dawn was breaking, a faint lightness in the East where the sun would soon show its face.

Aunt Sara came in from the back bedroom as Jane finished counting the big basket of eggs and folding towels to put between each layer in the basket, a pleased smile on her face, twelve dozen in all. That would buy a lot of the badly needed things.

"My! you sure got the old hens on the right track. I hadn't seen that many eggs in a coon's age," Aunt Sara said.

"Everything around here shows a woman's hand. I had me a good night's sleep. That bed's as soft as a cloud to sleep on, and smells so good and clean. My! look at all that dried pumpkin, you sure are a wonder, Jane, and so pretty," Aunt Sara continued.

Jane's face flushed with pleasure as she turned away. "I thank you for noticin', the pumpkin, I mean," she said with embarrassment.

The wagon was heard in the distance, "Have Will come fetch Madge and turn her to pasture. We will tie her inside the gate till he is up. The chores are all done. If you want he can bring more pumpkin to string. We have a lot. I expect to be back in time to milk and do the chores." With that Jane picked up the basket of eggs and hurried over to the road. Setting the basket well out of the way, she opened the bars to lead Madge through.

"You sure are a sight for sore eyes," Tom said as he brought the team to a standstill, "in your weddin' dress and your cheeks like roses."

Getting down from the wagon after carefully pulling the brake and wrapping the checkreins around its handle, he walked old Madge through the bars and laid them up again after tying her to a fence post inside the field.

Jane climbed up the wheel and waited for Tom to hand up the basket of eggs. She would hold them on her lap for safety during their trip in the rough wagon.

The wagon was piled high with sacks of wheat for the mill, one on the front of the wagon served as a seat for her and Tom. The sacks were covered with a tarp in case of rain.

Since there hadn't been any rain in two weeks or longer, each hoof of the horses sent up little puffs of dust at each step. Looking behind them Jane could see the dust from the wagon passing, hanging on the air till they went around a turn out of sight.

At a steady clip clop, clip clop, they were soon passing the Hall place where Aunt Sara and her daughter's family lived. A bunch of younguns were in the yard waving as they watched the wagon out of sight.

Leaving Beech Valley they topped the hill and started down through Big White Oak. "This used to all belong to dad," Tom told her. "He sold some off to Billie Conley. He has built a house and cleared some of it."

The wood section they were passing through came down to the wagon road on both sides forming a tunnel for them to pass through.

"When we pass Conley's farmhouse there is only one other till we reach the West Fork. That's my brother Sy's place," Tom explained.

To the East the sun was topping the hills with assurance of a fine day ahead of them. A big black snake slithered across the road in front of the horses. They shook their heads and snorted, starting to swerve to the side of the road. Tom brought them back sharply in line.

"That was a good six foot one, harmless though. Now a copperhead is something else," Tom said.

Like the team of horses, Jane didn't like snakes no matter what

53

kind they were, and was always uneasy in her mind about getting bit by one.

They made good time, soon passing the mouth of Little White Oak. "Dad owns all up that holler too," Tom said as he pulled the team to a halt beneath a big oak tree. "We will take a breather here," he said.

"Do you want to get down?" Tom asked.

"I don't think so, I'm alright and it's such a bother to climb up again," Jane told him.

Tom got down to check their load and the horses' harnesses to make sure everything was secure. Climbing back to his seat they continued their journey. Rounding a turn in the road, they could see the wooden bridge across the West Fork. The horses shied because they didn't like the sound of their shod hoofs and the rattle of the wagon crossing the boards. With a firm hand, Tom got them across without further ado.

They were now leaving the White Oaks and starting down the West Fork. It was a sizable creek and could almost be called a river, treacherous at times during heavy rains. Topping a small hill they looked toward the Jarvis homestead. The big white house by the tall cedar tree could be seen for miles.

In the big field north of the house were several horses and men milling around. Looked like fifty or more. "Wonder what that's all about? Suppose someone has died? Or are they having a horse race which they sometimes did in the big meadow." Tom was taking in all the movement, asking questions that didn't get answered.

As they got closer they could see that the crowd was in the big meadow away from the house. A big train of wagons was coming from the south up the West Fork toward them. Some of the men rode out to meet the wagon train, calling to the drivers and laughing loudly. The hullabaloo could be heard for miles, but Jane and Tom were still too far away to see what was going on.

Suddenly two men sitting tall in their saddles, both in uniforms, went toward the lead wagon, pointing and waving their arms as they directed the wagons to a knoll farther up the meadow.

"That's soldiers!" Tom exclaimed. "The war must be on and they're mustering here." His eyes began to shine as he slowed the wagon to take it all in. You could feel the excitement of the men and boys that were milling around the wagons.

Jane's heart gave a heavy thud at the thought of war. She had heard some rumors, never paying them any mind. Oh! What if my Tom has to go, she thought. Surely not with all the younguns, she could never manage without a man to help.

They arrived at the big house and could still hear the noise from the meadow.

Tom's mother met them at the front piazza. "Well, Tom, you have finally brought your new wife for us to have a look at."

"This is Jane, mother," Tom said. By that time his dad had come from one of the outbuildings to greet them. They shook hands on meeting. "This is dad, Jane," Tom said.

"How are you?" Mr. Jarvis asked. "Go on in with mother, I'll help Tom unhitch. Dinner should be about ready."

Jane and Mrs. Jarvis entered the house. A big cool foyer greeted them, the sittin' room opened off to the left with the dining room and kitchen beyond. Glancing around, Jane saw white lace curtains at all the windows. Big deep chairs with horsehair stuffing, covered in velvet and some in leather. She had been in lots of houses but nothing like this. Soft carpets covered the floors. There were so many places to sit she wondered how one made up their mind which chair to sit in. In a corner by the wide fireplace was a contraption she had never seen before. It was tall and ornate with a row of what looked like teeth peeking from under an overhang. Not wanting to stare she looked away, at the rows of books that were on the other side in shelves to the ceiling. Everything was polished till it shone and the smell of beeswax hung in the air.

"Sit down, Jane," Mrs. Jarvis told her. "Now tell me about Tom's children and how you are making out with them."

"We are making out just fine, and the younguns are well and growing. Will is a heap of help and Catherin is beginning to take her place and help, but they are all biddable younguns," Jane answered.

"I suppose you noticed the mustering in the meadow? The wagons that just arrived were the tents for the men, and the cook tents. Where they will find food for all of them, I don't know. Anything you have to sell will be at a premium," her mother-in-law continued.

"I have twelve dozen eggs with me in the basket I left in the hall," Jane told her.

"Some of the men were here this morning looking for eggs. I'll have one of the boys let them know, you will get more for them here than at the store."

"The girls will have dinner directly, I'll see how it's going, excuse me a minute."

Tom had told her that his mother's father was a doctor. That accounted for her fine manners and the rich furniture. The trip to see how dinner was coming gave Jane a chance to really look this room over. Her eyes were on a picture big enough for a tabletop. A stern looking old gentleman with a mustache and her Tom's eyes looked back at her from the gilt frame.

"That's my father, he was a wonderful doctor in Braxton County. He went out west to the Oklahoma Territory a few years back. I went with them, but came back to visit my sister and met my Tom. My family are still in Oklahoma. I doubt I will ever see them again," she said sadly.

A bell rang somewhere in the back. Jane could hear men's voices as they entered through a side door. Mrs. Jarvis rose. "Come," she said, "dinner is ready." They went down a long hall to a large dining room. The table was set with a white cloth and the prettiest dishes she had ever seen, paper thin, with pink rosebuds. A glass of water at every place, glistened in the light. A long wall, with several windows having snowy lace curtains, overlooked the creek and the back meadow.

There was so much food Jane couldn't name what she ate when she was through. Two pretty girls served them, which she knew were Tom's sisters. They joshed among themselves, remarking how pretty Tom's wife was, making Jane's face turn pink, and Tom's eyes sparkle. "This is Caroline, and this is Catherine, Jane," Tom's mother said with a smile. "Our other daughter, she is called Jane too, has gone to my father's. She wants to work as a nurse with him. She would like to have been a doctor, of course, but that is out of the question for a girl, so she will do the next best by being a nurse."

The dinner went along lively with joshing and talk of the war.

"Caleb, would you find the soldier who wanted eggs this morning? Tell him to bring a container to get them in, that we have twelve dozen for him."

Caleb soon returned with a young lieutenant carrying a big pan. The eggs were transferred from the basket. Jane had figured maybe she could get twelve cents a dozen for them, maybe fifteen at most. The young man gave her a five-dollar gold piece. "I hope

56

that is enough." "Oh, yes, thank you," Mrs. Jarvis answered for Jane.

"Isn't that too much?" Jane wanted to know when he left.

"Not at the prices they will have to pay, keep it, child. I'm sure you will need that and more for your houseful. If you don't take it, the men will spend it on whiskey, if they can find it," Mrs. Jarvis told her.

Tom had given her the eighteen dollars from the harvest pay that morning. Taking the drawstring bag from its hiding place where she had pinned it to her underclothing, she added the five-dollar gold coin to what she already had and it made a tidy sum. She had never had that much money before. The things she had decided to do without she now decided to buy. If prices were going up now would be the time to get them, Jane decided.

Soon after the meal was over the men went to hitch up the team. The wheat would be dropped at the mill to be ground, and another load brought the next week and the flour from this load picked up. The big store wasn't far away. Several people sitting on the long store porch watching a game of horseshoes in progress, and talking of the mustering, looked at Jane as she entered.

The big, long store was cool and dark with the smell of new cloth, leather goods, coffee, and lamp oil, all mingled together mysteriously. Jane's eyes couldn't take in everything for so many things were new to her. She was scared half to death but never showed it by the flicker of an eyelash, walking around looking at this and feeling that as though it was an everyday occurrence. The merchant followed her, explaining the merits of all that caught her eye. After all, this was a Jarvis, fine family and big farms. He had never seen this one before but she sure was a pretty little thing even if she was no bigger than a minute and he could see, also, that she had a mind of her own.

"What is the price of sugar?" she asked. "It was three cents a pound last week, this week five cents, probably fifteen cents next week," he answered, eyeing her as he told her the prices.

"I'll need two twenty-five-pound bags of sugar, fifty pounds of lard, twenty-five-pound sack of coffee grains, fifty pounds of salt, three pounds of baking powder, two of soda, three cans of lye, two boxes of matches. Measure me off one hundred feet of clothesline, six dozen clothespins, a number two washtub, two five-gallon stone jars, four one-gallon jars, a five-quart bucket, a pound of black pepper, one pound of nutmeg, three packages of turnips, and three of parsnips, and one of kale, one can of cinnamon; one black and one white number fifty thread. I want twelve yards of that blue and white checked three-cent gingham."

Still looking around she noticed an empty vinegar barrel, a twenty-five-gallon one. "What do you want for the empty vinegar barrel?" "I can let you have that for a quarter," the merchant told her.

"Do you have two? If so, I'll take them both," Jane said. Seeing a twenty-gallon kettle, she asked the price of it, but thinking it was more than she could afford he passed it up.

"Would you show me some boys' shoes, heavy ones for outdoors." Will would need shoes to help outside this winter.

The clerk showed her a lightweight pair for seventy-five cents, "I have heavier ones at one dollar and a half."

"I'll take the heavier ones for an eight-year-old boy. I will need five gallons of lamp oil, and a pound of peppermint stick candy, and that will be all for today. My man will be back from the mill directly to load it onto the wagon. If you will tally it up, and tell me how much I owe, I will pay you, sir."

Tom was soon back and was surprised at the mound of things on the porch to be loaded. Looked as though Jane had bought out the store.

The stuff she had bought had cost twenty-two dollars, but it would be saved in the long run when things went up in price. Jane had an idea how to even make it produce some more money.

The things were soon loaded and they were on their way home. They hadn't intended to stop at Tom's folks on the way back, but were waved in when they approached the gate.

Caleb carried out a big basket of peaches and gave them to Tom, "We have plenty and thought maybe the younguns would like some," he said.

"They're sure nice ones, we are beholden," Tom told his brother, as they said good-bye again. It was well on in the afternoon and would be sundown by the time they reached home.

There was much excitement when Tom and Jane arrived back at the cabin. Even Aunt Sara was out in the yard to see the wonders they had brought home from the big store, and to hear the news.

The kitchen was overflowing when the two big barrels were

brought and placed against the wall behind the door. The sacks of sugar, salt, and coffee stacked on top to make room for walking.

Jane went through to take off her dress and bonnet. She carried the pound of peppermint candy and put it on the high shelf, folded her dress and laid it on top. It would be kept till Christmas. The cloth was also put away for safekeeping.

Tom had offered to milk and help Will with the chores while Jane made the supper. She had decided on the way home to make a peach cobbler to be eaten with milk, and a big pot of fresh coffee. That would be a good dinner and everyone would think it a treat.

Soon the smell of cinnamon filled the kitchen, as the peach cobbler bubbled in the oven.

When the milk was brought in, it was strained to be put away, leaving out a generous amount to be put over the cobbler. Lifting it from the oven brown and fragrant made everyone's mouth water in anticipation.

Three bowls were found for the adults, and tin cups were put around the table for the younguns. Big helpings of the cobbler was at every place. They ate with oh's and ah's as Tom told Sara about the mustering. Will, not being able to contain himself any longer, asked, "Are you going, Pa? Are you gonna muster? Am I big enough to muster?"

Tom's eyes sparkled as he answered his son, "I'm afraid you would be a mite small. Those are big rifles, in fact, almost as big as you are. I doubt that Mammy Jane would let me go either, even if I had a hankerin' to do so."

Jane noticed she had been holding her breath while he answered and thought to herself, thank God. To change the talk from mustering and the war, Jane began to tell them about their grandma and grandpa's house. "There was a big-toothed mysterious thing in the sittin' room, and I still haven't figured it out," she told them.

Tom looked at her and started to chuckle. "That's a 'pennfort,' you play the teeth as you call them, and make music. My sisters both play, and they would have played for you if you had asked." He laughed again. "Lots of people never saw one or heard it played. Mother also plays, but not often anymore. It came from her father's home."

Turning to Aunt Sara, Jane said, "You may as well stay the night. Will can ride you home in the cool of the mornin'." Getting up from the table she went to the egg basket and brought a box of

Aunt Sara's favorite snuff and gave it to her. The new shoes she gave to Will. Both of their faces beamed with the surprise of the gifts.

Will took the shoes, turning them slowly every which way, his face shining like the sun was on it.

"You know what that means?" his pa asked.

Will tore his eyes away from his treasure. "It means I'll go out in the snow and help with chores this winter, and maybe do some trappin'."

The other younguns gathered around to touch and look, and smell the new leather shoes, "The man said genuine cowhide," Jane told him. "They are guaranteed to last till you grow out of them," she added.

"I'll take care, and then John can have them when I outgrow them," Will said. They all wanted to see if they fit, and went to the back bedroom where each had a turn trying them on for size. The clump, clump, as they walked, could be heard all the way to the kitchen.

Apple Pie and Vinegar

The mist came up the valley, beginning to rise toward the hilltop, as Tom got the horse ready to ride to the Cook farm. They would be starting the corn cutting this week and the cane for molasses would be ready soon, too.

Sara and Jane had coffee together. "Do you think you could stay a few days longer?" Jane asked her.

Aunt Sara seemed pleased to be asked. "I recon I can eat just as well here, in fact the matter is you are a better cook, ha, ha, ha, and I sure sleep good," Sara answered.

Tom will be taking another load of wheat for the mill day after tomorrow and I have in mind to go along," Jane told her.

Today she and Will had work to do. "Will, fetch the mare, maybe you had better saddle her. We are going apple picking, we can tie the sacks to the saddle so they don't slide off." The sacks, the basket, and new bucket were readied for the picking.

The sun had barely topped the first hill as they started up the "holler." Will seemed to know where all the trees were, and Jane was hoping they could find several. Following the cow path that wound along the run, finally Will pointed out the first tree, on a little hillock back from the path. It was an old gnarled tree and hung full of apples. The ground was covered with fallen ripe ones.

"We will take the windfall ones, they will do for what I want them for. The others we can pick for holing," Jane said. There were soon two sacks half full ready to be tied together to throw across the saddle to take home. With grunts from Will, and a heave-ho from Jane, they managed to load them.

Jane filled the basket to carry, they started down the "holler," leading the mare with her load.

Back at the cabin they unloaded at the kitchen door, half lifting and half dragging the sacks inside.

Jane started peeling the peaches they had brought from Tom's home, washing each one thoroughly. The good peels would go

61

into the vinegar barrel with the apple peels. She should have enough for the two barrels of good vinegar. There was already "vinegar mother" clinging to the barrel sides and would soon have the vinegar working.

The peaches would be dried starting them outside in the sunshine then stringing them on twine as they had the pumpkin.

The peaches were finished quickly and the apples started. Jane intended to bake twelve apple pies, and she figured by stacking them, adding four pumpkin pies on top, she could carry the pies in the big long split basket they had brought the peaches home in, and the egg basket. Considering the price the soldiers paid for eggs she figured she could get a dollar a piece for the pies; she knew she was a good pie maker. There would be some eggs to take also. The big copper kettle was as much as hers right now. She had seen some oilcloth she wanted for her tables. It would match the blue checked gingham she had gotten for curtains. It would add some homeyness to the cabin this winter.

When Tom came home to the smell of apple pies, and the news that she would be going with him, he was pleased. "That's a fine idea," he said.

Off they went bright and early with one basket setting at her feet with a folded quilt under it to absorb the jolts of the wagon, the big one rested on her lap for safekeeping.

The reception at the camp was something she hadn't expected. The men and boys took the pies so fast they were gone before half the camp knew what was going on. A moan went up when they found out there weren't any more. Jane could have gotten more out of them and decided the next batch would be more. She felt it was selfish but they wouldn't be there long and she would have to "make hay" while the sun shined.

Jane ended up with twenty dollars for the day's work. She was so pleased she could scarcely contain herself as they went on to the mill and store.

"Could you get me three smooth boards about ten inches wide, and four feet long, at the sawmill? I need shelves over my work-table," Jane said.

"With all the money you are making I might as well order you a new house pattern," Tom said, looking at her proudly.

Jane blushed at his joshing. The scene around the store hadn't changed. Seemed the same men were lounging on nail kegs or leaning up against the wall, spitting long streams of amber tobacco juice into the roadway.

The owner of the store, Mr. Cheniweth, seeing her enter, came up, "Well, well, young lady, what can I do for you today?"

"I would like the twenty-gallon copper kettle, seven yards of the blue checked oilcloth, another twenty-five pounds of sugar, and a fifty-pound-can of lard, and that will be all today. The wagon will be here directly."

"Will Tom be mustering?" he asked by way of conversation.

"He has five younguns, I surely hope not," she answered. "I'll take a penny's worth of gumdrops," she said as he finished carrying her things to the porch for loading.

Jane had to wait a while for the wagon to return from unloading the wheat, and the flour loaded and tied down with the tarp over it.

Tom knew she had in mind to buy the big kettle, and had left a hole down between the flour sacks to put it. The other things she had bought could be put inside the kettle.

Stopping at his father's farm to return the basket, they were asked to stay for dinner, as the family was ready to sit for the noon meal. Tom's mother turned to Jane, "Why don't you keep the basket? If you have use for it, Caleb makes them and we have several."

"She has already found a use for it," Tom said and went on to tell about the pies.

"What a wonderful idea, Jane," Mrs. Jarvis remarked.

"You want to keep your eye on her, Tom, the army is likely to take her along when they leave, to bake pies for them," Tom's father said with a laugh.

"I'm beholden," she told her mother-in-law, "It sure is a fine basket. I'll find many uses for it."

They arrived back at the farm in time for Will to ride Sara home. Jane gave her a quarter for her staying with the younguns.

"You just send the youngun any time, I'll come," Aunt Sara told Jane.

More apples were peeled and the peelings added to the vinegar barrel with sweet springwater. A cup of sugar for every bucket would be sufficient to make good vinegar. The other barrel would be used later. The peaches were wilted enough to be strung and not break. Jane had put them in pans on the kitchen roof to dry in the sun where the chickens couldn't get at them.

63

All the peels and cores that couldn't be used for vinegar was given to the chickens, nothing was ever wasted that an animal could eat.

There was work aplenty to do, the garden patch had to be leveled off and the turnips, parsnips, and kale sowed. Cabbage had to be gathered. All the big split heads, that had grown too fast, would be brought in to fill the two five-gallon churns for sauerkraut. That would have to be done before the rest of the apple picking. They would have to pick on a Sunday so Tom could help. It was too much for Jane and the younguns.

She planned to send Tom with more pies on Sunday to the "compound." Jane didn't think it "seemly" for her to go. He could take the big basket by horseback in front of him on the saddle horn. She didn't know how he would take to it, he would have to or she would go herself "seemly or not," she intended to make all the money she could, she wouldn't have to spend the money from this batch, it could be saved.

The week flew it seemed, the kraut got made, both churns filled with layers of plump green tomatoes throughout each layer as a bonus.

The seeds were planted and that side of the garden smooth and rich looking waiting for the new plants to peep through. More pumpkins had been strung, soon the first strings would be ready to be put away in a clean salt sack and hung in a corner to keep for winter use. Apples were strung and hung to dry also. Dried apple pies were even better than fresh ones.

The pies were all ready for Sunday delivery, all brown and fragrant with cinnamon and nutmeg. Tom seemed more than willing to leave early with them. Returning around noon he handed Jane twenty dollars. He was strangely quiet as they set off with the horses and wagon to the big apple tree. He had put a ladder made from saplings on the wagon. The younguns all climbed into the wagon enjoying the ride to the pickin'.

The afternoon was cool with big white clouds scuddling across the sky. The smell of the crisp apples, as they were loaded, was intoxicating. The feel of fall was in the air, the leaves falling like rainbows of color. Soon the frost would come.

Through the next days Jane and Will scoured the hills for apple trees, picking everyone they could find. Holing away the sound best ones and made the rest into dried apples or apple pies. The leaves were falling fast and nut picking was next. They picked up chestnuts by the bucketful, and gathered all the hazelnuts they could find, everything that was eatable by man or beast was hoarded away. Black walnuts were hulled by the younguns leaving their hands black with stains.

Tom had cut the field of corn against the hill. He and Will hauled it to the barn where it could be shucked later as Tom was still helping the Cooks. The molasses making was over and Tom had bought a five-gallon bucketful and brought it home. It would be a real treat with hot biscuits and butter for breakfast.

The morning came when Jane found ice on the water bucket. A few mornings later when she looked out at daybreak, there was snow on the ground. Everyone was excited to see snow, but it was gone by noon. There were still some leaves on the trees, even though it was mid-November. Everything was being readied for the cold winter ahead. Will and Tom hauled in trees for wood every spare moment they could find. Sawing and splitting, piling big piles close to the house where it would be easy to get to in the snow. They held off as long as possible on building a fire in the big potbellied stove in the sittin' room, staying in the kitchen till bedtime to keep warm by the kitchen stove. Late one afternoon Jane took a shovelful of fire coals from the kitchen stove and started a fire in the sittin' room to take the chill and damp out of the beds.

Tom and Will cut pieces from saplings and built a picket fence on the hillside surrounding an outcropping of rocks, for the pigs. Will dug some dirt from beneath the overhanging rocks, gathered dry leaves for them to bed in and laid rocks across the front, leaving them a hole for entering and leaving their nest. They would be warm and out of the bad weather.

The female runt had done well on old Blossom's milk, and Jane's and Will's care. You could hardly tell now that she hadn't been the pick of the litter.

Tom made the weekly trips to the compound with Jane's pies, eggs, and a few pounds of butter she could spare. He would bring the money home and hand it to Jane. The little pouch was almost full, she never bothered to count it but knew it was mounting.

Buying a Farm

This week Tom took the wagon so he could bring their winter supply of flour from the mill. He had taken wheat in payment for part of his work at the Cooks. He still had some money coming to him for his and the team's work and brought home a ten-dollar gold piece to Jane.

When he returned from the mill, Aunt Sara was with him on the wagon. Jane was surprised and wondered what the reason was for her visit. She came in and removed her wraps in the kitchen where Jane was.

There were tears in Sara's eyes as she told Jane and Tom that her son-in-law had volunteered and enlisted in the army and would be leaving in a week. He was sending his wife and children to his parent's home over in Lewis County. Aunt Sara had no one to run her farm and would have to go stay with another daughter who lived on the Kanawha River.

They had talked it over and had decided to sell the house and farm. There were sixty-five acres plus the house and barn. One cow and about twenty chickens. They had one horse but the son-in-law would take it to war with him.

"We wondered, Tom, if you and Jane would want to buy it since you join up to it with your farm?" Aunt Sara made the offer wiping tears from her eyes.

Tom looked at Jane and looked away without answering. Jane didn't know what to think, turning to Sara asked, "What do you want for it?"

Aunt Sara thought for a minute. "Fifty dollars for the farm, and ten dollars for the cow, she is with calf, and I recon two for the chickens. There will be most of the house plunder, too. They can't take much that far away," she added.

Jane mulled it over in her mind, there was cleared ground for crops next year, but could they feed the animals on the feed they had? She got up and walked around the kitchen thinking. "I'll

66

give you sixty dollars for everything if you've a mind to sell," Jane said.

Aunt Sara nodded her head. "That will do," she said. "And I'm beholding to you for buying it. I'll bring you the deed. We will have it signed over. We want to be gone before snow. My son-in-law's people are coming for my daughter and the younguns. I will go to my other daughter's with them."

"I'll take you and Jane over to fix the papers up, tomorrow if you want," Tom told them. "We can leave the younguns with your daughter."

That night Jane counted her money. There was over two hundred dollars. She took out the money for the farm to have it ready. Tied it in a corner of a big handkerchief and put it in the pocket of her weddin' dress.

This is the only way to get ahead, add to. That would make one hundred and two acres they owned. The extra cow would be a blessing when Blossom "freshened" and maybe she could sell more butter with two.

The details were all taken care of and their nearest neighbor gone. They all went to the new farm to fetch the animals home, and to see that everything was closed up for the winter.

One bed and the cooking stove, a table and benches, and a corner cupboard was still in the cabin. There was hay and some cut corn in the barn loft. It could be hauled home later to help out.

The next week after Aunt Sara left there came a foot of snow. The wind blew and the creek froze over. It was so cold no one left the cabin unless it was necessary.

"Thank the Lord for plenty of foodstuff," Jane said aloud. She now had time for some sewing. She sent the younguns to bed early and sat at the kitchen table sewing. She would make each of the girls a dress from one of their mother's old ones, for Christmas, and shirts for the boys.

Tom grew more restless than Jane had ever known. Being cooped up all day in the house, she decided.

The snow had stopped and the wind died down somewhat. After breakfast Tom announced it was time to go after the deer. Will's eyes lit up. "Can I go, pa?" he asked hopefully.

"No, son, we need the meat and it may be a long wait. I'll build a 'blind' close to the deer lick and lay in wait, may have to wait a spell." He pulled on his heavy sheep-lined coat Jane had found stuffed on the bottom shelf of the cupboard, and carefully washed.

He took a piece of tarp to lay on behind the blind and asked for a biscuit sandwich to take in his pocket. "Don't worry if I'm not back by dark," he told Jane as she handed him a butter and jelly sandwich. "Will, you see that old Madge is fastened in the shed, we will have to bring the deer home on her back," he called as he slammed the kitchen door.

Jane had gone to the shed to milk, and Will was bringing the firewood in for the night, when they heard a shot and then another following in quick succession. Will dropped his load of wood and ran to tell Jane. "Did you hear pa? I sure hope he got two, I sure hope so," Will said.

They had returned to the cabin when they heard the whoooo—ee yell of Tom. Going outside they saw him motion for Will to bring the mare, and a rope to tie the deer with, knowing he had at least one.

Will soon joined his pa at the edge of the woods where he waited.

It was dark when the two returned, and wrapped in the tarp tied to the mare were two young bucks. By lantern light Tom and Will skinned and dressed the deer, tied rope to their feet and hung them high in a tree for the night to freeze.

Jane put the liver, kidneys, and hearts in a big pan, taking them inside, she washed and sliced the livers. Pounding and rolling them in flour, she fried a big platter full for their supper.

While they ate Tom told the younguns about the kill. "I was sittin' there behind the oak tree branches I had propped up for a blind. It was almost dark. My hands were numb with cold. I heard something coming, crunch, crunch, in the snow. A big buck with a pair of antlers," he measured with his hands. "I don't see how he ever got through the trees they were so big. He come prancing out of the edge of the timber, snorting and pawing the ground. He knew something wasn't just right, but didn't know what. I sat there not even breathing in case he could see my frosty breath. He came on to the lick, slinging that rack of horns and sniffin' the air. He decided it was safe when he wasn't challenged, and called his herd out from the underbrush. They came slowly eating the fern tops sticking up out of the snow. I wasn't more than twenty feet from the lick. There were fifteen altogether, and these two young bucks were close together, looking right at me it seemed. I slowly raised my double-barreled gun, brought it to aim, and let her rip! First one barrel and then the other. Both went down like they was hit with a sledge.

"You never heard such a racket, that old buck let out a squeal as they fell over each other getting out of there fast."

"Boy!" Will let out his breath, "I sure wish I could have been there."

"Tomorrow I will cut them up, and take one to the compound to sell. We can take it on the sled since we have enough snow, and bring whatever you need, Jane. I can bring a load of feed from the Hall farm on the way back. How would you like to go and see the soldiers, Will?"

Will was speechless for a minute, then jumped up and threw his arms around his pa. It was a surprise to both of them as there wasn't much hugging went on in the family.

Will and Tom started at first light, Jane had stayed up to make pies by lamplight, wrapped the eggs so they wouldn't freeze, added five pounds of butter in a bucket with a lid. She had already made back most of the money she had paid out for the Hall farm.

Tom had said the new cow, old Brindle, would freshen sometime in February or March, that was an unlooked for bonus as she could still have milk and butter to sell.

Dusk was falling when they heard the horses and sled coming. Looking out she made out three walking, and wondered who could be coming with them.

The sled was piled high with hay, and the bed from the Hall farm on top. "Now what in the world?" Jane asked, as she watched.

With stomping of feet and brushing of snow, they came in the kitchen, and Jane had the surprise of her life, her older brother Harn was with them. "Harn! How in the world did you get here in all this snow? All the way from Gilmer County," Jane exclaimed.

"Oh! I got a ride here and there, and decided to come for Christmas. Hope I don't put you out," Harn answered.

"Of course not, I see Tom even thought of bringing you a bed," she said as they busily moved things around in the sittin' room, to make room for the extra bed over in one corner. Jane brought the girls' bedding in from the other room, and made up their bed for Harn in with the boys. She had been thinking of putting the girls in this room. They were getting a little old to be sleeping in the same room with the boys.

The menfolk unloaded the hay while Jane set another place at the table, and put the vittles on.

Harn brought in a sack of his belongings and took them in and put them under the bed Jane told him would be his.

"This is a nice house and farm, looks like you're doing fine. A lot of people are giving up when their men and boys sign up," Harn remarked. "Of course, I don't have to go with this limp of mine." He had one leg shorter than the other since birth, and had never married. "Everyone said to tell you hello."

Jane was still curious. There weren't that many who knew her, she had been hired out and gone so long. Something was in the wind, but she didn't quite know what yet.

Christmas came, the deer was cooked, and a big cake smelling of cinnamon frosted with a thick butter frosting. A big pot of the new turnips was ready. They were going to have a real feast.

Christmas morning was noisy with the gifts of new dresses and new shirts for the younguns. The big box of peppermint was passed around. It was the nicest Christmas Jane had ever had. The first one in her own home. Two months married and the changes were unbelievable. If things kept on she would be rich before she was twenty, the thought made her smile.

Tom and Harn had a toddy from one of the gallon jugs she had Tom get to have ready for her medicines that she made. When they were all comfortable and happy together, Harn decided to sing to them, and sang a Christmas song followed by a hymn. He had a nice voice, and they all went to bed feeling uplifted somehow.

That night Tom held Jane in his arms talking low, telling her how lovely and sweet she was. How much he loved her, and how proud he was to call her his wife. He made love to her until she was helplessly weak. Still holding her in his arms, stroking her hair he told her he loved her so much, then he said, "I'm going, Jane."

"Going? Where? Now?" she couldn't get her mind on what he was saying.

"To the war, I signed up today. I have to. I can't stand by and see the States go down and secede from the Union. I'll be leaving next week, January first. Harn has promised to stay with you and the younguns. They will let me come home in the spring to put in a crop. There is little I can do this winter anyway. I'll be going South with the next company leaving the compound."

Oh, My God! Jane thought to herself, what will I do? At times Harn was like a youngun and she couldn't depend on him, and she would have a baby from this night, she had been lucky so far. She shivered, not able to say a word.

70

Tom held her close kissing her hair. At this moment she hated him. Just like a man—off to the war and her left to look after his younguns. Not a word of this passed her lips, as the thoughts flew through her mind.

"We will make do fine," she told him, "if that's what you want."

"I knew you would take it like that. Three of my brothers are going, only—" there was a long pause. "Only two went to join the Confederate. Wess and me, we joined the Union. We will be fighting against each other," he told her. "Not a pleasant thought, we have been trying to talk each other into seeing the way we each see it, but we can't. Dad tried to talk to them, too, but we each have our own opinions and will have to fight the way we see it."

The days passed swiftly and the nights more so for Jane, and then Tom was gone. Her Tom with the ready grin and laughing eyes. Her heart broke as she stood in the chipyard waving to him as he rounded the bend in the road and she couldn't see him any longer. He had decided not to take the horses, but to leave them for the family and walked to the compound, saying "He might as well learn to march now."

Jane never allowed herself tears, and went about her work and plans as though Tom had never been.

If the soldiers were going to leave she would have to double her efforts to make money from them. Fortunately, new ones came all the time from as far away as Pennsylvania and had plenty of money. Jane intended to get as much as she could of it.

The pies, eggs, and butter continued to be sent regularly. Harn took what she had once a week and returned with the money.

This war would take her man, when they had been married less than three months. In return it would give her the big white house she had promised herself, the first time she had seen one, sitting in a big green meadow.

The last trip to the compound, Harn made his stop at her in-laws to see if there was any word from Tom. He had been gone over a month now.

Harn came back without any news, other than Tom had been sent somewhere toward the South where the big battles were going on.

A Mr. Middleton sent word that the farm he owned south of her was for sale, eighty-eight acres. Their house had burned along with every building on the place last winter. Tomorrow she would ride old Madge down and have a look at it.

The Rape

Most of the snow had melted, and the sun now sent feeble rays that warmed the air somewhat. The mud around the outbuildings was ankle deep. The animals tromping around the barn for warmth and lack of something else to do, kept it stirred up.

Jane waited until the sun had reached overhead and had Harn saddle old Madge. She would go look at the Middleton farm which wasn't far because she wanted to see what timber was available. She was planning to build a barn, and a good one, over by the road at the end of the meadow.

On days they could work outside, Jane had Harn and Will clearing every level spot for mowing, enlarging the meadow as much as possible. With the stock they were accumulating they would need as much feed as they could get to see them through the winter.

While she was out she decided to ride by the Hall farm, and see how much more hay and fodder was left to bring home. The next freeze she would send the boys to fetch it. During a thaw like now they could never get there and back with a wagon.

Mounting old Madge she pulled her cape more closely around her, and securing the shawl around her head, they started off down the Beech road. She noted how nice the new meadow had been cleared and that it would be a goodly size when finished. The rail fence surrounding the meadow butted up to the Middleton acres.

The ashes showed up black where all the buildings had burned the winter before. Some logs still lay with their blackened sides exposed to the elements. Several acres had been cleared for pasture, some meadowland lay to the south and there was a truck patch left untended by the burned-out area. There was fine timber and more than enough to build three barns, and it was close to the sight she had decided on so that it wouldn't have to be hauled far. Land was going for around a dollar an acre. She could buy it and still have plenty of money left.

72

Not feeling safe carrying her cloth poke she had fixed a hole under the house where she hid the growing amount of money. A big slab of creek rock covered it and the washtubs on top of that. Even in case of fire, it would be safe.

Feeling satisfied with the look of the farm she would send word, or go herself, and buy it from Middleton. All of this was going through her mind as she rode toward the Hall farm.

Coming in sight of the house she could see that all of the doors and windows were closed, everything looked secure.

Dismounting she tied old Madge to the yard fence and went toward the barn. Climbing into the loft, she inspected what feed was left and discovered a good amount was left to be hauled home.

While she was poking in a far corner, she heard Madge whinny, and stomping of hoofs. Thinking the mare had somehow broken loose from where she had tied her, Jane hurried from the loft. She sure didn't have a hankering to walk two miles in the mud. If old Madge broke loose she would head home and not stop till she reached there.

The barn door had swung shut and the light coming through the few cracks was dim, Jane made her way toward the door. As she reached to push it open, it swung outward. Two men stood in the door blocking her way. Surprise and shock numbed her senses. She was close enough to smell the sour odor of whiskey on them.

"Ha! Ha! Clem. Look what I found. A little barn kitten to play with." Their yellow teeth showed in drinking grins as they pushed toward her.

Jane backed into the dark barn, her knees shaking. There was no way out but the door they were in. "Get out!" she demanded. "This is private property," she told them with authority, standing straight and as tall as she could before them.

The one called Clem pushed through the door toward her. "Oh! Oh! Our kitten has claws, we will have to tame her, Billy Dan," he said to his partner. Jane could see they weren't going to stop, and there was no way out. Looking around she knew there wasn't a weapon she could use. Backing toward the ladder to the loft, she thought if she could get up there and somehow pull the ladder up, maybe they would leave her alone. She flew up the ladder, turned and tried to lift it. It was made from saplings and too heavy.

Both of the men shuffled and staggered toward her and caught the ladder as she tried to push it backward from the loft.

They started climbing toward her. She searched frantically for a loose club. There was nothing. "Don't you come near me. My man will be here in a minute," she told them.

"We watched you way down the road," Clem told her. "We were in a clump of trees finishing off our jug, there is no one in miles of here. Come here," he said as he made a grab for her, catching her shawl and pulling it from her head. Her blond hair tumbled to her shoulders.

"Hey, Billy Dan! She is a pretty little thing. Look at all that 'yeller' hair."

"Please, please," she begged. "I'm with child. You don't want to bother with me." She knew they were both too drunk to listen to any pleading. She also knew what they intended to do. "Oh, Merciful Lord, don't let this happen." Still trying to get away she ran into the farthest corner. The one called Billy Dan was in the loft by now. Both were penning her in the corner and grabbing for her. Dodging here and there, her hair over her face, "No! No! No!"

"I got her," Billy Dan said, catching her by her hair. Throwing her head back he found her mouth, with his foul breath he covered it with his own, forcing his filthy tongue down her throat again and again, making her want to gag.

Grabbing her hands, Clem shouted, "I'll hold her for you, Billy Dan. Down her and get at it. I want my turn. My cock's dancing 'Yankee Doodle' now."

Together they threw her down on the hay, Billy Dan clawing at her waist trying to get her clothing open to her breast.

Knowing there was nothing more she could do but submit, she lay still. "No need to tear my garments, I'll open them if Clem will let go my hands," Jane said.

"Let go, Clem," Billy Dan told him.

She opened her clothing exposing her young firm breasts. Her skirts were pulled up to expose her lower body.

"You sure are a pretty thing," Billy Dan told her as he let his pants fall around his feet, falling on her sucking and slobbering, making revolting noises while he devoured her breasts. Jabbing and grunting, he found her opening. She gritted her teeth at the pain of his cruelty. After the gentleness of her Tom, this was almost more than she could stand. Jab, jab, grunt, jab, and he rolled to one side in the hay. The wetness running down her buttocks. Clem was at her like a bull after a cow. He only lasted a minute

74

and he too lay off her in the hay. "Boy! was that good," he told Billy Dan.

Jane hurt so bad that tears stung her eyes. "You will pay for this, both of you," she said to herself.

"Hey, We gotta get back for roll call," Billy Dan said as he began pulling on his clothes and started down the ladder. Clem followed, buttoning his clothing as he went.

Jane calmly put her clothes to rights. "Oh, Billy Dan," she called as he was ready to go out the door. "I'm working at a farm near here. I'll be leaving tomorrow. How would you two like to meet me here, about the same time tomorrow?"

"Hey! She liked it," Clem said. "Most of these little old gals love it, once you break them in right." Pounding Billy Dan on the back, "What you say, Billy Dan?"

Billy Dan looked surprised, with a loud laugh, "Sure, barn kitten, we will be here," he said. "We will be here with bells on, you be ready for us."

They staggered out to their horses. Jane could hear their laughter as they mounted and went at a gallop toward the compound. It was five miles or more and she wondered how they had found their way over through the backcountry. They had found it alright, and also found what they were looking for, a helpless female for their lust. When she was sure they were out of sight, she came down from the loft. Her legs were bruised and weak as she went to the run. Squatting down she splashed the icy water between her legs washing away as much as she could of the vileness that covered her. No one must ever know, no one, it would follow her to her grave and her children's graves as well. She had told them she was with child to try to stay them, but it hadn't worked. Tom hadn't left her in the family way when he went off to the war, and she considered herself lucky.

Now she might not be so lucky. To birth a child for the likes of Clem or Billy Dan and who could say which, made bitter bile come into her mouth. She gagged and heaved there astraddle of the run. Dipping her hand in the cold water she washed her mouth and face, wiping it on her skirt. Looking for telltale evidence of what she had been through, making sure no hay clung to her clothing. The bruises she had collected in her struggle wouldn't show. Her breasts ached from their lust. Twisting her hair as best she could, she tied the shawl around it. Mounting old Madge she started home, making plans for the meeting tomor-

75

row. She knew they would come back, and she would be a willing partner for them . . . or so they thought.

Every detail had to be worked out, so there would be little rest for her this night.

The Revenge

It was well into evening when Jane returned to the cabin. She gave over the horse to Harn and started supper for them all.

As they ate, Harn and Will wanted to know how the farm looked. "It's a fair place. Plenty of good timber, and a good amount cleared for pasture and crops. We could put in more corn next year without having to clear. I'll buy, if the price is right," Jane told them. "There is no buildings so it shouldn't be too costly." Thinking of her plans for the next day, she quickly added, "I'll go back down again tomorrow. I want to look at another portion of the woodland." That should cover her trip back to the Hall farm without questions, she thought to herself.

All through the sleepless night the nightmare of Clem and Billy Dan pulling at her, haunted her. Tossing and turning, she thought of tomorrow and her meeting with them again.

Getting up at first light she took the saddlebags from the peg behind the door. Taking two half gallon jugs of her precious store of whiskey from the lower cupboard shelf she wrapped them in a towel and put them into the bags. A good thing she had Tom get two gallons before he left, for the medicine she made.

She then went to the barn where Tom had a blacksnake whip laying on a high log of the barn, stepping up on a lower log to reach it, she got it down. She knew how to use it holding firmly by the short handle she flicked it out and back several times, a twist of the wrist and the tip would cut with a sharp snap like a gunshot when it landed. Coiling it around and around she put it into the other pocket of the saddlebags. All of this was done before anyone was up to ask questions.

Breakfast was well on the way when Harn came through headed for the privy. "Morning," he said as the kitchen door slammed.

As they ate breakfast, Jane told Will and Harn to finish in the meadow by noon then come for dinner and cut wood in the afternoon as she would be gone and they would look after the younguns.

The morning didn't go fast enough to suit her. She was anxious for the meeting with Clem and Billy Dan.

Harn finished dinner and saddled the mare for her. Jane was ready and waiting by the chopping block, must be going on to one o'clock. She wanted to be in the barn when they got there. By the time she had reached the Hall farm it would be time for the boys to come, she didn't have much time.

Climbing up into the loft, she threw down a pile of hay around a center pole. Taking out the blacksnake whip she took it back to the loft and hid it under the hay, now everything was set. The saddlebags hung over a partition with the jugs showing.

Maybe they wouldn't come, she began to worry. She felt sure they would not turn down such an opportunity. Every nerve was on end as she waited and listened. She had waited a good half hour when the sound of shod hoofs could be heard coming down the road towards the barn. Looking through a crack she made out Clem and Billy Dan riding loosely toward her. Clem had a jug which they were drinking from, laughing and talking between drinks, looking like they were well on their way to being drunk already. It wouldn't take as long as she had thought or as much whiskey, she thought thriftily.

They started to trot their horses as they spotted her mare tied to the yard fence. As they dismounted and staggered toward the barn, Jane threw the door open, one hand holding it for them to enter.

"Welcome, boys!" she said. "Come on in."

"Hey! Barn Kitten! We didn't think you would be here." They both reached for her as she turned toward the saddlebags.

"Looks like you didn't wait for me," she said as she took a jug from the bag and turned it up as though she was drinking, then handed it to Billy Dan, who took several swallows and handed it to Clem.

"Hey, Clem, you know this here barn kitten is alright. Come on, gimme another drink of that," and he grabbed for the jug.

"Come on, boys, and sit down here on the hay I've fixed. Let me take your coat, Clem," she started unbuttoning it and Clem laughed with glee. "I like this," he said as he half fell onto the hay as she tickled his neck.

"I'm gonna treat you like you should be treated," she told them. Handing the jug to Clem, she started unbuttoning Billy

Dan's coat and shirt. "It's time for you, Clem," and the jug was passed to Billy Dan.

She had their shoes and pants off, a drink between each piece of clothing. The first jug was almost empty so she brought the second one from the saddlebag, pretending to take a drink from it before handing it around.

She pulled the long johns from Clem down over his feet. Deciding to leave them in a tangle around his ankles. Giving him the jug, he took another drink and fell over passed out onto the hay, his bare behind sticking up naked and white.

"You're some gal," Billy Dan said as she pulled his johns down around his feet, patting his white belly, as she did so. Seeing his manhood swollen and red she turned to him again with the jug, first taking her turn. He let the fiery whiskey go down his throat till he couldn't breathe. Moving close to him in the hay and urged one more drink on him. The jug fell from his limp hands into the hay, and Billy Dan toppled over beside Clem, dead to the world.

Quickly recorking the jug, no reason to waste good whiskey, Jane went to the loft to get rope she had hidden with the whip. Bringing them both, she tied Clem and Billy Dan's hands above their heads and to the post behind him. They were as limp and helpless as a newborn baby, the rope was a precautionary measure.

Standing up, she looked at them, naked and ugly. The rage built up in her. "Scum," she gritted through her teeth. "You will rue the day you picked on this barn kitten."

Taking the whip she stood back where the tip would just reach to sting and tease. "Too bad you aren't fully awake to enjoy this," she said, as she let the whip streak toward them. Moans escaped them as they tried to twist away. The whiskey had done its job, they couldn't move but little, and when they did it was toward the whip. Their brains were addled by the whiskey.

Blood was streaking from both their white skins, and welts raising angry red. "Scum! Wretch! Filth!" the words were forced out with each lash of the whip. Over and over it sent its wicked tongue to sting. Jane's arms gave out, letting them fall to her sides as she stood looking at her victims.

They were the victims now, not a helpless woman. As they turned in their agony, she could see clean skin and let go the torturous whip again and again, not an inch could be seen that wasn't bloody.

79

Rolling up the whip she returned it to the saddlebags. The empty jugs went into it also.

Easing out the barn door, she brought the two horses closer quickly unsaddling them. The saddles she took to the loft and pulling back the hay hid them underneath out of sight.

Looking at the beaten flesh of the men made her nauseous. They hadn't moved, but moans escaped them and she knew they weren't dead. She felt no mercy toward them. Taking the rope from their hands, she looked around to make sure there were no telltale articles of her being there.

She picked up the saddlebags and rope and went toward the horse leading the two others. Mounting she started back down the Beech road toward the Middleton farm. Opening the fence she went through and closed it behind her then keeping to the grassy places, rode up the first "holler." She knew she could cross from the "holler" out a flat to her farm. The horses followed without trouble. She reached the flat and followed it through the woods to the head of the "holler" that was Bear Run and the home farm.

There was grazing land cleared here. Not much of anything to eat now but the animals would be alright for a couple of days.

Using the rope she hobbled them so they couldn't come to the barn, hanging the bridles in a tree, and headed for the cabin.

The men were splitting wood and were surprised to see her coming from that direction. As they took old Madge to unsaddle, she explained she had wanted to see just how the farm butted up to hers. They never questioned her explanation. Taking the saddlebags she went into the cabin, putting away the telltale evidence of her last few hours, she sank down on a chair. Her legs quivered and she felt like she had stood over the washtub for a week.

It was done, and she had her revenge. There was little danger that two grown men would ever let it out that a slip of a girl had undressed them and whipped them senseless. They would think twice before attacking another woman.

It would please her to see them walking the five miles back to camp in the knee-deep mud.

She doubted they would look for her, and would think she had turned the horses loose and no telling where they would go. There was no one around to ask questions from. If they did look for her they would go down Beech, that's where they had seen her come from. There wasn't a house for miles in that direction if they did look.

It started drizzling rain by nightfall and Jane looked out the window with satisfaction. The horses' tracks would be washed away even if they could find where she took them into the field. Now all she had to worry about was the results of their vile act. She was midway between her monthlies, if a woman was like animals, they would have to be near their bleeding time to catch.

There was nothing she could do till close her time when she would have certain herbs she had heard of on hand to douse herself with.

The night was much like the last one, except with the sight of blooded flesh in her dreams, causing an uneasy sleep.

Morning came, Jane didn't feel like moving. Her arms and shoulders were sore from using the whip. Nerves had made her weak, and her legs still shook. She couldn't let on that anything was wrong.

After a few minutes she rolled out of bed and lit the fire in the kitchen. It had started to snow slightly and the kitchen was cold, but not freezing, a good day for baking pies and readying them for the compound. She had in mind to send Harn and Will the next day with eggs, butter, and pies. Having them both go would give her a chance to see to the two hobbled horses. They would need feed after two days on what roughage they could find. She was also anxious to know what was said at the compound, if any mention was made of the whipping.

Jane had her stacks of apple pies ready in baskets and eggs and butter ready. They would have to carry the baskets in front of them on the saddles as they would be going by horseback. The wagon would never make it through the mud. Jane saw the two off early and cautioned them about the horses and the things they carried.

They were to go to the store and see Mr. Middleton, if he wasn't there, leave word that she might be interested in his farm if the price was right.

As soon as she fed the younguns dinner, she put them to bed for a nap telling them she would have a surprise for them when they awoke, warm and cozy they were soon asleep. It was the only way she could leave them to go to the animals.

Going to the barn she put six ears of corn in a sack and started up the "holler." The two horses were standing in a grove of trees. As she approached, they threw up their heads and whinnied.

Separating them she put three ears of corn on the ground for each of them. They were so hungry they nibbled every kernel off and then started to eat the cobs. "That will have to do you for a couple more days," she told them. They wanted to follow her as she started back home, but with the hobbles they couldn't go far. A rope tied to a front foot and it pulled back toward their body and the rope tied up over their necks. This let the animals eat and drink and at the same time kept them from wandering too far. They were both fine animals, well-bred. If worse came to worse, she would turn them loose and let them go where they would. They had belonged to the boys, not the army, and she figured she had more than paid for them with what they had put her through.

Going back to the cabin she busied herself with the work at hand. It was getting colder and the snow had started again as she heard the horses in the woodyard.

Bringing the basket and money in, Will stomped the snow from his feet. Harn was putting the horses in the barn, and he was soon stomping on the steps as Jane put supper on the table.

As they ate they told the news. The compound was deserted except for a few. Most of the soldiers had been sent on march South early that morning. The cook took her pies and such saying another group was coming down from the North tonight or tomorrow and then move farther South in a few days.

"Is there any sickness at the camp." Jane asked.

"No, everyone there was up and about. There was some talk of the soldiers drinking, some weren't too glad to start on march, but they all went," Harn answered.

"What about Mr. Middleton? Did you see him?" Jane asked again.

"No, he wasn't around, the storekeeper said to tell you likely he would be over the next break in the weather. He wants to get rid of the farm and move over on the Kanawha with his brother. Likely, you can get it at a fair price," Harn told her.

That night as Jane settled herself in bed, she thanked the Lord that she hadn't been found out.

She knew that Clem and Billy Dan wouldn't talk. They could be shot for their part in it. She would suffer all her life, if it was ever told.

Sleep came slowly, but the nightmares were there to keep her tossing and turning, moaning in her sleep.

Back at the Barn

The two men awoke to cold and darkness, both reaching their hands out feeling in the hay discovering each other at the same time. "Billy Dan, that you?"

"It's me, Clem, what the hell happened? Oh! I ache all over, and I'm baby assed naked. Clem, I'll kill you for this. What the hell did you do to me?" Billy Dan said as he tried to get up from the barn floor.

"Honest to God, Billy Dan, I didn't do nothing. I'm half froze and scratches all over me. Oh! Lord, I'm sick." He got up on his knees and started to heave, gagging, and coughing, moaning every breath. With one hand Clem tried to brace himself while trying to pull his long johns from around his feet.

"Some son-of-a-bitch took my clothes off and beat the shit out of me. I'm nigh frozen to death, too," Clem said, getting to his feet staggering around getting his arms through the sleeves of the long johns.

Billy Dan was gagging and staggering around doing the same thing. "I'll shoot the son-of-a-bitch who did this. Oh! God! I hurt. My back is raw and bloody. Someone horsewhipped me. I'll kill him. I'll kill him. The son-of-a-bitch."

They didn't have a light, but feeling around as they staggered they found their clothes. Trying to pull them on over sore backs cursing every breath.

"I don't hear the horses, Clem," Billy Dan remarked, as he pulled his jacket on shivering and his teeth chattering till Clem couldn't hardly hear him. "Where did we put the horses, Clem?" he asked.

"They are out by the fence, Billy Dan, I'll go see to them," Clem opened the barn door, standing back out of the wind listening. No sound could be heard but the wind in the naked trees beating the frozen branches together.

"Hell, Billy Dan, the horses ain't here. Whoever done this to us, took our horses or turned them loose. They are to hell and gone by now. Recon we will have to ride 'Shank's Mare' back to the compound. Come on, Billy Dan, we have to hoof it back. The old horses won't be around here, you can bet. They might have gone back to the compound, maybe we can catch up with them."

They left the barn door swinging in the wind as they made their way across the run to the road.

"Clem, you recon whoever done this, snook up and took that little gal? She drank almost as much as we did and musta been passed out, too," Billy Dan asked.

"I recon maybe that might could be, Billy Dan, she sure was a pretty little thing," Clem answered.

They were staggering up the muddy road stumbling over rocks splashing into water-filled tracks making slow headway up the first hill. There wasn't even starlight to see by as the clouds rolled in the sky. Their voices trailed off, their breath coming in loud gasps as they climbed and slid around. As they reached the top Clem said, "Oh, Hell! I need a drink. I hurt so bad I'm about to piss myself." He opened his clothes and Billy Dan could hear the splash on the road and hitting puddles of water. "Oh, My God! I ache all over. I never hurt so bad in my whole life. I don't think I can make it, Clem," Billy Dan whined.

"You got to, Billy Dan, I sure as hell can't tote you. I'm hurting, too. We got to keep tracking or we will freeze to death out here. It's cold now, if we're not back for roll call, that hot-headed 'Lewie' is likely to shoot us for desertion," Clem told him.

It was just breaking dawn as they limped and half fell into the cold tent they shared.

The sound of "roll call" gave them only minutes to rest. They had to fall out with the other troops who eyed them up and down as they lined up in formation.

"You two look like you already been in battle," and a snicker went through the group close enough to hear. Billy Dan and Clem's drinking bouts were no secret in camp.

After roll call the orders were—"Pack your gear, saddle your horses—you that have them, strike your tents, we are moving out soon as chow. We take the train South, Sergeant, man your groups, let's 'hussel' it."

"I can't go, Clem, I'll never be able to walk for a week," Billy Dan whined.

"We have to go, boy. I'll scout around and see maybe we can

84

ride. It's twenty miles to the depot from here. You pack, I'll look for our horses, too." Clem headed for the corral to look over the mounts that were being saddled. Theirs weren't there, and they couldn't even look for them now. They had to move out. Clem returned as Billy Dan painfully finished rolling up their bedrolls and packing their few belongings.

"I'll help you strike the tent. I made a deal with the 'Mule Skinner' to ride on the tent wagon and help out, as long as that 'Lewie' don't catch us, we will be alright."

The milling around and confusion was deafening. The cavalry finally moved out. The foot soldiers would go next, then the supply wagons.

The horses would be loaded on the train by the time the supply wagon arrived, and that would take most of the day. The trains only moved at night, anyway.

That was it, the big war was just down the road.

The jolt of the wagon caused them to hurt with every turn of the wheels. Billy Dan had managed to find a drink that helped him bear the pain. He soon snuggled beneath the tarp and went to sleep.

Clem watched for the officers, but seeing them all ride ahead, the temptation was too much and he crawled on his belly out of sight under the tarp and was soon asleep, also.

When the unloading started the two tried to slip away in the confusion, they were still aching, their backs stiff and sore, their clothing sticking to the dried blood, clung in spots.

Still they were ordered to unload the tents and put them aboard the train. They swore under their breath mumbling vengeance on the "Mule Skinner" who was making them work.

The horses had been loaded and the cook fires started, they would be fed before the train pulled out.

It was getting colder and the snow clouds were rolling up in the West. By morning the train would be deep in the mountains towards the southern battlefields.

There were jokes and loud talk about what they would do to the Rebs when they arrived, never thinking they could be laying cold and stiff soon on a battle-torn field, or in a mountain gully.

The Middleton Farm

Jane had made up her mind that the Middleton farm would be a good addition to their acres and would buy it even though the price would be high. It was all fenced and would be good farming and pasture for the animals.

Tom had been gone well over two months, and still no word from him. They were together for such a short time, it didn't seem that they had been together at all. Oh, well, she would make do, so far she hadn't done too bad.

The weather cleared up and in a few days Mr. Middleton came to the cabin. Jane had the money carefully counted out and put aside for the farm. However, she hoped to get it for less than the eighty-eight dollars she had counted out for it.

Mr. Middleton was a big man and filled the crowded kitchen till there didn't seem a place to walk. Jane seated him at the table and gave him a cup of coffee and as luck would have it, she had made a cobbler for their dinner. She gave him a big bowl with plenty of milk over it.

The blue-checked curtains, with their wide ruffles, Jane had made and the oilcloth to match made the kitchen cozy and homey.

"This sure is a fine cobbler, Mrs. Jarvis," Mr. Middleton informed her between bites. "I understand your man joined up, you seem to be fairin' pretty well."

"We get along, my brother is here to help me and the younguns," Jane answered.

"I understand you want to buy my farm? You look like just a slip of a girl. Do you do business yourself?" he asked.

"I'm a married woman with five younguns and I've been doing business for sometime now," she said with dignity. "They tell me you want to sell your farm," she said. "I may be interested if the price is fair."

"There are eighty-eight acres. I'll take a dollar an acre. It's a

86

good farm and all fenced. I lost my only son in the war. My wife and I want to move back to the Kanawha where our family lives. My wife is poorly, you know."

Jane listened carefully to what he told her, weighing every word. "We have more than we can rightly take care of now, and without buildings that seems to be a bit costly to me," Jane told him.

Mr. Middleton looked at Jane in surprise. "Tell you what I'll do, if you have the cash, I'll let you have the farm. There's two stacks of hay in the lower meadow, and I have an almost new mowing machine over at my friends where we are staying on the West Fork, I'll throw that in, you can have the whole 'kit and caboodle' for eighty-five dollars."

Jane looked him in the eye, never letting on how excited she was. A mowing machine, she had seen one once, one man could cut in a day what six men took a week to cut by hand. Thinking fast she decided that the machine would cost that much alone. Not answering him, he continued.

"Young lady, that's a bargain you won't find often. We are in a hurry to get my wife where there are doctors. We've had nothing but bad luck this past year, and my wife wants to get away."

"How would we have the deed done?" Jane asked.

"We can have Mr. Cheniweth, at the store, notarize the signatures. He's the justice over there at Minnora and can do all the paperwork."

"The hay and mowing machine included with the farm for eighty-five dollars?" Jane asked, to make sure she had heard correctly.

"Right you are, little lady," Middleton said.

"I will have to have a little time to study on it, I will be at the store tomorrow by noon, you be there with your deed and we will see if we can seal the bargain. I'm beholden that you come to see me," Jane said, all business.

"Alright, little lady, I'll be there at noon tomorrow, with the papers, that's fair enough," he said rising. "I'll be on my way. Thank you for the coffee, and that was fine cobbler."

Jane stood in the door watching him ride down the road. Poor man, seems bad luck don't miss many people in this life. She was so excited she could hardly wait to tell Harn and Will who had waited outside during the business talk.

87

The supper talk was about the farm and they all agreed she had herself a bargain.

"How many acres will that make us?" Will asked.

"Thirty-seven and a half here at the homeplace, sixty-five at the Hall farm, and eighty-eight in the new one. That will be one hundred ninety-one acres altogether." Jane said, counting silently.

"Will we be rich then?" Will wanted to know.

"We are on our way, but not yet. It will take a heap of work and planning just to keep going, without being rich," Jane told him.

The evening chores were done and Jane still was thinking of the farm. She felt sure it would be safe to go over to the store since the soldiers had been transferred out of the area.

The next morning the sun was trying to shine, but the clouds scuddled across the sky making light and dark shadows as they covered the sun. Leaving the house early, she took her little cloth poke with the eighty-five dollars in it and had it pinned securely inside her clothes. Giggling to herself she thought, I'm carrying a farm inside my clothes. How excited she was to think she could say nay or yea, and hand over all that money and be the owner of a farm. She didn't stop at the compound even though she had a basket of eggs to sell. She would take them to the store. That's where she would soon have to sell them if the army left the compound.

The talk was that the war was becoming big and going to last for sometime. Men were pouring into the South by the hundreds, many sent back minus arms and legs, or sick with fever. The healthy men and boys that joined up came back as wrecks of their former selves.

Jane didn't dare dwell on it. She tried not to think of her Tom. He would do his job as she was doing hers.

She arrived at the store and saw Mr. Middleton standing on the porch. "Howdy there, little lady," he said, tying her horse up for her at the hitching rail. "I see you made it," he said, stepping aside to let her enter the warm, cheerful store.

There were several people around the potbellied stove. Conversation ended as she walked in, but it resumed as she looked around and saw them staring at her.

Mr. Cheniweth knew why they were there and motioned them to the back of the store where he had a cluttered office in a corner by the post office. They all sat down at a table and Mr. Middleton laid the deed down, smoothing it out. "Here's the deed, little lady," he said. "What say ye?"

Mr. Cheniweth picked up the deed reading, "Eighty-eight acres on Beech. This is all clear and legal," he said.

Turning to Mr. Middleton, Jane said, "Now I understand you want eighty-five dollars for the eighty-eight acres, two haystacks, and the almost new mowing machine."

"That's right, little lady. If you have the cash, we can sign the papers and close the deal right now," Middleton answered.

Mr. Cheniweth looked over at her and remarked, "That's quite a buy I'd say. A new mowing machine like that costs sixty-five dollars, F.O.B., Mrs. Jarvis. Now, Mr. Middleton, do you swear that all these holdings in question is free and clear and that you own them outright?"

"That's right, all free and clear," Mr. Middleton answered.

"Mr. Middleton, I've decided to take the farm off your hands," Jane told him. "I have the cash for you. Mr. Cheniweth can fix the proper papers, if he will." Reaching in her pocket where she had transferred the money from her poke before reaching the store, she counted out eighty-five dollars in bills.

Mr. Middleton reached for the money.

"Not so fast," Mr. Cheniweth told him. "The papers have to be signed first." He was adding a bill of sale and revising the deed as he talked.

"Now, Mrs. Jarvis, sign right here." He pushed the papers toward her.

Never batting an eye, Jane said, "I'd be obliged if you would sign my name for me, Labanna Jane Jarvis."

Not wanting to embarrass her, he signed, saying, "Put your mark right here." She was a smart little thing even if she couldn't write, he thought, and a "go-getter" from what he had seen.

Mr. Middleton signed his name. Jane turned to him, "It's also understood that the machine will be left at my father-in-law's place."

"Yes, mam, it will be there this afternoon," he told her.

The storekeeper turned to her. "I'll give you a receipt that I have the deeds, they have to go into the courthouse for recording, but I'll get it back to you. There is a twenty-five-cent charge for recording. It's the law, and has to be done," he told her.

Listening to every word, Jane said, "I have another deed that hasn't been (she couldn't remember the word) done, yet. If I send it by the boys when they come for the machine, can you have both done? I'll pay you the money today for both."

"Sure Mrs. Jarvis, I'll be glad to record them for you."

Jane was glad to see he treated her with some respect and didn't call her "little lady."

Jane finished her trading, sold the basket of eggs and filled it with the few things she had to have. Receiving enough money back to pay for the recording (she had remembered the word this time) and was on her way, owner of another farm. She thought of her Tom and the surprise he would have waiting when he was released. Happiness filled her heart at the luck she had in such a short time.

Stopping by her in-laws she received an enthusiastic welcome which always surprised her. They urged her to stay for dinner which she decided to do, keeping her eyes and ears open for any comment on the soldiers. The conversation around the table was always lively and full of laughter, and today there was a distinguished guest at the table. When they were all seated, her mother-in-law turned to him, "Judge Howard, I would like to present my daughter-in-law, Tom's wife, Jane. Jane, this is Judge Howard."

"How-do-you-do, my dear? Tom's wife? What do you hear of him? I understand he joined up sometime ago," Judge Howard said.

Not knowing how to handle such a formal introduction, Jane just nodded her head at being presented to the judge.

Mrs. Jarvis spoke up, "Yes, Jane is taking care of Tom's children and the farm while Tom's away, with her brother helping her. We haven't heard anything of Tom as yet."

Jane was grateful for her mother-in-law answering for her. She admired the way Mrs. Jarvis handled herself and the way she talked. Jane could never talk as fine as her, but learned every time she was around her how to handle different situations. She would not forget them and would make use of every well-learned lesson. Turning to her father-in-law, she decided to bring up the machinery. "Mr. Jarvis, Mr. Middleton will be sending a mowing machine that I have bought. I told him to leave it here, I hope it's alright? The boys will come and fetch it home as soon as they can, if the weather holds, should be a day or so."

"Well! Well! So you bought yourself a mowing machine? It's a

90

fine one, I've seen it and it really does a fine job." He looked at her in surprise.

Jane wasn't sure she should tell them about the farm, but they would think it odd later when they found out, so decided to tell them. "I bought his farm, too. Mr. Cheniweth fixed the papers today and will take them and record them for me." (There, she remembered.)

Mr. Jarvis and the rest looked at her surprised. "The farm, too? I congratulate you for managing that, Tom will be proud, it joins his farm, I believe?"

"Yes, there is eighty-eight acres with quite a bit cleared. No buildings because they burned last year, you know. There is some meadows and a couple of haystacks which we need for the stock. We have two cows and the horses to feed." That was a long speech for Jane, and she flushed slightly as everyone sat listening to her talk.

"Two cows? I thought Tom only had old Blossom," Mrs. Jarvis commented.

"We got one and about twenty head of chickens when we bought the Hall farm," Jane explained.

"Old Aunt Sara Hall's farm?" Mr. Jarvis asked.

"Yes, I bought it and some feed when they left, right after Tom signed up," Jane explained.

Mr. Jarvis's eyes got bigger and bigger. "Just watch yourself, Jane, getting in debt can be a fearful thing."

"I'm not in debt," she remarked. "They are all paid for, with clear deeds and title." She was bursting with pride to be able to tell her in-laws who owned so much that she was making her way too.

"Well, I never!" her mother-in-law said, looking at Jane with astonishment and a glow of pride. This little dainty, pretty girl, was full of surprises and strength, she added to herself. She would get along alone or otherwise.

The judge coughed behind his hand, a smile lighting his face. "Well, Tom, looks like you had better get better acquainted with your new daughter-in-law, looks as though she could show you a thing or two. She will soon own as much land as you do," he said as a chuckle escaped him.

Jane blushed scarlet as they all looked at her.

"I'm astonished," Tom, Sr., said, "and proud of you. Tom will be surprised and bursting with pride at what you have done. I

91

knew you were working hard but never dreamed you could accomplish so much." Turning to his wife he said, "Mother, I think we have a real Jarvis in the family. One who knows how to make a dollar and how to spend it. If the soldiers stay your pies and eggs will buy out half the county," he laughed. "We have been hearing plenty about them."

"When the Lord makes a road, you take it," Jane said.

"If one can make good out of bad, we are lucky and should thank the Lord," her mother-in-law replied.

They rose from the table. Judge Howard turned to Jane, "It's been a pleasure meeting you," he said, and extended his hand. Jane put her work-worn hand in his big one, looking up at him and smiled.

"If you are ever over our way, we would be pleased to see you," she said.

"He travels the circuit to Charleston, but you never know when the road could open through Sandy, it may be nearer that way to Charleston," her father-in-law remarked.

The men continued to talk as they moved out to a side door.

Saying her good-byes, Jane left for home feeling a satisfaction she never dreamed of before. If only my Tom was here to share it, she thought. Only the Lord knew where he was or what hardships he was going through. "Keep him safe, Lord," she prayed. "Keep him safe for me. I had him such a short time, and I need him so."

Jane arrived home and had to go over every detail at the supper table for Will and Harn.

"How are we ever going to work it all?" Will wanted to know.

"It will all fall in place," Jane told him. "We have a bunch of workers growing up," she said as she looked around the table.

"We will work, we'll all help," they said.

The Mowing Machine

The boys were most interested in hearing about the mowing machine. "I seen one, and they do a fair job, cut more than ten men, in the same length of time," Harn told them.

"Well, we'll know, come haying time," Jane said. "If the ground freezes over, you and Will can go fetch it home. I want it where we can keep an eye on it." She didn't admit it but she could hardly wait to see the contraption herself and weigh its possibilities.

Sure enough the ground froze over in the night and a skiff of snow covered high places. The first thing Jane always did when she got up in the morning was to note the weather. Today looked like a perfect one to send for the machine. She would get them up and off so as to be back before the ground could thaw. The mud was bad when it wasn't frozen over and she didn't want to take a chance of them getting the machine hung up in it.

Harn and Will had been doing the outside chores. Today she would milk and feed and send them on their errand.

It was just breaking day when they harnessed the horses and left one astride each horse. There were no eggs to take this trip and they could make better time. Warning them to go slow and easy on the way home and not break anything, she sent them off.

Jane had to go up the "holler" to see about the horses again. and this would be a good time. She thought it would be safe to bring them home. What she would tell Will and Harn she hadn't figured out yet, but she would study on it and something would come up. "Everything would fall in place" was her saying.

Collecting the bridles first, she removed the hobbles, then leading them, she brought them to the cabin, and tied them both in the shed, giving each an ear of corn and putting hay in the manger for them. They had begun to look a little gaunt, but otherwise hale and hearty, and glad to be around humans again.

Jane was sitting working on covering a quilt late in the afternoon, when hearing the sound of wheels on frozen ground and guessing th' looked-for machinery was arriving, grabbed a shawl and walked outside. The younguns were all at the window, trying to be first to see the mowing machine.

It advanced toward her in all its majesty, a long arm in the air as though saluting her as she had seen the soldiers do.

The boys stopped in the woodyard, pointing out the different parts, the gears which Will was most interested in, the cog wheels, and cutter bar, all came under the minute inspection of Jane, with Harn telling her how everything worked.

"Put the tarp over it and tie it down good. We will have to build a shed to get it out of the weather. It's a fine looking machine and cost a heap of money. We have to take good care of it," Jane told them.

The boys unhooked the horses and went toward the shed.

Jane went back to the warm kitchen knowing she would have a lot of questions to answer about the contents of the shed. She was making herself busy at the stove when Harn and Will came back to the cabin.

"Mammy Jane, there are two strange horses tied in the shed. Do we have company?" Will wanted to know.

"No, no company," she continued with her cooking.

"Whose horses are they? Where did they come from?" Will wanted to know.

"I come by them, they likely belong here. Tomorrow I want them took to the lower farm. There is hay and they can be fed there. We will be breeding them as soon as we find the—uh—equipment for it. Until then we will forget they are there, unless we have to feed them," Jane finished.

"Oh!" Will said. He and Harn looked at each other. They weren't too surprised at anything Jane could do. She sure had been working, planning, and getting, since pa left, and all to the good. Will could hardly wait till "haying time" to see the machine in action.

The cabin was quiet as Jane banked the fire for the night. Her thoughts were on the events of the past month as she settled herself in her lonely bed. Most of her plans were made before going to sleep at night. Her monthly time was drawing near, but so far she hadn't experienced any of the symptoms she had seen in women when they were in the family way, but she would not take any

94

chances. Tomorrow, she would send Harn for some things she would need.

With the additional horses and the new machine, it was time to start planning the barn.

Another time, she thought as her tired eyes closed for the night. The nightmares of the cruel rape kept her tossing and turning, for she hadn't had a real night's sleep since it happened.

The Miseries

As usual all were up with the coming of daybreak, except the littlest younguns. The boys went to the barn to take care of the beasts, while breakfast was being put on the table.

It had snowed some in the night and the ground was still frozen over. The chores were mostly done by Harn and Will leaving the housework to Jane. She had found time to start young Catherin and Elizabeth sewing. They were learning to mend clothing, and darn socks. Trude seldom wet herself or the bed now with the attention she had through the winter. Will's birthday had been a few days after Christmas. He was now nine and Catherin almost eight. She was starting to do the dishes and be a big help.

When breakfast was over, Jane sent Harn to take the two saddle horses to the new location on the Middleton farm. Jane instructed him to fill a manger with hay for them and make sure the fences would hold. Also to come back as soon as he could, she wanted him to go to the Cook farm for her. Harn returned as a weak sun tried to break through the overcast.

"They're fine horses," he told her. "However you come by them, you done good. I'll bet the army would pay you two hundred dollars a head for them."

"They are not for sale," Jane answered quickly. "We are going to have some fine foals from those two."

"I want you to go to William Cook's this morning. Mind you don't go into great detail about the mares, but find out if there is a breeding stud anywhere around, and send word if there is that we need one. Take two five-gallon buckets and see if we can buy some molasses. Here is two dollars," she handed him the money tied securely in a corner of a big red handkerchief. "I need a bunch of cane heads to make a broom. Find out if Jimmy Boggs wants to work for a few days riving boards, and building a shed on the other side of the barn for me, and when he can come so I can send for lumber. Tell Mrs. Cook that my pig come out real

fine and will make a good brood sow come spring. Find out anything else that you can, that's going around," Jane finished her
list of orders and sent Harn on his way riding old Madge.

All morning as Jane worked she thought of Clem and Billy
Dan, and of the awful ordeal she had been through, and wasn't
finished with yet. She didn't need the cane heads for a broom as
much as she needed the cane seed for a brew. She intended to
douse herself with it and not take any chances. She had heard all
her life that it worked.

February had been cold and dry so far. With snow at times but
not as heavy as the one around Christmastime. Her apple pie
making would soon come to an end, though the apples had lasted
longer than she had expected, but they were almost all gone now.
She still had lots of dried pumpkin, but pumpkin pies were too
hard to carry and deliver all in one piece. Jane had been studying
on how she could still make money from the soldiers. With the
nuts she and the younguns had gathered, she could make nut
cookies and a nut cake. Yes, she decided she would try that, when
the apples were gone, maybe take some of the turnips and kale.
She could sell them for there were plenty, twice as much as they
needed, which were planted for that purpose.

Harn returned in late afternoon with her two buckets of
molasses and a large bunch of cane heads tied to the saddle. Anis
Boggs walked beside the mare and accompanied Harn home. He
was a sort of distant relation somewhere along the line, and
traveled around working here and there, but like Harn had never
married, and carried around what he owned in a gunnysack on his
back.

Jane was in the woodyard when they came up, mist from the
mare's breath and the men's floating like smoke in the cold, frosty
air.

"Howdy, Jane," Anis said.

"Howdy, Anis," Jane said. "Come on in by the fire. You look
like you are frozen," noticing the thin sweater he wore.

Harn handed down the molasses and cane heads. Anis and Jane
both took a load and headed for the back door.

"Well, Jane, looks like you have a right nice place here. Warm
and snug, and I hear adding to it all the time," Anis said as he
warmed his hands at the potbellied stove.

"We are doing fair, Anis, you know my man joined up and has
been gone for almost three months now?" Jane answered.

"I heard, I come to see maybe you would rent me the house you bought? I could batch there the rest of the winter, till work opens up, come spring," Anis looked doubtful at Jane.

"Well, now! What would you eat? How would you keep warm? Without bedding or food. I recon you had better stay here and share Harn's bed a day or so, then we will see," Jane told him. He was just what she had been looking for, another man to work. They could start getting out logs for her barn while the ground was frozen to make hauling easier, and Anis was one of the best notchers and hewers she knew of. "The Lord works in mysterious ways." Providence had lucked her again, if she could talk Anis into it, and in the middle of the winter, a full stomach and a warm bed would hold a lot of sway.

After supper when everyone was in around the sittin' room fire Jane shelled off a handful of the cane seed and sat them to seep in some hot water on the back of the stove. Before she went to bed she intended to drink some of the brew. A cow would lose a calf if she ate cane heads full of seed. It should work on a person the same, she was thinking to herself. She had heard farm women whispering together about cures and naming cane seed brews.

Everyone went off to bed. Jane banked the fires for the night, took the brew from the stove and drained the black-red liquid off into a cup. Taking some sugar she mixed that into the liquid, stirred till it melted and measured out two tablespoonfuls and swallowed it. The taste wasn't so bad. She threw the cane seeds outside and went to bed. Figuring "an ounce of prevention is worth a pound of cure."

Jane was sleeping soundly when the first pain hit her. Starting in her lower extremities it seemed to wash upward till it hit her brain setting it on fire. Her face and neck got hot and sweat broke out on her brow. A cramp set in doubling her up in bed. Bile flowed into her mouth with the intense pain. The pain flowed out and she caught her breath with relief. No sooner than it had subsided when another one rolled in, just time for a breath and it began again and again.

It went on and on for the better part of an hour. What have I done? she asked herself. I may have poisoned myself. The last pain seemed to hang on and on suspending her in the air by a rope of pain. Then she began to sink down, down, and down. Her body weak, covered with sweat, and it was over.

Jane awoke sometime later a sticky feeling on her thighs. She

98

got up and went into the kitchen and lit a lamp to see to herself. It had happened. She was safe. Thank God! The chapter of Clem and Billy Dan was closed. No one would ever know it had happened, with that she buried it deep in her mind never to let it surface again.

In bed again, the relief was so great that tears stung her eyes as she offered up a prayer for her deliverance.

Anis

At breakfast Jane was still weak and shaky from her night of pain. There was a hearty breakfast of hot biscuits, pan gravy, butter and molasses, with a pot of strong coffee. Jane noticed that Anis ate as though he had been starving, which she suspected he had.

"Well Anis, how did you sleep last night?" Jane asked, sitting down at the table.

"That was a good warm bed, and Harn's not bad as a bedfellow," he said and laughed. "I had me a good night's sleep. You set a fine table, Jane. I don't recon I ever tasted better biscuits. Hope I'm not making a pig of myself, them 'sargums' sure are good," Anis told her.

"Anis, how would you feel about staying here, and helping out? I've a mind to build a barn soon, and I need a shed built on the end of the barn here for the machine I bought."

"Well, now, I'd just as soon be here as anywhere. You feed good and I sleep good," he laughed again.

"It's settled then, you go out and I'll show you what I want built. You figure out what it takes in lumber and you and Harn can take the wagon to the mill today and get it, and get started right on it."

They both got up and went out to the barn measuring and figuring what they had to have. This would put a shed around two sides of the main barn and make more covered space.

Harn had the wagon ready to go when they finished figuring nails and two-by-fours and such.

Jane quickly fried some eggs and made them a lunch of biscuits with eggs between for their dinner on the road. She gave Harn money for the material and gave two dollars to Anis saying, "buy yourself a warmer jimmenson, you'll need warm clothes for outside work." She had seen to it that Harn had clothes when he first came to her.

100

Jane sent a sack of turnips and one of parsnips, ten dozen eggs all covered with a quilt so they wouldn't freeze on the way. "Mind you don't get my quilt dirty," she told them as they were off with a creak of the harness and a rattle of wagon wheels.

Harn had told Jane that Jimmy Boggs would come to rive her boards. Tom had a stack of chestnut logs cut to "bolt" length stacked by the barn. Jimmy could start anytime the weather permitted.

Tom had left his good gun when he went away saying that the army would furnish him one, if she remembered right, Anis was a fair shot. She would see if he could get them another deer, some of the meat would go good.

Before the weather got bad, Jane had picked kale, 'parcooked' it, squeezed it into balls as big as her head, and put down a barrel full in brine. She had bought two hundred pounds of pinto beans which should last through the winter with sauerkraut, turnips, and parsnips. There wasn't a substitute for meat in a man's meal, now she had two to feed. With two men working, they should get a lot done before the time came to put in a crop. She would see to it that their's were in early and Harn and Anis could "hire out" for some money of their own. Everyday would be planned to get the most out of it. The men would bring the studding, and would cut logs for the foundation. When they got it started, Anis could work while Harn went back for more lumber. The main barn was hewed logs and was worth building around. It would last a lifetime.

The men were hardly out of sight when Jimmy Boggs came ready to do the riving. He brought his own tools as was the custom.

"Howdy, Jane," he called as he came into the chipyard.

"Howdy, Jim, looks like you come to work? Come in and warm yourself, and have a cup of hot coffee." She figured it had been a long time since he had "bought coffee." He came into the kitchen where the younguns were still eating.

"Sit down, Jim, by the table. Have you had breakfast? Have a biscuit and 'sargums' with your coffee," as she put a tin plate with three biscuits before him. He only hesitated a minute, before he poured a generous helping of molasses over them and began to eat. Jane explained that the blocks were ready, "so you fix a place out of the wind wherever you've a mind to for working."

"Them were fine biscuits," he told her as he got up from the table, "and that coffee sure gives a man 'get up and go.' "

Taking her shawl, Jane followed him out to show him the blocks and get him started.

He picked the sunny side of the barn and fixed himself a riving foundation and soon the splitting boards whined in the morning air.

Well, everything is going fine, she thought. If the weather holds, they should get the shed under roof this week. Keeping the fire going in the kitchen stove, Jane put a big pot of beans on to cook. They could cook and simmer most of the day to make a good thick broth. She had to think of things that were filling to keep the men up to their best work. Jim would be eating dinner with them, but he would go home for supper. While she could get him to work, she planned to have him make boards for the big barn roof. They would be ready when the barn was built, and if he would help they would have it done to hold the hay in the spring cutting.

The men were back with the load of lumber in time to go up the "holler" and cut a log for the foundation and snake it in. They would be ready for Anis to start in the early morning on hewing it.

Will had taken on the job of stacking the new boards for Jim. By the end of the day there was a pile as high as he could reach, held in place by stakes driven into the ground.

The bark sides of the blocks were used for firewood. Will split it, in between stacking boards, to fill the big woodbox high.

Jim left in time to get home by dark. It had turned colder as the weak sun sank behind the hills, and the days were short from dawn to dark, however, a lot had been accomplished by the hardworking men, and Jane was well pleased. She never skimped on her praise to her workers. She found a pat on the back and a "well done" would get good results.

The weather held without rain or snow and the men worked. The shed had begun to look like a barn, with the rafters up and the siding almost finished. Soon the roof would be done and a big, wide door made so the team and machine could be driven through from one side to the other. Jane was pleased with the progress, having the men come inside every three hours for hot coffee and to get warm. They all talked and laughed as they drank, pleased with the treatment and the job they were getting done. Harn had

102

brought another load of lumber from the mill and the compound had bought the turnips and parsnips and was clamoring for more, especially eggs. The money Harn brought back was almost enough to pay for the load of lumber. The hammering went on all week, the boards were ready for the roof and put in place. Jim helped nail the last ones on, each overlapping the other. They finished the last one and put the mowing machine in before Jim went home. He promised to come back the following week to start on the boards for the big barn Jane planned. Jane and the men were pleased with the job. The doors had to be made yet, that could be done even in bad weather, now that they had a shed to work in. As they sat at supper that night the snow started to fall in big fluffy dabs. The younguns all ran to the window to look. "God is shaking his feather tick," they laughed.

It continued snowing most of the night, slow and easy, by morning there was a good eight inches on the ground.

Jane decided the horses should be brought from the other farm and kept in the shed and sent Harn after breakfast to fetch them. Anis decided to go along, and took a couple of traps from his things. "I think I may catch myself a mink," he said as they started off. Jane told him about the deer and the gun. "No use to take it now, he would see if the blind was still there, if so he would take a look-see about dusk," he told her. "Sure would be good eating, guess maybe I can get us one."

The men came back with the horses, having to move the harness and saddles to the new shed to make room for them.

Anis pulled on an extra pair of socks and wrapped an old muffler around his ears, then took the piece of tarp to sit on and went to wait for the deer. It was cloudy and almost dark by four o'clock. Going up the hill, he circled around and came into the blind from the upwind side. The snow was blowing some and covered his tracks in the snow.

Anis settled down behind the blind on the piece of tarp, he was out of the wind somewhat. He knew he would have a long wait. On a day like today the deer might hole up in a thicket and not come for water at all. The better part of an hour had gone, Anis was getting cold and cramped. The light was getting bad and if there wasn't any action in another quarter hour, he would call it quits for the day.

Keeping a sharp eye out for any movement, if they were coming, it would be in the next few minutes. He caught a movement out of a corner of his eyes, quickly scrunching down as far as he could behind the blind. Hardly breathing, he slowly turned his head, a big buck stood with just his head and front feet showing, on a knoll to his left. Anis counted sixteen points and watched as the beautiful animal flung his head up, testing the air in every direction. It was several seconds before he ventured his full bulk onto the knoll. Stomping his front feet he again tested the air. He wasn't sure it was safe to call his harem in to drink. Standing on the knoll, his breath sending white puffs around his head, he called the does out from the safety of the trees, sending them to the lick while he stood guard. The does, about ten in all, came daintily through the snow, some were heavy with calf. Anis didn't intend to kill a doe, only as a last resort. He waited until a couple of young bucks came toward him from farther down the hill. The old buck slung his head and stomped, and snorted, not wanting the young bucks close to his females. Anis's finger itched on the trigger, he waited wanting a closer shot. The bucks waited till the does were through drinking, and started back into the woods. They moved in quickly to drink, before the old buck moved down for his turn. The nearest buck took a drink and raised his head, seeming to look Anis right in the eye. He had the gun sighted and pulled the trigger. The young buck sank where he stood. There was a squeal of surprise and fright from the knoll and the deer were gone, in a cloud of kicked up snow. Anis had his kill and a good one, too.

Harn was watching from the house as Anis walked up the hill where he could be seen and waved for him to bring the horse to help bring the meat home. Anis dragged the buck over the hill to the road, traces of new spilled blood on the snow.

Together they wrapped it in the tarp and tied it to the mare, each holding on as they walked the horse home.

Jane brought out the dishpan to hold the offering of liver, heart, and kidneys. Going back to the kitchen she quickly made a pan of biscuits, the men expected liver for their supper. The butchering of the deer was finished, and left in the shed to freeze overnight.

The talk around the table was of the hunt and kill. Will wanted to know every detail, comparing it with the time when his pa got a deer. "When your pa comes home, he can teach you how to hunt deer, and shoot the gun," Jane told him.

Will didn't say anything, his eyes glowed with the thought of what he termed as becoming a man.

All went to bed that night with a full stomach and the satisfaction of the tale of the hunt.

Timber Cutting

When it thawed the men went into the woods and with a sharp eye selected the logs for the new barn. The trees had to be straight and tall. Each tree was looked over carefully and the area where it would fall so as not to crack the body of the tree when it fell. Anis would help with the hewing and knew what to look for so that they would square nicely, and not warp. They had decided it was to be twenty-eight by forty-eight feet, with stalls along each side out of cut lumber. There would be a drive-through with a loft for hay. This would be about twenty-four to twenty-six logs high, to allow for a full-loaded wagon or sled to drive through, with four double stalls on each side, to accommodate eight teams.

Jane had in mind to raise horses, from the fine ones she had "acquired."

On days that weren't fit to cut timber, the men sawed blocks from the chestnut logs in the yard for "Board Bolts," to have them ready when Jimmy Boggs came. There was a stack left from the shed, so he already had a start. Jane wanted them ready when the barn was ready to roof.

February had been an unsettled month, cold, snowing, and then thawing, time and again. A wind that didn't seem to stop, found its way through the layer of clothes they wore. When Jane hung the wet clothes outside they would freeze almost as fast as she got them on the line. She had to wash in the kitchen and boil the white things on the kitchen range.

Elizabeth had come down with the croup. It took all of Jane's medical experience to get her up after a week. She doused her with the cough syrup she had ready. Mullein leaves steeped slowly and drained, to which a half cup of honey, two peppermint sticks, and two tablespoons of whiskey were added. She also had a rub made from lamb tallow, fresh mint from along the run and seeped mullein leaves. Between rubbing and taking medicine she got well, but she looked peaked for several days and Jane kept an eye on

105

her for a relapse. She felt lucky that none of the other younguns had caught it.

The hens had almost quit laying with the cold wind, even though Jane had bought some cracked corn for them through the winter.

There was little to send to the compound now, only the nut cakes. She would make a big three-layer cake, full of nuts, and covered with butter frosting sprinkled with more nuts. The soldiers never complained at the five-dollar price she charged them. This week she had made three, there wasn't enough eggs to sell. She sent a sack of turnips which she decided to charge three dollars for. Things were getting scarce, she could have sold some of the deer meat, but as long as the weather stayed cold, it would keep. She had decided the men and younguns needed meat to keep well, and to work in the cold. She cut six nice slices to send to her in-laws, for a gift. She felt better having something to give them.

Harn was sent off with her wares while Anis worked on the doors for the shed.

Dark was falling by the time Harn returned, bringing great news. There had been word from Tom. He was well and hadn't been in anything but what they called "skirmishes" so far. It had been a bad winter for the army he had said and to Jane's surprise, had sent a telegrammed money voucher to her for fifty dollars. Jane could hardly believe it and thought to herself that he should have kept it for himself.

The family had wired back that all was well with her and the younguns, they thought that she would want them to.

Just knowing he was alive and well and thinking of them made Jane so happy that tears of joy stung her eyes. "I'm glad to hear and that a message was sent to him. I'm sure that he worries about us all," she said.

"When's pa coming home?" Will wanted to know.

"He said he would be back to plant crops, so when you hear the first 'pee-wee' you can start looking for him," Jane answered.

"They said, 'thank ye,' for the venison," Harn added. "One of the girls was in bed with a cold," he said.

"I'll send some of my cough syrup the next time you go. I made plenty last fall in readiness," Jane told him.

"Did you get the hinges for the doors?" Anis asked.

"Sure did, and they were dear, seventy-five cents each pair,"

106

Harn answered. "Looks as though you have them ready to hang, if we can't cut logs tomorrow, we will hang doors," Harn said.

Everyone was cheered about the news of Tom and went to bed with a light heart, as the wind whistled around the eaves.

The Stallion

February came and went, the wind and cold continued. The piles of logs over by the barn site mounted. They would cut when it thawed and haul when it became frozen again. There were several more logs stripped of branches, ready to bring in. Some of the big ones needed two teams, Jane had Jimmy bring his team of big dapple-grays to help.

With the extra money she could afford to have an extra team. She planned at least to have the main barn done by hay cutting time.

They again had luck and a man came with a beautiful black stallion. The men took the two mares and went up the "holler." Jane could hear the screams of the mares as the stallion mounted them, each in turn. The charge was five dollars apiece, but Jane thought it well worth it. Her herd of horses was on its way.

Both cows were getting heavy with calf. Old Brindle was slowly going dry, they would have to stop milking her soon. Blossom still gave plenty of milk for the family. Jane was so thankful for milk for the younguns. They had all been lucky not to have more sickness through the winter. Jane felt that good food and warm clothing had been "saving grace." She had the time to make extra things for the younguns and an extra shirt apiece for the men. Also, had covered the ragged quilts with new flannel. There hadn't been a moment of idleness all during the cold weather.

March came in with swirling snowstorms. The wind blew gusts that rattled the stovepipes and anything else that was loose.

The animals stayed close to the barns huddled together for comfort and warmth. It was cold and windy for two days, then the men sat around the fire, only going out to take care of the stock.

Anis decided to go around his traps, and came back late in the day with icicles hanging to his clothes, but he had caught a beautiful mink.

108

It looked like a number one. He had reset his traps hoping for its mate. Going to the barn he made a board and skinned and stretched it, the fur side in. It had to cure before he could take it to be sold. There would be enough from the hide for spending money to last him all summer. Will and Harn were in and out till the job was done. Everyone talked of the weather, "in like a lion, out like a lamb" was the saying for March. The third day the sun rose bright in the East, a joy to see. What snow that had gotten trapped in the fence corners was soon gone in little rivulets of water.

The animals began to stir themselves and looked for new blades of green grass that might be peeking up. The day was a promise of the spring just around the corner.

The men went at their sawing in a fury, knowing that soon plowing and planting had to be done. On such a beautiful day Jane couldn't help leaving her work and standing by the window or in the woodyard looking at the road in the distance. She longed for her Tom and felt in her bones he wasn't far away.

With the break in the weather Will went to the woods with the men. He had grown to be as tall as his Mammy Jane, and could swing an ax as well almost as a man. He trimmed branches and limbs from the felled trees, while the men downed more of the big giants. They told Jane if the weather held they might have them all on the ground in a week.

The weather held and Jane decided to make the trip to the compound this week herself and leave the men to their work. She spent the day, before she was to go, baking cakes and cookies. She could still spare turnips and fixed them ready to load.

The horses wouldn't be used that day. Old Madge was saddled for Jane and left in the shed till she was ready to leave. She intended to start riding the new horses soon. If someone didn't they would become wild. She always took along the blacksnake whip. And kept her eyes open and watched the mare, she would give the alarm if anyone or anything was near, never again would she be caught like a fly in a spiderweb.

The trip through the woods made her jittery, since there was hardly a ray of sun in the summertime that could get through the overhanging branches. Thank heavens, with the leaves off she could see through them. Coming in sight of the compound she could see there were lots of soldiers and animals around. She would go to her in-laws and send someone to sell her wares. She had no desire to get close to any of the men in the compound, or for any of them to see her.

Jane was greeted with warmth by her husband's family as always. Her horse was taken to the barn and Caleb sent for the soldier in charge to pay her and take away the foodstuff.

Jane had been thinking of having a "barn raising" and wanted to see what her father-in-law thought.

They all commented on how good the venison was and how much they appreciated her sending it. The conversation got around to what was going on at her house. She told them about the log cutting and how well the men had done on such a big job.

"Will you have a 'raising?' " her mother-in-law asked.

"I wanted to ask you and Mr. Jarvis about that. There are very few men over our way," Jane answered.

"We will help, we can cook and bake," both of her sister-in-laws volunteered.

"I think I can get a few men from around here. Caleb and I, of course, can come, and I think Tom's brother, Sy. We can round up a few and some teams," Mr. Jarvis told her.

"I'll come over and help put in the foundation so as to be ready. What day do you think?" he asked Jane.

"Whatever day you can come. The men can drop whatever they are doing to help you," she answered.

"If the weather permits, Caleb and I will come tomorrow. As soon as the soil is dry enough we want to start our plowing and planting," he said.

"We want to get started early too, we hope to put in crops on all the cleared land on the three farms, and want to have the barn ready for haying," Jane said.

"I've ordered fruit trees to put in an orchard and have to see if they are in yet," Jane remarked.

"They should be planted soon," her father-in-law said. "If they are in, Caleb and I will bring them over tomorrow. We will bring our team and can manage them. You won't be able to carry them on horseback."

"I sure do thank you. I'll do that," Jane said. She went on to the store and stopped on the way back to tell them that the fruit trees were in. It had cost her a whopping twenty dollars for the trees to be sent. She had asked Mr. Cheniweth to help her order them and together they had selected a dozen trees. There were "Winesaps," which were best for apple butter; "Maidenblush,"

110

"Johnsons," "Russets," for winter use and "Roman Beauties," and one tree of "Spice Sweets." She hadn't bothered with peaches and pears, they couldn't be holed for winter and seemed frivolous to Jane for the little use they could be put to. She would put down stakes where she wanted them. The orchard would be in front of the big white house she intended to build, with a yard in between. In her mind's eye, she could see it in full bloom in the moonlight and the house in shadows behind the lovely trees, she and her Tom sitting on the veranda.

The Barn Raisin'

Everyone was up early. There was a glow in the eastern sky where the sun still hid behind the horizon. While Jane got breakfast the men fed the animals and harnessed the horses.

It was just a good day when the rattle of harnesses and sound of hoofs were heard. Looking out, they saw Caleb and Tom, Sr., coming through the gate at the road.

Jane went out to meet them in the chipyard. "Good morning, Mr. Jarvis, Caleb," she said. "Would you like something to eat? A cup of coffee? We just finished."

"I don't think so," they both answered. "We want to get started. Now where is this barn to be," he asked.

Jane went back for a shawl saying she would walk to the site with them. "Will, stay with the younguns till I get back."

"Ah, shucks," he said, knowing he should never talk back, as he headed back to the house.

They all walked over to where Jane, Anis, and Harn had staked out where the barn was to be built.

Mr. Jarvis looked around and examined each corner carefully to make sure there was solid ground, remarked, "Looks like a likely spot. Seems you have studied out every angle, Jane."

She blushed with the compliment, "I've been thinking on it quite a spell, Tom and I never had time to talk over things before he left," she added.

"I'm sure he would approve. I do," Mr. Jarvis told her.

"Let's get at it, men. First we will dig four corner holes and fill them with rocks, pound them down solid then we will have to find some big cornerstones for the foundation logs to rest on."

"Have you located the cornerstones," he asked turning to Jane with a smile.

"Yes, I've kept an eye out and there are two fine ones up the 'holler' a little ways; one down there at the edge of the woods," she pointed to the left, "and one up along the road there. There are some in-between ones along the road," and she waved her hand in the direction.

Mr. Jarvis laid out the area for the corner holes to be dug. He put one man to digging and told Caleb to take their wagon along the road and pick up rocks no bigger than his fist to fill the corner holes with, the other team would get the cornerstones out and drag them to the site. The men made a drag from poles to roll the big rocks on to drag them along.

"If I can't be of help, I'll go send Will back to help pick rocks, mind you keep an eye on him, Harn," Jane said as she went back to the house. She was so thankful to have her father-in-law in charge. She knew everything would be done right. She could hear the ring of the shovel on rock as the hole digging went deeper. The sound of the rocks rolling into the bed of the wagon sounded like distant thunder. It was music to her ears as everyone worked together.

Will was like a young colt let loose from the house. He was anxious to be out working with the men and wasted no time getting to the work area.

Jane fixed the churning and put Catherin to doing it while she fed the chickens and pigs, and milked the two cows. She hurried as she wanted to get back and bake some dried apple pies for the men's dinner. She planned to fix a really good dinner for it would be the first time her in-laws had ever eaten at her table.

As she worked, she was bursting with excitement. At last one of her dreams were coming true. They would have a big handsome barn that anyone could be proud of.

The morning went quickly with so much to do. The cabin had to be sparkling for her father-in-law's and brother-in-law's first inspection.

Catherin's hair had been freshly braided with calico strings tied in bows on the ends of the braids. Wrapped in Jane's shawl, she went to tell the men dinner was ready.

They all came in muddy and full of talk. A big washpan of warm water awaited them on the bench outside where they could splash as much as they wanted. Catherin stood by holding a long clean sack towel for them. The pan was emptied and refilled several times before they were satisfied they had enough of the mud off to wipe on the towel.

The table was loaded with steaming dishes. The menfolk looked around and remarked, "Sure looks and smells good." With a clat-

113

ter of chairs being pulled into place, and everyone getting seated the vittles were passed around, a big platter of venison, mounds of mashed potatoes and gravy. The men talked and laughed and as if by magic they made the heaped up dishes of food disappear.

"We may make this job last several days," her father-in-law told her, "if you continue to feed like this," as Jane placed the apple pie on the table and refilled the coffee cups.

"I expect a lot of work for this dinner," Jane told them with a faint smile, joshing didn't come easy to her, neither did laughter.

With a scrape of chairs being pushed back they all trooped from the kitchen. "That was a fine dinner, Jane. Tom can be proud of his wife in more ways than one," Tom, Sr., said as he went outside to join the others who were on their way back to their jobs.

The girls sat down now to eat, there hadn't been room with the four men and two boys at the table.

The weather held and it was decided to have the "barn raisin'" on Saturday. Will was sent to the Cook farm to spread the word of the "barn raisin'" and ask them to come with their women-folk, and to tell anyone else they might see.

Jane rushed around all the rest of the week, washing and cleaning. On Friday she made two large nut cakes using plenty of eggs. She got out the last big pumpkin and made it into pies. Also made some dried apple pies and filled the corner cupboard with the good baked things.

Saturday dawned clear and bright, warmer than expected. The men and teams started to arrive shortly after sunrise. The women, in their best bonnets and colorful dresses, alighted from the wagons each carrying covered baskets and buckets.

Jane would make the last ham of the deer, had it ready to put into the oven, with herbs to baste it with. A big kettle of the dry pinto beans were simmering on the back of the stove to be cooked till dinner time. She had sent Will to the garden for two heads of the "holed cabbage." He came with two heads so big he had trouble keeping them from dragging along the ground as he carried them by their stems. She would chop a big pan for cole slaw. She had a pan of the kale balls soaking in water to get the brine out.

Jane knew the women would all bring something, and usually they brought tin plates and knives and forks as no one had enough for all the extra people.

Jane had Harn take down one of the new barn doors and put it on sawhorses in the yard for a table, there wouldn't be space in the kitchen for them all.

This was a social visit for the men and boys as they talked and laughed and worked.

They all stood around admiring the new-laid foundation, marveled at the size the barn would be, then got to work at the job they were partial to, full of high spirits.

Jane went into the woodyard to welcome Mrs. Cook and her daughter, Ora Jane, Mrs. Boggs and her two girls were just behind. They all went into the cabin, looking around, they all admired the pretty ruffled blue-checked curtains, and the tablecloth to match, and the shelves with their scalloped edge of blue-checked oilcloth. "How in the world did you ever find time to hem all those ruffles?" someone asked. "Jane, you certainly have been busy, I can see," Mrs. Cook told her, as they took their things into the sittin' room, laying shawls and bonnets on the beds.

Catherin had been instructed to take the younguns in the back bedroom to play and keep them out of the way. Soon she heard them playing "Ring Around the Rosie," that Jane had taught them in a moment of foolishness.

The women all admired the cabin and the well-behaved younguns, each one talking till none could be heard.

Mrs. Cook had brought a basket of fried chicken and four loaves of bread. Ora Jane had made her molasses layer cake, fourteen layers with cinnamon apple butter between, just like the one she had made for Jane's wedding.

Mrs. Boggs had brought pickles and a wonderful looking salad made from potatoes.

"I do hope there will be enough food," Jane said anxiously looking out the window to see the new arrivals.

Mrs. Jarvis arrived in her buggy with Catherine and Caroline. They had word that Jane, with her grandfather, were doctoring in the war. Tears showed in Mrs. Jarvis's eyes when she told of her father and her daughter. From her buggy she took an enormous pan of baked beans and a large baked ham, plus a fifty-pound lard can that was full of sugar cookies.

The table was beginning to be laden down with food. Another wagon was pulling in the yard, Jane didn't know the people. Ora Jane and Mrs. Cook introduced them, "Mandy," she called her. Mandy Ellis and her young girls were carrying covered baskets and blushing prettily.

115

At last count, there were about fifteen men and ten young boys. Lord a Mercy, how will we ever feed them all? Jane thought to herself.

The women and girls brought in the bench from the boys' room and all found places to sit or stand, the talk and laughter made Jane's head spin trying to sort it out.

About eleven o'clock the young women decided to take a walk over toward where the men were working, gathering wraps, they all went out chattering like geese.

Jane took time out to walk outside for a breath of air with the older women, showing Mrs. Cook where her orchard and her new house would be some day. She showed her the half-grown "runt" that she gave her for her wedding present.

"Jane, there is no one who deserves it more, and I'm amazed at that pig, she will make a good brood sow," Mrs. Cook said.

Noon came, the barn had risen miraculously from the ground. It was taller than Will's head and going up fast, the new hewed logs shining in the sun.

The men laid down their tools and stopped at the creek to wash, knowing they couldn't all use a washpan. Jane sent Catherin with several towels for them to dry on.

They all stomped into the kitchen where plates were stacked on the end of the table. Ora Jane, Catherine, and Caroline, with some of the older girls, stood behind the table to dish up their plates. They grabbed a fork and hurried outside to find a block of wood to sit on at the big table Harn had fixed.

Jane sent Will with ten cups, and asked Ora to take the big pot of coffee and pour for the men.

The other girls took up dishes of food and going outside passed it around. Several platters were placed on the table for them to help themselves. They were joking and talking, joshing the young girls who blushed and lowered their eyes, loving the excitement.

By three o'clock the barn was ready to be roofed. The men swarmed up the rafters catching the new-made boards as they were flung up to them. The ones who weren't roofing, hauled boards and stood waiting to throw them up, and giving advice.

The men who like to do carpentry started on the pile of new lumber that Jane had bought and was stacked nearby, and the big double doors began to take shape. The sawing and hammer-

116

ing was deafening, but the men enjoyed themselves, working together.

Both sides of the roof was being done starting at the bottom and worked toward the rooftree, where it would meet. The logs were carried up in the square where rafters of smaller logs formed the roof with crosspieces of sawed lumber. The gable on each end was filled in with sawed boards leaving an opening to load hay into or throw it out of, and a door would be mounted in the center of each end of the gable.

Jane couldn't believe they were making such headway. She could understand now why the big plantations of the South wanted black slaves. But, Lordy me, how could they ever feed them all, she thought.

The women washed dishes and tidied the kitchen, talking all the time. This was a wonderful social gathering for them all, as they compared recipes, quilting information, and the many farm things that interested them.

There was so much food left that Jane suggested they have it reheated and make more coffee and let the men eat again before going home, that way, the women wouldn't have to make late supper when they got home.

Looked as though the men would be working late to finish the barn. It had been a beautiful sunny day and warm for that time of the year. As the sun sank lower, it started to get cool.

Jane shook up the fire in the sittin' room and kept the one in the kitchen range going. There were yells from the men and boys that could be heard for miles, causing the women to all run outside to see what the commotion was about, and saw that the roof was on and the last door was being fitted in place. They all stood and admired their men's work. "How nice it looks, how proud you must be," they all turned to Jane.

"It's a fine barn," she said, "and I'm beholden to you and your good men for all the work you have all done this day. I'm a very lucky woman to have such friends, and if there is anything I can ever do for any of you, let me know," Jane said.

"We enjoyed ourselves so much," they all remarked in unison.

"I'll make coffee and get things ready. Someone tell the men, and tell Harn to come directly, I need him," Jane said.

Harn came to the house to see what was wrong. Jane handed him a jug and a tin cup. He didn't have to be told what to do. Another yell went up when he joined the group of men by the

117

barn, where they were all standing back, admiring their work. The jug was handed around with laughs and whoopees from them all. There would be a nice swig for all of them but not enough to get any of them in trouble with the womenfolk.

The men would talk for days about the barn raising and the swig from the jug to top it off. They all came back to finish off the food, talking and laughing among themselves, joshing Jane, wanting to know if she had another barn to build next Saturday, they had had so much fun building this one.

Blushing, Jane thanked them everyone as she took charge of the coffee pouring. "My Tom will thank you himself when he comes home from fighting the war. You're all fine neighbors and built a fine barn. I thank ye."

The dishes were washed and separated, each woman finding her things and rounding up her younguns, while the men hitched the horses to wagons for the homeward journey.

"This has been a fine party," they all told Jane as they took their leave, wishing her well, and inviting her to visit them anytime.

Mrs. Jarvis kissed her cheek, "I'm so proud of you, Jane. I'm sure Tom will be, too, when he sees all you have done by yourself. Good-bye dear, come soon."

They were all gone, the quiet descending around her as she waved the last wagon out of sight.

She must see the barn, even though dusk was falling, and the chores not done. Walking across the creek stepping on the rocks jutting out of the water, she reached the big new doors, lifted the latch and walked into the new smelling dimness. She would do the same many times in the future but the thrill would never match what she now felt.

"Oh, if only Tom were here," she said out loud as tears stung her eyes.

Returning to the cabin she turned to take another look at the new barn and under her breath said, "Thank you, Lord."

Everyone was still excited about the day and all the company. Marveling about the way the barn had gone up and remarking on this one and that one, how they did their work and what they said.

The men had to go outside and take a last look at the silhouette of the new barn against the meadow before going to their bed for the night.

Jane knelt by her bed, "Thank you, Lord, for this day. Keep my Tom safe and bring him back to me soon. Amen."

The Orchard

The next few days were warm and sunny, with the ground warming and drying quickly. Young grass started to green up along the creek and in the fencerows.

Jane went with the men to lay out and plant the young fruit trees. Her father-in-law told her how they were to be planted, a deep wide hole the bottom to be filled with rotten manure, then filled with water and the tree gently unwrapped and placed with more dirt over the manure. The soil crumbled and tamped in good.

It took them all day to haul manure, carry water from the creek, and dig holes for the trees. The young trees looked brave standing in the spring sun with their skirts of burlap. The sacking that balled the trees was cut and wrapped around the bottom of each tree to keep the rabbits from eating the bark which they did as high as they could reach unless the tree was protected.

Jane could imagine the sight of them in bloom and in the fall full of fruit.

They were tired and proud of what would be a fine orchard, no better anywhere in the county.

It would be Will's and the girls' job to water the new trees each day, and to check the burlap, seeing it didn't slip, letting the rabbits at the tender trees.

The ground had dried enough to start turn plowing. The potatoes should be planted by the fifteenth of the month when the moon was dark, below-ground crops were always planted in the dark of the moon and above-ground crops in the full or light moon.

The earth smelled fresh and new as they turned the dark side to the sun. They would plant enough potatoes to use in the kitchen in the gardens here at the homeplace, and plant the winter potatoes at the Hall farm in the garden there, leaving room for the kitchen garden close to home. This year they would grow

119

their own molasses cane. The problem would be storing everything that Jane had in mind to grow.

As always Jane said to herself, "There will be a way."

She had asked Anis to make her some shallow boxes from the scraps of lumber when he had made the shed, she had grown tomatoes, cabbage and pepper seeds. They were starting the third leaf and would be ready when the time came to set them out. She wouldn't bother with a "hot bed" this year; by next year, they would need one. She would have more help, the younguns would all be bigger and, of course, would eat more, too.

The garden was plowed, harrowed, and the potato area furrowed out by noon, so they should get some planted in the afternoon. She would open the "potato hole" for the seed and cut them herself while Will and the men planted.

She had the younguns gather around her to watch the potato cutting making sure two eyes were in each piece cut to plant. Cutting around the larger potatoes, she saved the centers in a bucket of water to use for cooking.

Will came for the first bucket and the planting began. They had decided on six rows through the garden which would be enough for the table use. The planting was done and the men ate an early dinner. They would go to the Hall farm and start the plowing there. They took tools and nails and such. While one plowed the other would check and repair any down fences, and if everything went well the potatoes would be planted there the next afternoon. All the potatoes saved for seed would be used. Jane reckoned about two hundred pounds. That should make a good crop and would be more than they could use, with good luck.

They would have to wait a bit to plant corn, however, the fields would have to be prepared. The barns would be cleaned and the manure from them spread over the fields and plowed under for fertilizer.

As soon as grass came up the two saddle horses would be taken to the lower farm to graze. Old Brindle was turned dry to wait for her freshening next month. The grass could almost be seen growing and the animals were searching every nook and cranny to find greenery to eat.

Jane sowed a big bed of early lettuce to make an addition to the vittles with wilted lettuce. She planned to go along the creek bank soon to look for greens. Milkweed, meadow lettuce, whitetop, "shonnee," wild mustard, "wooley britches," and many

120

other weeds made a tasty meal cooked with plenty of bacon grease.

Everyone was starved for new greenery in their diet as well as were the animals and looked forward to that first mess of greens in the spring.

To be able to leave the windows open for an hour to air out the house was a treat for Jane, and to hang out wash without it freezing, to see the clothes flapping in the sunlight on her new line was a pleasure.

She still looked longingly down the road. The feeling of Tom being near still persisted.

The days were longer and the work went along at an even pace. A lot was accomplished by them all. The first few days of spring work using new muscles made for sore aching back and legs. Even the team seemed sore and stiff when they started out in the early morning to a new job. They all soon "toughened in" and could soon work the day through without aches.

Tom's Homecoming

The day dawned bright and sunny as the men were off to the lower farm plowing for corn.

Jane had her wash out early, taking the younguns with her to the garden, she made beds along the edge out of the way of the plow and planted radishes and beets. They were an early crop and would come on in a short time.

The corn would soon be in and a big field of cane was to be planted at the lower farm.

When Jane was through with her planting she went back to the house, noticing on the way, that old Brindle was showing signs of dropping her calf. Putting her in the shed she gave her hay in the manger and put down a layer for her in one corner of the shed.

She had put the younguns down for their afternoon nap, more to get them out from under foot than anything else.

She had seen an old "domernick" hen clucking that morning. She wanted to set her. She would be a good settin' hen and could cover a good twenty-three or twenty-four eggs.

Deciding that it was time to make new nests, Jane brought armloads of hay from the barn and taking out the leaves that were nothing but shreds, placed hay along the nesting area, making shallows for nesting. The old "domernick" was in one corner, not wanting to be disturbed, Jane gently picked her up by her back feathers and sat her on the floor until she had the hay in the nests.

The old hen clucked to herself and with a fluffing of feathers settled herself where Jane had set her down. When the nests were all done Jane firmed some in between the corner nests and the rest as a "sorta" partition to give the settin' hen privacy from the layers. Lifting her back on the nest, the old hen patiently settled herself deep in the hay nest. "I'll have you a setting of eggs in a day or two," Jane told her. "So you won't be wasting your time." Twenty-four eggs would be carefully selected, the most perfect

122

ones picked and marked with rings around them in bluing. They were then put into the nest where the settin' hen took care to keep them warm and turned them with her beak everyday.

Not wanting to go inside Jane stopped on her way back to the cabin and looked in at her two pigs. They had become hogs now and were fat and healthy looking.

Turning as she stepped in the doorway, Jane looked off down the road, there was someone walking in the distance. She could barely see them as they topped a rise almost a mile away. Her heart gave a leap. The walk—she knew that walk. Her Tom, it has to be, gladness filled her. She hurried inside, washing her hands and put on a clean apron, smoothed her hair not having time for more. She looked out again as the figure came closer.

It was Tom! It was Tom! in his soldier's uniform. She went in and awakened the younguns. "Your pa's coming! Your pa's here," she said.

They all came tumbling out of bed, rushing outside and down to the creek to fling themselves at him.

Jane wanted to run and do the same but stood quietly in the chipyard till he came to her. He came slowly toward her, his eyes never leaving her face, the younguns clinging to his hands and clothes, asking questions that no one heard.

Jane had tears in her eyes as he spoke her name, "Jane, my princess," he added under his breath. Regardless of the younguns he folded her in his arms, kissing her eyes, her face, and finally a long, lingering kiss on her soft mouth.

She pushed him away, "The younguns, Tom, mind the younguns."

"Is this the Thomas P. Jarvis farm?" he wanted to know. His eyes taking in all the newness that had been added. "Looks like some rich farmer's place to me," he told everyone.

"Mammy Jane did it, we all helped, too," the younguns told him together. "Did you see the new barn?" they all asked with pride in their voices.

"I surely did, and the new shed, and the new plowed garden, and the orchard," Tom was smiling his wonderful smile at them all.

As they all entered the cabin, Tom stopped, "Oh, Jane, you don't know how good this feels, and you have made a home out of it. You have all worked every minute, I can see. What pretty curtains! I'm so proud of you. This don't look like the scraggly

123

bunch I brought you home to. You and everything looks so good to me."

Jane blushed with pleasure, "How was it, Tom?" she asked.

He hesitated a moment before answering, "I never dreamed that humans could be so ungodly, or that they could stand so much. I'm home now and I don't want to think about the war while I'm here. I just want to look at you all and enjoy the quiet and goodness that surrounds you, I'm so tired."

"Take off your outer things, and go lay down while I fix you something to eat, you look worn-out and you're nothing but skin and bones," she said ushering him into their bed.

"I haven't had a good night's sleep in weeks, I think I will rest for a while," he began to remove his uniform as Jane turned down the bed.

"My Princess," he said with a sigh as he sank into the feather bed only to be asleep in minutes.

Jane folded his clothes and her heart ached with sadness at the paleness and tired look on her Tom's face.

Returning to the other room she reminded the younguns to keep quiet so their pa could rest.

She had some of the venison that she had fried and put down in grease, she would get that out for supper. She wanted Tom's first supper at home to be extra special. Hurrying around to build up the fire she decided to make dried apple pies for supper. Peeking into the sittin' room to look at Tom every few minutes, he slept on and on.

The sound of the horses coming as Harn, Anis, and Will returned woke Tom; he came from his sleep, looking somewhat better to Jane.

She had managed to milk old Blossom between her cooking, and doing her chores. The kitchen smelled of baking and meat cooking.

Tom went out to greet Will, Anis, and Harn, talking to them as they cared for the animals. Will hugged his pa, coming up to his shoulder in height. "I've grown, pa, I've been working hard," he told him.

"You are a good boy, Will, and I'm proud of you," his pa said as he patted him on his shoulder.

As they all gathered for the evening meal it came out about the new farm when Jane and Anis told Tom they were plowing for cane there and expected to plant about a three-acre patch.

124

Tom looked at Jane unbelievingly, "Another farm?"

"Yes, Tom, and a new mowing machine and some hay to boot," she answered.

"Well, well, looks like I'm not needed around here," Tom said with a proud smile.

Jane looked quickly at him not knowing if he meant it. Seeing the smile, she answered, "You're needed, Tom."

"We have been lucky and everything just seemed to fall in place," she told him.

"We had a good winter," Anis said. Harn nodded in agreement.

"Thanks to you two, and the Lord," Jane added.

"I've never ate better or slept warmer through a winter," Anis told them. "I may never leave, Jane."

"You always have a home here, Anis, you and Harn, both," Jane answered.

"I'm beholden to you both for staying and helping Jane. You are one of our family, we want you to feel that way," Tom said.

Anis, when building the shed, had fitted and made a door between the sittin' room and the back bedroom. The men could have privacy for their wash down bathes. It was only closed while that was in progress, or when they were dressing, but as they went to bed that night, it was softly closed.

Tom was in bed as Jane banked the fire, seeing everything was secure for the night.

As she got into bed Tom reached for her and gently pulled her close. His arms holding her, he kissed her hair, her eyes, murmuring words of endearment, his mouth found hers, all her strength seemed drained from her body, her legs were weak, and her head swam. She felt a hunger that surprised her in its intensity.

They melted together down, down, down, then high on the crest of a wave. Their tears mingled as a sigh escaped them both.

Jane lay in his arms all night to be gently awakened time and again, by his urgent kisses. "My Tom," she said, over and over, "My Tom."

The next morning Jane discovered that Tom had a whole month at home to do his crop planting. Jane was glad to have him there to see to everything.

The time went so quickly it was unbelievable the morning he donned his uniform to leave.

Jane decided to take him to catch the train back to his outfit. She had managed to get the saddles from under the hay in the

Hall farm barn. They would saddle and ride the two horses, it was time she got some good out of them. Will had to stay home from the field to be with the younguns.

Jane made a lunch for Tom to take along, wrapping it in a clean red handkerchief.

Tom stood in the chipyard looking long at the farm around him before mounting to leave. They rode slowly talking and planning, sometimes holding hands across the space between the two horses, each hating the time for good-bye, for it came all too soon.

The train pulled out, and they waved good-bye. Jane stood alone, her Tom gone.

The trip back she went over the last two weeks in her mind, sometimes a smile on her lips and, at other times, tears in her eyes.

The spring continued into summer, every day busier than the last.

Old Brindle dropped her calf while Tom was home, a beautiful little heifer. A month later old Blossom had her calf, another heifer. The crops were doing well. On rainy days, the additional stall section of the barn went up slowly.

Jane's tiny waist began to thicken, for she, too, was with child. Never doubting she would be, it was no surprise to her.

The new mowing machine was oiled and polished, the grass fell in even rows before it, a sight to behold. Jane counted her blessings as the new barn filled with hay.

The compound was empty of soldiers, all gone to fight a war that was the longest and bloodiest in history.

There would be no more trips to the compound, the eggs Jane took to the store. She only bought what she couldn't do without now. What was left over from the eggs, she had credited to her account, as the merchant didn't pay cash anymore, only goods.

When the crops were in, the two men went to help other farmers. The Cooks hired them both.

The days went into midsummer. Another voucher from Tom had found its way back to Jane along with word that he was well. That's all she could hope for.

They had all been invited to Ora Jane's wedding in late June. She had married someone from Ohio. A tall, handsome, soft-spoken man with curly black hair and a mustache. They had bought a small farm in the next county and moved there.

126

There was a lull between work after the crops were laid up and time for the second haying, and the harvest.

Jane spent some time planning on her new house, walking over every inch of the location. Measuring in her mind's eye, just how everything would be. The cliff over there would be cut out for a cellar, and the stones used for the house foundation. The spring tail could run through to keep milk and butter cool. A bridge would go there across the run, just outside the kitchen door. "When my Tom comes home," she said with a sigh. She went back to the cabin and the work now at hand.

The beans would be ready to work up next week. There were bushels and bushels to be strung and threaded to dry. There wouldn't be soldiers for ready money, they would have to "make do" on their crops this winter and from now on.

Summer

The news of the war was terrible and the fighting was getting closer. There had been a battle at Harpers Ferry and another on the Kanawha River. The number of men and horses that were being slaughtered was overwhelming, and no word of Tom had reached his family in weeks. One of the Boggs boys had been killed somewhere in Tennessee and buried where he had fallen. The war raged on. Jane thanked the Lord that they weren't in the thick of it. The word of fires and looting, rape and murder was heard from the battle-torn countryside.

Prisoners were an everyday occurrence, killed and mistreated beyond belief. The farms laid waste, and the cities burned-out.

In the hills, it was quiet and hard to believe a war was raging all around them. Word came to Jane that there were scouts coming through the country looking for men and horses. Jane had the two horses taken up the "holler" and hobbled there. She had let them take her Tom but had no intention letting them have her two mares. She would keep them hid until the scare was over.

There wasn't danger they would take Harn with his bad limp, and Anis was too old to go, even though he looked much older than he really was, letting his gray hair and beard grow long. Jane never asked him to cut it, knowing it was for a purpose.

They all worked hard. Their crops were doing well and it looked like there would be a heavy yield.

Jane and Will, with what Catherin could do, tended the kitchen garden leaving Harn and Anis to the rest of the farm work.

One of the big vinegar barrels was now full of crisp cucumber pickles, strings of beans hung in rows from the clothesline to dry in the sun, and brood hens with little chickens clucked and scratched in the chipyard. Jane had set three hens and now there were fifty-three little biddies hatched in all and another two hens were starting to set. She would put eggs under them, for the chickens could be eaten or sold at the store for staples.

128

The orchard had grown well with the exception of one tree which she and Will had talked to and babied. It still looked puny, but maybe would get enough of a start to make it through the coming winter.

The men were ready to start the second cutting of hay. They wanted to finish it by the last of July. The wheat and oat harvest would start in August and they wanted to be ready to hire out for it.

Anis had all the studding in for the stalls at the new barn. He had worked on it everyday it was too wet to work in the field. It wouldn't take long to close it in once the roof was on. The boards were stacked in the shed ready for the roofing. The mowing machine was moved to the new barn and left there to be ready for the mowing. The shed that had been built for it was turned into a shop house to do work on the farm tools, with a grindstone for sharpening scythe, hoes, and such.

Anis knew of an anvil for sale and a bellows, so Jane had given them the money and sent them for it. They could now sharpen and temper their own plow blades and shovels, or shoe the horses themselves without taking a day and going miles for the job. One end of the shed had been enclosed for saddles and harnesses where the animals couldn't get at the leather, for it didn't take an animal long to chew up a good saddle or bridle.

The lower farm was no longer called the Middleton farm, because Anis and Harn said there were so many yellow jacket nests there, that it oughta be called the Yellow Jacket farm, and so it was renamed. The hay was cut there and several loads hauled to the new barn. The second cutting would be stacked and left there. The barn would be full by the time the corn was cut and put in.

By cold weather the horses would be moved to the big barn, leaving the shed for the milk cows. A big bin had been built in the horse barn for shucked corn. They would have to be thinking of a granary before long. Anis had built Jane a "cool box" for the spring tail early in the spring. It was needed badly but was unhandy to use. A heavy lid had to be raised then the milk crocks set down inside, however, she was thankful for it. She hadn't wanted him to spend much time on it as she said it would be temporary.

She had in mind to start her cellar, and had been asking around for a stone cutter to begin, but the cliff of rock stood waiting. Jane was finding out that waiting was a part of living. She would

129

wait, too. She could picture the finished cellar in her mind as she went back to the cabin.

That evening the men said the haying would be finished on the morrow. The last haystack was in the shock. There were fifteen shocks left. Will would snake them in (it was done by tying a rope or chain around the shock and dragging it slowly to the stack) while Harn and Anis stacked. The hay had to be placed around an upright pole very careful to get it evenly tromped down and topped off just right on the top so rain and snow didn't get in to rot the stack before it could be used. If properly done, a stack would last two seasons without damage. The Cooks had sent word that they needed all the men they could get for the threshing, and if they wanted to work to come Monday.

Anis had made enough from his furs to buy his shoes and much needed clothes. He wanted enough for a gun of his own, and more traps for next winter and was now saving towards that. The pay for the team would be used for flour for the winter.

Jane was restless and irritable, not being able to settle to any job with pleasure. Nausea had been plaguing her in the mornings and made her strength flow from her body. She had seen other women take to their beds for weeks when they got in the "family way." She had thought them pampered and spoiled, but she was finding even the strongest could become weak with morning miseries.

Making herself a glass of cold water with a teaspoon of honey and one of apple cider vinegar settled her down and gave her strength to do her work.

She put the younguns to shelling beans, a tub full had been fixed for them to work at. They all worked getting ready for the long winter ahead.

The harvest would soon be over and the garden put by for another year. Jane wanted her crops in earlier than last year for her winter things.

The men would dig the potatoes at the Hall farm and haul them home to be holed. She and Will would do the ones left in the kitchen garden if her strength held out and didn't fail altogether.

Old Stoney

The men were away at harvesting, and Will had gone up the "holler" to see about the hobbled horses. They had kept them hobbled and out of sight for a month now, but Jane wasn't sure the danger was over yet.

The rattle of wheels on the road brought Jane and the younguns to the kitchen door.

There was some sort of a two-wheeled contraption coming, pulled by the ugliest horse Jane had ever seen. It was a dirty gray with the worst swayback she had ever laid eyes on. It looked like its belly almost dragged the ground and so bony you could count every rib.

"Who in the world?" she asked of no one in particular. "Must be a peddler," she told the younguns. "No one else would drive a contraption like that."

"What's a peddler?" they all wanted to know.

"Oh, someone with wares for sale. They carry shoelaces, ribbon, thread, scented soap and such," she told them.

"He's turning in," with that they all went to the woodyard. The younguns staying close to Mammy Jane's skirt.

The stranger came through the gate and across the creek toward them. His head moving on his neck like a pivot, looking first one way and then the other, taking in everything as he came. He pulled the old nag to a stop a few yards from the waiting group.

"Howdy! You be Mammy Jane? You be wanting some stone-masoning done?" Not waiting for an answer he pointed a gnarled hand toward the cliff of rock. "That's a likely looking quarry. My name's Joe Stone, everybody calls me 'Stoney,' don't know why," and he chuckled.

Stepping to the cart, Jane reached up a small hand. "I'm Jane Jarvis, wife of Thomas P.," she told him as they shook hands. Looking him over as she did so. He didn't look like much but she decided she liked him. "Get down," she told him, "unhitch your

131

brute. You can take him around back to the shed and give him a feed of hay. Recon you ain't had dinner? We were about to have some." Watching for him to come from the shed, she had a wash pan of sudsy warm water ready and handed it out the kitchen door. "You can wash up there on the bench. Catherin will bring you a towel. Come on in and set then." There was a big pot of beans bubbling in their thick brown broth on the back of the stove, and corn bread baking in the oven. There hadn't been enough left from supper to last and she had to make more. She quartered a couple of nice Dutch onions and put them on the table. He would have to eat what the rest ate. Looked like he hadn't had much for a long time, for he was as bony as his horse.

Jane set a big plate of beans and gravy in front of him and handed the plate of steaming corn pone to him.

"That sure looks good, one of my favorite meals, beans and Dutch onions and a good pone of corn bread," he said as he took a big bite from the onion.

The younguns all ate without a word, taking peeks at old "Stoney" from under their lowered heads. Will came as they sat for eating, and joined them, "Everything is fine up the holler, Mammy Jane."

"This is your boy?" the old man asked between mouthfuls.

"This is Tom's son, Will," Jane answered.

After they had all eaten, the old man got up from the table. "That was a fine dinner, you know how to cook beans. Some cooks don't put any taste into them. I'm partial to taste myself," he said.

"Well, let's take a look at your rocks. You can tell me what you are gonna do with them."

They walked toward the cliff, Jane stopping to point out the orchard and where the house would stand, the bridge would go across the run. The old man took it all in till she finished.

"That's a fine orchard, well-planned and your house sounds like it will be a fair one," Stoney said.

They continued across the run and then the spring tail to look at the rocks more closely. "I have in mind to cut out the rocks to form a room in the cliff for a cellar. Let the spring tail furnish cooling for the milk. Use the cut out stone for the foundations for the house and for the chimney stones," Jane informed him.

"There'll be quite a lot but not enough for all that. This here rock will do fine for a foundation for your house and for your cellar. I favor a softer sandstone for chimney rocks though. Any good chimney man will tell you that, and I know a good one when you're ready." He was poking with an iron bar here and there at the cliff as he talked. "Might as well get started. Maybe can have one done 'fore nightfall," he told her as he started back to his cart he had pulled in by the barn for his tools.

"We are a mite crowded for sleeping," she told him as they walked back.

"I can sleep in your harness room for the time being. I'm not choosy, I sleep on the ground half the time. I got me a tarp and a quilt in the cart."

Jane could hear the peck, peck, peck of the hammer on the rock as she cleaned up the dinner things.

Will had followed the old man back to the site, watching and listening as the old man talked. She let them be till her chore was done.

Stepping to the door she called, "Oh, Will. Come, I have a chore for you." She took the broom and met Will. They went to the shed to see if they could fix the old man a place to sleep. Together they nailed some boards against one end high enough for a bed, swept down the cobwebs, moved as much as they could to the other walls. Jane had Will bring down some fresh hay. They piled it and formed it into a bed on the framework. The old man came for some of his tools. Will called him to look and he brought his things. They spread the tarp and quilt over the hay making a fair bed. "That's a fine bed," he told them. "I'll sleep snug in there."

"It will do for the present. We don't usually put people to sleep in the barns," Jane told him.

"Don't you worry none, I'll get back to me rock, that's a fine blue ledge, makes fine cornerstones for your house, misses," he was scuttling across the run as he finished telling her. It was clear he loved his work and liked to keep busy.

"Mercy me, another man to cook and look after," she said to herself. "This place is starting to look like a compound." There was so much to be done and it took men to do most of it. Her house was started, and that sent a thrill through her, even knowing it would be years before it could be built. She hadn't counted her money but there wouldn't be enough to buy lumber and build the kind of house she wanted. She planned to put the men to cutting timber and taking it to be sawed, if they did that, it could be built in time without much layout of dollars.

133

Molasses

The two men always left before daybreak, riding the harnessed horses so as to be in the field by sunup. The threshing was in full swing, and the men were getting fifty cents a day, plus Jane was getting fifty cents for the team. It was finished in about three weeks and then the molasses making. They felt that Jane had enough cane to warrant moving the machine for her crop after the Cooks were finished. Some people on down Beech had stopped to see Jane and to know who would be making her molasses. They would bring their's to her set if she could get someone to make them. Since her field was at the Yellow Jacket farm, it wouldn't be far for their cane to be hauled. It was a certainty now that they would come, and it would be worth their while.

The first load of wheat to go to the mill, Jane wanted to go, too. She would need more churns to put the molasses in, and before cold weather wanted to buy what coffee, lard and such things they would need to see them through the winter. She would need flannel for the baby's things. She wanted to see her in-laws and see what news they had of the war.

The men told her the next day they would be going and she was to be ready. She made a nut cake to take her mother-in-law for a gift, readied her basket of eggs, and was ready when the wagonload of sacked wheat arrived. This wagon would be coming back empty so she could bring back what she needed.

Mr. Cheniweth greeted her cordially and wanted to know how she had been and would wait on her himself.

"Will you count my eggs today and total my credit I have coming, please?" she asked. "I want to go to the sawmill for some business and will be back directly."

Upon reaching the mill, she introduced herself, "I'm Mrs. Thomas P. Jarvis. I would like to speak to whoever is in charge."

A gentleman came from a back cubbyhole office. "I'm Brown, owner of the mill, Mrs. Jarvis, what can I do for you?"

"What will it cost me to have a house pattern cut?" she asked.
"We have to have something to work from, such as measurements. How big a house did you have in mind? We have to know how much studding and such."

"That I'm not familiar with, say a house the size of my father-in-law's."

"That's some house," he said as he looked her up and down.

"We have a sizable family now and will no doubt have more in time," she said as color stained her cheeks. "My man is away fighting the war, but I intend to start the building in the spring, if possible, before." Jane told him with a toss of her head.

"On an order that size I can take some logs for the sawing and some cash."

"Very well, you will hear from me." Offering her hand she bid him good-bye.

While she did her trading she talked to Mr. Cheniweth about sawing, and the price he reckoned for a sizable house pattern.

"Well, Mrs. Jarvis, that depends. I'd say maybe one hundred fifty dollars or two hundred dollars for the sawing fee. Course if you did some 'horse trading' you might get it for half that much by trading timber for sawing."

"I thank you for all the information, now how much credit do I have coming?" she asked.

"You haven't used much of your egg money all summer, so it comes to twenty-one dollars and seventy-five cents, with what you brought in today," Mr. Cheniweth said.

"I'll need a hundred pound of coffee grain, a fifty pound can of lard, fifty of sugar, twenty yards of flannel, half white, half blue, thread, nutmeg, and she named some more spices, and two pairs of shoes." Will's will be handed down to John, Catherin's to Elizabeth, Trude would still be barefooted this winter. She bought a roll of batting and enough calico to cover a quilt, and heavy thread for knotting. She had gotten extra jars for the molasses and had traded the merchant out of another vinegar barrel. She had to pay eight dollars from her poke. Oh, well, she wouldn't be coming in again till spring and eggs would start adding up to her credit. She could have charged the eight dollars and let eggs pay for it, but had found that cash money got more respect, she needed all of that she could get being alone.

Stopping at her in-laws on her way home she brought in the basket with the nut cake. She was welcomed with pleasure, as she

135

explained she would have to hurry. Her mother-in-law was so pleased with the cake, she gave the basket to her daughter telling her to refill it with peaches and have it taken out to the wagon.

"Jane, you are just blooming, you grow prettier each day." She looked at her carefully. "I think you have a secret," she said with a smile.

Jane blushed and nodded. She wanted her mother-in-law to know, but didn't know how she would ever tell her, now it was done for her.

"We have good news. Tom is well and sent you a money voucher that his dad cashed for you." She handed her twenty-five dollars.

"Thank you. Did he say when he will be coming home?" Jane asked.

"No. The war is going badly for the South, and the North have an epidemic in the hospitals of yellow fever, so many are dying. I had a letter from my Jane, she wrote that father and she work from morning till way in the night, doing what they can. It isn't much as medical supplies are low, and no food to speak of to feed the wounded." Silent tears rolled down her cheeks. "May God keep them safe, and send my children home to me," she said in a whisper.

"I thank you for the money and the news. I'll have to go now, but if you hear anymore, send word. I'll have the men stop when they come through with the wheat." Jane went to the door.

Mrs. Jarvis kissed her cheek, "Take care of yourself, child, and try not to worry. It won't be good for you at this time."

"I know. Good-bye." Jane climbed into the wagon for the homeward journey, pleased by the news and the money to add to her little hoard.

Bad News

The peck, peck of the hammer on stone could be heard from daybreak until dusk. It had become a part of the farm sounds, no note taken of it unless it stopped.

The wheat hauling continued, leaving a day between to give the miller a chance to mill the load so it could be brought on the return trip. On one trip they brought word that Tom had been wounded. Harn tried to break it to Jane gently. "Sister," Harn began, Jane looked at him in surprise. He had never called her sister since a little boy.

"There's news of Tom." She knew without being told. She had been uneasy the past two days even though they had just heard that he was well.

"How bad is it?" she asked, looking at Harn and squaring her shoulders.

"They don't know yet. If they send him back he will be on the train tomorrow," Harn told her.

Jane sank onto a chair. Her weak legs wouldn't hold her, she became dizzy. It took a minute to make her body behave.

"He's alive," she said. "He will be alright, I know he will be alright," with that, relief flooded her heart. She allowed herself to sit a moment before going on with her work.

Her Tom hurt, how bad she didn't know, maybe a leg or an arm, Oh, Lord, no! her mind was in a tumble. Somehow she managed to get their supper and the evening chores done.

Someone had told Stoney and his ever present chatter was silent during the meal, but she could feel his eyes on her. As he left the table he gently touched her shoulder, "Mrs., if he was hurt real bad they would leave him in the hospital, not send him home on the train."

Jane looked up at him, the gentleness causing tears to come to her eyes, "I recon you're right," she told him, "thank you for your concern."

137

Stoney gave a "harrumph"—and left the kitchen.

"What a gentle little man," Jane said to herself, "that's why I like him, he reminds me of my Tom."

The night seemed long and weary with Jane turning and restless, sleeping little. As she awoke at daybreak and got out of bed, a pain hit her in the lower back, making her grab onto the bedstead and gasp for breath. "No, no, not that, too!" She dressed and went to the kitchen, making herself some hot water and honey, with a dash of whiskey. There had been no more pain, just a nagging feeling low down. She decided she couldn't go to meet Tom in the jolting wagon, she would just have to send Harn and wait at home a while longer to know how bad her Tom was hurt.

It was one of the longest days she had ever endured, waiting, and waiting, trying to think of something to fix that Tom would like, she decided to kill a chicken and make a big pot of chicken and dumplings. That would take her mind off Tom, for a while, anyway.

The younguns were on their log horse in the woodyard, watching for the wagon that would bring their pa. Will had split wood till he got tired and then would help Old Stoney. He was learning from him how to chip a straightedge on the stone, and how to size it up to split it with the grain.

A yell went up interrupting the chip, chip. "They're coming, they're coming, they're coming," as the wagon came up the rise a mile away. Slowly making its way up the dusty road, now behind the big barn, slowly to the gate. Harn got down and came around to help the other passenger out of the wagon and through the gate.

Jane went at a fast walk to the creek, eyes glued to Tom. He was walking! with a bad limp, but walking, nevertheless. "*Thank God, Thank God*," Jane mumbled as she took his arm for him to lean on her, saying his name "Tom, Tom."

"I'm all right, Jane, just a little tired. It's only a nick, a piece of shrapnel in the leg. The doctor took it all out, but it just don't want to heal."

Tears were running down her face though not a sound came from her. "Come, I'll put you down for a nap and you will feel better soon," Jane said.

"You younguns say hello to your pa and then skedaddle so he can sleep," she told them.

138

She brought him a drink like she had made for herself that morning, it did wonders for a person.

Tom didn't ask what it was, just drank it and smiled, putting his head down on the pillow. Jane helped lift his legs on to the bed, sat holding his hand till she heard the even breathing of sleep. The wound would need tending to, but she would let him have his sleep first.

Tom slept until supper time. He didn't look quite so pale and ate as though he was starved. He and the men talked all through the meal. Not much was said about the war, Tom didn't seem to want to talk about it, just that shrapnel had hit his leg, and that he was lucky it hadn't caused much damage.

Everything had settled down for the night. Jane asked Tom about his wound. "Come, sit here and let me look about it," she told him.

He removed his trousers and sat at the kitchen table, his leg up on a chair.

Jane carefully removed the dirty bandage. She could smell the pus from the ragged hole in the calf of the leg, bringing hot water in the wash pan she poured in turpentine, made hot packs holding them till they cooled down. Tom winced as the hot rag went on the tender wound, after about the fifth one he said, "I think it is feeling better, it don't throb so."

"It will take time to draw out all the 'matter,' it's deep," she said, going to the cabinet she found some clean rags. Bringing her mullein leaf ointment, she spread a square of cloth with it and put it over the wound and then wrapped it and pinned it with a safety pin. She walked him to the bed and brought him a hot tonic, this would assure him of a good night's sleep.

Jane was weary, the pain had quieted and her back felt better, maybe she wouldn't "miss" after all. A good night's sleep would tell the tale.

Tom looked better next morning, but she kept him quiet with his foot on a pillow on a chair. Taking the bandage off, she reapplied the hot turpentine packs, then at noon and evening she did the same, the angry red and swelling was starting to leave. The healing would take time, but it would heal and he wouldn't lose a leg.

The two talked more the next few days than they had since they had married. Tom teased her about putting on weight, knowing all along she was carrying his child.

139

It took three weeks for the wound to heal, and for Tom not to limp. He was his old self, walking around the farmyard, and going over to watch old Stoney and talk to him as he worked.

By the time the molasses mill was set up at Yellow Jacket, he insisted on going down to watch the molasses making, and the younguns were all let go along. They were made small wooden paddles to eat the "skimmin's" with. Molasses making was an occasion, with people coming for miles to gossip and lick "skimmin's" and just visit. It was a slow relaxed job that took lots of time to do. The molasses makers took pride in their work and didn't hurry it one mite.

The fall days were bright and crisp with frosty air turning the hillsides to rainbows of color. Each day Jane knew was numbered and waited for the time Tom would have to leave.

The day after the molasses making was it. After breakfast Tom told her, "I must go. Don't worry, I'll be back. This war can't last much longer, a year, at most. You are doing a fine job, and you're a much better doctor than any the army has," he said with a smile.

"I'll leave today. I want to walk. I'll have to do plenty soon enough, might as well get used to it," he told her. He readied his things, put his knapsack over his shoulder, kissed Jane, long and tenderly, hugged each of his younguns and left, whistling cheerfully as he started down the road.

Jane slumped into a chair, the waiting over. She never knew she could feel such loneliness, and Tom was barely out of sight.

The Harvest

A year had gone by since Tom and Jane had married. Out of that year they had spent less than half of it together, and a lot had happened in that time. Jane felt she was finally a woman. She had turned eighteen in May of this year and would have her own child before reaching nineteen.

The harvest was almost finished. They had harvested all the apples they could find, drying some and holing the rest.

Harn and Anis were bringing home the last of the potatoes from the Hall farm, to be holed. There was a good harvest of them.

Jane had readied Will and Catherin and took them to Minnora and entered them in the school there. They had been riding one of the mares since early September, Will in the saddle and Catherin on behind. They would go as long as they could, then the roads and weather would keep them home soon enough. They could learn some and go again in the spring. The five miles was a long way for younguns to have to go alone.

The old straw from their beds was ready for use in the tater hole. Jane had renewed it with new wheat straw after the harvest. She would supervise the tater holing.

The stalls on one side of the big barn was finished. The horses and the calves would be fed there through the winter. The two mares would foal in December, and could be in out of the weather. The two cows had been driven while Tom was home. They would have late spring calves again. She had hopes that her sow would breed and have pigs in the spring.

Jane was feeling better than she had a couple of months ago. Her child would be born around Christmastime, how she would manage she didn't know. She would have to have someone with her, she had helped tend enough women to know what to expect.

Looked like old Stoney would be here most of the winter, she had rearranged the bedroom so as to fix him a bed. He couldn't

141

continue sleeping in the shed when it got colder, so she had sewed together flour sacks for a tick and filled it with straw. Harn could turn the boys' bed around and make a narrow one to fit in the other corner. The calico she had bought had been worked into a nice, new comfort, it would go on her bed then she could switch hers to the girls' bed and give Stoney one of the old ones.

Jane wanted to get all the washing done before cold weather, she wasn't too comfortable leaning over the washboard now, and there was still two more months to go yet.

All the pumpkins, beans, and dried apples had been put away. Stacks of stone jars, the three big wooden barrels, one of pickles, one of vinegar, and the other would be filled with kale, pickled in brine. They all lined the walls of the kitchen. Anis had put a high shelf over them to line up the lard cans on that held nuts, dried apples, and beans. Jane had stored away enough for an army, so there would be plenty to eat through the winter.

There was barely enough space to walk in the kitchen. It would be really crowded to wash clothes, but it would have to be done in the winter months.

The last of October the drizzle of rain started. Everything was dripping wet, the leaves falling and the gloom of winter settled in.

Jane started on the little gowns and shirts, and bellybands, making them from the blue flannel, hemmed three dozen white flannel diapers. She worked by lamplight after the others had gone to bed, thinking of the little body they would clothe, and of her Tom. If ever a baby was conceived of love, this one was. She felt it would be a boy. She wanted a son, one that would look like her Tom. Oh, if only he could be here for the birthin' of their first son. Jane didn't want to think of the ordeal ahead, and tried to put it out of her mind. There was a finger of fear tickling up and down her spine that wouldn't go away on command.

The days passed, one into another. The first snow fell on November 7. The two younguns had to give up going to school. It was too cold and dangerous for them to go so far. The mare had to be kept close at home too. She was heavy with foal, if she happened to fall it would kill her. She would have to be watched so as not to lose her foal.

Anis had started the stringers on the other half of the stalls. The lumber and studding had been brought as a wagon came back from taking wheat to the mill.

Old Stoney kept up his tap, tap. He had moved into the bedroom. Jane had asked for his clothes and had told him to wash from the skin out and change.

The cut stones were hauled and placed around where the foundation was to be built.

Anis wanted to finish the barn before starting on timber cutting. They would have all winter. With two working it wouldn't take long to finish the stalls on the barn. The hay from the two cuttings had filled the barn loft and overflowed into the main floor leaving enough room for the mowing machine. The barn at the Hall farm was full of hay and cut corn to be shucked through the winter. The barn at the house was full also. The cows would be kept and fed there. There would be plenty of feed for all the animals.

Jane had a flock of seventy-five laying hens. Several fryers to use or sell. The farm was more than doubled in the one year and still growing with animals and people. They would have to have a house before long. This one is bursting at the seams, Jane thought to herself.

The hammering and tapping continued through November with its snow, rain, and sunshine at times.

The kale was ready to be picked for the brine barrel. Jane and Will got at it, he carried plenty of water from the spring to wash it in. Every leaf was swished separately to get any grit off. The biggest kettles and pans filled the stove top while the cooking took place. This would be the last of putting away winter food. The smell and steam didn't set too well with Jane. Even Will complained how could it smell so awful and still be good to eat.

Anis went out with his new gun and brought home ten squirrels. They made a tasty meal for them all and enough broth for a hearty soup for a second meal.

Jane had in mind to send Harn to Minnora before long. Christmas things had to be bought and she had to make some arrangements for her "laying-in." Maybe Harn could approach her mother-in-law and she would have an idea. It would have to be done soon. Jane figured she had less than a month to go.

She and her two mares would be due about the same time, she thought with a smile.

Anis had gone down the creek on Sunday to set out his traps. He had bought himself four more. Now he had a string of six. When he came back, he said, "We have new neighbors in the mouth of the holler across from Yellow Jacket. A man with a limp, came back from the war wounded bad. He has just got married. They have dug a cellar and put a room above it to live in. He just bought the farm, name of Jed Hicks. His woman's name is Florence," Anis finished his long description.

"Do they have younguns?" Jane asked.

"No, just the two of them, seems like nice folks," Anis answered.

"How will they live? Do they have brutes?" Jane asked again.

"Seems that her family spared them some food. They have it in their cellar. He has one old mule. Said it can live off brush mostly. He wants to work if he can get some with his bad leg. Looks like they need the money."

Visitors

Sunday was a nice sunny day. The men had gone off hunting or just trudgin' through the woods as they liked to do on a Sunday.

Jane was tidying the shelves in the kitchen. She wanted everything in good order when someone else had to take over. Stepping outside to empty her cleaning water she was surprised to see a man and woman coming through the bars at the road.

The man was limping, must be the new neighbors. Taking the pan back inside she reached behind the door for her shawl and went to the chipyard to meet the new arrivals.

"Howdy," she called out. "You must be our new neighbors?" Reaching out her hand she shook hands with them both.

"Yes, we're your neighbors," the man Jed answered. "This is my wife, Florence."

"We're so glad to have someone near. Come on in," Jane said, leading the way.

The younguns were down for a nap except Catherin, she sat by the window with a storybook. She could read some and loved books.

"Have you ate?" Jane asked.

"Oh, yes, we had dinner," Florence answered.

"Sit down here at the table. I'll pour us some coffee, it's still hot," Jane put cups in front of them and one for herself.

"You have a real nice kitchen," Florence remarked. "I like your ruffly curtains and tablecloth to match."

"Thank ye, took some time hemming them but it 'pleasures' me to look at them," Jane told them.

"We don't have much yet. We have been busy fixing a place to live. Jed's family come and helped. It's small but warm and Jed says we will have a big house someday," Florence said.

Jane had time to look her new neighbors over. Florence was tall and thin with black curly hair and black snapping eyes, that took in everything at a glance. Jed wasn't as tall as Florence, slight of

145

build with reddish-blond hair that stood up all over his head and of course the limp. He had a bellowing laugh that was startling in its intensity; it came roaring out at unexpected moments.

Jane cut a piece of apple pie for each of them. She had it warming in the warming closet of the stove. She had made three after cooking dinner. Usually she baked for Sunday supper.

"You're a good cook," Jed informed her, with that bellowing laugh again.

Jane couldn't help smiling. "Thank ye, I hope you can eat it," she said as she watched him scrape every crumb from the plate.

"I recon I'll walk around a bit, leave you womenfolk to gossip," Jed said as he left the kitchen.

"Help yourself, the men should be back directly," Jane told him.

"Florence picked up the plates and cups. Took the pan from the nail behind the stove and poured water from the teakettle, then began to wash up. Jane was amazed and pleased to see her make herself at home in her kitchen. Maybe this was just what she was looking for.

"When are you due?" Florence wanted to know, as she swiftly dried the dishes. Jane was still sitting at the table.

"Very soon, I'm afraid," Jane said. "I've not made arrangements yet. I really don't know who to try to get."

"You leave it to me. I'll ask old Aunt Mandy Ellis, she has brought a heap of younguns into the world. She is good. I'll come myself and see to you and your family. I like you and your kitchen." She turned to look at Jane, taking in her surroundings with snapping eyes.

"Oh, what a relief, I like you too. Maybe we can help each other, 'The Lord works in mysterious ways,' " Jane said.

"I recon I won't be needing Aunt Mandy for a while," Florence answered with a laugh.

"What in the world do you have in all those barrels and stone jars?" Florence asked, looking curiously at them.

"Food," Jane answered, "That one is vinegar, that one sauerkraut, that one greens in brine, that one molasses," she pointed as she talked. "And in the cans sugar, lard, coffee, and seeds."

"You have a regular storehouse. I don't recon we will eat so well. We didn't get in much. I have a nice cellar but not much in it."

146

One thing Florence didn't lack for words and told it straight out.

"There's lots of kale, if you want you could put down a barrel of it before snow. There is turnips and parsnips, more than we need. You can have as many as you want," Jane told her.

"You just tell me how and I sure will put it down. You sure you don't need it?" she asked.

"No, there's a plenty. Let's go out and I will show you." They walked to the garden. The bed of kale was fresh and green in the sun. Jane pointed out the holed potatoes and apples to her. They took a walk by the "stone quarry" and "the house site." The orchard was admired by both women. "I always wanted an orchard," Jane told her.

Jane had never had a girl friend even when a child. She had never realized what a pleasure it was to talk and visit with someone near her own age. As they walked back to the cabin, Florence asked, "How old are you, Jane?"

"I just turned eighteen this spring," Jane answered.

"I'm twenty-two," Florence told her. "We never got married because Jed was in the army even before the war. Then he was wounded and in the hospital for a while." With a sigh she said, "We got a late start. But we will do alright."

"Sure you will. We have had some good luck. You will too. I would rather have my Tom home," Jane told her. When they returned the younguns were up from their nap.

"These can't all be yours," Florence said in amazement.

"No," Jane went on to tell her the story, as she sent them out for a walk in the sun. She wanted to show Florence the baby things she had been making.

"Let me take a couple of the gowns and put some fancy work on them for you. I would like to," she said as Jane hesitated.

"Alright if you really want to, I don't do much in that way."

"You sew nice though. I want me a sewing machine someday," Florence said.

"What is that?" Jane asked.

"It's a machine that sews the littlest stitches you ever did see. You sit at it like a table and pedal it with your feet. Feed the cloth in and it does all the sewing." She sat at the table to demonstrate. "It goes ever so fast, you can make a whole dress in a day," Florence's eyes flashed and her laugh rang out.

147

"What a wonder," Jane remarked. "I surely would like to look on one of these machines," she said.

Jed had wandered over to see the big barn and was coming back towards the house talking to the younguns in the chipyard.

"If you want some kale we could pick it while the sun is out. You can put it in your cellar till you get it cooked." Jane explained how it was to be done. "Do you have a churn or barrel to put it in?"

"I have a big twenty-gallon churn my mother gave me. I don't have anything in it," Florence answered.

"Alright, let's take the tub and fill it, you can bring it back. Do you have salt?" Jane asked.

"Some though I don't allow it's enough," Florence said.

"I'll loan you some," Jane said.

They took the tub from under the house. Jed and Catherin came to help. Jane couldn't stoop to pick and bossed the job. Telling them how to pack it down. Soon the tub was full, mashed down as much as they could. Jane sent Catherin for a flour sack to tie over the tub to keep it from spilling. "You can get more if you want, fill your stone jar full. You can add more in a couple of days, it don't hurt," Jane told them. Greens and corn pone wasn't bad in the winter.

They decided they had better get home, they would carry the tub between them.

Jane gave them a pound of salt, and pulled a cabbage head out of the dirt for them. "It will keep till you want to eat it." Jed carried it by the stalk and Florence carried the salt.

"I had a real nice visit and we both enjoyed the pie and coffee," Florence told her as they took their leave.

"Now you send for me just as soon as you get a twitch, you hear?" Florence laughed as they crossed the creek and out through the bars.

Jane sighed with relief, she wouldn't have to worry now. Help was close. Such a cheerful person, it made you feel good just having her around. Jane slept peaceful and relaxed, the first in a long time.

Finishing the Barn

The weather held for a few days. Florence and Jed came back for another tub of kale. Jane urged them to take all they could use and to dig some turnips and parsnips to put in their cellar.

Jed returned the tub, bringing his mule and a couple of sacks and dug about a bushel of each to take home.

The men were busy on the barn trying to get the roof on before another snow. Jed stopped at the barn to talk to the men and see what they were doing. Anis was nailing shingles on the roof as Will brought armloads up the ladder to him. Harn followed just above with the second row of shingles.

"I'll come tomorrow and help you put up the siding. I'm a fair carpenter," Jed told them.

Sure enough, by good light the next morning, limping, Jed was there with his own hammer, ready to work. Jed started the siding while the other two worked on the roof. They were just ready to tie it in when it started to rain. The temperature dropped rapidly as they hurried to finish and came down the ladder as the first snowflakes started to come down. They all worked on the siding, starting on the northwest side where the wind blew in. If they got that side done they would be protected from the weather.

Jed was good with a saw and hammer. Will carried boards in under the new roof to keep them dry and in reach of the workers.

They all came to the cabin around three-thirty for a cup of hot coffee and to get warm by the fire. Jane was expecting them and had a big pot on the back of the kitchen stove ready. She hadn't been feeling too perky all day but had washed out some of the men's clothes and had them hanging behind the stove. She had continued all afternoon at her work. Being heavy on her feet they had begun to swell some. No wonder, she thought, the load I'm carrying.

"Harn, you and Will will take over the milking. I'll not venture out in this weather," she told them.

149

Harn and Anis looked at her with concern. "Alright, Jane. You don't need to be out."

Jed got up to say good-bye. "Guess I better get on down the road before I get snowed in here," and his booming laugh rang out. "If you need my Florence you send one of the boys. I'll get her here if I have to carry her on my back." Ha, Ha, Ha, he was still laughing as he reached the chipyard on his way home.

"He's a worker, a good carpenter too," the boys both said.

"He sure likes to laugh," Will put in. "Makes you feel good around someone who laughs a lot."

The snow didn't let up, by the time the chores were done and supper over everything was covered with snow.

"Harn, make sure the mares are fed and safe in the barn. Keep them separated. They could foal anytime now. Might as well pen the cows in the shed too. It looks like this will last a spell," Jane told them.

Harn said, "We are in better shape this year than last. We have plenty of feed for the animals and looks like Jane has put down enough for all of us."

"That poor old mule of Jed's, I hope it don't freeze or starve to death," Will told them.

The next morning the wind had died down. There was about six inches of snow on the ground, it didn't seem near as cold as when the wind was blowing. The men were up and had the chores done and were deliberating whether to work a while on the barn or not.

There was a "hello the house," looking out, they saw Jed leading the old mule with Florence aboard. She slid off nimble as could be and came in while Jed tethered the old mule to a log in the woodyard.

Stomping the snow on the step, her cheery, "Good morning, all," brought a chorus of "good morning" from all in the cabin. Jane went to greet her and take her shawl.

"You look fair-to-middlen," she said, eyeing Jane up and down.

"I feel better today. I didn't feel too pert yesterday, but today I'm fine," Jane answered. They both went into the sittin' room. Florence brought out the two little blue gowns worked beautifully with fancy work. Little pink and yellow flowers and feather-stitch all down the front.

"Oh! They are too pretty for a boy," Jane told her. "You went to a heap of trouble. I appreciate it. I never expected to have anything so nice for my baby."

150

"I'll teach you how and you can do any number of things. Towels and pillow covers. Even bed throws," Florence told her.

Catherin came in and saw the gowns on the bed. "Oh, how pretty, I love pretty things."

"There," Jane said, "you can teach Catherin, I don't have time for such fancy things."

"Oh, would you? Would you? I'll try real hard to learn fast," she said as she turned her earnest little face to Florence.

"I sure will and I'll teach you to knit too. You can make a pair of mittens just like these," and she held up a pair of red mittens.

The sound of muffled hammering came to them. "I guess the men decided it wasn't too cold to nail boards. I just had to bring the gowns myself," Florence told them. "And see how you were. I have a feeling it won't be long. The full of the moon is first of the week and that's a good time."

"I'll be glad to have it finished," Jane said wearily. "I've just been dragging my feet lately."

While the men worked Florence and Jane knotted the comfort that Jane had started. She was making a flannel wrap for the baby. Blue on one side and white on the other. "Batten" in between and knotted with blue thread. It would last and be warm and serviceable. Catherin helped tie knots and became part of the group. Jane wanted to keep her out of things for a while longer. She was past eight now. I was helping bring babies at ten, Jane thought to herself. It's not a pretty sight for a young girl. The women gossiped and finished the wrap. "It's pretty and so soft," Catherin said with her shy smile. "I love little babies. They're so sweet."

"You'r' sweet too and a pretty girl," Florence told her as she gave her a squeeze.

"She likes women's work and will make a fine wife one day," Jane said. "I hope the men had sense enough to put your mule in the barn and give it a good feed," Jane said, looking out the window. "It'll snow again before mornin'," she prophesied.

"It usually does when there's a baby due," Florence commented. "No matter, I'm close enough to get here."

"It's a comfort to have another woman near," Jane told her.

It was getting on toward evening, the men still hammering away.

"Catherin, go punch up the fire in the kitchen stove. I'll put on some supper," Jane told her. "The men should be here directly. What do you think of a big apple cobbler?" Jane asked Florence. "We have plenty of milk and it will fill everyone up."

151

"That sounds real good. I haven't had apple cobbler in a coon's age," Florence answered.

"Let's peel the apples then," Jane said, giving herself a push to get out of the rocking chair she was sitting in. They both sat talking, peeling, and slicing apples for the cobbler. Jane made the dough and lined the biggest bread pan she had. It just barely fit into the big oven. Adding plenty of brown sugar, cinnamon, and nutmeg. Long strips of dough between each layer of apples and crisscrossed on the top, it was soon bubbling in the oven. The spicy smell penetrated throughout the house making everyone hungry. The usual big pot of coffee boiled on the back of the stove.

They heard the men coming just in time for the supper to come out of the oven. "Um—um—something smells good," Jed commented as he came in.

Florence had started setting the table for them all. They would eat before starting their trip back to their cold home.

They all enjoyed the hearty tasty cobbler, some having third helpings. Cup after cup of coffee was poured around the table. The men got up patting their full stomachs in contentment, remarking how much they had enjoyed the feast.

The chores were done as Florence and Jed started on their way home; Jane calling to them, "Be careful and don't let the mule break a leg." It had begun to look a little more alive getting fed while they were there.

Water was brought in from the spring to fill every container. It would be frozen over by morning.

"We just have the two doors and the doors on the manure holes and the barn is finished excepting the stall partitions; we can build them on rainy days," Anis said.

"Then you can soon start on logs for the house pattern," Jane said.

Old Stoney had left to visit a sister during the worst of the winter and said he would be back as soon as the weather cleared some. After Christmas probably.

"Thank the Lord," Jane told them, "we have been very lucky and you have all done well."

"Let's go to bed," Anis said, "I'll go around my traps in the morning, I feel lucky, may have a mink."

"If this keeps up we will try for a nice fat buck for meat." They settled down for the night with contentment, Jane thinking of her Tom as she drifted off to sleep.

The Colt

The wind whistled around the eaves of the cabin blowing snow-drifts into every crevice that would hold it. Toward morning the baby's kick woke Jane from a deep sleep. The cabin had begun to get cold, the wind finding every crack. Getting out of bed she punched the fire up and added wood, checked to see if the girls were covered. She couldn't have them sick and a new baby almost here.

Harn came in from the back room dressed for the outside.

"Where are you going at this hour?" Jane asked.

"I'm uneasy about the mares. I think old Babe is ready to foal. She showed some signs last night. I'll take the lantern and see about her. Anis wants up early anyway to track deer." Harn was putting on his outdoor boots as he talked.

"You be careful of the lantern," Jane cautioned him. She sat by the stove with her shawl around her till she was sure the new logs caught. They couldn't have things frozen in the cabin. Not to mention the sickness it could cause. She waited a while for Harn to return and when he didn't, she went back to bed. She dozed a couple of times but never really got to sleep. Turning over she picked up the clock by her bed. She could see the face by the flickering light of the fire. It was a quarter past four. Time she got the kitchen fire going so the men could eat before going hunting. Harn came back just as she was making up her mind to put her feet on the floor.

Coming close to the potbellied stove to warm himself, he said, "Well, we have a new addition. Babe has a beautiful little filly colt. As pretty and pert as can be. I dried it off and fixed it a nest of clean dry hay. She birthed it just as I got there, got along fine." Harn was pleased with himself and the new colt.

"I'm glad there was no trouble. It's a cold night for a little feller to come out into the world," Jane remarked. "Put a

153

shovelful of coals in the kitchen stove. I'll start breakfast," Jane told him.

She was dressed when he came back to the fire. "How is the other mare?" she asked.

"Pet? Oh, she's fine. She will foal anytime now," Harn answered.

The boys had named the two mares finally, Babe and Pet, Jane thought them a little fancy but didn't say anything.

The kitchen range was sending out plenty of heat and the kitchen was cozy and warm. Jane soon had coffee boiling on the back of the stove and biscuits in the oven. They had plenty of butter and molasses for a good filling breakfast. Jane always thought to say, "Thank the Lord," under her breath.

The weight in her belly made her slow and clumsy. It was becoming most unhandy, and troublesome to her as she tried to work. The baby seemed to always be shifting and to her notion putting her off balance. Oh, well, it will be over soon, she thought.

The biscuits were puffed up brown and crisp, ready for the men as they came in to eat. They talked of the new colt and the other one that was due, and of course the hunt. Nothing seemed to excite men so much as getting out tromping the hills looking for something to kill.

She hoped they could get a deer, they hadn't had meat for some time now. She knew the men especially craved meat.

They took the gun and left before daybreak, going in a different direction than where they wanted to be, having to circle the "lick" and not alert the deer that came to drink. It was so cold and snowy they might eat snow instead. It had to get terribly cold for the "lick" to freeze, it was fast running.

Jane had seen the two men stop at the barn to check on the new colt and the mares before being on their way. Jane sat and had a peaceful cup of coffee, the crackle of the flames and the wind to keep her company. She rarely had time to herself. Soon the cabin would erupt with the noise of the five children. Someday she would have a big house where she could go into a room and close the door and be alone. Her mind seemed as heavy and full as the rest of her body this morning.

Will would have to do the chores and milk unless the men came back soon. They couldn't stay out too long in the cold. If the deer didn't come shortly after daybreak they wouldn't come at all.

Jane sat on thinking of this and that and, of course, of her Tom. Hoping he was in a warm place.

All of a sudden Jane had a peculiar feeling. Like a wave washing up from her feet to the top of her head. Sitting still, feeling the warmth and closeness of the cabin around her. It was unusual for idleness to find Jane. Rarely did she take time to sit and eat let alone just sit. A faint ray of light came through the window. Jane arose and going to the window pushed the curtains aside. There was just a hint of the sun in the East, standing there she watched the pink flow up into the morning sky.

It's coming up in waves just like I felt a while ago, she mused to herself. Maybe it means the birth of a new day and the birth of a baby.

"I'm getting peculiar in the head," she said out loud, talking to herself.

Just as she turned from the window she heard a shot and then another like an echo of the first one.

One birth, one death, Oh, no, mustn't think like that. No, No, No.

My Tom is out there somewhere. A silent tear rolled down her face. Watching out the window she saw Harn coming at a fast walk. He went into the barn and soon emerged with old Madge. Well, they got a deer, she said to herself, that's why they needed the mare.

She tidied up the kitchen getting the milk things ready. Laying out knives and the big pan for the butchering of the deer. Jane didn't look out again, having no desire in her condition to look at a dead animal.

She heard the two men at the shed. Harn came to the door, knowing she would have things ready.

"We got a big one," he told her as she handed out the knives and pan.

"Good! We need it," she answered.

The butchering and chores over, the deer hanging high in the shed to freeze, the men started off down the valley to run Anis's trap line.

The younguns had their breakfast and had settled down with a book that Florence had brought with pictures of everything through it and sat talking between themselves.

Jane was restless all day, looking out the window seeing

nothing but snow, looking for she knew not what, not being able to settle herself at anything.

The men came back in the early afternoon with their catch. Anis had two muskrats and a possum. They left them in the shed and came hurriedly in to get warm. They had to skin and stretch the hides on boards before they froze.

After supper the men both went back to the barn. They had been several times in the afternoon. The other mare was having some trouble but they didn't think there would be a serious problem. Will was right at their heels. Jane let him go knowing he was old enough to start learning such things.

The younguns had all gone to bed, and Jane had started to get ready for bed when the men came stomping in.

"We have another fine filly colt," they told her, grinning from ear to ear. "They are doing fine, it sucked and is on its feet."

"You want to get yourself a fine buggy, Jane, you now have a matched team of fillies that anyone would be proud of," Anis said.

"That's what I need just now," Jane said sourly. "I'm glad they are finally here, and that they are alright. Now let's go to bed."

Sleigh Bells

December 16 dawned bright and clear, the air frosty and crisp. Jane rose early, her night had been full of dreams of being chased by something unknown. The terror made her weak and breathless even after she awoke.

The men finished the chores looking after the new colts, staying in the barn much longer than necessary. They would be going around their trapline again, this was the kind of weather the best furs were trapped.

Jane wrapped a piece of the liver and heart and cut a big slab off a shoulder of the deer to send to Florence by the men. They usually went in to get warm when they were near. It now awaited in a flour sack by the kitchen door. They went off in a crunch of snow glad to be away from the cabin for awhile.

Will had to stay behind, Jane was so near her time that she felt safer with someone around she could send for help if need be. The other younguns were much too small. The restlessness was still with Jane as she put the milk things away and tidied the cabin.

Catherin got at the churning early. Jane hated the job, the girl was biddable and didn't seem to mind sittin' serenely pounding the dasher up and down.

Jane washed out some socks in the wash pan and hung them behind the stove to dry. She found some mending and settled herself in the sittin' room in the rocker by the window. She wanted some peace and sent the younguns to the kitchen table to leaf through their "Wish Book." The day was sunny but too cold to melt any of the snow. Jane sewed and rocked, at times found herself just sittin' holding her work in her lap. Her eyes misted as she thought of her Tom, how she longed for him. With his arms around her, she always felt safe and secure. His laughter would lift her spirits. Jane never laughed much but oh, how she longed to hear his laughter. This terrible, terrible war; it had been going on for such a long time.

157

She sat rocking and thinking when the sound of bells jingling came to her on the crisp air. "Whoever heard of such a thing?" she said to herself, "I am getting peculiar in the head."

The younguns came tumbling into the room. "I hear jingle bells, I hear jingle bells," they all yelled. "Is it Santa Claus? Mammy Jane, is it? Is it?"

"Couldn't be," she answered. "He only comes at Christmas and that's two weeks away."

They all rushed to the windows craning to see down the road. "It's a funny sled," Catherin said. "No, it's a sleigh with bells! I saw one in a book at school when we sang 'Jingle Bells.'" She started to sing in her high sweet voice, "Jingle bells, jingle bells, jingle all the way."

Jane went to the window to look. "I believe it's your Grandma and Grandpa Jarvis come to call."

"Oh, isn't it wonderful? the sound is so pretty," Catherin remarked. "I love it. I never thought to ever hear the bells."

"I love it, too," John and the rest sang in chorus.

The sleigh was through the fence and coming across the creek, now in the woodyard. It was a picture to see the horses stomping and snorting, sending clouds of frosty mist around their heads.

The sleigh was bright red, the occupants covered in a heavy red plaid blanket. Bundled so only their noses and eyes could be seen.

Jane held the door open as they came inside, laughing. "Oh, that was fun," Mrs. Jarvis said, pulling off her wraps as she told everyone hello.

"Come by the fire," Jane said, pulling chairs for them, "Catherin, put their things on the bed."

"How are you, Jane? My! You look fine. And my grandchildren?" She gave each a squeeze.

Will put on his coat to help his grandpa take the horses to the barn out of the cold. And to show him the new colts.

"I'll put on the coffee pot, you must be frozen," Jane said as she went toward the kitchen. She had a big pot of the deer meat cooking and a big pot of dry beans, which sent a welcoming smell through the kitchen.

"We just had to know how you were, Jane," Mrs. Jarvis told her as she joined them in the sittin' room again.

"I'm feeling fine, things are getting a little worrisome, but will soon be over," Jane told her.

"The moon fulls tomorrow," her mother-in-law said, "so you can be ready. I find it always happens before the waning moon. "We haven't any news of the boys. The war is getting worse, the fighting increasing. The Northern armies are being sent further and further into the South. They say 'no news is good news,' but the waiting wears a body down."

Her father-in-law and Will came back from the barn. "My! You have a fine team of fillies there, Jane. I never knew you had the two mares. They sure are fine horses and have done you proud with the little filly colts."

"I've not seen them myself, the boys say they are fine ones though. I got them right after the Middleton farm deal. We now have ten brutes on the farm. They are adding up fast." She talked more than was common for her, not wanting to get into the "acquiring" of the mares.

"Harn and Anis went off around their trapline awhile ago," she told them. "They have been catching some good furs."

"As soon as it thaws they will start cutting timber for the mill, for the new house. Old Stoney got out most of the stones for the foundations. He works on the chimney, the cellar, and the foundation depending on the type of stone he comes across. She continued telling them about his going away for the worst of the winter."

"Will, put a couple of sticks of wood in the cook stove. I'll finish dinner directly," Jane told them.

"Oh, Jane, don't bother. We wanted to see you and the children. It was such a perfect day for a sleigh ride, we couldn't resist," Mr. Jarvis said. "I think my Tom enjoyed it as much as I did," she smiled up at him.

The younguns had to tell her they thought it was Santa. They both laughed merrily at that.

Jane went to the kitchen, her mother-in-law following, leaving the younguns with their grandfather who was telling them a tale.

"Jane, why don't I take the younguns home with me till this is over? I didn't want to ask while they were around in case you wouldn't favor it," Mrs. Jarvis said.

"I've been wondering what to do with them. The cabin is so small. It would be a heap of bother to you," Jane answered, her eyes on her mother-in-law.

"Not at all, Catherine and Caroline will love having them," she said.

159

"Well, if you think it is alright. I don't mind," Jane said.

"It's settled then," Mrs. Jarvis said.

Jane filled coffee cups for the adults and set them on the table. "Maybe we can have some coffee while my dinner finishes cooking," Jane said. They sat talking while they drank their coffee. The men returned from the trapline with some "catch." Will and Tom, Sr., joined them in the shed while they skinned and stretched them.

Jane put dried apples on to cook and got out three pie pans, started making crusts for pies.

"Oh, Jane, don't bother. I know you must be uncomfortable, you don't need to go to so much trouble for us."

"It's no trouble, I've made so many the past year I can do it with my eyes shut, it may be some time before I make pies again." The apples came to a boil as she rolled out the dough and lined the pans. It took her a very short time till the pies were in the oven. The meat was almost done. She peeled potatoes and turnips and added them to the pot to cook. She would make a stew out of it. The leftover pie dough was rolled thin for dumplin's. She set the table steaming with good things.

While they ate, their grandma told the younguns about their visit. Their eyes shone. They couldn't hardly contain themselves for their excitement.

Will kept looking at Jane and then away.

Jane noticed his intense looks and began to wonder what was on his mind. When they finished their dinner the men all went to hook up the horses to the sleigh for the return trip.

Will hung back as they all left the kitchen but he and Jane. "Mammy Jane, I don't want to leave you. I don't have to, do I? I want to be here in case you need me."

Her heart went out to him. "No, you don't have to go. You'r' a man now, you will miss a nice sleigh ride," Jane told him.

"I'd rather be here close to you," he told her, as he took off after the men.

The cabin was a flurry of getting together the things they needed. Jane was thankful she had kept all their clothes washed and mended. Soon everything was ready. They wrapped Trude in a quilt from the girls' bed. The others bundled in shawls over their heads were settled in the sleigh and the big heavy plaid blanket tucked in. It was a joyous bunch that took off in the cold afternoon with good-byes ringing in the air.

160

Jane finished the churning. She had Harn lift it to the work table where she could take up the butter. She could hardly get the kitchen put to rights she was so tired. As she set the big pot with the beans to the side, a pain hit her in her back. "Oh!" she said in surprise, and sat down at the table. She sat for a minute, nothing else happened. With an effort she finished the kitchen work, going to the sittin' room she let herself down in the rocking chair.

Will came in unexpectedly, "You alright, Mammy Jane?" he asked.

"I'm alright, just a little tired," she answered.

"Florence is comin', she will do for you. If you need me, just call," he told her as he went back outside.

Florence opened the kitchen door calling to Jane as she came in. Unwrapping her shawls, her black eyes looking Jane up and down as she did.

"How are you, Jane? You look tired and a little pale. Has the pains started yet?" As usual Florence didn't give a body time to answer her string of questions. Pulling up a chair she sat down across from Jane.

"You didn't give me time to get out of the chair," Jane told her. "It takes some doing and I'm tired. The younguns went off to their grandma's. I'm thankful for that, for the past two days all I seem to want is peace and quiet. The noise tires me so," Jane explained. "I did have a sharp pain while clearing the kitchen. It only lasted for a second and there's been no more," she went on telling Florence.

"You'll likely start in the night sometime," Florence answered. "The moon is right for the baby to come. I'd better stay the night. The girls' bed is empty now."

"There is a clean sheet in the cupboard," Jane told her.

"Knowing you, the one on the bed will be just as clean, Jane," Florence said with a laugh. "Have you got things ready?" "I think so, I bought a rubber sheet for the baby. We will put that on my bed tonight and some padding just in case. I feel as though I'm about ready?" Jane said.

"Are you scared?" Florence wanted to know. She was one to talk about the most private things that Jane wouldn't let herself think about.

"Oh, I don't know," Jane answered. "It's something I just want to have done with. I don't really let myself think about it. When the time comes it's a job that has to be done."

"It's a hard job, I think I would be scared to death," Florence continued.

"Have you had supper?" Jane asked, wanting to end the conversation about being afraid.

"Oh, yes, I fixed some of the deer liver and we had a feast. I'll tell you it was good. Jed ate and ate, said his belly hurt it was stretched so," Florence's laughter rang out.

The two women sat talking, Florence doing most of it, laughing every other breath. Jane felt cheered just having her around.

"I'm so glad you came," she told her as she pushed herself up out of the chair.

"Tell me what you want, I'll get it for you," Florence said.

"I have to move about, I feel peculiar," Jane told her.

"The baby is probably turning to be born," Florence informed her. "The head has to be pointed down into the birth canal."

Jane had never heard this talked about, she said nothing, wanting to hear all Florence had to say.

"Sometimes when they don't turn themselves they have to be turned or you have a breech birth, and that is the hardest one of all for a woman. It's unnatural," Florence continued. "You'll be alright. I can see the baby has turned and has fallen. You will birth it tonight or tomorrow for sure."

The feeling, Jane couldn't describe it to herself, the quivering had stopped, and she sat down again. As she did a pain hit her in her lower back, making her catch her breath, and her face flushed.

Florence noticed, "It's started," she said, "I can tell. Well the sooner the better. It will take some time with the first one. You show me where everything is, and do you have some whiskey? You may need something to ease the pain."

"Everything is in the trunk there. You will find clean rags on the bottom shelf of the cupboard. Yes, there is a bottle of whiskey in the kitchen cupboard. Maybe we had better fix the bed while the menfolk are out. The rubber sheet is in the cupboard where the rags are," Jane said.

Florence got it and a pad that had been sewed out of old rags and knotted by Jane in readiness. She turned Jane's bed down and placed the things in position. "I'll set the flatirons here on the heater to get hot. A warm iron at the bottom of your feet helps a lot," she told Jane.

"You seem to know a lot about this, never to have had any yourself," Jane said. "I've helped some, but I don't know all you

162

do. I'm obliged that you have told me so much. It does seem to ease my mind," Jane told her.

The men came in stomping snow and slapping their hands to the fire, ending the talk between the two. They all looked slyly at Jane when she wasn't looking to see if there was a change.

"I'm staying the night, Jed," Florence said. "I'll be needed before this night's through."

Jed looked quickly at Jane. "Anything you want done?" he asked his wife.

"Nothing to do yet," she answered.

Will took a couple of steps near to Jane and didn't say anything. He kept looking at her to see if she was alright.

"You better leave that old mule in the barn," Anis told Jed," or you won't have him to plow with next spring."

"Well, I could do that," Jed said. "It's a lot nearer through the field home anyway. If you need me, come for me. I'd better get home before our fire goes out." Florence went through the kitchen door with him.

Anis and Harn talked about their traps and the furs they were accumulating, and the likely price they would get. Jane knew they were nervous and didn't know what to do.

"If you want coffee and a piece of pie before you go to bed, it's on the table," Jane told them.

They went into the kitchen, she could hear them banging the coffee pot and pulling out chairs. Soon they all came through the sittin' room and went to bed.

Jane and Florence soon followed. "You call me. I'll be awake in a snap of the fingers," Florence said with a laugh as she snuggled under the covers.

"I will," Jane said as she sank with a sigh into her own bed, not expecting to sleep. The bed felt good and to stretch out on her back felt better than she had all day. Soon she was fast asleep.

163

Firstborn

Jane slept for some time. She awoke suddenly not knowing
what had awakened her, she lay still listening to the sound of
sleeping people in the cabin. She felt the quivering wave start and
flood up her body to her head. A sharp pain followed like a echo.
She caught her breath, bit down on the corner of her lip till it receded. The relief flooded over her as she relaxed, waiting, to see
what would follow. Talking to Florence had made her more aware
of what was happening to her body and didn't frighten her as
much as she had thought she would be. She picked up the clock
and could see it was close to three o'clock. Thankful to have had
almost a full night's sleep, she felt much rested for the ordeal
ahead. It would be on her shortly.

Oh, Tom, where are you? she thought. I need you so. Then
smiled to herself. He would probably be as scared as the other
men were of her and what was happening. Finally she dozed off
again, to be brought back from sleep by a wrenching pain in her
back that seemed to embrace her body in a vice. Leaving her
shivering and weak, her breath coming in gasps. She knew there
would be more to follow and tried to let her body relax to prepare
for the next one. Looking at the clock she found an hour had
passed, it would soon be day. The day's work she put in this day
would be the hardest she had ever known. Another pain hit low
down in her belly, echoing and ricocheting down her legs. Laying
still waiting for another onslaught, she dozed off to sleep again in
the relief of none following.

Jane didn't awaken till daybreak and heard Florence starting a
fire in the kitchen stove.

Getting out of bed, she dressed for the day and went to the
kitchen to help with breakfast.

"Are you alright, Jane?" Florence asked, raising up from putting wood in the stove. "Why don't you stay in bed? You look
pale this morning."

164

"I'm fine, I had a couple of pains in the night. I'd rather be moving around. I'll have plenty of time in that bed later on," Jane told her.

"I guess you'r' right. Sometimes staying on your feet helps the birthin' sooner. Do you show any sign?" Florence asked.

Jane looked up in embarrassment and surprise, "No, not yet," she answered.

They could hear the men moving around readying for the day. Jane sat down at the breakfast table. She didn't feel like eating but would have a cup of coffee. They were all eating, peeking under their lowered heads at Jane every now and then.

Feeling the wave start again, she quickly left the table going into the sittin' room where she doubled over holding her sides. Suddenly she felt warmth on her thighs and knew she was "showing."

Florence followed her in and said, "Young lady, I think you should be in bed."

"Directly," Jane answered, she could hardly get her breath after the intensity of the last pain. Going to the cupboard she got a clean soft rag, raising her skirt placed it between her legs.

Watching her, Florence said, "You'r' showing."

Jane only nodded and got out a long flannel nightgown to get into.

Florence straightened the bed and left Jane to get undressed, went to get the milk things and send the men to do the chores. One of them would have to go fetch Aunt Mandy soon. Florence knew she could deliver the baby herself but in case of trouble, it being the first one, she wanted someone with more experience around. They had plenty of time but she would send them as soon as the chores were done.

It took the men about an hour to do the chores. When they brought the two big buckets of milk she told Harn, "It's time, you had better fetch Aunt Mandy, we will need her soon."

Noticing the scared look on Will's face, she told him. "You can be a big help, Will. Bring a couple of buckets of water from the spring. Then you can fill the woodbox for me," Florence told him.

"I will right away." Grabbing the water bucket, hurried off as though the house was on fire.

"I'm going to work on the stalls in the barn, if you need me, holler," Anis said.

Now that Florence had everybody busy, she went in to see

about Jane. She found her sittin' in the rocking chair in her nightgown with a shawl around her shoulders looking like a little girl waiting for a bedtime story.

"I'm glad the younguns are away, takes a heap of worry off my mind," Jane said.

"It will give me more time for you," Florence told her. "You'r' not to worry about anything. I'll take care of everything."

Jane moved quickly out of the chair, her clumsiness gone. Walked to the window and back, her lips compressed tightly across her teeth, a gasp escaped as the pain receded.

"I'll make you a cup of hot tea with a drop of whiskey in it, maybe you can nap and rest while the house is quiet." It worried Florence that she couldn't get her patient in bed where she could do for her. She made strong sassafras tea with a good jolt in it and plenty of sugar. Taking it back to Jane, found she had finally gone to bed, her face as white as the sheets, scrunched up as another pain hit her.

Florence lifted her head, putting another pillow behind her and held the tea to her lips.

It took a full ten minutes for the tea to start its work. Jane closed her eyes and the color came back to her face.

Florence sat and watched her, seeing her relax and breathe evenly. It was some time when the next pain hit, raising her half way up in the bed, a soft moan escaped her lips. Florence took her hand, Jane held it tightly as another pain drained the color away from her face. "You'r' getting there, Aunt Mandy should be here in another hour and you will be ready for her. You are doing fine," Florence told her.

"I'm—so—glad—you'r' here," Jane panted. "I couldn't do without you."

"Hush now and rest," Florence told her, as she smoothed the covers that didn't need smoothing. She took one of the flatirons and wrapping it in an old shirt slid it in at Jane's feet, and sat by the bed. There was little she could do for her. It wasn't good to give her too much whiskey till she was farther along. The pains were fairly regular now, about twenty minutes apart, there was a long way to go yet.

Florence had taken the remains of the deer stew cutting up the meat and vegetables, she added more water and simmered it for soup. She would give that to Will and Anis for their dinner when they come from the barn. They should be coming soon to get

166

warm, even if they weren't hungry. It was close to twelve thirty when they finally gave up and came into the warm kitchen. Florence gave them a big bowl of soup and the news that Jane was holding her own and was fairly along in labor. Most women didn't talk about such to men, but it didn't seem to bother Florence one mite.

They warmed themselves and sat at the table longer than necessary. "Is there anything I can do?" Anis wanted to know.

Will still looked scared. Florence finally figured it was because his maw died shortly after birthin' with "childbed fever."

"Jane is going to be just fine, Will, don't you worry, you'll have a new brother or sister this time tomorrow," Florence told him.

"Yes'm," Will said and dropped his head. Putting on his coat he hurried from the room.

"He seems more worried than he orta be, I expect he thinks of his maw. He puts a heap of store by his Mammy Jane," Anis said and smiled.

"I figured as much," Florence replied.

Anis had just entered the barn when Florence, standing by the window, spotted Harn and Aunt Mandy coming up the road. Glancing at Jane she saw she had her eyes closed and was lying quietly. She stood watching the horses through the fence and across the creek into the woodyard. Aunt Mandy rode sidesaddle and was so bundled up if she would fall off she would never be able to get up again.

Harn dismounted and led old Madge over to the choppin' block so as Aunt Mandy could slide off with his help, stepping on the block and then to the ground. As she clutched at Harn's shoulder you could hear her laugh as she half slid, half fell to the ground. She came bustling into the cabin bringing the fresh smell of the outdoors with her.

Florence helped her unwrap from all her shawls and mufflers. Helped her take off her "arbuckles" and settle her by the fire to thaw a moment.

Jane's blue eyes followed the action glazed with pains that were coming regularly now.

Florence had a pan of water with a few drops of turpentine in it on the stove ready for Aunt Mandy when she wanted to examine Jane.

"How's our girl?" she asked Florence.

"She is doing fine. The pains are regular, about eight minutes apart now," Florence answered.

Aunt Mandy went over to the bed, "Howdy, Jane," she said as she gently lowered the covers and placed both hands on Jane's protruding stomach, firmly pressing here and there. Another contraction started, she pushed downward feeling the baby move in the birthin' position. "It will be sometime yet. I'll examine her directly," Aunt Mandy said. "Do you have a cup of coffee, Florence? I'm nigh frozen to death," she said with a laugh. Aunt Mandy and Florence went off to the kitchen to have their coffee. Florence told her about the tea she had given Jane.

"That's fine. Get ready to fix some more soon. I think the pains will speed up from now on. I'll see if she is dilating soon as I finish my coffee."

Going back to Jane, Aunt Mandy washed her hands in the turpentine water. Went to the bed, raised the covers and asked Jane to raise her knees in bed while she examined her. When it was done, she washed her hands again at the stove. "You are coming along just fine. Another few hours and you will have a new baby."

Jane let each pain roll over, up, and away, lips tight, no sound to let the women know how bad she was. Oh, to have it done with, she thought, as another pain crested.

Aunt Mandy, watching her face, knew the pains were closer and getting harder to bear. She wanted to wait a while before they started working with her. Save her energy as much as possible.

The men came to do the chores and Florence had started supper. She sliced and pounded venison, rolled it in flour to fry. Warmed the leftover beans. Got out a dish of sauerkraut, made gravy and corn bread, and a big pot of coffee. She fixed another cup of tea—strong and with lots of sugar. Took it to Jane, helped her drink it while the others ate. Sat down by her till the whiskey took effect relaxing her, giving her time to rest before the ordeal ahead.

She went back as the others finished. Aunt Mandy went in to sit with Jane while she cleared the kitchen.

"Do you need anything?" the men asked.

"No. Why don't you take the lantern and go visit Jed for a while?" Florence asked them.

None of them wanted to go out in the cold to visit but said,

168

"Now that's a fine idea. Old Jed's down there all alone and lonesome I bet." Getting themselves together, they started off.

Florence went back to Jane and could see things were starting in earnest. The pains were coming one on top of the other with only minutes between.

"I sent the men off to visit Jed, out of the way," she told Jane. Jane's eyes were glazed with pain as she nodded.

"Pull the bed out, Florence, and get on the other side," Aunt Mandy told her. "We have work to do."

Taking Jane's hands from both sides, told her to push with the next pain. Pulling on one arm as Florence pulled on the other —push!—push!—Jane half rose with the effort and fell back limp. Sweat standing out on her face. Again and again the demand to push—push—push—harder.

The tearing pains were so intense that Jane half passed out between each one.

Aunt Mandy washed her hands again and worked at the foot of the bed. "Its head is cresting," she told them. "Careful, Jane, push steadily now with the next one. Florence, put both hands on the top of her stomach and push too. Now all together."

In spite of herself, an animal grunt escaped Jane as another pain hit and the push—push command. "A little more, I can't help you yet," Aunt Mandy told her. "This is a big baby, its head isn't giving any."

"Take a hold of the bedstead above your head, Jane, and when the pain hits, push!—."

Jane did as she was told, pushing with all her might. She felt tearing below and warmth trickling down her hips.

"Once more easy now, the head is almost through, don't tear yourself more," Aunt Mandy told her.

Jane pushed once more and felt the blessed relief as the baby's head came through and Aunt Mandy pulled it into the world. Stuck a finger into its mouth to remove the mucus, held it up by its legs and gave it a half shake and a spank.

"A fine boy," she said as a baby's scream filled the room.

"Here you are, Florence, he is all yours. I'll cut the cord, hold it now. You clean him up. I have work to do yet."

"There will be another pain, Jane, to bring the 'after birth' and we are all through." Another pain shot through Jane and she felt an emptiness and what relief.

Aunt Mandy cleaned Jane and removed the mess of birth. Jane was asleep by the time the clean covers were tucked around her.

"It's beautiful," Florence said as she held the new baby wrapped snug and warm. It too was sound asleep. They looked at the clock, it was nine thirty. The men should be back before long. The women were both glad it was over and that things were alright.

"That's not too bad for a first one," Aunt Mandy remarked.

"You can't tell with Jane. She never shows how she feels," Florence said. "I'm glad it's over. She suffered more than she let on and is completely worn out." Florence laid the baby by Jane's side. "How about some coffee, Aunt Mandy? I'm going to punch up the fire and make a pot.

"You don't plan on going home tonight, do you? Half of my bed is empty."

"I'll stay the night. I don't like to leave till I know everything is alright with the baby and mother," Aunt Mandy said.

Florence had the coffee made when she heard the men outside, afraid to come in even though they were frozen. Opening the kitchen door she let them in. "Quiet, Jane's sleeping. We have a fine ten-pound boy and everything is fine," she told them, a big smile on her face. "You'r' just in time for some hot coffee and some cookies." She set out a glass of milk for Will.

They finished and tiptoed into their room first peeking at the new mother and baby.

They left a lamp turned low in case they had to tend Jane and the baby and the two women turned in for the night.

Christmas

All had gone well with Jane and the baby. She had plenty of milk and the baby nursed without trouble, had filled out and gained weight.

Florence was still with her. Jed came each day and ate with them, helping the men finish the barn stalls.

The morning of the seventh day Jane got up and dressed and was sittin' in the rocking chair when Florence awoke.

"You'r' not supposed to be up, it takes twelve days for your insides to go back in place," Florence informed her, surprised at seeing her up.

"My insides are back in place. I just didn't realize I would be so weak. I can't stand that bed another minute," Jane said. "I can see I won't be doing the wash though," she said with an effort at humor.

"You take it easy and don't get cold. You will make the baby sick as well as yourself. I'll fix breakfast, Jed will be up soon. He has to go to Minnora today about some papers." Florence told her.

"He can stop at the Jarvis farm and have the younguns brought home. They have been there long enough. I'll be able to do for them in another day. I don't want to impose on my in-laws," Jane told her.

"I can go home and come every other day," Florence volunteered. "I will do the wash for you a while. You don't need to take a chance and it's so cold."

"I have to get ready for Christmas, the younguns won't have much but I'll have to do something," Jane said. "I'll send Harn with Jed, he can get some things at the store, candy and such," Jane continued.

"No money coming in we can't get a lot. We can send what eggs we have."

"I've not used any, there is a basket full," Florence said. "You

171

and Jed have Christmas with us. We can do what needs to be done together." The two women went on planning the dinner and treats for Christmas day.

Jane walked around the cabin to get her strength back. Florence washed out diapers and hung a line behind the stove.

The men returned late in the day. Harn had news of Tom, and a voucher for twenty-five dollars. "He and Weeden were together and so far well. The war is speeding up it seems with fierce fighting on both sides. They are somewhere in the mountains of Tennessee or in Kentucky, they weren't sure just where," Harn told Jane. Trying to cheer Jane, Harn said, "It don't get too cold there anyway. They will bring the younguns home the last of the week. They are all well."

Jane got stronger each day. Her baby was good, sleeping most of the time without fuss. She had named her first son Calvin, for no reason other than she liked the name. The cold weather continued. The snow melting only slightly through the day, then freezing at night with a light fall to cover all the tracks and make the winter look new again.

Jane looked for the younguns each day. Finally the sleigh bells were heard and with the sound of voices ringing in the cold air and the bustle of getting in by the fire they were home.

"We have a gift for you, Mammy Jane," they all tried to tell her at once.

Mr. Jarvis was bringing in a big bundle wrapped in a quilt. It had been tied on the back runners of the sleigh.

The younguns' eyes sparkled as it was put on the floor and unwrapped. Jane watched in wonderment from the rocking chair.

The most beautiful cradle she had ever seen sat before her. Shining with polish, the grain of wood showing through.

"Isn't it pretty?" Catherin asked as she gently rocked it back and forth.

"It surely is," Jane answered, looking up at her father-in-law.

"Caleb made it for you, Jane, and sends his love to you and your new son," Mr. Jarvis explained.

Jane's face flushed with pleasure. "Tell Caleb it's a fine cradle and I'm beholden," she said.

"We have had a grand visit with the grandchildren," their grandmother said. "I'm afraid we spoiled them some. Where is the baby? I want to see it before I go," the new grandfather said.

They all "tippy-toed" to the bed to see the bundle that was the new baby.

There was a fat pillow in the cradle for a bed. Jane lifted the sleeping baby and placed it in the cradle by the fire. The younguns were all patting and touching the wrapped bundle of sleeping baby.

"Oh! He is beautiful," Catherin said. "I love him so."

Jane could never understand where Catherin got her way of expressing herself. Maybe from her grandmother. She talked like that. Jane decided it was nice to hear and never said anything.

"I've got to get back, Jane. You have a fine son. We will let you know if we hear from Tom. Merry Christmas to you all," he said as he went outside to the sleigh.

"Good-bye, grandpa, Merry Christmas," the younguns followed him, waving till he was out of sight.

Someone wanted to rock the baby all the time. The new cradle lost some of its polish with all the little hands that touched it.

Florence loved children. They were always at her heels wanting to hear a tale or to learn a new rhyme or song.

Jane listened and learned herself. She had never had time in her girlhood for the foolishness that Florence seemed to take for granted.

Now that the younguns were home, Florence went back to her house with Jed. Jane took over the household again.

Jane gave Florence two dollars for the time she was there. She didn't want to take it but Jane insisted. "You earned it, Florence, buy yourself something you need."

The weather broke and the thaw set in. The creek and runs were full of muddy water from bank to bank.

The men had finished all the work around the new barn and were ready to start cutting timber for Jane's new house, right after Christmas. Jed and Florence were in and out and came to help cook the feast they would have on Christmas Day.

When they sat down to Christmas Dinner, Jed insisted on saying a blessing and Florence led them in a Christmas song after dinner was over. All the younguns singing along with her, Catherin's sweet voice could be heard above the rest.

Florence had made ribbons for the girls' hair and Jed had made tops for the boys to spin.

Jane brought out candy and popcorn balls and a big bowl of apples polished till they shone.

173

Their grandma had sent a package to be opened for Christmas. Jane sat in her rocker, all eyes on her as she untied the wrappings. There were knitted mittens for all the younguns, Red, Green, Yellow, Pink, and Blue. A larger pair of black was for Jane.

The excitement was contagious as the children all tried their's on thinking the ones they had chosen the prettiest.

The day ended with full stomachs and a good feeling of being together, well and happy.

Jed and Florence took their leave amid good-byes from the younguns and the invitation to come again soon.

Jane went to the door with them. "Florence, I couldn't have gotten along without you. You are a good friend and neighbor. Maybe I can do as much for you someday."

Florence laughed, "I've enjoyed it so much."

They were off down the meadow leaving their old mule where he would have hay to eat and a warm place to stay.

Jed helped the men enough so as not to feel beholden about the old mule being stabled and fed.

Logging

The thaw continued. Water in every low place. The horses and young colts were turned out for exercise in the warming air. They ran and kicked, churning up the barnyard to a quagmire of mud.

Anis, Harn, and Will went to cut timber. The sap had thawed and their saws bit into the big trees as it was pulled from each side by the men. Will trimmed the smaller branches leaving the big ones for the men to cut.

Jane was feeling her old self now with the baby a month old. She had been studying on the lumber cutting. Thinking of a sawmill coming to them instead of them going to a sawmill. She had seen saw sets moved from one place to another and knew it could be done.

Jed and Florence came home with the men that night. Jane had been sending milk to them and they brought back a couple of the buckets and to visit Jane and the baby.

They all sat down to supper. Jane brought up her idea of the mill. Jed spoke up, "I want to have some lumber cut too. I think that's a fine idea. We could have a set together. It would save a heap of hauling and time." The men all agreed.

"Do any of you know of a mill?" Jane asked.

"There used to be a McCulty that had one. I think he lived 'sommers' over on Otter Creek," Jed said.

"Your pa-in-law should know someone," Florence put in her two cents worth.

"Since you all agree and I think it's what we should do, we will find out," Jane said. "We will have to keep an eye out for a location where the most trees can be hauled the easiest and where there is water, I believe," Jane said with satisfaction.

The evening was spent talking and planning, the conversation going this way and that, each of the men giving their opinion about the location. Night had fallen. Jane and Florence finished the kitchen chores. Jane poured a bucket of milk for Florence to take home.

Jed lit their lantern and they started home, he carrying it and Florence the bucket of milk.

The men were soon off to bed, tired from the saw. Another day would be on them before they knew it.

Jane sat in the rocking chair going over everything in her mind. January had been a wet month without freezing or snow since Christmas. The men had ten trees down in that many days. They had to be trimmed and some would make three cuts of twelve feet. They weren't using the horses and Jane was itching to ride to her in-laws about the sawset. She didn't dare take the baby out yet and with nursing she couldn't be gone long.

The next day, Jane's mind was still on the sawmill. She knew she couldn't do anything yet. She would just have to be patient. Going for a walk to look over her orchard and examine the spot her new house would stand, Jane's spirit rose. "It will all fall in place," she told herself. It takes time. This was her second winter here and they were coming through it better than most.

"When my Tom comes home things will be different," she told herself. Work went on as usual as the days slid by, with the men still cutting timber. Jed was at his timber cutting too. Florence's brother came and was helping Jed with the crosscut saw. They were both hoping that they could find a sawmill and working toward that end, anxious for a new house of their own.

March came in like a lion with snow and freezing. The animals kept in the stable grew restless for summer weather as did the rest of them.

Hopefully it would be the last bad spell. Plowing time would soon be there.

The baby was growing fast and was little trouble. Catherin took care of it and did as well as Jane could. She was such a little mother to them all and a big help around the house.

The snow melted and the rain set in. The men still cut timber, coming home to remove their wet clothes, hanging them on the chairs around the stove to dry. The steam from them followed the stove pipe up and up. They dried overnight to be put on again in the early morning.

Jane was growing restless. All her mending was caught up. Catherin had gotten good at sewing and helped. All the things from the trunk that could be made over had been used. There

176

were only scraps left. Jane and Catherin started cutting strings
and tacking them together winding them into big balls. When
enough were ready they would hook a rug from them. The strings
would be finished quickly with both of them working on them.
The wind died down and the air got somewhat warmer. The
downpour turned to a drizzle and one morning the sun peeked
over the highest hill. Everything was bathed in blessed sunshine.

End of Winter

In a week's time the willows by the creek had turned from yellow to a lovely delicate green. The doors of the cabin could be opened for a few hours in the middle of the day to air it out.

The old hens began to cackle and scratched in the yard. The boar hog was separated from the sow, and penned in the barn. The sow would have a litter of pigs very soon now. The cows wouldn't calf till late April or May this year. They were still giving plenty of milk but were heavy with calf.

After the baby was put down in the afternoon Jane headed for the hen house. She had decided to make fresh nests for the hens. They usually scratched the nests to pieces through the winter. Bringing hay from the barn, all of the old straw was thrown in the yard for the chickens to scratch in.

One old hen was already clucking. She would set her in a few days. Jane wanted to give Florence a hen and chicks for her a start.

In the afternoon Florence came by with the bucket. "Howdy, Jane, I just couldn't stay inside another minute and had to tell you the news."

Jane looked expectantly at her, not knowing what to think with Florence.

"We have our own cow! She has a new calf too. And gives plenty of milk. My pa gave her to us as a weddin' gift. They brought her over two days ago," Florence was bubbling with the good news.

"I'm so glad for you," Jane said, "A cow is the biggest blessing you can get. If you have milk and bread, you can get along."

Jane was still at the chicken house. They both heard the sow making a noise and went over to the pen. They could see she was having her pigs.

Nothing would do Florence but climb the fence to see how she was doing. "She has six already," she told Jane. "There is one

178

don't look too good." Taking it up in her hands she brought it to the fence for Jane to see. Jane untied the old apron she had on and wrapped it around the little fellow. "We had better get him by the fire and get some warm milk down him, Jane," Florence said, cuddling him like he was a baby. "It's not a him, it's a her," she added as they went into the kitchen.

Giving the wrapped pig to Catherin to hold, Florence went to look for an elder to make a nipple for the pig to suck. Soon she came back and asked if Jane had a bottle. Jane had saved one that turpentine had come in. Florence fussed, washing and scalding it. Wrapped a rag around the hallowed out elder stick till it fit the opening. Filled the bottle with warm milk and was ready to feed the baby pig. With her doctoring and petting, the pig was more active by the time she was ready to go home.

"You just take that pig home with you, I don't have time to take care of it," Jane told her. "I hope you can get it to live, I doubt it."

"I'll make it live," Florence said with a laugh as she started out, the pig cradled in her arms like a baby.

"I'll bet she does," Jane said to Catherin as Florence got out of hearing. If it didn't, she would give her another one. There were eight at the last look. That was quite a litter of healthy pigs.

By the middle of March the wind and sun had dried the ground till plowing could be started. The men had cleaned out the barns, driving the sled close to the manure holes and throwing out the manure. It was then taken to the garden, spread, and plowed under. The potato patches were the first to be ready. Jane and Florence had sowed their lettuce beds the first sunny day. The days were warmer now, the younguns could come outside, the clothes were now hung up to dry in the sun and wind.

Timber cutting was laid by for now till the planting was done.

The new orchard budded out and there were a few blossoms that warmed Jane's heart. All the trees lived. Will and Jane went to each one to make sure little buds were on them all.

Old Stoney came one day and the tap, tap of his stone tools could be heard from early morning till dark.

He marveled over the baby and told Jane what a handsome young man he was.

There had been no word from Tom. He was where the fighting was the worst. If he was killed or in the hospital they reasoned they would have heard.

A sawmill had been located. They had two sets to saw and it would be late in the summer before they got to Jane's set. They had agreed to come after coming to look over the location.

A family down Beech wanted sawing done too. There would be logs from three families to saw.

Jane was itching to get her house started. She intended starting the cellar as soon as Stoney had the stones out. She hoped to have it done before harvest this year.

Everything greened up fast. The mares with their new colts were turned out to roam at will.

The planting went along at record pace, the men in a hurry to get to the timber again.

Florence and Jed visited only on Sunday now, when they came to have dinner with the family. Florence's pig grew and followed her everywhere. Jed had somehow gotten another mule and was busy plowing every level spot and planting too.

Jane planned to try to sell some of the pigs before long. They were now fed milk and growing fast.

They all worked long hours every day. Jane couldn't help but look longingly down the road for her Tom. He never came. At times she doubted he ever would.

It seemed so long—so—long.

Copperhead

All the garden was planted and doing well. The cornfields had little green shoots three inches high. All the cleared ground on each farm had been filled with growing things.

The men had a few weeks before the first cutting of hay to work at the timber.

The day was sunny and bright. Jane was in the chipyard at the washing. She had been washing up all the winter things and putting them away.

The two youngest were on their log horse. Elizabeth was at the stone quarry with Stoney or watching the old man Stoney had brought laying the cellar stones.

Catherin was working on the rug they had started together and watching the baby.

Will's play time was over. He worked each day alongside the men. The day was beautiful and Jane was doing what she liked best, hanging clean clothes in the sun to dry. There was a loud yell from the quarry. "Jane! Jane!"

It was Stoney coming at a run with Elizabeth in his arms. Jane ran to meet him, "What is it? What happened?"

"Snake," Stoney almost sobbed. "A snake bit her. Oh, Lord what will we do?"

"Fetch her to the house quick." Jane ran on ahead. "Put her on the kitchen table. Catherin, come quick. Get some potatoes, about three, grate them on the grater, don't take time to peel them, Hurry! bring them to me." Jane grabbed a dish towel and tied it above the little girl's elbow. The snake had struck her in the top of her hand. The teeth marks oozing blood and already the hand starting to swell.

Jane grabbed the sharpest knife she had. Cut a deep gash, pulled a pan over to catch the blood. "Stoney get the can of lamp oil from under the house." Jane sucked the blood and spit it into the pan. Again and again. She poured lamp oil over the open cut once, twice, three times.

The child was laying limp and unconscious. Old Stoney had tears streaming down his weathered old face. "I didn't see them. There was a nest holed in from winter. Joe's digging them out and killing them. Oh, Lord in Heaven, don't take this little angel," Old Stoney prayed. "It's my fault. I should have smelled them."

Seeing he would be of little help, Jane said, "Help Joe and be sure you get them all. And be careful."

Catherin was standing holding a big bowl of the grated potatoes, tears in her eyes but not saying a word.

Jane slapped a handful of the grated potatoes over the gash and waited. They turned green in a matter of minutes. She clawed them off and put another handful on. She continued to do this till the bowl was empty. It took longer each time for them to turn color.

"Make another bowl," Jane told Catherin. "First bring me a cover from your bed." She wrapped the child leaving only the hand out. Removing the tourniquet she saw that the hand hadn't swollen much more than when she was brought in.

"Build a fire in the kitchen stove and put the flatirons on, Catherin."

Jane continued the poultices of grated potatoes, wrapped the last bunch with the dish towel and left them on as she gathered the little girl in her arms and took her in to her bed. Placed her gently on a pillow and sat beside her. Feeling her rapid heartbeat she knew it was still touch and go. It wouldn't take much of the poison to kill a child that small.

Catherin soon brought the warm iron wrapped in a rag. Jane put it to the bottom of the little feet and wrapped the little girl again.

"Make more potatoes and fetch them here," Catherin hurried to do so; she was quick and sure and soon back.

Jane continued with the poultices. "Is the teakettle hot?" she asked. "It's hot," Catherin answered.

"Sit here and change the poultices as I did," Jane told her. "I'll make a tonic to give her." Taking hot water, a couple spoonfuls of honey, added whiskey and brought it back to the bed.

The child's eyelids fluttered open as she raised her head holding the cup to her lips. "You must drink this," Jane told her as she got her to swallow some of the tonic. The little head was dry and hot. The fever had hit. She continued working over the limp child. Not knowing if it would do any good or not. They could never get a doctor here in time to save her, it was all up to Jane. She was doing what they did for the animals when they got snake bitten. It might not work on a child.

Jane sent Catherin for a cool bucket of water from the spring. They put cold packs on the hot little brow to keep the fever from climbing.

Elizabeth had started to fret, tossing and turning, mumbling in her delirium.

"Is Lizzie going to die?" Catherin finally asked Jane.

"I just don't know," Jane answered. "I've done all I know to do. Maybe Florence would know something that I don't," Jane said.

"I'll go fetch her," Catherin volunteered. "Do you want I should?"

"No, we will wait. Maybe she will come directly. I hope so." They sat by the bed doing what they could, not knowing if it would help or not. A couple of hours had gone by and Jane made another tonic and got it down the child.

The potato poultice was changed again and again. It was no longer turning the peculiar green as before. The little hand was red and swollen, ready to burst. Jane decided to try hot turpentine packs and did away with the potatoes. The little hand was wrapped in steaming cloths, the turpentine causing their eyes to sting and water.

Catherin continued to change the cold pack as the rag became warm from the fever.

Stoney came to see how the little girl was and reported that they had dug out five copperheads and killed them. "We searched the quarry. It was the only place they could hole up."

"It could have been worse. The other younguns could have been with her and them all got bitten," Jane told him. "Don't blame yourself. No one is to blame. It's just something that happens. She seems a little easier," Jane told him and sent him back to his work.

Florence came late in the afternoon. Jane was so glad to see her. She wanted to know if she had done everything possible to save little Lizzie.

"Oh, my God, Jane, what happened?" she asked.

183

Florence was told from beginning to end all that happened and what was being done. "Do you know of anything else?" Jane asked anxiously.

"Seems you know more about this than I do, Jane," Florence said. "My specialty is babies," she said with a laugh.

"I don't know," Jane answered. "I don't know more to do. I've done my best. Seems she is easier now. I think the swelling has stopped. We just have to wait and see." She continued the hot compresses as she talked. It was good having Florence near for comfort.

"Let me do that, Jane. You rest a bit. Catherin and I will take over." The flatirons were changed to keep a warm one at the feet at all times. The cold compresses for the brow and hot ones on the little hand.

Toward evening the tossing quieted and the little girl seemed to sleep peacefully.

"I think she will be alright, Jane," Florence said.

Jane was sittin' in the rocker nursing her baby. "Oh, I hope so. I hope so," Jane said with a sigh. "I've never been so scared in my life."

"You done real good," Florence told her as she got up to take her leave. "If you need me, send someone," she said.

Jane finished the evening chores checking on the child every little while.

Catherin sat faithfully watching her and keeping the cold packs on the little brow till Jane finally sent her off to bed.

Leaving the lamp on, Jane lay down around midnight. She never undressed and kept a watch all through the night.

The little hand was still swollen and red. The fever seemed to have broken somewhat.

At daybreak Jane heated more water and gave Lizzie another cup of the hot tonic, changed the cool iron for a warm one.

By noon of that day the swelling had gone down. Jane bathed the cut she had made in turpentine and tied a clean rag around it.

Little Lizzie slept peacefully most of the day. Toward evening Jane fed her some bean broth and she fell asleep again.

Jane got up through the second night a couple of times to examine the child. She slept on.

The crisis was over, the little girl would be alright.

"Thank you, Lord," Jane said simply as she went to bed and fell into an exhausted sleep.

The Sawmill

Little Lizzie was wan and peaked for days after her ordeal. Stoney didn't want the younguns at the quarry anymore even though he loved them and liked their company. He would send them back to the house.

John was hurt the most by being sent back. He "helped" Stoney, chipping away at the stone alongside him.

Jane liked the younguns to learn all they could about any work that went on. They had very little ways to learn as it was.

Jane went to the quarry, "Stoney, you are a good man. No one is faulting you about the youngun gettin' snake bit. They can't go through life afraid of every rock they turn over. They just have to learn to watch out for harm. It don't do no good sending them somewhere else. That snake could just as well been in the woodpile. Just tell them how to watch out for them. It's harmin' them sending them away."

Wiping the sweat from his brow with a big red kerchief, part of it Jane suspected was tears, "You'r' right, Jane. I'll tell them how to watch for snake dens. They can come when they've a mind to. I thank ye fer not putting me to blame. I blame myself. I love them younguns, Lord knows, and don't want harm to come to them," Old Stoney said.

"I know," Jane said as she turned and went back to the cabin.

Word came that the sawmill would be there the next week. Harn, Anis, and Will were hurrying with the haying, finally asking Jed to help. They wanted to get the first cutting laid by in time to work on the mill.

The Cooks sent one of their younguns to see if the men could help them. They had to send word that it was impossible due to the sawmill set, but would try to be ready for the threshing.

By working part of Sunday the hay was all up. With a sigh the men washed themselves in the creek and slept the rest of the afternoon.

185

Jane had decided the new sawmill would be set up in the bottom up the "holler" from the garden. It would make the lumber close. The slabs could be sawed for wood. The "holler" had the best maple and poplar which would be used for siding and flooring, oak for foundation and studding. The trees they cut at Yellow Jacket would be hauled here. Jed and the people down Beech could bring their's here too without too much bother.

In case of trouble they would be close to the house. The day long looked for finally arrived.

The big teams of Belgian horses were straining in the shafts bringing the heavy machinery to the location. Another wagon followed pulled by oxens, the shining saw standing on end in a crate in the middle of the second wagon.

The younguns were all astraddle the log in the chipyard, big eyes taking in the procession as they entered the gate and came over the creek. The men yelling at the horses to make them lean into the traces up the bank.

Stoney and Old Joe had left their work, crossing the run to see the big wagons arriving.

They called a halt at the woodyard, for the horses to blow and of course for everyone to have a closer look.

Jane sent Catherin for a fresh bucket of water and a dipper for the tired men a cool drink.

Harn and the main sawyer went up the "holler" to see where the mill would be set up. They already had a pile of logs close to where they thought the mill would be.

The mill would be set close to the run, where water would be handy. It wouldn't be set up completely today. They had to return with the wagons to bring the rest of the equipment and tools.

Jane felt elated that finally she could see some headway toward her house.

The men went off up the "holler" to mark the trees that would be cut and figure out a road to haul them into the mill. It was decided that they would cut on the high point above where the mill set. The logs could be skidded down the hill then hauled the rest of the way, driving in a "dog ring" and snaking them with the horses.

Jed brought a load up that afternoon. His mark was on the end of each log so as not to mix them and the sawyer would know who the lumber belonged to. With everyone bringing logs, it should

186

keep the sawyer busy. Once the sawing started, they didn't like to shut down.

Old Joe had most of the cellar stones laid up. He knew his job of mixing mortar and fitting stones and had done a prime job. Cut stone steps led down to the dirt floor of the cellar.

Jane sent Will to Jimmy Boggs for him to come and make shingle boards for the roof. Jane intended to have him help build the cellar house if she could get him to. When it was finished she could move the men over there to sleep and have more room in the cabin for her and the younguns.

The mill was being set up as soon as they could saw. They would slab the logs and use the slabs to build a shed. That way the machinery would be protected and they could work in any weather. They would be going home at night for the time being and brought their dinner in buckets that hung high in a tree to keep ants out.

Jane might have to put them up once the sawing started. She didn't know how they worked it.

Things were starting to move again and Jane was at her best when planning a project and carrying it out. She was blooming with good health and had never felt better. After the baby was born, Jane felt that at last she had become a woman. If only her Tom was home everything would be alright.

By the spring her house could be started in earnest. The lumber would have to dry before it could be used in a house.

The farm animals were multiplying rapidly. She now had six cattle and six horses and a passel of pigs.

Tom would find changes when he came home and she hoped he'd be proud. The fighting went on. No one had thought the war could last so long. Stories of starvation in the South and terrible conditions of the prisoners that had been taken came almost daily. Tom and his brother Weeden was somewhere in the thick of the battles, with no word from them in weeks.

Calvin was crawling now, a big healthy happy seven months old baby. Jane was proud of him. He had been no bother at all with Catherin's help in tending him.

Jane and the younguns were busy stringing and shelling beans. They had a fine crop. Jane hoped they wouldn't have to buy any this year. There was little money coming in and no way to make any. She would have a calf to sell but hoped to keep it to a yearling. Old Blossom had a big bull calf. The other one had been a heifer which would be kept. She was fattening the pigs for a fall market. Her father-in-law had advised her to keep them and send them to Charleston where he would be driving a herd of his own. He could use one of the men to help and hers could be taken too. She planned to keep one to butcher.

By the end of the week the scream of the saw was heard cutting through the first tree. Then there was a time of quiet while something was adjusted to suit the sawyer.

The younguns all had strict orders not to go around the mill. Jane had only paddled John once since she had been their ma. The younguns were all biddable and did as she told them without bother.

Jimmy Boggs had come and was at the shed riving boards. The men had cut a stack of chestnut bolts for them in the winter. Jane planned to let him work as long as possible. The boards would be ready for the new house when it was built.

Jane would like to start the house now but the timber would have to season first. So it would have to be in the spring and not before. She needed patience. Everything would fall in place in time.

First Frost

Jane opened the kitchen door to a frosty world. Every blade of grass stood stiff with a coating of frost. It was so heavy as to almost be snow.

The summer days had gone quickly. The sound of the mill and men's voices were loud in the hazy Indian summer days.

The stack of new lumber mounting, standing bright and fragrant in the sun. Teams came and went bringing logs and taking away lumber on the return trip.

Anis and Harn had hauled the timber they had cut in the winter and had a backlog for the sawyer. They were then free to help the Cooks for the three weeks of threshing. When it was over they went back to timber cutting, having enough to keep the mill rolling.

The cellar was finished. The cellar house done all but some framing inside and a coat of whitewash outside. It looked grand standing there high above the run.

The younguns were back in school, three of them this time. Jane was doubtful about sending little Lizzie, she had wanted to go so badly that Jane finally gave over.

They had started riding the two mares, the men first and found them gentle enough. The three younguns went off each morning, Will in the saddle and the two girls behind. The colt frisking along beside its mother kicking up its heels and making them all laugh.

The harvest was almost all done, just potatoes to dig and they could be put in the bins that had been built in the new cellar. Shelves lined the walls where pumpkins could set, with all the stone jars of things.

Jane was so proud of it and of what a blessing things were so easy to get to. Three little windows had been put in the walls. They were only about a foot square but let in light and air.

The sawyer had built a slab shanty where they slept and their wives took turns coming to cook.

Jane was glad she didn't have to do for them. She was busy every minute putting away food for the winter. With the men cutting timber she had to do more gathering in from the different farms than she would have liked.

The sawyer's wife came in the afternoons to stay with the baby and the other two younguns. She could do her fancy work setting in Jane's rocker. In exchange Jane gave them things from her garden so they didn't have to bring food so far.

Jane sent word by the younguns to her father-in-law that she would like to see him. She wanted him to look over the lumber and see if she had enough of everything for the house. She wanted plenty and maybe enough for a barn for the cows too. And being so proud of her new cellar, she wanted him to see it.

The orchard had grown over the summer, each tree sending out new branches, some of them were taller than her head now and she had found one apple on a tree that excited them all.

Each day Jane would say, "Thank you, God." Now that Catherin could read, Will could too but he didn't take to it like his sister. Jane wanted to order a Bible and have her read it aloud each day. She would ask her father-in-law when he came to order one for her.

The men were busy from start of day till after dark. All the barns were bulging with hay. The corn and cane were still to be cut.

They would have a big crop of cane this year. Molasses could be used so many different ways. They wouldn't have to buy costly sugar that was shipped in from over the waters, from a place called Cuba. Jane had asked once about it and Mr. Cheniweth had explained it to her. Seems it was grown and milled somewhat like molasses. Oh, if only I could read I could learn so many wonderful things, she said to herself, more than once. I wouldn't have to ask, I could learn for myself.

The Cooks decided they needed some lumber and brought six or eight trees to be cut. The sawyer had been busy with hardly a day shut down now for eight weeks. They wanted to finish if possible and get their mill home before the roads became impassable.

Mr. and Mrs. Jarvis finally drove over one afternoon in their buggy to see Jane. After saying hello Mr. Jarvis went to the sawmill to look things over. Jane walked around the place showing her mother-in-law the cellar and the cellar house. And all the food she had put by and of course the orchard.

"I'm so pleased, Jane. You have done wonders. It's unbelievable that a mere girl could get so much accomplished."

"I've had help," Jane said, her face pink with pleasure and embarrassment at the praise. "If only my Tom was home." It was the first mention of him. Each woman not wanting to spoil the visit for the other.

"I don't see how the war can keep on. The South is ravaged and we hear they are starving, very little crops could be planted with the fighting surging back and forth." Mrs. Jarvis said. "If we could only hear something, I know it worries you, Jane. It does me and Tom's father."

The women went back to the house where Jane made coffee for them. Her father-in-law came back from the mill by way of the cellar house.

He came into the kitchen as Jane started to pour the coffee and set a platter of cookies on the table.

"Jane, this is starting to look like a real farm. When Tom first bought here I don't need to tell you I didn't think much of it. I think you have enough lumber cut for your house and barn. If I was you while the mill is here, I would let them cut as long as they can before winter. Good seasoned lumber always comes in handy. You won't be having another saw set in some time I'd say. There may be a market after the war for good lumber. Men coming back wanting to build. So far your judgment has been solid and you have planned well. I'm proud of you. I know Tom will be too when he gets back. He made a wise choice in you," Mr. Jarvis said with a laugh.

Jane blushed and didn't answer.

Her mother-in-law spoke up. "Don't josh her, Tom. She is a fine wife and mother."

They talked on for a while, Jane mentioned wanting a Bible. They promised to get one for her as they took their leave.

The Skirmish

The valley lay below them. The mist rising slowly over the cornfield.

The orders to dig in had been given. The sound of shovels and picks on the rocky terrain resounded and echoed through the hills as everyone snapped to.

Tom and his brother Weeden piled up rocks in front of them forming a breastworks. They had picked a ledge with a good view of the valley. A natural fortification with an overhang of rocks. Being mountain boys and hunting all their life they knew how to blend with their surroundings.

Taking their short-handled shovels from their packs, they shallowed out a hole and threw the dirt up on the rocks they had carefully placed atop their trench.

"I think that's safe enough," Tom said. "At least we will have some shelter and it's fairly dry here."

"I think I have a 'Reb' lookin' me right in the eye from the hill across the cornfield," Weeden said. "I can see the light flash on his gun barrel."

The men both had excellent eyesight and were good shots. Their captain had given them this point for a lookout spot.

Weeden was to hold the point while Tom carried information back down the hill where the Command Post had been set up.

This war wasn't what they expected when they signed up. Half the time there was no food or ammunition to fight with. They had to live on "hard tack" and water for days at a time. The farther South they penetrated the less food was to be found. What the Southern armies hadn't eaten, they had destroyed.

So far they had only been in light "skirmishes" and no real battles.

This looked like it could be a real one with the "Reb" army occupying the hill on one side and the Union on the opposite hill. There could be plenty of bloodshed in the valley between.

Some of the new troops, young boys mostly, were anxious to get in the thick of battle. They hadn't seen men's guts trailing over bushes like a woman's clothesline, or come upon an arm or leg in the brush with no one there to claim them.

The terrible waste of war was something the two brothers disliked most: the burned over fields, the beautiful farmhouses and barns in ashes, and the awful waste of young men. Both being family men they were careful of their own safety every moment and watched out for each other. They were hoping they wouldn't be separated if they got into battles.

However, Tom had been ordered to carry messages. He was small and quick and a good runner, good in the woods and mountains.

They were snuggled in and lay on their knapsacks all afternoon without a shot fired. No one came to them with food and they gnawed their "hard tack" taking turns sleeping while they could. They were out of the wind and reasonably warm. The sun was out part of the day and warmed the rocks around them.

Clouds were rolling up to the West with thunderheads building up. There would be a storm tonight. Nothing would please the "Reb's" more. They liked attacking in storms. So a sharp lookout had better be kept tonight. Old "Reb" would be on the prowl.

Darkness descended quickly, with the approaching storm. Flickers of firelight could be seen far back in the woods on the opposite hill. Too far away for sighting anyone.

Thunder began to rumble and flashes of jagged lightning streaked across the mountains.

Taking out their small tent tarp, the men rigged it over their trench tying it to trees close to them, readied themselves for the downpour soon to come.

They could hear action below them. Tents put up and talking and laughing among the soldiers.

Tom kept a sharp lookout toward the opposite hill. Every flash of lightning his eyes swept the cornfield below them. It would be hard to see men sneaking through the cornstalks that were still standing.

Weeden lay in the trench, comfortable as he could make himself, trying to sleep. He knew once the fighting started, he wouldn't get any rest. A few splatters of raindrops hit the tarp over their head sounding to the occupants underneath like gunshots.

In a flash of lightning Tom thought he saw movement in the field below. "Hey Weeden, come look, I think the 'Rebs' are sneaking up on us."

Weeden was wide awake and alert immediately and lying on his belly next to his brother. They waited patiently for the next flash of lightning, almost holding their breath. Thunder rolled in the distance, several flashes of lightning one on top of the other lit up the valley.

"They're there, all right," Weeden said, "and moving fast." Keeping his eyes on the field he said to Tom, "You best get down the hill and warn the Cap."

Tom, grabbing his brother's shoulder, said, "Hold tight, I'll be back," and started down the hill in the dark. Scrambling over rocks and around trees. He reached the headquarters, gave the pass word "Old Blu" to the guard and hurried into the Captain's tent.

"They're moving, sir, I'd say 'summers' between a hundred or a hundred fifty comin' across through the cornfield. They're aimin' on surprisin' us in the storm," he reported.

"Very good, soldier, go back to your post and alert us to anything different."

The rain was coming down now in earnest. Tom was soaked by the time he got back to the lookout post. "What they doing now, Weeden?" he asked.

"They're still sneaking through. They're halfway over to our side now. I saw some commotion on the hill, can't make out what they're doing up there yet," Weeden answered. "Come keep a sharp lookout and see if you can tell and keep down, you never know when the fools will start firing at this hill."

Tom crawled up beside his brother to look. There were such long waits now between the flashes of lightning, they couldn't see much.

The wind shifted and they could hear some action on the cliff on the opposite hill. "Recon they have a cannon?" Tom asked.

"I wouldn't be surprised, and if they have you can bet it will be aimed right at us," Weeden told him. "Does the Cap still want us to stay put?" Weeden asked.

"Yep!" Tom answered.

They both had their eyes glued to the hilltop. Waiting to catch any motion whatever.

The captain was smarter than they thought as they watched,

194

firing started from their sides. He had a line about fifty feet from the foot of the hill. They must have dug in after dark. The first volley resounded with yells of hurt and dying men in the cornfield. There was cross fire now coming and going; a fast exchange. The men in the field got the worst of it and started retreating. A wave of cavalry came pounding from the other hill.

"Oh, my God," Tom said, "they will ride right over our troops." No sooner did he say that than he heard cavalry on their side going at a run, jumping breastworks where the first firing had taken place to meet the "Rebs" in the middle of the cornfield. It was all happening so fast there wasn't time for Tom to tell the Cap about the charge.

Fortunately the captain had anticipated it and was ready. "I think we have a smart Captain," Tom told Weeden.

"Looks that way. I'm sure glad we ain't down there, must be Hell," Weeden said. "I think they have a cannon on the hill, better go tell the Captain fore it's too late."

Tom jumped out of the ditch and headed down the hill again. The storm had swept over them and it was getting lighter. He could at least see the trees before he got to them.

The captain was walking up and down. A bunch of papers lay on a table where a lantern shed faint light on them.

Runners came in from below where the battle was being fought. Gave their report to the "Cap" and hurried off again. It was Tom's turn, "We think the Reb's are readying a cannon atop the lookout. Can't see much but can hear clinking from over there," Tom reported.

Captain nodded his head. "I expected as much," he answered. "Keep a sharp eye out and keep reporting," he said. "By daybreak all Hell's going to break loose."

Tom could see wounded being brought in. A tent was set up below the captain's for them. Looked like a lot of them.

When Tom arrived back at the lookout he told Weeden, "We're losing heavy. But the Cap sure seems to be on top of it."

The "Reb's" cavalry had retreated back to their ranks and the night was still from the guns. There were yells and anger from the troops this side. "Come on, Reb, I got something for you."

All quieted down as the night wore on. Everyone watched and listened. There was little sleep on both sides the rest of the night. As they licked their wounds and readied themselves for the break of day and the battle to come.

The Battle

The first faint rays of dawn brought plenty of action on the opposite hill. The flash of a spy glass could be seen from the highest point.

Men gathered behind a rock formation where Weeden and Tom were sure the cannon was located.

"Better report to the Captain, Tom," Weeden told him.

When Tom reached headquarters, everything and everyone seemed in motion. Horses were hitched to a mean-looking cannon being pulled up the hill to be positioned on a jutting point overlooking the valley and opposite hill.

Everything was being readied for an all-out battle, which Tom knew would start very soon. He gave his report and was sent back again to his post.

Tom was halfway up the hill when the firing started. The boom of the cannon from the opposite hill resounded and echoed among the rocks. Tom didn't think the captain had time to position their cannon yet when the deafening roar that shook the ground under his feet and caused him to hit the dirt and flatten himself, sounded so loud he couldn't hear anything for a few seconds.

As soon as he quit shaking, he started humped over at a run back to his position.

"What's going on?" Weeden asked as he jumped into the ditch beside him.

"All Hell's broke loose," Tom answered. "I think we had better find us a more secure spot."

"Can't," Weeden said, "We are supposed to keep watch and that's what we have to do. So get to it and see if you can make heads or tails of what's going on in Reb territory."

Tom strained his eyes watching with every nerve taut and quivering.

"Looks to me like they're going to storm our location," he told Weeden.

"Wait a little till we try to sort it out before you report again," Weeden told him.

They could see the cavalry forming at the hill. It would be first this time, sweeping the valley, then the foot soldiers to mop up afterwards. This would be a bad one. There must be thousands on the "Reb" hill, with at least five hundred mounted men.

"Better go, Tom, and for God's sake be careful. Good luck," Weeden slapped him on the back as he started.

When Tom reached the captain and gave his report he nodded and put his hand on his shoulder. "Well done, boy," he said.

Tom had to smile at that. He must be almost twice the Captain's age. He started back up the hill. Firing of the cannons were spasmodic in the early morning. As Tom topped the first rise he suddenly fell to the ground as though a giant hand had slapped him down. Dazed for a minute he thought he had slipped. Trying to get up, he fell back again.

"My God! have I been hit?" he thought his legs and arms seemed alright and his belly (where he had always been afraid of being hit) on examining it seemed intact.

Blood started dripping down all over him. He started examining his face with a hand which came away with blood and teeth mixed together. "Oh, my God! I'm hit in the face." It felt only numb as he keeled over in the leaves and dirt. Tom didn't know how long he had laid there. When he came too, the sun looked a couple of hours high in the sky.

He started to crawl up the hill toward the lookout and Weeden. He found he was weak and shaking but kept going, pulling himself up halfway by trees till he could see the point where Weeden was. He tried to call to him but found his mouth wouldn't work. A broken jaw, he decided, resting for a minute, he crawled on to where he could toss a rock and get Weeden's attention.

Weeden looked over the edge and saw Tom all bloodied, looked like half of his face was gone. He let out a moan, "Oh, my God!" and started toward him as Tom again slumped down in a faint.

When he came too this time, he was in the hospital tent bandaged and lying on a cot. His whole face ached and he couldn't see out of either eye, feeling himself he found his head was as big as twice its size. He could hear voices in the distance and the sound of cannon and rifle fire. The moans of the wounded sounded all around him. He heard someone praying and another calling, "Mom, mom."

Jane, Jane, he thought as he again became unconscious from the pain.

Tom awoke, someone shaking his shoulder. Looking up through the slits that his eyes had become he made out his brother Weeden.

"How are you, Tom? Don't try to talk, I know you can't anyway. They're sending you back. It's been three days since you was hit. You'r' bad but the Doc says if they can get food in you that you will heal in time. They wired your jaw together. The minie ball ricocheted or you wouldn't be here. Broke your jaw and you lost a few teeth."

"No hospital," Tom finally got out so as Weeden could understand.

"I don't know, Tom, they are carrying out the wounded to the nearest depot and will put you on a train North. You've got to try to eat and get your strength back. Here, I got some broth for you." He started spooning it into Tom. All he could do was let it run down his throat and try to swallow. Every motion sent stabs of pain to the top of his head. It was hard but he felt better after the warm broth hit his stomach.

"The battle has been fierce," Weeden said. "That cornfield is covered with dead horses and men. The losses have been high on both sides. I'm staying behind. I'll see what I can do to get you home instead of the hospital," Weeden told him as he left.

Tom nodded weakly.

Weeden found the orderly and talked with him telling him that Tom didn't heal too good and that he would be better off at home if he could get there. Some money changed hands and the orderly promised to see what he could do. He would be going with the wounded.

Tom was loaded on a wagon of hay with several other wounded packed together as close as they could be. The journey to the railroad was rough and uncomfortable. They stopped at noontime and a bucket of soup was heated over a fire for the wounded. Tom hurt so, he didn't feel like eating but when the orderly brought him a cup of steaming soup, he got it all down slowly having to feed himself.

The jolting ride came to a finish as the sun sank in the West. The train was waiting and as the group was loaded, Tom could see there were many more coming from other directions.

The orderly wanted to know if Tom thought he could sit up? "I'll try," Tom told him.

"If I can get you walking maybe I can get you sent home," the orderly informed him.

Tom nodded and slumped in a corner seat where he half sat and half laid . . . his swollen eyes seemed some better. He could see more. But the pain was almost unbearable. The jolt of the train wheels sent shivers of pain all through his body. He fought to keep his senses about him, finally he put his head back and fell asleep from exhaustion.

When the train pulled in to a stop for the men to be fed, the orderly brought him a bowl of soup with a long quill made of several overlapping ones. Showed him how to mash the vegetables and suck them through the quill. He got along much better than trying to eat from a spoon, forcing it between his swollen lips.

He was told they would change trains at daybreak. Tom had no idea where they were. Somewhere around Tennessee he thought. Maybe Kentucky. It didn't matter much as long as he could get back to Jane, she would make him well again. My beautiful little girl, wife he thought.

That afternoon the orderly made him stand, holding on to the rack overhead. Seemed to Tom an hour but was only a few minutes. He still felt wobbly but had more strength in his legs.

By the time they changed trains, Tom leaning on the orderly, half walked and was half dragged aboard. At least he didn't have to be carried.

The orderly found a seat that leaned back in a corner and tucked an army blanket around him. The farther North they got the colder the train became. He was asleep by the time they moved out.

Tom awoke during the ride several times but dozed off again, the clickity-clack of the train's rhythm helping in the process.

Three days went by and the train was now jammed with bandaged soldiers. A gruesome looking lot moaning and hollering in their sleep.

It was impossible to give them much food, there were so many. There was plenty of hot coffee handed around. At stops along the way the women handed out pieces of cake and sandwiches to those who were able to eat.

After numerous stops for loading and unloading along the way they arrived the fourth day in Charleston.

The orderly came through to tell Tom that he had arranged leave for him to go home. Also told him yellow fever was raging in the hospitals and that he didn't blame him for wanting to pass it by.

He arranged for a hack to take Tom to a rooming house for the night till he could make arrangements to go home. His strength had returned somewhat and the hack took him to the rooming house he was familiar with where he had been before with his father. Tom gave a prayer of thanks for his deliverance.

Weeden had sent a cable ahead that Tom was on his way home. Tom wasn't sure it had been received. When he got to the boarding house he found his younger brother Caleb who had been there for two days meeting every train that came in. He found out later that the one he had been on hadn't been a scheduled one.

Caleb had brought his mother's spring seat buggy to fetch him home. They stayed the night so Tom would get a good night's rest before starting the long trip home the next day. It would take them several days to get home from there.

"I think a doctor had better look at you, maybe change your bandage. It looks like it needs it," Caleb told Tom. Inquiring of the innkeeper, they found there was an old doctor not far away.

Tom sat waiting his turn in the run-down office of the doctor. Finally he was told to go through a door to the inner room where he found the old doctor. He could hardly get around but seemed to know what to do as he cut the dirty bandage from Tom's face and head.

"Looks like you might have a headache there," the old doctor said with a chuckle. "Um—how long ago did this happen?" he asked.

Tom managed to get out, "A week or so."

"It's not healing too good. Can't do much, try to keep the 'proud' flesh down. Just have to wait for nature to do its job, get as much broth into you as you can. Keep your strength up to fight it. The wires will have to stay in your jaw till it knits." The old doctor bandaged his head and jaw again, charged two dollars and sent him on his way.

Tom felt so shaky, almost passing out again, that Caleb decided to wait another day before trying to start home.

He brought milk and broth for Tom and helped him eat it.

200

Found a bottle of whiskey and laced a cup of coffee for him which put him to sleep for several hours.

The next morning they started home. Blankets and pillows were in the buggy, their mother had put them in to make it more comfortable. Caleb bought food and started out. He knew the whiskey would do Tom more good than anything else and got a full bottle for the trip.

If Tom could have sat on a horse they could have made better time. He did well to sit up in the buggy, he was so weak. Caleb arranged the pillows in a corner of the hack and wrapped the blankets around him. The spring seats rode well and while they were on good road Tom dozed.

Tom was still in pain, a swallow of the whiskey every little while helped him bear up. They could only make twenty-five miles at most in a day. That is, if they had good roads.

Toward evening Caleb stopped at a farmhouse to ask about lodging for the night. About five miles ahead they were told they could find a place for the night.

The innkeeper made a thick broth for Tom. He ate and went directly to bed. The trip had worn him out.

On the way to Charleston, Caleb had camped out. He had only stayed one night in an inn.

It took them three days of hard traveling to get back home.

Tom's mother and father were overcome at seeing him after such a long time. They had butchered a sheep and his mother had thick mutton broth for Tom.

"Oh, Tom, it's so good having you home." Tom's mother said as she brought clean rags to dress his jaw. Helped him wash up, and put him to bed on soft feathers to rest.

Tom had the first real night's sleep in a long time. "Home," he said as he dropped off to sleep.

Tomorrow he would really be home. Home to Jane. He would feel safe then. Jane would take the hurt away and make him well again.

Two Buddies

The trench was waist deep. Weaving in and out among the trees and rocks. The two men by the clump of hickorys brought out their jug.

"Hey! Billy Dan, you want a little warming drink?"

"Sure do, Clem. Let's have that jug, gotta keep my eyesight sharp for them damn Reb's." Billy Dan laughed as he let the white hot whiskey down his throat. "Whooooo—ee that's good! That old whiskey makes the hair stand up around your Cock."

"You said it, Billy Dan," Clem was gasping for breath as he lowered the jug.

"What you think them Reb's got planned?" Clem asked.

"Hell! I don't know. I recon the same thing we plan, to put as many bullets where they will do the most good." He thought that was funny and rolled in the bottom of the trench laughing.

They had stuck together ever since enlisting. They had been in one skirmish that didn't amount to much. To them the war was a big joke, a reason to ride and drink and spin yarns. Usually about the women they had and what they had done with them.

As the night wore on and the liquor took effect, they became louder and their stories wilder.

"Sure wish we could find us one of them little Southern Belles, Billy Dan. One could do me a heap of good along about now."

"Hush up, Clem. You want me to get a hard on? Some damn Reb's liable to shoot it off." He doubled over with laughter.

Off to the right someone called, "You fellars keep quiet over there. You want the Rebs to lob a cannon ball over here?"

"Shit! I bet they don't even have a cannon, Billy Dan," Clem boasted.

"Don't you bet good money on it, Clem. Them Reb's are tricky, T-R-I-C-K-Y—I say."

"I gotta piss, Clem. Where in Hell am I gonna go?"

202

"Don't piss here unless you want to sit in wet and stink. Go over to that clump of trees," Clem told him.

"I'll do that, yes, sir," Billy Dan got up staggering and falling in the dark making enough noise to be heard miles away. Clem couldn't tell if he was coming back or still going out, till he suddenly fell on top of him in the ditch.

"Billy Dan, what the hell are you doing? Trying to kill me? Get down in here, you horse's ass, before you get your fool head blown off."

"Quiet, you two! That's an order!"

They finally settled down. They were supposed to be watching for any movement across the wheat field in front of them, propped against each other they were both soon asleep.

The night was quiet on both sides, only a glimmer now and then of a campfire and the distant braying of a mule gave witness of both army camps.

The mist was still hanging over the valley when the two awakened to the faint sound of a bugle.

"I'll be damned, Billy Dan, they're playing music over in the Reb camp," he laughed uproarious.

"Shit, I don't feel like music this mornin'. My head hurts and my mouth tastes like a hog pen." Billy Dan rolled over and sat propped against the trench wall.

Clem was up looking over the top of the trench trying to see where the bugle sound was coming from.

"What are you doing, Clem?" Billy Dan asked.

"Hell, I don't see nothing. That was probably the call to breakfast," Clem said.

A runner came down the trench toward them. "Get ready, men, that was a 'reading to charge' call. They're gonna be coming through that wheat field any time now. The cap'n says stand firm, don't fire till the order, then fight like hell. This is gonna be a bad one." He was off running on down the trench carrying the order to those strung out in the trench to the right.

"I wonder—they gonna feed us?" Clem wanted to know.

"I don't think so Clem. Anything left in that jug?"

Clem pulled the jug from under their blankets. "Sure is. Just enough for us both a snort to start the day." He turned the jug up taking a couple of good swallows and handed it to Billy Dan.

Billy Dan turned the jug up and drained it. Threw it over the breastworks toward the Reb line. "There you are, Reb, you can have it now," he let out a loud laugh.

"Ain't no good to us anymore," Clem added.

A cannon roared from the woods on the opposite side of the field. The round tore a hole about halfway between the woods and the breastworks.

"They got a cannon, Billy Dan. Look at that hole, you could bury a wagon and team in there. What we gonna do?"

"You heard the order, Clem, sit tight. That old Cap'n knows what to do, you wait, we'll whomp the living hell out of them," Billy Dan told him.

They could see men starting to advance from the other side straight toward them.

"Keep your head down, Clem. You're gonna get it shot off."

"Shit, Billy Dan, I've got to see what's going on." He raised his head again to look. A cannon ball exploded closer this time, sending fragments in all directions. A piece of metal hit the jug Billy Dan had thrown out, broke it into a million pieces that went every which way. A handful of glass found a mark, buried itself in Clem's face and scalp, cutting deep into an artery.

He fell back in the trench, blood gushing down over his face. An animal scream resounded down the trench as Clem fell. "I can't see, Billy Dan, I can't see. I'm hit bad."

Blood spurted over Billy Dan as he leaned toward his buddy, seeing nothing but blood and torn flesh. Billy Dan's stomach churned, vomit flew from his open mouth as he half raised from the trench to get away from the awful sight before him.

Rifle fire followed the last cannon shot as the Reb soldiers ran toward the entrenchment.

One found Billy Dan, hitting him in the back of the neck, shattering his spine. He fell before even a moan could escape him. His sightless eyes glued on the morning sky.

"Billy Dan, help me. Get a doctor," Clem pleaded.

"Where the hell are you, Billy Dan? Don't you go off and leave me." There was no answer to his plea. The blood was forming puddles around him draining away his life.

"Oh, God, I'm hurtin'. Billy Dan! Damn you, Billy, where are you?"

Clem started feeling around him, his hands were covered with blood that he couldn't see. When he leaned too far, he fell forward on his face where he remained, the last of his life's blood draining away. No more words left his lips, a long moan and a sigh. Clem had joined Billy Dan, his buddy, again.

Their rifles never fired. The two foolish wicked boys were no more.

The battle raged for two hours. Men screamed like wild beasts as bullets found their mark.

The orders were given to retreat as cavalry overran the dug in troops.

Very few found their way out of the battle. By noon the vultures were circling overhead in the quiet of midday.

Many a mother's son would not darken the door of the old homestead again. The war raged on. To many it ended that bloody morn in an unknown wheat field.

End of Summer

Old Stoney was still chopping away. The sawmill whined in the crisp sunny autumn. Stacks of lumber were piled high around the mill.

Jane still had Harn and Anis cutting timber. The sawyer told her he would only stay one more week. She wanted them to cut as much as possible in that time.

Jimmie Boggs had stacks of clapboards mounting every day. They would season for the new house and be ready when needed.

Jane had sowed her winter turnips, parsnips, and kale. The nights were getting colder. Soon they would need to fire up the heaters in the house. Jane had ordered one for the cellar house. It was a spacious room big enough for three double beds, a cupboard, the potbellied stove and chairs to sit on.

Molasses making would start the week after the mill moved. They had a big crop of cane and with what the neighbors brought, it would take a week or ten days to make them all.

Jane had ordered several two-gallon stoneware jugs for the molasses. They would fit nicely on the cellar shelves. She could hardly resist entering to look around each time she passed. She was so proud of her new cellar. "My girl, be careful," she told herself, "Pride goeth before a fall."

The fall days flew by. The molasses making over, the cellar shelves lined with jugs. Big stone jars holding twenty-gallon set on the floor—molasses, vinegar, sauerkraut, pickles, pickled tomatoes, and a spot was left for the big barrel of kale in brine that would be added before snowfall. Jane was very pleased with the stores for winter, they had worked hard to put by.

Her kitchen would seem empty this winter, only the dried things still lined the shelves against the wall. They couldn't be put in the cellar due to the dampness.

The men were cutting and hauling the corn to the barn at the house. It would be shucked later filling the big bins that were built for it.

The younguns were still in school, loving every minute of it. Coming home full of teacher said this and teacher said that, and teacher thought that. Jane listened to every word. This school room thing was a whole new world to her and she listened and thought about what came to her secondhand, and formed her own conclusions. Something she wanted to know more about, she would say to the younguns, "Why don't you ask your teacher so and so?" They would bring her answer back to Jane in the telling at evening time. She never said anything but learned lots from the children's lessons as they learned and talked.

The saddlebags were always part of saddling the horse. One evening Jane's Bible came, wrapped in a piece of cloth. Jane unwrapped it and looked at the gold lettering on the outside. It was a big book with covering in black leather.

Catherin said there were pages to put down marriages, births, and keep a record of everything. Carefully turning the pages of the big Bible on Jane's lap, she found the lines. There—this is marriages, the page with hearts and flowers. This is births and the next page is deaths. You have to write in the date and name.

Jane looked at the flowered borders around each of the pages —daisies and roses around births; cupids, hearts and flowers around marriages; and crosses and lilies around deaths. "Can you read it, Catherin?" Jane asked timidly.

"I don't know all the big words but I can read some. Grandma marked with a bookmark where I was to read," she told Jane.

Jane noticed a satin ribbon marking a page that Catherin pointed out. "Do you want I should read it, Mammy Jane?' she asked, looking up at Jane.

Jane nodded, turning the Bible so Catherin could see.

"This is Psalms—twenty three," Catherin said as she started to read.

"The Lord is my shepherd; I shall not want. He maketh me to lie down in green pastures: he leadeth me beside the still waters. He restoreth my soul: he leadeth me in the paths of righteousness for his name's sake.

"Yea, though I walk through the valley of the shadow of death, I will fear no evil: for thou art with me; thy rod and staff they comfort me.

"Thou preparest a table before me in the presence of mine enemies: thou anointest my head with oil; my cup runneth over.

"Surely goodness and mercy shall follow me all the days of my life; and I will dwell in the house of the Lord for ever."

Jane sat silent, a lump in her throat and her eyes misted. "Read it again to me, Catherin, I want to get the meaning clear in my mind."

"That's what teacher says to do," Catherin said as she read again, her sweet voice bringing out each word like a song being sung.

Jane cherished her Bible and each night had it read to her while they all sat and listened to the Holy Words. However, the first reading seemed to take on more meaning for Jane.

The days grew colder as the last of the harvesting was done. The clouds began to roll in from the Northwest with a promise of snow.

Jane picked kale and put it down in brine. She was one step ahead of the snow this year.

Florence had things to work at and didn't visit so often. They were planning their house. Jed and his brother were going away to work the coal mines. He wanted to make money for the building. They had put up a shed for their team of mules and had enough feed to see them skimpily through the winter.

They came on Sunday for dinner and told them about the job.

Florence would stay at home and take care of the animals. She had twenty chickens now. Jane had given her an old hen and chicks in the spring. And her little sow pig and of course the cow and two mules.

They had started getting a little ahead and with Jed working the winter would help considerable.

Jane never commented but wild horses couldn't drag her down in a black coal mine, no matter how much she needed money. She would find another way.

The first skiff of snow fell the day after the brothers left for the mine.

The younguns would have to quit school the last of the week. Jane couldn't have them riding so far in the cold. She was always worried they would catch "Quick Consumption." There was little could be done for it.

The last day at school they stopped to tell their grandparents good-bye and told them that they wouldn't be coming anymore till spring.

They had word from Tom. He had been wounded and was being sent home. He refused to go to the hospital because of yellow fever.

There had been a wire from Weeden to that effect. He was fine and they didn't know how bad Tom was.

Caleb had gone to Charleston with the team and buggy to fetch him home. They didn't know how long he would have to wait before Tom arrived or how fast he could travel when he did get to Charleston.

The blood drained from Jane's face when the younguns told her. "Thank God he is alive. No matter how bad he is, he'll be home soon," she said.

There was a flurry of cleaning and washing the following day. The men's beds were finally moved to the cellar house. Jane rearranged the rooms to allow more space. Everything was ready for Tom's homecoming. They all waited.

Tom Home

The autumn days were clear and sunny. The work went on around the farm. Finishing up outside so winter didn't catch them with things undone.

The men were repairing fences, hauling in wood to the wood-yard, and getting ready for snow.

Will chopped wood, keeping the younguns busy stacking it. They carried a big pile and stacked it at the cellar house for the big potbellied stove they had installed.

Jane looked down the road each time she passed a window. She would go outside standing with her hands on her hips looking and looking. A week went by and still no more word about Tom. Jane didn't think she could stand another day. She managed somehow.

The clouds rolled up from the North their bellies full of snow. The wind came from the Northwest with icicles in it.

The horses and cows were penned at night out of the wind, glad to be inside together.

Jane awoke to four inches of snow and the wind whistling under the eaves. "Oh, I hope my Tom isn't out in this. Let him be somewhere warm," Jane whispered. It had been two weeks since the first word of Tom's homecoming. Surely he should be here by now. The wind died down toward evening. Snow continued to fall softly now. It was warm and cozy in the cabin. Looking out Jane could see smoke coming from the stovepipe in the cellar house. It was a comforting sight.

The men liked their new quarters where they could talk and tell tall tales and not be disturbed.

Will wanted to move in with them too. John was too small yet and they would have to share a bed. Jane had promised that another bed would be added in the summer and he could spend next winter with the men.

In the afternoon of the fourteenth day, they heard the sleigh bells, the younguns hearing them first in the cold air.

Jane punched up the kitchen fire. Will added wood to the heatin' stove. A big pot of coffee was put on to boil.

The men had gone rabbit hunting the day before and brought home four big rabbits. They were in a big pot simmering for stew. The vegetables set in water ready to put in. Jane added turnips, potatoes, onions, and seasonings. It wouldn't take long for them to cook. She would add dumplings to the pot when everything was done.

The sleigh was coming across the creek. The younguns' noses glued to the windows, "Pa's with them. It's pa," they yelled. They all ran for coats and shawls to dash outside to meet the arrival of their pa.

Jane threw a heavy shawl over her head. The baby was on the rug Catherin had made in front of the fire. It would be alright for a minute. She too rushed outside as the sleigh came to a stop in a flurry of snow.

Her heart sank as she looked at Tom. His head and face swathed in bandages. He was wrapped in blankets till only his nose and one eye looked out at her.

Maybe he is blind, Jane thought, her heart fluttering in her chest. Oh, God, no.

His brother helped him from the sleigh, half carrying him. Tom's arms around him to help balance his weight. They got him inside, Jane giving orders as they went, "Catherin, get the baby out of the way! Pull the rocker over here," They lowered Tom in the rocking chair.

Caleb finally said, "He is tuckered out Jane, but alright. Mother wanted him to stay over there till he was stronger but he thinks you will get him well sooner. We stayed the night at home. It took us four days from Charleston. I waited there most a week after we got the word he was coming."

Jane helped take Tom's coat off and his heavy boots. She could see little of his face, still not knowing where or how bad he was wounded.

"He was hit in the jaw with a spent minie ball, Jane. Broke his jaw and took some teeth. It's not healing. I had a doctor in Charleston dress and look at it. His jaw is wired together. He can't talk much or eat much, only soup or broth. There's not much can be done, only keep the wound clean and let nature heal it. It will take time and patience," Caleb told her.

She nodded, understanding. "His eyes?" she asked.

211

"They are still swollen. He can see some. It'll take a month, the doctor said, for the swelling to go down. His eyes are alright," Caleb added.

Jane nodded again. "Take your coat off, Caleb. I'll bring coffee to warm you." She went to the kitchen, made two cups of coffee with honey and a slug of whiskey in each, stirred them well and returned to the sittin' room.

Caleb rummaged in Tom's coat and came up with the quill for sucking through, put it in Tom's cup. Jane held it for him till his own hand came up and covered hers. What she could see of the one eye sparkled as he tasted the whiskey.

"That's a fine cup, Jane," Caleb said. "Takes the icicles out in no time."

During the time Jane had waited, she had made Tom a long flannel nightshirt. "You younguns go in the kitchen, I'll put your pa to bed for a nap. Supper will be ready directly." Jane undressed him like a baby, seeing his thin body before slipping the nightshirt over his head. Helped him to their bed and in, tucking the warm comforts around him. She took an iron from the stove, wrapped it and placed it at his feet.

Tom patted her hand as his eyelid drooped.

"Sleep will do him good," Caleb told her.

"Thank God it wasn't worse and you have him home. There are three more we have to worry about."

"I know your mother has a burden to bear," Jane answered. She went to the kitchen to finish supper. Anis and Harn were siting in the kitchen with the younguns.

While she finished cooking, the men and Will took Caleb to see the new cellar and their sleeping quarters above.

They came back as she took the corn bread from the oven and put the food on the table. Leaving plenty of broth to simmer for Tom. She looked in and he was sleeping like a baby, warm and safe.

They all finished supper and Caleb took his leave, everyone going to see him off.

"If there is anything we can do, Jane, send word," the bells jingled merrily as the sleigh started off.

"I will, I'll let him rest tonight. I'll start my doctoring tomorrow," she said.

The cabin quieted as the men went to their quarters and the younguns went to bed. Jane sat rocking the baby and watching

212

Tom, he had slept through their supper and Caleb's leave-taking. She had the stew still simmering ready to feed him when he awakened.

Noticing Tom starting to awaken, Jane put the sleeping baby in the cradle for the night.

Going to Tom she fluffed the pillows putting another to his back raising him to a sittin' position in bed.

"You stay right there, I'll bring your supper. A couple of days in bed and you will feel a lot better," she told him.

Going to the kitchen, Jane dished up a big bowl of the broth from the stew, bringing it back she fed him with a spoon. His eyes following her every move. The broth was soon gone, some color coming back to Tom's cheeks.

He nodded to tell her, "Good," he got out.

"I'll fix you a tonic and you can go back to sleep," pouring hot water, she mixed whiskey and honey stirring till it was well mixed, put the quill in the cup and held it for Tom to drink.

"There," she said as he drained the cup. "Go back to sleep," she removed one pillow and arranged the covers to suit her.

Banking the fires, Jane readied herself for the night. Slid in beside Tom. He reached for her and holding each other they soon fell asleep. "My Tom home," Jane said softly. "Thank you, Lord."

Convalescence

Tom remained in bed for almost a week, he had caught a slight cold coming home.

Jane fussed over him, mixing this and that for him to take. When she unbandaged his wound, she almost passed out. A big chunk of his jaw had been blown away, leaving a deep gorge in the flesh. Fortunately none of the bone had been lost, only flesh and teeth. Jane examined it carefully. She decided to try some hot turpentine compresses to take down the swelling and to help with the healing.

Tom said a few words to her as she worked.

"Glad—to—be—home—Jane."

"I know I'm glad you are home where you belong." Deep in her heart she resented his leaving her to join up when he didn't have to.

"You'll be well in no time," Jane told him.

The time came when Tom finally insisted on getting up. He had let Jane mother him long enough and been pleased that she did.

Jane let him sit by the fire, a comforter around his shoulders and wrapped around his legs. Still she wouldn't let him go outside, he didn't insist.

Heavy broth was kept simmering for him. Chickens had been killed to make broth, when there wasn't rabbits. Jane gave him apple cider, vinegar, and honey which would do instead of eating vegetables. She knew it helped somehow in healing. His color had returned and he had more strength now.

The day came when she couldn't keep him wrapped in a chair by the fire any longer. He insisted on going out to the privy, tired of the chamberpot under the bed.

It had snowed off and on since he arrived home. There was a path knee deep to the outbuildings tromped down solid and glazed with ice.

Jane decided to have the men butcher the hog for Christmas. It would butcher out three to five hundred pounds. She had made up her mind to keep a young sow and breed the two and double her crop of pigs. The four she had sent to Charleston had brought a hundred dollars. That would be a way to make money for her house.

It was time for Tom to see the doctor about taking the wires from his jaw. Florence promised to come and stay while Jane went along. The baby was almost weaned now. Could eat and drink from a cup.

The team was readied. The sled filled with hay. Jane wrapped stones she had heated on the stove to put at their feet. Just she and Tom set out together.

They arrived at Tom's father's in time for dinner. Found out that old Doc Dye would likely be home and could remove the wires.

Jane asked her father-in-law to get her a gallon of whiskey. She knew Tom would need some on the way home. There would be pain in removing the wires. The jaw had healed. Only a red ragged scar remained. It had taken a month and a half to do so with lots of attention from Jane.

Tom's father decided he would take Tom to the doctor while Jane went to the store to shop. She had brought two big baskets of eggs and would buy things for Christmas which was two weeks away.

Shopping carefully, looking over the many things in the big store house, she bought a shirt for her Tom, stockings for the girls, and a pair each of socks for the men and boys. A pound of horehound candy and one of peppermint sticks. Some spices and flavoring for her Christmas baking. She wouldn't go into her poke of money and bought only what the eggs would pay for.

There were rumors of the war ending. It could drag on for months before that happened. The men were starving and freezing. Yellow fever was raging through the hospitals and the prisons.

"Thank God my Tom's home," Jane said to herself. Keep the other brothers safe, Lord, Jane prayed.

The old doctor gave Tom something to deaden the pain while he removed the wires and dabbed something on the unhealed holes that oozed blood and looked angry red around each place where the wires had been. Tom would have pain when the medicine wore off. The old doctor had done a ragged job of removing the wires.

Tom could talk some but found it still a little strange not hav-

215

ing talked for two months. Everyone slapped him on the back and told him how lucky he was. They all wanted tales of what went on. Tom didn't seem to want to talk about it. Just informed them that "war was hell" and started talking about something else.

Mr. Cheniweth informed Jane that he heard a man that had owned the land south of her, had been killed in the fighting and that his widow wanted to sell the farm they owned. "There's about sixty-eight acres," he said. "Are you interested, Jane?" he asked.

"If it joins our land, I'm interested," Jane told him.

"I'll find out the particulars and let you know. I don't think many people would be rushing to buy it. The woman's name is Keaton if you hear anything."

"I'm obliged, Mr. Cheniweth," Jane said.

"I hear your saw set was a big success," he added.

"Oh, I guess so. We have new lumber stacked everywhere. We hope to start our house in the spring. Most of the chimney rock and foundation rock is ready. Old Stoney will finish when he comes in the spring."

"I hear you are going to have the finest farm in that part of the county."

"It's shaping up," Jane said modestly as she said good-bye. Tom shook hands with the men he knew as they took their leave.

Their bundles were put into the sled and they were off, dropping Tom's dad at his gate.

"Take care," he called to them. "If we hear of Weeden and his brothers we will let you know."

Tom drove the team at a fast clip over the frozen ground, anxious to be home.

"How is your jaw?" Jane asked as they topped the hill toward home.

"Hurts," he remarked bluntly.

"You want I should drive," Jane asked.

"No," was the short answer he gave Jane.

They were soon home. Will took over the sled and team. When they got inside Tom collapsed in the rocking chair without even removing his coat. Jane knew he was still weak and now in pain.

Removing her wraps, she hurriedly made a tonic for Tom, helping him out of his coat she gave him the tonic.

Jane had bought Florence a piece of flannel, she was now pregnant. She never asked her to stay with the younguns without giving her something.

"Thank you, Jane, I'll use it to make a 'kimono,' that's sorta like a gown," she explained, "only a little more fancy," her cheerful laugh rang out. "I'll go now before dark. I have to milk and feed yet."

"You be careful you don't fall," Jane cautioned her.

"I'll be fine, Jane, don't worry about me. I'll see you Sunday." She was soon out of sight down the meadow taking the short cut by the creek.

Jane put Tom to bed early, his jaw was aching. Hot packs of turpentine eased it and helped the gorges the wire had made.

Jane rocked the baby and nursed it before putting it down for the night. It's good to be home, she thought. Even from such a short trip. She knew how Tom must have felt to be back. Each day was full now with her Tom home. There was more satisfaction in all she did.

"Thank you, Lord," she said as she went to bed beside her Tom.

The Butchering

The hog was butchered before Christmas to give time to make the sausage and get it out of the way before Jane started her Christmas baking. It was a fine hog—fat, tender, and tasty. Jane rendered out about seventy-five pounds of lard. Every crackling was saved and put away in jars to make crackling bread. She could also use them in cooking beans. The sausage was ground, seasoned with sage, pepper, and salt. Some was fried and put into crocks, covered with grease, and set in the cellar. It would keep till way in the summer.

Florence came to help and was given a bucket of meat to take home with her.

"I don't know what I'll do when you get a bunch of younguns, Florence, and can't help anymore," Jane told her.

"Oh, that won't keep me from working," Florence said with her ringing laugh. "It didn't stop you yet, Jane."

They worked together getting the meat put away. Then it was time to get ready for Christmas—baking cookies, pies, and a couple of big cakes, and popcorn balls were made, making sorghum taffy to hold them together.

Jed would be home from the mines, they would come to Jane's for Christmas dinner as usual.

The younguns were excited about the coming of Santa. Talking among themselves about the jolly old man.

Catherin had them all in the back bedroom practicing a "program," she called it. They planned to put it on for Christmas Eve.

Jane could hear them singing and saying pieces. Tom went out for a walk every day now. His head and face wrapped in a muffler from the cold. He walked to the barn and went to the cellar house to visit the men. Sometimes Jane would see him in the bottom at the saw set looking over the new lumber. His eyes took in everything.

They were all ready when the big day finally arrived. The gifts were given and Catherin put on her program after dinner.

She, Lizzy, and Will sang "Silent Night," Catherin doing most of the singing.

John said a "piece" about Santa and the reindeers. He forgot part of it, Elizabeth had to fill in for him. There was laughter from them all as John went to hide behind his sister in embarrassment.

"If we could have gone to school, they were having a tree, and all trimmed with strings of popcorn and stars and all," Elizabeth explained.

"You did just fine," Florence told her, giving her a big hug. "You all did. We enjoyed it a lot."

Jed told them all a Christmas tale about how Santa came to the coal mines and had to go deep into the mountain to find all the papas and give them a candy cane from their younguns. How he got black coal dust in his white whiskers and had a terrible time getting them white again. Mrs. Santa wanted to boil them with lye soap like she did the Sunday shirts. Old Santa explained that they were fastened to his chin and couldn't be taken off. It was a long tale with lots of Ho, Ho, Ho's. The younguns took it all in as gospel. Everyone laughed uproariously after the telling.

Tom sat smiling, his eyes shining, looking at Jane over the others' heads. Telling her with his eyes, it's good to be home.

They all had a glass of milk and a big piece of cake before Jed and Florence went home. The stars were out and the night clear as they saw them to the door.

"Let's go deer hunting tomorrow, Jed," the men called.

"Sounds good, I'll be up before day. See you then," his booming laugh rang as they started off down the valley together.

They all called "Merry Christmas," as the men took off for the cellar house and the younguns got ready for bed.

Tom and Jane were the last to go. Turning to her, Tom said, "Jane, it was the best Christmas I've ever heard. I never appreciated home so much as I do now."

"I'm glad you are home and hope you never have to leave again. I think of all who are in the war and away from their loved ones today," Jane answered him.

"No one knows unless they have been through it," Tom said.

"Forget it, and let's go to bed." Together they readied the

house for the night, banking fires and seeing that the younguns were snug and warm.

They lay holding each other in their love, that Christmas night, all the world forgotten as sleep found them.

Last of Winter

January was cold and windy with snow swirling in clouds to block one's sight, finding every opening around one's face and neck to dampen the clothes inside.

Tom still would go outside, not being able to sit at the fire as Jane wanted him to. Toward the beginning of February he tossed and turned in the night, waking Jane. She felt his head and found he was burning with fever.

Getting out of bed, she built up the fire putting hot irons to his feet and soon had water hot for a tonic. She mixed turpentine, water, and honey and with a fuss got it down him. She sat by the stove waiting. He fell into a fitful sleep, still tossing and throwing the covers off which she patiently replaced each time. Tucking them in around his arms and legs.

By daybreak Tom was burning up with fever. The wound on his face almost purple, she could see his face was swollen. Examining him carefully she found that where the wires were removed from his jaw, one had become abscessed. It was red and oozing pus.

Jane started the hot packs, then decided on a poultice of grated potatoes to draw out the infection. She doctored Tom all that day and most of the night. He talked in his sleep, mostly to his brother Weeden and about the war.

Jane heard things that she would just as leave not heard.

Tom finally started to get better after the better part of two weeks. He seemed weak and haggard and it was no problem getting him to sit by the fire.

The men kept busy feeding, wood chopping, running their trap lines, and hunting. They made enough each winter from it for their clothes and whatever else took their fancy.

The winter continued, each month getting worse it seemed. Florence came through the snow to visit and for someone to talk to. She showed the girls how to do fancy work and was helping Catherin make a pair of mittens for her pa. Jane rocked the baby

221

who was now walking and watched as they worked. The days were worrisome with them all penned inside.

The men hunted, bringing home rabbits for the pot. They kept Florence in meat too. They hadn't had any luck yet getting a deer, but said when this spell broke, they would try again.

March came in with sunshine. The snow melted sending gushing water down every gully. Florence couldn't come for days. The mud and water was everywhere. Even the animals hated to go outside to tromp through the mud. It looked as though winter had gone into hiding. They all knew the old saying: "In like a lamb, out like a lion." They didn't have long to wait, awakening in the night to shrill winds under eaves. Anything loose banged and clattered or got blown away altogether.

When they got up in the morning, a frozen world greeted them. The ground was covered with half an inch of snow. The men talked at breakfast, "This is the day we get a deer." "We will go late in the afternoon, they will be out then," Harn said. Preparation was made and they started out. The wind died down in the day, a weak sun shone for a few minutes in the afternoon.

Tom commented, "They will get one today," as he checked the weather from the window.

It was almost dark when they heard both guns go off. Two shots from one gun and one from the other one. Watching they saw Harn come for the horse and knew they had been lucky and would bring home a deer.

Jane knew the routine and had things ready for the butchering. Lanterns had to be lit for the job as night fell before they got home.

When they did come they had two big bucks on the horse. "One is for Florence," they told Jane.

"That's good, she can use it," Jane said. They still had meat from the hog. The hams and shoulders were salted down and would last even in hot weather. The deer meat would be welcome on anyone's table.

A big pan of liver, heart and such was brought to the door. The men expected some for their supper while they finished cleaning the deer. It would be hung to freeze overnight. Jane instructed them to cut the one they intended for Florence and take only part of it to her. She could never use a whole one with the men gone.

By the time they were finished, Jane had platters of liver fried for them. The supper was lively with the telling of the kill. Tom

222

wanted to hear every detail. Jane knew he was itching to get out and do things on his own. His health wasn't good. He would have to be satisfied to stay in till spring.

Jane was so thankful she had him home where she could care for him. He would have died without good care. "Thank you, Lord, for sending him home to me," Jane never forgot to say each day she looked at her Tom.

Spring

The sun came out and the ground warmed. Plowing and planting got into full swing.

Old Stoney came back to his tap—tap—ing. With one more for an audience. Tom was still weak and his walks were short. He would sit on a sun-warmed rock and watch Old Stoney shape the stones into squares. Sitting by the hour as work went on around him.

Jane was pregnant again. It was a burden getting the younguns off to school in the early dawn. The morning sickness leaving her weak and shaking. Her tonic of vinegar and honey in hot water began to help after awhile.

The younguns went to school three months in the fall if they were lucky and about six weeks in the spring. They learned well during that time. They could all read and write. Jane was so proud of that.

She sent word to her father-in-law to send a builder to start her house. He came one day bringing a tall skinny man with him, a Mr. Weaver who he said could do a good job.

Harn and Anis took time to help get the foundation in and haul the studding to the site as he directed.

Mr. Weaver was slow moving but Jane could tell he did everything the way it should be done. Leveling and squaring every corner with precision.

When Jane first talked to him she had told him she wanted a house that would stand a hundred years. As slow as he was she sometimes thought to herself it might take him that long to build it. Then decided it was her condition that made her impatient.

Florence came, she had on a loose-fitting dress, her baby due any day. Jed was home now, back from the mines, plowing and planting as were all the farmers.

Florence's cow would freshen soon as would Jane's two. They were both out of milk. Florence told her what a godsend the deer

224

meat had been. She had put down some in grease till Jed came. Florence talked and laughed about her "laying-in." "You are likely to have it on the way home, coming all this way and you so near your time," Jane told her.

"Oh, I'm fine, my sister will come this week. She will be glad to get away from home and will stay what time I need someone. I will be glad to get it over with," she laughed her loud laugh.

"Send if you need me," Jane told her. "Send if there is anything we can do."

"You don't look so good yourself, Jane, kinda green around the gills," and her laugh rang out. "My guess you'll have a surprise again around Christmas."

"It won't be a surprise," Jane said, no humor in her remark.

"Oh, Jane, you are a caushin," and Florence giggled.

"Do you plan to start your house this spring?" Jane asked Florence.

"I don't know. We would like to. We may have to wait a bit yet. Jed made good money in the mine, but we need more. He wants a barn first for the animals and may build that first. We haven't decided yet."

"As long as you have a place to live, a barn is important," Jane answered. "We are not so crowded now with the cellar house for the men. We could get along a while but I'm glad ours is started. Tom may have to go back to the war. He is still not able, he can't seem to get his health back yet," Jane told her.

"It's not your fault, Jane, Lord knows that you've doctored him all winter. If he had been in an army camp you wouldn't have got him back."

"I'm afraid not, Florence."

The two women talked, the only enjoyment either had during the long work-filled days.

The house foundation went slowly. Jane could hardly see a difference from day to day.

Tom would have to go to Charleston soon to check in at the army office there. The war went on. More and more men were killed and wounded.

One of his brothers who fought for the South was missing. Weeden was still in the thick of it. So far he was alright.

Jane could tell that Tom wasn't anxious to go back and insisted he give himself another week before the trip.

Tom walked regularly now. Up the "holler" out of sight, to the barn even all the way to the Hall farm where the men worked. Trying to regain his strength. If they sent him back to the battlefields he would be on his own. He doubted he would find Weeden or be put in his outfit again.

The day finally arrived when it could be put off no longer. With his knapsack over his shoulder, he started off. Jane standing in the woodyard silent, tears running down her face. Tom's family would take him to the railroad or to Charleston.

When he was out of sight, Jane wiped her eyes with the corner of her apron and went back to the cabin. Preparing herself for the long wait of empty days without her Tom.

Back to War

Tom sat in the office waiting his turn. Papers must be filed and then an examination by the doctor. He had sat in the office of the capitol all morning through time for dinner and now afternoon.

He was hungry and tired. His head ached and the old wound in his leg had stiffened up. He walked around the room a couple of times. The weary eyes of others following him.

Around three o'clock they were all told to leave. Not wanting to spend money at the rooming house, Tom asked some of the men where they stayed and found the army had a barracks close by. He followed the rest there to spend the night.

Back the next day to sit again. Tom couldn't see that any of them were being processed. The room was full and still more coming, crowding it further. A young orderly came out in the late afternoon telling them to all go home until they were called again.

They didn't understand but gave a whoop—and laughed, slapping each other on the back, left.

Tom's heart did a flip. Feeling like a young boy, let out of school in the spring. He decided to go to his uncle's farm about twenty miles from town. Maybe he would borrow a horse for the trip back or catch someone going his way.

Found on arriving that they were expecting the circuit judge to stop on his way back to the county seat and Tom could go back with him as he usually drove through by buggy.

The old judge arrived, stayed the night and welcomed Tom as company on the long drive back.

Talking on the way the judge told him about meeting Jane at his father's and what a fine girl she seemed to be, how smart she seemed. He asked if she had bought any more farms?

Tom laughed, pleased at the remark. "She sure is making that few acres I owned into a real homestead," Tom said. "No telling how much more she will add to it. Right now she is building a house as big as dad's."

"Is she now?" laughed the Judge. "I'll have to visit there. I have an invitation to, you know."

They both laughed. Enjoying each other's company, talking about whatever came to mind.

Tom was weary by the time he reached his father's farm, not as strong as he thought he was and glad to stay the night before going on home. It would be as much a surprise to Jane as it was to his mother and father.

They all decided at the supper table that maybe it was a sign the war would soon be over.

Passing Times

The days flew by, season after season, year after year. The farm flourished and more acres were added. Jane had bought the farm north of her and another sixty-nine acres that joined the Yellow Jacket farm on the south.

The war had ended and those who came back seemed restless, wanting to move on. The road West called many.

Mammy Jane's house stood tall and majestic. The white porticos trimmed in lacy patterns were something to behold. It had taken four years for Jane to realize her dream house.

The orchard was thick and tall reaching to the upstairs portico, filled with blossoms each spring and full of fruit each fall.

The new furnishings she had had made filled every room. Lace curtains hung at the tall windows of the big airy rooms.

A well had been drilled outside the kitchen door. That enclosed in a room connecting the house to the cellar house.

The girls were young ladies. Catherin now sixteen and Elizabeth fourteen, Trude an unruly ten.

James Calvin was now seven. The cradle had held three since him. In the eight years Jane and Tom had two boys and two girls. Jane was two months along again.

Old Stoney was long gone from the scene. Jane had heard that he had passed on. She missed him. He was a nice old man.

Tom's folks had bought a big farm close to Charleston and moved there selling the homestead on the West Fork.

Jane was sad each time she passed the big white house where she used to stop on her way to the store.

Tom took over the farm work with the help of Jane. He had never fully recovered his health since the war. He came down with unexpected fevers that left him weak and shaking.

They talked and planned, Tom leaving a lot of the decisions to Jane. When they decided, Tom would ride his mare and supervise the planting, fence building, and such.

Anis and Harn still made their home with them. Harn was getting old and had rheumatism in his crippled foot. He could still do a day's work and complained little.

A new barn had been built up the "holler." The bottom where the saw set had been was fenced in. That was now the cane patch. It covered about five acres and grew enough cane to keep molasses on the table at all times.

The cellar in the cliff where Old Stoney had spent so many hours had been built. The spring tail routed through to have a water box to keep things cool.

The new barn was for the milk cows and called "the cow barn." The cabin had been turned into the chicken house. The old shack that had once housed the chickens had been torn down.

There were geese now for feathers, a pair of feather pillows filled with snowy feathers on every bed. Each one would soon have feather ticks to sleep on.

There was a herd of twenty beautiful horses roaming the pasture. All from the two Mammy Jane had "acquired" and their offspring. They had a sizable bunch of cattle, some for market each year now.

The old judge came regularly on his rides through to the state capital.

There was hardly a week went by that the company room didn't hold some important personage passing through.

With a big barn to house their teams and a full table with plenty of company, it was a favorite stopping place for the doctors, judges, legislators, and preachers riding circuit.

Tom made them all welcome, calling out, "Jane, add another place at the table."

Catherin was a fine cook. In fact anything she did turned out well. Elizabeth was learning fast too. Jane left the teaching mostly to Catherin, interferring only when necessary. Will was grown now. He went off to work at other farms during harvesting.

Mammy Jane expected him to come home with a wife anytime now. So far he hadn't found one to his liking.

Florence still was a regular visitor bringing her three younguns. The foundation and studdings were up for her house. It went slowly, Jed doing much of the work himself. They had added stock to their farm and fared well. Jane and Florence hadn't the time to talk and visit as before, each with their families to see to.

Florence's younguns were wild compared to Jane's. And like

230

their parents, full of loud laughter, whooping and hollering like Indians.

Jane wondered at times how Florence could remain calm with so much noise around her. She joined them in their laughter and seemed to enjoy the commotion.

Jane had bought fancy wire to fence the yard, with scroll work on top. Painted white with whitewash it looked like a lace edge around the smooth green lawn.

This fall she was having the graveyard fenced with the same wire. The locust posts were in, soon the wire would be stapled on.

The tall stone at Martha's grave standing tall and snowy white could be seen for miles. Jane had Old Stoney cut it out of the quarry when he was there. She had promised Will she would have it done.

When Tom came back from the war, there it stood. "First wife of Thomas P." it read and a Bible verse that Catherin had selected, short enough to be cut into the stone.

Each spring it was whitewashed and could be seen even in the moonlight at night.

Jane had a few sheep around. Some were turned in the yard to keep the grass short and even. The graveyard would soon have its grass eaters too.

Jane had been thinking of raising a flock of sheep. They had two salable crops a year, lambs and wool. Tight fences had to be built to hold them where you wanted them. Scroll work fences couldn't be put around a sheep pasture. Jane smiled to herself, sure would be pretty though.

Jane now owned a fine buggy with two seats, the wheels painted yellow. The top had fringe all around in yellow that shimmered in the sun.

The first foals her mares had were her team. They were both bays with black mane and tails. Fat and slick they made a picture pulling the big buggy.

Jane sometimes went all the way to the county seat. She and Tom sitting high in the front with the smallest younguns in the back.

They always had to stay the night so it wasn't often that they went. Only when there was some business Jane didn't want to trust to others.

Mr. Cheniweth had done her business for her many years, for which she was beholden to him.

Mr. Hamiliton would advise her on his stopover at her house. "Don't look like you need much advice," he would say. "You are a shrewd business woman. You should have studied law, Jane. You would probably be the first woman governor of the state."

At times Jane didn't know if he was praising her or making fun.

Tom would say, "He sure is fond of you, Jane. I have to keep my eyes open or he is likely to run off with you." His eyes sparkling, a shy smile lighting his face.

"That would surely be a sight," she told him. "Old Mr. Hamiliton and me with a string of younguns tagging along behind rushing away together." They would both laugh. "You sure do paint a picture, Jane," Tom said, still laughing.

The days of Indian summer came. The haze in the "hollers" hung like a veil over the tall hills, the trees showing through like a shadow.

Harvesttime came again with the full wagons of wheat, corn, and oats. The threshing crews were hot and hungry to see to and bed down at night. They had help with the harvesting and planting now. Each year more and more ground was cleared to plant in crops.

Both cellars were filled with food. Jane now canned in big stone jars with lids sealed with sealing wax.

Peaches, tomatoes, early apples, and apple butter. They all worked from early to late, their tired backs sending them to bed before the last light of day was gone.

Jane sent for one of the Boggs's girls to help stir the apple butter and peel the apples to fill the big copper kettle.

It all seemed to come at once. The harvest and the canning and drying and gathering. Even with the best of planning it was a tiresome chore. The stone cellar shelves were full of jars. The bins waiting for potato digging and the harvest of apples. The big "cliff cellar" held the big barrels of vinegar, sauerkraut, pickles, and the stone jars of molasses. There was always plenty of food and it took plenty of work to put it by. Mammy Jane had the name of getting it done and done right. Her harvest was in and finished before most got started good.

Thanksgiving

The fires had been lit in the big twin fireplaces warming the tall ceiling rooms, sending cheery heat and light to every corner. The harvest over, Tom sat in his rocking chair by the fire, as Jane went about her work keeping the household running. Seeing that the girls did the upstairs room and that the company room across the hall was sparkling, the bed made with clean sheets and the best comforter, no telling when there would be company coming. There wasn't quite as many riding through in the winter as there were in the spring and summer.

Jane had bought a flock of twenty Southdown sheep. They were being housed in the shed where they once kept the cows. Tom didn't like the bleeting and wanted them out of sight and sound.

Harn, Anis, and Will were cutting logs to build a barn for them. Jane had selected a knoll out from the graveyard for it. Mr. Hamiliton had explained they had to be high and dry. This seemed high enough for them to Jane and the rain water could drain off in every direction from the barn. After going to look over the sight, she reckoned it would do.

The logs were piling up fast. They wouldn't be hewed, just laid up in the round, notched and fitted together snug. With the heavy wool the sheep didn't have to have an airtight structure. Later she would add a running shed shelter around the outside of the square log center.

Old Jimmy came to make clapboards again and help with the fitting of the logs when enough were hauled in.

The men used two teams and the work went quickly. The barn should be up before winter was over.

The first heavy snow came just before Thanksgiving. It fell at night soft and slowly with no wind to let the sleeping household know it was falling.

Jane looked out her upstairs window in the early light seeing a fairyland.

The orchard was a picture to behold with snow hanging to every branch, the trees etched in white, very little of their dark branches showing.

She stood and looked, taking in the beauty and stillness below her. Hearing Tom stir behind her she called, "Tom, come and look." Not knowing what to expect Tom hurried out of bed to the window. Standing beside Jane, Tom put his arm around her. They stood for sometime each lost in their own thoughts, taking in the winter beauty before them.

Jane said, "Thank the Lord, Tom, for all he has given us."

"I do, Jane, and for him giving me you. I've been happy these last years. You've given me a reason for being."

Saying nothing for the tears chocking in her throat, Jane turned and dressed for the day.

Tom slowly started pulling on his trousers, "I think I'll go rabbit hunting today," he told her.

"It will be a good day for it," she answered as she headed for the kitchen and the big breakfast that had to be put on the table. The girls would soon be in to help and the day would begin.

The feast for their Thanksgiving dinner had to be planned and the baking started.

All through the day the kitchen sent out smells of spices, pies, and baked bread. Jane left most of it to the two girls, only making a tall layered nut cake with chopped nuts covering the butter frosting on the outside. This was Tom's favorite and she always made it for him.

Catherin could make pumpkin and apple pies as good as she could. The cookies were left to Lizzie. Catherin scolded her for being so messy, spilling flour on the rug in front of the work table, and fooling around cutting fancy shapes. Lizzie still took her time and enjoyed every minute.

Jane stayed away from the kitchen after making her cake, letting the girls do what they liked.

She could hear Catherin calling Trude to peel apples. She would do one job and disappear, Catherin having to look for her again. Trude was flighty and hard to keep at anything long.

Jane wondered if she would ever settle down to housework. She liked the animals and caring for them and hated the things that made a clean smooth running house. Jane pitied the man that married her. He would have a handful.

Calvin and John had gone to tell Florence that they were invited for Thanksgiving dinner. They had come for years but Jane wanted to make sure they knew they were welcome, younguns and all.

Boards would be brought in and put on sawhorses for a table. A bench was made with a board on two blocks of wood on each side to seat the younguns. The adults sat at the main table.

Jane had Will kill two fat hens, they would be stuffed with a dressing made of biscuits, corn bread, onions, salt, pepper, sausage, chopped black walnuts, and broth from the necks and giblets cooked until tender. A big pan was baked separately with broth over the dressing. A big ham was baked, Jane taking care of making a coating of honey, sprigs of dried mint, a touch of vinegar and brown sugar made into a paste. It would bake most of the night before the big day. The fire kept low to bake it slowly for tastiness and tenderness.

Big dishes of buttered pumpkin, creamed onions, turnips, kale, cole slaw with a sweet and sour dressing, pickles, dried beans with thick broth, fried apples rich with butter and sugar, sweet potatoes, steaming bowls of fluffy mashed potatoes with dabs of melting butter on top, deviled eggs, pickled tomatoes, hot biscuits, butter, honey, and apple butter. The two tables groaned under the load. A happy hungry bunch sat down to a feast fit for a king.

Heads bowed, all quiet as Tom said grace—"Thank you, O Lord, for the many blessings you have showered on this house. For the fruitful harvest, for good friends to share and a loving wife. Amen."

They all raised their heads as the food was passed around the table, each helping themselves to the dish in front of them and passing it on.

The younguns talked and laughed and bragged how much they would eat, especially the boys.

By the time the cake and pies were served, they could hardly find room for them. Big pieces disappeared, however, and cup after cup of coffee.

Snow was softly falling as they all left the table to gather around the fireplace in the sittin' room, for some jokes and talk before Florence and Jed would take their leave. They had come by sled with the younguns nestled down in hay with quilts covering them.

Florence never tired of seeing Jane's house and the two women and the girls went across the hall to the company room where a fire burned in the grate. Florence was with child again too. Jane's would be born in early spring and Florence's a little later.

"Looks like you will have a big family, Jane," Florence remarked.

"If you count every two years till I'm too old, I would say so," Jane answered.

Florence laughed. "It took a while but mine are a little closer than that. Looks like we will neither be lonely in our old age."

The women talked on, Jane telling about the new barn being built and the flock of sheep.

Florence told of how their house would be finished for sure by summer if she had to nail every board herself, she laughed loudly. "Our cellar house is full now. There's not room enough to turn around without someone stepping out on the porch first to make space." Again her laughter rang out.

Jane smiled, enjoying her company and the chance to sit without feeling guilty.

The afternoon wore on, some of the younguns were asleep by the hearth, Florence finally getting up reluctant to leave. "It's time to go," she said. "I'll have Jed get the team ready," she crossed the hall to tell him. "Jed, time to go," she called.

"All right, woman, I'm coming."

The younguns were scurrying around finding their wraps, putting on shawls and mittens. With a flurry of good-byes, they saw them to the door and out to the sled, the girls helping tuck the smaller ones in.

"It was a wonderful day, Jane, the dinner was the best I've ever had," Florence told her. "It sure was," Jed added. "The only thing is my stomach is stretched all out of shape. Take a year to get back where it's supposed to be."

"Whoooeee"—he laughed as he flecked the mules with the lines, they were off in a flurry of snow and laughter.

Catherin and Lizzie went back to finish putting things away in the kitchen. "It's a joy cooking for such happy people," she said.

"It was a good day," Jane said. "One we will remember for a long time. You girls done real good. You'll make fine cooks and good wives."

The girls blushed with pleasure, "I don't know about Trude," Catherin said.

"I don't care, I don't want to be a wife and cook," Trude yelled as she stomped from the kitchen.

"She will change when she finds a man she likes," Jane said.

"I hope so," Catherin said with a sigh.

Sleds at Christmas

The snow kept falling after Thanksgiving, there was perhaps ten inches, covering everything, no wind blew to drift it, laying silent and white through the winter nights.

The sun came out the middle of December, melting the thick snow, filling the creek beds to overflowing. It warmed enough that the men were out in shirt sleeves, no longer needing heavy winter outer clothing.

Jane couldn't keep the boys inside. They were out throwing tree limbs and trash in the creek watching it swirl in the current as it washed out of sight. It was much too warm for this time of year. The breeze felt warm on the skin.

Jane predicted there would be sickness after such warm weather. It lasted for most of two weeks. Going to bed to warm weather they awoke to a frosty world again.

Some of the younguns had sniffles, Jane dosed them with tonic.

By Christmas there was more snow. The younguns were happiest playing out, building snowmen and the girls making angels in the snow. Laying on their back their arms spread wide they moved them back and forth to make the imprint of the angel wings.

Looking out a window Jane even saw Catherin in the snow making an angel. Catherin, comin' in, her eyes sparkling and cheeks rosy seeing Jane, knew she had been caught.

"The angel prints in the snow are so pretty," she said.

Jane turned her head and smiled to herself. She would be tempted to make one herself if she thought no one would see. She loved a snowstorm, liking to walk hearing the crunch of fresh snow under her feet. She had never told anyone in her life about such foolishness.

Christmas came with cold, windy, snowy weather. Catherin and Jane spent hours baking and cooking for another feast. Jed, Florence, and their brood was going to her family for Christmas.

There would just be Tom and Jane's family. She had bought Christmas things the time they went to the county seat. Material for shirts for the boys, which she, Catherin, and Lizzie had made, closed in the company room in the afternoons.

Jane had bought one of the newfangled sewing machines. Catherin had become quite expert at pumping the peddle and sewing on it.

Jane had bought silk in a pink with dark pink and white rose buds for Catherin, and a length of sateen for Lizzie, calico for Trude.

The girls could make them after Christmas during the long dark days of January and February.

Jane was waiting for the look on Catherin's face when she saw the silk. It was quite a treasure. Catherin was such a fine girl and loved pretty things so.

Her girls would never have to be "hired out girls" like she was. They had been raised to be respected from a good home. Jane hoped for a good husband for each of them. She had tried to implant that desire into each of them.

Christmas Day came. Anis had made sleds for the boys. The gifts were given around, Catherin had made Jane a lovely lawn handkerchief with tatted lace around the edge. Jane figured Florence had probably helped her get the material. Her face lit up, she was so pleased that she had been thought of. A big white square had been painstakingly hemmed for Tom.

The day was full of laughter. For once Catherin was speechless. Tears coming into her eyes as she held the pink silk and smoothed her hand over it.

The boys were out against the hillside with their sleds. Shooting off the steep hill by the cliff cellar, their sleds just stopped short of the creek.

Jane couldn't watch, expecting one to tumble headfirst into the icy water. She didn't say anything. They were young for such a short time.

She left them play longer than she should. They finally came in at dusk, their cheeks rosy, their noses red with cold.

She made them all wash up and change into dry clothes before supper. It had been a happy day for all. Another Christmas together in good health.

The house seemed dreary after all the hustle and bustle of the holidays were over and they went their separate ways for the night.

The house quieted as Tom and Jane went to their room up the curved oak staircase. They talked of the day and how much each had enjoyed it.

"Thank you, Jane, for being so good to my children. Catherin was so happy with her silk. You have never had anything so nice yourself." Tom put his arm around her full body.

"I don't need anything so fancy," she said as she turned back the "comforts" and they climbed into bed.

The wind whistled under the eaves as they drifted off to sleep.

Calvin

Calvin was coughing at the breakfast table. Jane didn't like the sound of his cough and told him he wasn't to go out that day.

After everyone was off to the chores, the girls cleaning the kitchen, Jane went into the sittin' room and found Calvin and his pa sitting by the fire. Calvin's cough seemed to be worse. Jane felt his head, it was dry and hot.

"Young man, you get into bed!" She turned one of the beds down in the sittin' room for him. Brought an iron that was always on the back of the cookstove and put it at his feet. She brought the cough syrup giving him two tablespoons full. He drifted off to sleep, Jane checking on him every little while.

Tom sat looking through a book of farm tools, he never tired of inspecting the pictures on each page.

Calvin coughed in his sleep and each time seemed more rasping to Jane. "I think we had better put him in our room away from the other younguns," Jane told him.

"I'll go make up the fire," Tom said, taking some wood from the box by the fireplace. They had a small woodburning stove with a flat top for heating things in their room. It was the smallest room in the house. Jane planned it purposely to hold only one bed. All the other rooms held three full-sized beds with cupboards and bureaus for clothes.

Tom and Jane's room was cozy and a perfect place for sickness away from the others.

Calvin had just turned nine before Christmas. A small addition of Tom, he was slightly built with blue eyes and Tom's sense of humor. Jane's firstborn and she loved him dearly.

The room warmed, Tom wrapped Calvin in a quilt and carried him up the stairs.

Jane had hot irons in the bed and waited to tuck him in, the bottle of cough medicine ready to give him another dose.

He was half asleep when she raised him up to give the medicine.

241

"My throat hurts," he said hoarsely. Jane could see he was burning up with fever and sent Tom for cold water to put cold packs on his burning head.

"Jane, why don't you let Catherin do that? You will wear yourself out," Tom told her.

"No. I don't want any of them around him," she answered Tom.

"Open your mouth, Calvin, stick out your tongue," she told her son. She could see his throat was red and swollen.

"Tom, change your clothes, put on another shirt and pants. Leave the ones you have on here, and don't come in here again. Anything I need, I'll call, set it in the hall."

"What is it, Jane?" Tom asked, coming toward her.

"Do as you'r' told," she said quickly.

Tom changed clothes and did as she said. He left the room and went back to sit at the fire.

Jane put cold packs on the burning brow time after time. The fever got worse as did the cough.

"Oh, my God, I hope it isn't what I think," Jane said out loud.

She called to Catherin, "Make me a mustard plaster as soon as you can." Soon she heard Catherin in the hall. When she heard her go back downstairs, Jane opened the door. She applied the plaster to the hot little chest, well up towards the throat. Calvin mumbled and tossed.

Jane gently opened his mouth, could see the tongue had started to darken. Tears streamed down her face. "Not my firstborn," she said to herself. "Oh, Lord, not that." Knowing as she prayed that it would be a miracle if Calvin had another birthday.

Going to the door she called, "Tom! Tom!" He quickly came into the downstairs hall starting up the stairs toward Jane who was leaning over the banister.

"Don't come any nearer, send for the doctor. Calvin has diphtheria." Tom clutched at the stair railing. Jane thought he was going to fall. "Oh, my God, Jane, not that."

Numbly Jane nodded her head, the tears starting again. "Hurry," she said, "send Will. Don't let anyone near here." She closed the door and went again to her little boy in the bed. He slept fitfully through the day, his fever high, Jane changing the packs time and time again, his little chest rising and falling with the effort of breathing.

Jane had heard Will leave on horseback leading a horse for the doctor to ride. It would take several hours for him to fetch Old Doc Dye. Doing what she could she worked over her son. Nothing seemed to help much. If she could keep the fever down that would help.

By late afternoon she was walking from window to bed looking first at the restless little body on the bed and then out down the road for a sight of the doctor.

Calvin's breathing got worse toward evening. Still the doctor didn't come. It was pitch-dark by the time Jane heard the horses at the barn.

Opening the door she heard Tom and the doctor talking as the old doctor removed his great coat. Catherin brought a hot cup of coffee with a slug of whiskey. The old doctor gratefully drank it as he held his hands and feet to the open fire to warm.

"I'm most frozen," he told them. "I'll go up as soon as I'm limber enough." Jane soon heard his tired feet on the stairs. She opened the door as he reached it and ushered him inside.

"How is he?" he asked Jane. He opened his satchel and adjusted his glasses, moved toward the bed.

"He is bad, doctor, seems his breathing is worse. His throat and tongue is black," she told him.

"Oh, Lord, diphtheria." Listening to his breathing with his stethoscope, his hand on the boy's pulse.

Jane watched, hoping for a word of encouragement.

Taking the stethoscope from his ears, leaving it dangling around his neck, he placed a wooden paddle in Calvin's mouth opening it as much as he could to see inside. Jane held a lamp high above the bed for him to see.

"It's diphtheria all right, Jane. There's no question about it. It's almost always fatal. I'll do what I can. Just hope none of the rest catch it."

"I've kept them away," Jane said. "They were all at breakfast together but not since."

Taking some medicine from his bag and a long swab he asked Jane to hold the boy's head while he swabbed the throat. "Sometimes we can break the blisters and they can breathe easier," he explained.

As the doctor ran the swab down again and again, the little body went limp in Jane's arms.

"He has fainted," the doctor said. "It's just as well. He will be relaxed and maybe the air passages will open."

243

"What can I do, doctor?" Jane implored, tears in her eyes.

"You've done all you can do. We just have to wait and hope and pray."

Jane heard Catherin call, "Mammy Jane, I've brought you both a plate of supper."

"Alright Catherin, set it in the hall," Jane cleared a place on the bureau and set the rockin' chair for the doctor by the window and went to fetch the supper.

The old doctor sank gratefully in the chair, ate as though he was starved. "I just finished delivering a baby up Walnut Creek. Your boy met me coming back, didn't have anything since breakfast, sure tastes good. You must have a good cook."

"Yes," Jane answered. "Catherin is a fine cook." Cups rattled outside in the hall as Catherin brought a pot of coffee.

Jane opened the door and sat the coffee pot on the stove till the doctor was ready for a cup.

Jane tried to eat, having to force the food down.

The doctor looking her over said, "I'm not sure you should be here, Jane. Looks like you'r' near your time."

"I know. I've a month yet and I don't want the girls exposed to this."

Calvin tossed and turned, throwing the covers off, mumbled in a hoarse voice, once even laughed. His small face screwed up to resemble a smile.

Jane covered him, changing the cold compresses, holding his hot little hand in hers.

The doctor listened to his breathing, shook his head and turned back to his chair. "We just have to wait. It's always worse in the night it seems."

Jane threw a shawl over the old doctor as he dozed in the chair by the window. She walked the floor silently praying and doing what she could for the sick child. Nothing seemed to help. She sat on, holding his hand, trying to help him breathe.

Toward morning he seemed easier, Jane thought. His little head wasn't quite so hot to her hand as she changed the cloth.

Dawn was breaking when the doctor roused himself and examined the boy again.

"I think he is some better. He doesn't seem quite so hot," Jane told him.

"Don't get your hopes up, Jane. His throat is almost closed." The doctor shook his head.

All through that day and the next night, the doctor and Jane kept watch. Toward morning of the second night, Calvin went into convulsions. His small body arching and jerking like the devil himself had hold of him.

The doctor tried to swab his throat again. Blood came out on the swab. The child lay limp and still exhausted from the convulsions. His eyes closed in his waxy-looking face. They could hear his rasping breath on the floor below at daybreak.

Hearing someone, Jane went out on the landing. It was Tom, his face turned up to her's from below.

Sobbing, her hands held over her face, she told him. "Oh, Tom, we are going to lose him. There is nothing we can do." Jane shook, the sobs tearing deep inside her. "Oh, Tom, our first baby."

Tom came up the stairway and took her in his arms. "Don't cry so, Jane. You'll hurt yourself. Don't cry, you did all you could." Tears were streaming down Tom's face as he held her close.

Jane turned from him, thoughts of the others causing her to control herself and her sorrow. "Go back, Tom, wash your hands. Don't come up again. There is too much danger to the other younguns." Going back to the sick room, seeing the pale face of her son, the breathing grew more shallow. Jane knew he was sinking fast and that there would be little hope for her boy as she sat by his side stroking his brow, his hot limp hand in hers.

A plate of ham and eggs and hot biscuits was brought for the doctor. He went to the hall to get it, leaving the coffee pot outside to be filled again.

Jane told him not to bring her anything. She could not swallow with the lump that remained in her throat.

The day wore on, Jane at the bedside and the old doctor near. As the pale sun sank behind the hills sending the shadows across the room a long rasping sigh came from Calvin's lips. His fingers grasped Jane's, his blue eyes opened, looked at his mother and closed never to see the light of day again. Another breathless sigh and the little body lay limp, all life gone from it.

A sob escaped Jane as her head fell forward on the bed. Burying her face in the covers, long ragged sobs tore through her.

The old doctor came to the bed and raised Jane up, wrapped his arms around her, patted her on the back. "There Jane, you will hurt yourself. You mustn't question the ways of the Lord." Tears ran down his weathered face as he held the mother of the dead child in her sorrow.

He opened the sick room door, seeing faces lining the hallway below. Leaning over the banister he told them, "Young Calvin is gone."

Lizzie crumpled to the floor in a dead faint. Her father gathered her in his arms and took her to the sittin' room, laid her on the bed that had been hung out and aired.

Catherin's sobbing could be heard as she ministered to her sister.

Jane sat at the window in the rocking chair, her sorrow under control. There were things that had to be done for Calvin yet.

The doctor stood outside on the portico in the fresh winter air. Jane finally joined him, "I know you did all you could, doctor, we're beholden to you."

"There's not much can be done in cases like these," he told her. "Keep a close watch on the rest, if they show the slightest symptoms, put them by themselves."

Jane heard sawing in the shophouse. She knew Anis was making a coffin by lantern light.

Jane went back to the room. Took the kettle of water and washed Calvin. Had his best clothes brought and dressed him for the last time. Straightened the bed and laid him on top of the covers, just a sheet covering his lifeless body.

"Air out the room, Jane, and don't let anyone in for a few days. The bedding should be boiled and if you have sulphur, burn some in here, it sometimes helps." The tired doctor told them he would leave now. The horses were brought around to the front so he wouldn't go through the house where the family was. He asked about Lizzie, she had come to quickly and was resting now.

Catherin wouldn't be consoled and hid out in the kitchen alone with her sorrow.

The doctor took his leave in the sadness that surrounded the big house. Harn would ride home with him and bring back the horse.

Jane took clean clothes from the hall cupboard and changed, leaving the ones she had worn inside the death room. The windows were wide open. The damper turned on the stove so the fire would die out. Jane closed the door and went wearily down the stairs.

"Send Will to me," Jane told Catherin. He was in the shop-house where the men were building the coffin.

When Will came, Jane sent him to the store to get batting and white material for the casket. "Mr. Cheniweth will know what is needed. We have clothes, just things for the coffin. He will be closed but go to his house and see if the preacher can come. Late tomorrow I think. I'll send John to tell Jed. He will help dig the grave at daybreak. Bring the things as soon as possible so the coffin can be finished tonight. The doctor says it can be opened at the grave out in the air. Calvin will have to be left alone till then. I'll place him in the coffin when the time comes. We don't want to danger the younguns."

Will hurried off to saddle his horse. The sound of hammering continued through the night as the coffin and rough box was made.

Jane saw that all the younguns went to bed, and that none had a sore throat.

Catherin with red swollen eyes finished with the house and went to her room.

Jane made Tom go to bed in the sittin' room. Telling him, "You have to be up early to see to the grave."

Jane took a box of soda and fresh water, wet cloths, and put over Calvin's face. It was to keep the body from turning before the funeral. Jane would have to change them herself, not wanting anyone else exposed. She knew Florence would come but sent word for her not to chance it. They could come for the funeral but not to bring her younguns to the house.

The room was icy cold where Calvin laid, his little hands crossed on his chest.

Jane lay down by Tom. Exhausted from the ordeal, she still went up the stairs every hour to change the cloths. Finally towards daybreak, she fell into a restless sleep.

247

The Burying

Catherin slept little. She went to bed with the other girls. She tossed and turned, finally got up to sit by the window most of the night. She was heartbroken over Calvin. She had mothered him and had taken care of him as much as Jane. She loved him so and felt as though part of her was gone.

Before day broke, she went to the kitchen and started the fire. Will came in, told her that the casket was finished and that they were bringing it to the kitchen for her to line.

The little new wooden box was brought in. Boxes of tacks and material, a big bundle of cotton batting soft and white to line the inside.

With tears in her eyes, Catherin started her painful task. Will stayed to help. They did the inside first, smoothing the batting in and covering it with the material and tacking it in place. Then the outside was done. Lace had been sent to go around the edge of the box to finish it off. Catherin soon finished.

Will put the hinges for the lid and the hardware outside, a handle of ornate hardware went on each side and on each end to carry it by.

Will took the box upstairs. Jane was there standing looking out at the orchard, her face pale and tired, dark circles rimmed her eyes.

"Leave it, Will. I can manage. I don't want any of you exposed." Each time Jane went into the room, she put on a long robe over her clothing for some protection and removed it on coming out again.

Catherine hurried to get breakfast ready. The men were ready to start on the grave. Jed came as the tired men got up from the table. They got their tools and went on the hill. The ground was frozen for a couple of inches but not so badly that they couldn't dig. Tom measured off the grave by the side of the baby girl that had died two days before his first wife.

248

Jane could hear the spades and tools hitting rock as the men dug, each sound weighing heavy on her heart.

Will had located the preacher and he would be there at three o'clock for the burying.

Jane had pulled two chairs together and placed the little white box on them, gently lifting Calvin for the last time, she placed him in his coffin. He was such a pretty little boy and had always been so loving and good. Jane's tears fell gently as she finished her sad task.

"Good-bye, little son, little firstborn, may God watch over you now and keep you happy." Silent sobs shook her as she left the room.

The grave was finished by noon. The rough box was carried on the hill ready to receive the little coffin. Boards stood by to cover over the rough box.

Catherin had gathered a big bunch of winter fern and tied them with a pink hair ribbon to lay on the coffin. All was in readiness now. They would have dinner, the men washed up and lay down for a couple of hours before the preacher came. They had been up all night working on the coffin and then the digging of the grave.

Jed went home. Said he and Florence would come back for the burying.

The preacher arrived just before three o'clock. Mr. Cheniweth arrived, riding along with him. The men went up the stairs to fetch the little coffin, going out the front door so as not to carry it through the house.

The younguns all waited with Catherin and Lizzie in the kitchen. Their wraps on, ready to go on that slow journey to the cemetery.

The preacher talked to Catherin, she had written down the birthday and name and other information he needed.

Bible in hand, he stood behind the casket, waiting for Tom and Jane. They came and stood behind him. The younguns lining up two together for the procession to the hilltop grave.

The men in front carried the little white coffin gently as the saddened mother and father, brothers and sisters followed.

Jed and Florence were already up at the grave waiting. Florence had brought a song book which she and Mr. Cheniweth were looking through to find a selection to sing.

The coffin was set on top of the rough box. The lid was opened for the last look at the dear little face.

Florence started the song. Catherin and Lizzie joined them to

249

sing with them. Mr. Cheniweth and Jed sang well, their voices booming out, Catherin's sweet voice could be heard carrying the melody.

All the younguns stood solemnly looking at their little brother. Trude holding three-year old Etta in her arms.

Sobs shook Tom, Jane's eyes were dry as she put her arm around him. She would have to be strong. There were others to think of and watch over. She could do no more for her firstborn.

The preacher's voice shook as he read the Twenty-third Psalm. Jane knew it by heart having had Catherin read it to her many times. It was comforting. Maybe that was why her mother-in-law marked it for her when she got her first Bible.

"Though I walk through the valley of the shadow of death, I shall fear no evil." The preacher's voice came clear on the winter air. The wind blew riffling the lace on the little coffin, moving the hair on Calvin's forehead as Jane looked. For a moment her heart stopped with the motion of it.

The little coffin was put in the rough box and lowered into the ground. The bunch of ferns laid to the side to put over the bare clay once it was shoveled into the grave.

The first clods hit the box with a hollow sound. Jane's head bowed and her shoulders shook in silent sobs. Florence came to Jane putting her strong arms around her. All the younguns were crying now.

"Oh, Jane, I'm so sorry. 'The Lord giveth and the Lord taketh away.' We don't always understand but he has a reason."

The preacher, his job finished, shook Tom's hand, "Have faith Tom, God has a reason for all things. We mustn't question him."

They all went back down the hill. The men finished rounding out the little grave. The late shadows were falling and flurries of snow blew around their faces.

"Come, have some hot coffee and get warm," Jane invited Mr. Cheniweth and the preacher. Florence and Catherin hurried ahead to put the big pot on.

Jane stopped halfway down the hill and looked at the big, beautiful house, smoke curling from the chimneys on both ends of the snowy structure.

The kitchen stove sent up blue puffs of smoke and she knew the girls were building up the fire to make coffee.

It's been a happy house, she thought to herself. This is the first sadness to touch my dream.

No doubt there will be much more. Maybe worse ones but today there could be nothing worse. Leaving my baby in the cold, cold ground. Lord, keep him in your arms safe from pain and sorrow, Jane said the silent prayer as they went on to the big house where life must go on.

Namesake

Everyone left, leaving the family alone. Jane had eaten little the past two days and had no sleep. The weariness seemed to drag at her, pulling her to the nearest chair.

"Mammy Jane, you must rest; come, I'll put you to bed. Lizzie and I can take over the kitchen," Catherin pleaded with Jane.

Mammy Jane followed her obediently as a child as she turned the big bed down in the sittin' room. Helping her off with her clothes and holding the big flannel nightgown for her to put her arms through the sleeves. Jane sat on the side of the bed while Catherin unbuttoned the many buttons on her shoes. Lifting her legs up into bed, and covering her.

"I'll bring you a tonic," Catherin told her. Soon she was back with honey whiskey and hot water, helping Jane to a sitting position, held the cup to her lips.

Catherin wrapped an iron and put it at Jane's feet.

Jane's head felt peculiar and she was too weak to move it seemed as Catherin administered to her.

Catherin stood looking at her, tears running down her face. There was a limit to even Mammy Jane's strength. The even breathing told her that Jane was finally asleep. She had added a good portion of whiskey to the tonic and Jane would sleep through the night. If she didn't rest she might lose the baby she was carrying. She could never stand the loss of two in such a short time.

Catherin went back to the kitchen to see that all were fed and that the younguns were put to bed. Thank heavens, Jane had taught her to be strong.

Her pa was out walking around going to the barn pretending to check on this and on that, knowing full well that the other men had taken care of everything.

Looking out the kitchen window, she saw him standing looking at the new mound of clay on the hill. Her heart ached for him, tears burned her eyes as she went about her work.

As dark fell, they all went to their separate beds. Tom got quietly in beside Jane, careful not to awaken her. Her face was pale and drawn-looking even in sleep.

Jane got up with the first cock's crow, made the fire up on the hearth, sat for awhile watching the flames sending sparks and smoke up the chimney.

Taking a shovelful of coals to the kitchen, she started the fire that Catherin had laid the night before. As she bent down she could tell the baby had dropped sometime in the night. It would be born soon, a death, a birth, how many times she had said just that. Going to the kitchen window she looked at the hills and the new clay that now covered little Calvin. Her heart ached for her lost child. None could ever take the place of a firstborn. Life went on, those left had to wait their turn to travel the dark valley.

She could hear Catherin starting the fire in the company room across the hall. It would have to be readied for the birthin'. She wouldn't dare go back to her own bed before it was washed and aired and sulphur burned. She had sulphur candles that she burned in the chicken house to kill the lice in the spring. Tom could light one in the room today, rugs put at the door so none of the fumes came into the other parts of the house.

Thank heavens the baby things were in a bureau in the downstairs hallway.

The low back pains started late in the afternoon. One just once in a while, Jane knew she would have another trying night.

When Will came in for dinner she told him to take the horses and fetch Aunt Mandy, that there was no rush but she had better come spend the night.

It was cold and a few snow flurries blew on the wind. The ground was frozen enough to keep the mud down.

Jane went about her work as usual. With the help of the girls there wasn't a lot for her to do only see that the younguns were warm enough and well. She lined them all up that night and looked at all their throats and felt their heads, then sent them off to bed, they all seemed alright.

Aunt Mandy had come just before supper. She was in by the fire talking to Tom. A bed was readied for her.

Jane's pains were closer but they both knew there wouldn't be much action till close to daybreak. They could both try to sleep some before then. It was never as bad as the first. This would make five for Jane. She knew all the symptoms now and what to expect.

Jane slept off and on. Aunt Mandy slept soundly across the room. Toward morning Jane got up and made a fire in the kitchen. The kettle full of water was already on. Jane put a pot of coffee to boil.

Her pains were closer. She would move into the company room for the birthing, so as to be away from the main household traffic.

A soft snow was falling. She washed herself and made up the fire in the company room, got the bed ready with the extra padding and such. Checked the chamber pot, brought in the baby things, and the cradle sat empty by the hearth waiting for its occupant.

Jane sat alone at the big table drinking a cup of the scalding coffee. A searing pain hit her low down making her gasp. She had been "showing" for some time. It was time she got into bed for the birth.

Going through to the company room she saw that Aunt Mandy was awake.

"Good morning, Jane. How are you this morning?" she asked.

"It's about time. I'm going to bed now. There's coffee in the kitchen." She went on to prepare herself for the ordeal ahead.

Catherin was coming downstairs, looked anxiously at Jane. "Mammy Jane, are you alright?" she asked.

Jane nodded.

Catherin followed her and helped her into bed and to get settled. "Why didn't you call me? I would have gotten things ready."

"I need something to keep my mind off this," she said as another pain came long and hard.

Aunt Mandy came in, a coffee cup balanced in her hand. Watching Jane's face she knew the pains were in earnest now. She examined Jane and told her "It won't be too long now."

The curse of Eve climbed to its intensity and came to an end.

Around nine o'clock a baby girl was born. Florence came in just in time to wash and clothe the baby.

"I'm naming this one for my friend. I'll call her Florence," Jane said, as her eyelids became heavy with sleep.

Jane slept as the baby was laid sweet smelling into the cradle by the fire.

254

Florence was pleased at Jane naming the baby for her. The two women went into the kitchen for a late breakfast and to wait for Jane to rest after her ordeal.

Catherin tiptoed into the room to see the tiny baby, not being able to wait another minute.

The women sat talking still with their coffee cups as Catherin reentered the kitchen. "Oh! she is beautiful. Such a perfect little face, I love her already."

Aunt Mandy commented, "Jane always has such pretty babies and they are always healthy, she didn't have too bad a time. I was worried about complications with all she has been through. Maybe this will help her get over her loss."

"She is a fine mother and a strong woman," Florence added. "I never had a better friend."

Aunt Mandy went to check on her charge and then would be on her way back home.

"I'll go now, too," Florence said, "tell Jane I'll be up again soon."

First Lambs

Jane was up in record time after the birth of little Florence.

The men worked steadily on the sheep barn, Jed came to help and Jane urged them on. The logs rose steadily and soon the roof was being put in place. It would be finished for the lambing.

The weather was on-again, off-again with no really bad storms while the work went on.

The younguns would all gather and walk to the graveyard on Sunday to stand silently by the new mound. Jane couldn't bring herself to go to look at the earth covering her lost child. She centered all her attention on the ones left to her.

Catherin still grieved but having the new baby to care for seemed to fill the loss.

The day came when the new barn was finished and the sheep were moved to their new quarters from the shed.

Hay was hauled to fill the loft and mangers and to bed the sheep.

All the men, even Tom, went one day to help Jed in return for his work. A lot could be done with so many working.

When they came home Tom said they had put on most of the siding, the roof and studding was already done and the rough floor in. It was beginning to look like a house now. They would help a couple of days and Jed could do the finishing.

"Old Jed sure did appreciate all we done to help," Harn said. "He can finish one room at a time no matter what the weather now."

Their chimney had been built last summer so they wouldn't have to wait for that.

Florence was due anytime now. Jane had told her to send her younguns up by Jed and leave them a couple of days. So Jane expected them any day now.

The sheep seemed content with their new housing. Tom was glad not to have to listen to them bleat anymore.

Anis said that lambing would start in about a week. The weather suddenly turned bitter cold with wind blowing little round balls of snow that stung when it hit a bare spot of skin. Everything was closed up tight against the wind. It blew for a couple of days then snow came down softly to cover everything in sight.

Jed came with the sled full of younguns. Most of them had "snotty noses" which Jane couldn't stand. Laughing and whooping as usual. There were three boys and one girl. Jane sent the boys to the cellar house, she wouldn't have to listen to them. Maybe they could play checkers till she could feed them and put them to bed for the night.

They had been looking forward to a stay in the big house when their ma was having the new baby. Catherin and Lizzie saw to them and tried to keep them away from Mammy Jane and their pa.

They stayed three nights. There were popcorn balls made and Trude got them all working at a "taffy pull." Jane could hear the commotion in the kitchen. The younguns could be heard for miles laughing and talking. The time finally passed and Jed came for them.

"It's the best time we ever had," they yelled as they were bundled off in the sled. Jed laughed. "Hope they weren't too much trouble, Jane."

"Oh, no, not at all. Tell Florence I will be down to see her and her new baby when this spell breaks."

The house with its normal noises seemed quiet after the younguns left.

Harn went up on the hill late in the afternoon to see to the sheep. Came back with a big smile. "We have two little lambs. The prettiest little black faced things you ever did see."

The younguns were all ready to go tearing up the hill to see them if Jane had let them.

"No one is to go around them while they are lambing. They are unsettled enough. You can see them in a few days. In fact we may have to feed some on a bottle and then you will soon get enough of them," she told all the younguns.

"So far the mothers have owned them but you never know when one won't own its lamb," Anis told them.

"Why don't she own them when they belong to her?" the younguns wanted to know.

"Well, I don't rightly know. Maybe it don't smell good to the mother or maybe she thinks it's ugly. Or could be that the mother is just ornery and don't want a baby hanging after her," Anis watched to see how the younguns took to that.

"Why don't she want to be a mother when she has a baby?" Trude asked.

"Maybe she is like you, Trude, and don't want the responsibility," Catherin said.

"Fiddlesticks, that's not so," Trude came back.

"Watch your language, young lady," Tom told her.

The lambing went on with or without the approval of Trude or the new mothers. And sure enough out of twenty ewes, there were sixteen lambs and one mother wouldn't claim hers. Anis and Harn brought it to the house where a suck bottle was rigged out for it. The younguns never tired of petting it and feeding it.

"That lamb has to be put in the shed, I don't want it in the house," Jane told them.

"You better let them keep it in a few days, Jane. It won't live outside alone in this weather," Tom told her.

So a box was made and it was let stay where it was warm. It followed the younguns around like a kitten and was a pretty little thing, Jane had to admit.

The winter finally wore itself out and the bright sunny days of April came with plowing and planting.

Jane rode down to see Florence and her new baby. Her kitchen was finished and she had moved into it. They still slept in the cellar house but had more room now that the table and cookstove was out. Her sittin' room would soon be done and they could sleep there.

"I just couldn't have spent another winter in there so crowded up," Florence said.

"You have a nice home and it will be finished before long," Jane commented.

"I sure hope so. Looks like we will have it filled with younguns by the time it's done," Florence laughed.

It was nice but nothing like the Jarvis house. There wasn't another like it anywhere near.

Tom was out from early dawn with the men plowing and planting more and more each year. They were finished in time for Anis and Will to hire out with other farmers. Harn wasn't able to go away to work anymore. It was enough what he did at home. His

258

rheumatism got worse each year and he limped more. He was a good man and seemed content with Jane's family. It had been a blessing that he came to her during the time Tom was in the war. The farm had taken on a different look since then.

White sheep and lambs roamed the hills. There were new colts and little calves running and kicking up their heels in the pasture fields.

The whole farm was surrounded with fences now to hold the animals. The country had changed too since the war, more people were moving in. A church was being built over on White Oak and there was talk of a school next year. Jane's younguns wouldn't have far to go then and they could go to church some in good weather.

Jane could go whenever she wanted with her fine team of mares and big buggy. Secretly she still would rather ride horseback.

Tom was proud of his big house and healthy children. They had done well and he never forgot to tell Jane that most of it was her planning and work while he was gone.

Time flew for the busy household, seemed planting was barely over when canning of the harvest started.

Everyone had a job to do down to the smallest child who could pick up wood chips and fill baskets for kindling. Jane saw that they all learned to work early in life and got pleasure from a job well done.

The Girls' Journey

That fall Tom drove a bunch of hogs and lambs to Charleston to market, the men went to help, all but Harn. He didn't go, not being up to walking so far. There was Tom, Will, John, and Anis. The girls wanted to visit their grandmother and grandfather. Tom thought it would be alright for them, that is Lizzie and Catherin, to go in the buggy. Catherin could manage Jane's team without any trouble. They could all ride back together and bring whatever they wanted to bring in the buggy.

The girls were so excited, washing and starching their dresses till they could stand up without being in them. Catherin's pink silk would be at its best in her grandmother's house. They planned and packed.

Trude stomped around and pouted because she wasn't allowed to go along.

A big basket of food was fixed to take with them. They could eat their first meals from it. This would be such an adventure for the two girls. Jane was glad they could go in style in the big comfortable buggy.

Catherin was nineteen now and pretty as a picture. She had little chance to meet an eligible man. She did know some that she had gone to school with but none she seemed interested in.

Jane knew it was time she was settled but hated to lose her, she had become so dependent on her to help run the household.

Little Florence cried and cried when she saw Catherin getting ready to leave.

The time finally arrived. The girls had outerwear coat-like garments over their clothes to keep some of the dust off. They were dressed in starched dresses with bonnets to match, smelling of soap and water, their hair clean and shining in the sun. They sat tall and lady-like in the buggy with Catherin holding the lines.

Jane was proud of her girls and also of the animals going off to market. They were off in a flurry of good-byes. Florence had been put down for a nap by Catherin. Jane thanked heaven for that, otherwise she would have been screaming after her.

Trude wouldn't come outside to see them off. Still pouting because she wasn't let go too. Jane meant to take some of the "muleness" out of her in the days ahead. She hadn't had to toe-the-mark like the other two girls. Jane had been lenient with her, she meant to correct that.

They all went about their chores. Jane put Trude to filling the big wash kettle, told her that she wanted a wash on the line by noon.

"I can't wash, I don't know how," Trude told her, tossing her head.

"Then, young lady, it's time you learned. So get busy. Fill the kettle and get the water hot. I'll gather the clothes together."

"Catherin can wash when she gets back from her fancy trip," Trude made bold to tell Mammy Jane. She made the mistake of being in reach of Jane when she said it. Jane's hand went flying, landing a loud smack on Trude's cheek.

"Don't you sass me, young lady, and get busy now. I'll take no nonsense from you. You've been 'spoild' by your sisters. They aren't here to cover up for you. Now get busy and do as you're told."

Trude turned her back snubbing and crying as she built up the fire.

Jane went about her work gathering clothes that had been changed for the trip, keeping an eye on Trude all the while. She would have to learn to take her place in the household. Catherin might meet someone anytime and go off to her own home.

Jane's own child Minerva was a good worker, always wiping and cleaning. She loved shining the windows till you didn't know there was glass in the windowpanes. She was a pretty little thing with blue eyes and curly hair. All her younguns had curly hair like hers.

Trude finally got the tub ready for the first wash. Jane filled it with diapers and white underclothing and put Trude to scrubbing. She watched her for a few minutes as she awkwardly scrubbed with her knuckles.

"Let me show you, Trude, you hold your clothes so and rub with the ball of your hand or you will have blisters in a minute on your knuckles."

Trude watched and took the clothes like Jane had instructed.

261

"There is pleasure in hanging clean fresh clothes on the line, Trude. There is pleasure in a job well done anytime. I hope you learn to find that pleasure. If you don't, your life will be filled with woe," Jane gently told her.

Having the two older girls gone, Jane and Trude would have to step to keep ahead of the work. There wouldn't be so many to cook for but the same amount of chores had to be done.

Jane finished in the kitchen and went to check on Trude. She had most of the white things on to boil.

"You're doing fine," Jane told her, "when you finish that tub, you can put this pile in. I've sorted them for you. Then this pile is last." She pointed to the dirtiest work pants and socks by the side.

Trude didn't answer but kept on scrubbing as Mammy Jane went about what had to be done.

By noon Trude had the first batch ready to hang. Jane went out, "You hang that basketful, Trude, I'll wash awhile." Soon the snowy clothes were flapping in the breeze. Jane could see Trude arranging them on the line all the diapers together. The little shirts next all in a row.

She is learning, Jane said to herself. Jane didn't miss seeing Trude standing back surveying her work before coming back to the wash tub. Jane let her take over again. She would be a tired little girl by the end of the day. And maybe not such a stubborn one.

The day was a busy one for them all. Harn kept the boys busy splitting wood and stacking it for winter. The little ones loaded their little sleds with wood and hauled it to stack beside the cellar house for winter. Nathan especially liked doing this.

Jane had made a big pot of apple dumplings for supper. The smell of cinnamon and brown sugar filled the kitchen.

Trude finished the wash late in the afternoon. The white things were dry and could be brought in. The colored would have to remain on the line overnight.

There was one tired little girl who came in to supper. She didn't do any complaining, only ate in silence.

"Your wash looks nice, Trude," Jane told her.

Still Trude said nothing, getting up from the table, she started stacking the dishes.

"You go bring in your white clothes, Trude, take the big basket and fold them as you take them from the line. The diapers won't

262

have to be ironed if folded right away. That's the best part of washing, taking in the sweet smelling clothes."

Jane started doing the dishes. Glancing out the window, she saw Trude burying her face in the fresh dried clothes. Jane smiled, maybe she would find pleasure in doing the wash yet.

The days flew by and it was time for the girls to come home. A week and a half went by before they heard the sound of wheels on the road, and rushing outside they were home.

Catherin and Lizzie hugged everyone talking a mile a minute. The buggy was piled high with packages of all shapes and kinds. Everyone had an armful to carry into the house. Presents were bought for everyone.

A beautiful black hat with a large feather plume on one side and a veil to tie it down with came out of a fancy box that was handed to Jane.

"They don't wear bonnets in the city, they wear lovely hats," Catherin explained. "Please try it on, Mammy Jane. I know it will look lovely on you."

Jane went to the bureau mirror and put the hat on over her dust cap that she always wore.

"Oh, no. Not like that," Catherin said, real shock in her voice. "Let me help. Take your dust cap off, please." Jane reluctantly removed the cap. Catherin adjusted the hat to the side and tied the veil under the chin. "Oh, my! you look grand," Catherin told her.

Jane turned to look at herself in the glass and didn't recognize the grand-looking lady she saw looking out at her.

"You do look grand, Jane," Tom told her. "No more bonnets, you must wear hats, they look well on you."

"I feel foolish," Jane told them.

The attention was turned from Jane and other presents were unwrapped and admired. They were mostly things that none of them had ever seen before, including Jane. A small music box for Trude which seemed to enchant her. A small woolly lamb for Florence that she proceeded to eat. Everyone was happy with the lovely things. Nicer than any Christmas ever was. There was excitement and talk about all they had done.

"There was a lovely party," Lizzie said. "Several young ladies and men, Catherin had a beau."

Catherin blushed scarlet, "Hush, Lizzie, he was just a nice man." Jane's heart skipped a beat, "Tell us about him."

Tom listened, his eyes sparkling. As no one wanted to answer Jane, he did. "He is a very nice businessman, quite a bit older than Catherin. He seemed taken with her. Gave her lots of attention. The family says he is well-to-do and has a nice house in town."

Catherin was still blushing.

"How old?" Jane demanded.

"Oh, I'll say close to thirty," Tom answered.

"That's an old man," from Trude.

"He is not an old man," Catherin came to his defense. "In fact he is quite distinguished looking. Tall and graceful."

"She probably won't see him again," Jane said, "so let's forget about it. Go change your clothes, girls, you are home and there's work to do."

Jane wanted to put an end to the teasing of Catherin. She would talk to Tom about the man and see just how serious it was.

They were all tired and went to their room soon after supper.

Jane and Tom had their talk that night about Catherin's beau.

"He is a fine man and I could tell how he felt about Catherin. She could do a lot worse. She would be around all the nice things she likes so," Tom told her.

"He's too old for her and she would go so far away we would never see her. I don't like it," Jane said.

Tom smiled, "How often does your mother see you? And I'm older and already had a family when you married me. It worked out."

Tom's arms were around Jane, his hands in her lovely hair. "I missed you. Seems I've been gone a month. I can't sleep when I'm away from you," he told her.

Their lovemaking was long and satisfying that night. They fell asleep in each other's arms, the question of Catherin and her beau not settled.

The Beau

The girls were up early. Catherin had breakfast started when Jane arrived in the kitchen. They were all still chattering about the many things they saw and did.

"Oh, it was such a lovely time," Catherin said to Jane. "I thank you and pa for letting us go."

"The stores are all so grand, with upstairs and downstairs full of things I have only read about. Mammy Jane, you would love the stores, you must go sometime. Grandma says you are very observing and know style instinctively, and that you soon would like the things they have there."

Jane listened and watched and said nothing.

The girls pitched in and soon the big house was spotless and running smoothly again. Jane hadn't realized just how much she had missed their help till she had them back home.

Most of the canning was done. Jane still would make another kettle of apple butter for the winter and more honey had to be gathered from the bees that Tom now raised, and in time for them to make it back before frost.

Everyone started peeling apples, soon the big copper kettle sent out the wonderful fragrance of newly cooked apple butter. Before the day was through there were fifteen gallons of rich red apple butter to add to the cellar shelves.

The apples and potatoes were to be gathered soon. That and pumpkins were always last of the harvest.

Rain set in a couple of days after the apple butter making. It went on for most a week. The wash piled up, no place to do it but the kitchen and hang it on the porches.

We have to have a place to do the wash, Jane decided, instead of in the kitchen. A body can't get anything else done when there are tubs of steaming clothes all over the place. We will build a house! A washhouse right across the run, that way it will be close to the spring water and will make a fine place to wash. All day

Jane thought about the washhouse. In the afternoon she threw a shawl over her head to go and look at where it would be.

Catherin saw her from the window and wondered what she was stepping off now. She would go twenty steps or so turn and go another ten and look this way and that. Whatever could she be doing, Catherin wondered, as she worked baking bread in the kitchen.

Soon Jane came in shaking the rain from her shawl and hanging it behind the door. "Well, I've decided. It's time we had a washhouse here. I'm tired of wash day cluttering up the kitchen so a body don't know if they are coming or going. It will be built across over there. Have a fireplace in one end to heat water in winter and be warm to wash in, with lines to hang up clothes inside. We will use the same lines outside in summer. We can have an extra bed for work hands when needed over there too," Jane told Catherin.

"That sounds very nice. It would be better to have a washhouse. I hate getting the kitchen so cluttered myself," Catherin answered.

"We will start the men on it right away. Give them something to do this fall and keep them from under feet."

At noontime when the men came in from the barns and whatever they had been doing, Jane brought up the building of the washhouse.

"When you've a mind you can cut and bring in the trees for a foundation. There are enough scrap cut stones around for the corner stones. There is enough younguns to fetch field stones to build three fireplaces." They all listened to Jane till she had finished her planning and telling.

Tom spoke up. "I agree, Jane, you women do need a place to wash. I myself hate the mess wash day makes in the house and take myself as far away as possible at that time."

"I've noticed," Jane said as she looked at Tom with a grin.

"I'll see to it, Jane, you just tell me how you want it and we will get at it." Tom went off up the "holler" right after dinner, Jane knew to select the trees to be cut for the foundation. He had asked her how big she wanted the cabin. "Somewhere around twenty-six feet by thirty-six feet would be big enough," she reckoned.

The fall rain kept drizzling for several days. The logs were cut regardless of the weather and snaked in to be hewed and set in place.

The younguns took their sleds, Anis had made a wooden box on them to haul rocks to pound in the end holes where the corner stones would be set to give a solid foundation.

Jane was happiest when she was getting things done.

Anis said there were plenty of dry clapboards for the roof.

They would have to have some two by fours. He would hitch up the team and go to the mill tomorrow and have them ready to put in place as soon as the foundation was laid.

It was scarcely daybreak when Anis went off to fetch the studding. If there were no problems he should be back by noon.

Jane sent a couple of baskets of eggs to the store and told him what she needed. They were just finishing the noon meal when the wagon came with its heavy load of new cut beams. Anis brought the basket to the door and called for Catherin. She went to get the packages and basket.

Anis handed her a white square. A letter! Jane following to help asked, "What's that?"

Catherin took the letter, her face turning scarlet then white. Jane, thinking she might 'swoon', took her arm. "You had better sit till you catch your breath."

"What is it? What is it?" The girls were all gathering around as Catherin sank into a chair, the letter in her hand.

"It's a letter from Charles from the Capitol." Again she blushed scarlet.

"Well, well," Tom said as he to came over to look. "Seems he hasn't forgotten you. It's been two months since we were there."

"Excuse me," Catherin said as she left the room to be alone.

The girls started to follow. "Leave her be," Jane told them. "She needs to be alone now. Go set a clean place for Anis and then get at the dishes."

Catherin finally came from the company room where she had gone to read her letter. "He wrote to thank me for the nice time he had at grandma's party. Says he is busy and that he likes me," she blushed as she told them this. "He asked me to write to him."

Jane looked long at her pretty stepdaughter's face and knew that Catherin was in love with the young man. Well, she would have to give her up soon and better to someone who could give her a home where she would be taken care of.

"Since he is so polite to write and thank you, I think it would only be proper for you to write to him. Don't you, Tom?" Jane asked.

"Certainly, Jane, she should write," her father answered.

"Oh, thank you for helping me make up my mind. I wasn't sure I should," Catherin said, the color coming and going in her face.

"That's settled. Let's get on with our work," Jane said.

Catherin took the letter to her room to put away and if Jane was right to keep always.

That was something Jane had never had to cherish—a love letter. I've managed without it, she thought, and have plenty of keepsakes of my love if one just looked around, and soon to have another one. Jane would have another "keepsake" one born from Catherin's first love, the night they returned from their trip to the Capitol. Jane remembered and smiled. Yes, love could hold a firm hand on a woman's heart. It now had a hold on Catherin's or she would miss her bet.

"Thank, God, it's to be a decent man," Jane said to herself.

The Washhouse

It took a week to set the foundation to Tom's satisfaction. Jed came to help raise the framework which took the men several days. The rain had finally stopped. They wanted to get the roof on before it decided to start again. Jed knew an old man Kemper who would come and build the chimney and would help put on the roof. He had built Jed's chimney and fireplace. Rocks were pounded in firmly where the chimney was to go. There were plenty around working, including all the younguns.

John was grown now and could drive a straight nail. Anis said he would make a fine carpenter. Jane noticed he liked that better than some of the farm work they had to do. Now Will was another story. He loved teaming. The men had started calling him "Wild Bill" during the timbering for the saw set. Jane thought he took too many chances at times. He was a fine worker and good with a team, but at times had a tendency for carelessness.

Will was now twenty-one past, looked like he was waiting a long time to wed. I reckon he will surprise me some day like Catherin, Jane thought to herself.

In two weeks the washhouse was up with a roof, only needing windows and doors and finishing. The old man was slow laying up the chimney and fireplace. As Jane said he had very small rocks to work with and was doing a prime job with what he had.

"It looks nice enough to live in," Catherin said one day.

"Is that where you and Charles plan to live?" Tom teased her. "So that's why you wanted it built in such a hurry?"

"Oh, pa," Catherin said, turning scarlet and rushing into the kitchen out of sight.

"You shouldn't josh her so, Tom. She will be afraid to see the man again," Jane told him.

"I'm glad we will have a warm place to wash in this winter. It really looks nice." Jane stood with her hands on her hips admiring the building before her.

269

The apple picking started, the big apples brought in basket after basket to be sorted and stored in the bins in the cellar. Jane's orchard had some of the nicest fruit she had ever seen and a nice variety. Mr. Cheniweth had done a good job selecting her fruit trees.

Jane had planted fruit trees on the other farms. Not so many but some on each, some of the trees had fruit this year.

The potatoes were dug last. They had so many that bins were built in the cliff cellar and part of them stored there. Tom thought they might sell some in town. Next year they would take some to Charleston when they took the stock to sell.

By the time the first snow fell, the washhouse was finished. It had been whitewashed outside and looked neat and tidy across from the back kitchen door. Jane and Catherin were proud of it and were so thankful for the comfort it afforded on wash day. A bench had been made along one wall just the right height to hold the tubs. Two could wash at once and still have room.

There were a back door and windows overlooking the big garden. It could be used for lots of jobs they didn't want to bring into the house.

"It's starting to look like a town around here, Jane," Tom told her at the supper table that night. "I don't know what else you can think of to have built," and he laughed.

"Well, we need everything we have. Our family isn't getting any smaller, it seems only bigger," she blushed at the last remark.

Tom looked at her questionably. He left the question till they were safe in their room that night.

"My golden-haired angel," he said as he held her close. "I should have guessed, after our return from the capital was a precious time to me." Jane didn't answer. She lay close and fell asleep in her Tom's arms.

Will's Logging Job

Winter set in with snow and wind, too quick in the fall for most people. Some weren't finished with their harvest. Of course there were always some who never finished and left their crops laying in the fields to rot.

Jane couldn't abide wastefulness in any form. Their crops were in and stored before the first frost.

A man came to see Will and wanted him to help with a logging crew that winter over on the river. He had heard how well he drove a team and would pay him top dollar of seventy-five cents a day and keep.

"It's a chance for you to get a start, you will be wanting to marry before long," Jane and Tom told him.

"I doubt that," he answered. "I still like Mammy Jane's cooking," he said with a laugh.

"You're a fine man, Will, just see to it that you don't live up to that name some give you," Jane told him as she helped him ready for the trip. She didn't like seeing him go but knew it wasn't fair not to let him. He was a man now and should be on his own.

"You come home when this job's over, you hear?" Both Jane and Tom told him. "And take care of yourself," they called advice as he rode away.

Catherin kissed him good-bye with tears in her eyes. "You come back to us, Will."

"I'll be back, sis. Then you will be going off to marry that old man and leaving me. Don't do it till I get back," Will told her and rode away laughing.

Jane stood watching him go. The first to leave the nest. She didn't like her younguns off hired out to someone. It was different with a man. At least her girls didn't have to hire out.

Catherin received letters all that winter from Charles Wentworth. She bloomed with love and good health.

At Christmastime she received a big box containing a selection

271

of books from Charles. She took each from the box stroking the beautiful covers with gold lettering. Some were poetry with passages underlined by Charles that sent blushes playing over her lovely face as she read.

"These are classics," she told Mammy Jane.

Jane waited for her to explain. Now what is a "classic"? Jane wondered. It was enough to see how Catherin enjoyed them.

"Just don't forget the Holy Bible," Jane told her. "These 'classics' can't take the place of it."

"Oh, I read the Bible every day," Catherin said. "As you know, each evening, for all of you."

"I know, girl. Just don't forget it when you are away from here." Jane turned away, not wanting Catherin to see her concern over her leaving some day.

Will didn't come home for Christmas and they all missed him.

The winter wore on with the usual spells of bad weather. Tom came down with one of his fevers. He hadn't had one for some time now with Jane's careful tending. He was in bed for a week and finally came downstairs to sit at the fire looking pale and weak.

Harn's rheumatism bothered him all winter. He not only limped but now walked with a stoop. Jane hated to see him suffering and made a tonic each night so he would sleep the night through.

Toward spring Catherin received a letter from Charles. She usually went to her room or across the hall to the company room to read them away from prying eyes.

She soon returned where Tom and Jane sat at the fireplace. "Mr. Wentworth wants to come for a visit in the spring," she told them. They both looked at her with surprise in their faces. Jane turned to Tom, left without words for once.

"Well," Tom said, "He is a serious man and I respect him for wanting to come here. I wouldn't like him if he asked you to go there to see him. I don't see any reason why we wouldn't welcome him, Do you, Jane?"

"We have lots of company and I'm sure we can deal with Mr. Wentworth. I for one want a look at him," Jane told her.

"Oh, thank you, I want him to see our home and meet my family. I wish he could come when the apple blossoms are in bloom. That's my favorite time. The house looks so lovely with the snowy orchard in front."

272

"I doubt the roads will be in shape by then for him to travel so far," Jane told her.

"You are right, of course, he will have to wait till later. He could come by train and we could pick him up," Catherin continued.

"Whatever he plans we will be here," Tom told his daughter. "I hope you know your own mind, Catherin. I'm afraid he is serious and I don't think you should continue this unless you have decided."

"I don't know. I like him a lot but I hate to think of leaving home. Mammy Jane needs me to help with the younguns and the house." Catherin was becoming upset talking about it.

"Catherin, if you love him and want to be a wife to him, then that is all you are to think about. You are old enough to have your own home now. It's a serious matter. Your pa thinks he can take care of you. The rest is up to you to decide," Jane told her firmly.

"I get so scared thinking about it then when I get a letter I'm ready to go with him," Catherin told Jane and Tom in a little girl voice.

"All girls feel that way about leaving home," Jane told her. "When the time comes everything will fall in place. You will see. Now don't upset yourself pondering on it. Time will take care of everything."

The willows by the creek were turning yellow ready for their new veil of greenery in the spring. The air was somewhat warmer than usual, making everyone restless wanting to be outdoors after the cold winter.

Will came home walking in on foot to surprise them all.

"Will! what are you doing walking home on foot?" Jane asked.

"I got a ride on a lumber wagon to the forks at White Oak. The mill is shut down. They're moving to a new location. I decided not to go with them. I figured you would need me for the plowing anyway," Will talked on.

Jane knew there was something more on his mind. He was hanging back now. He would have to get it out, so she gave him time, studying his bent head as he twirled his hat between his knees.

Suddenly he looked up, first at Tom and then at Mammy Jane. "I want to get married," he blurted out. "I found a nice girl and we want to wed. Her name's Catherin Sutton. Her pa's head sawyer on the mill where I was driving team."

Tom and Jane were both surprised at the news tumbling off Will's tongue.

"Well, it's about time," Jane said. Tom nodded. "You plan to go there or bring her here?" Tom asked.

Will dropped his head again. "That's what I wanted to ask you, pa, and you too, Mammy Jane."

"You and your wife are welcome here, Will, you know that. If you want to live separate there's the Hall house and the other farms," Jane said.

"Why don't you come here for awhile, Will, till you both decide what you want," his pa told him.

"When is all this planned for?" Jane asked.

"A week from Sunday one way or another," Will answered.

"Fine! You can take my buggy and team and bring your wife back with you. You will have space if she has belongings," Jane said.

"Oh, I feel better, I don't rightly like the country over there. I like it better here," Will said. "I'm glad you are letting us stay here for a while."

"Then it's settled," Tom said.

"You go get the dirt off, supper will be ready directly," Jane told him.

Will had a big smile from ear to ear as he came to the supper table. He looked at Mammy Jane, she nodded her head and made the announcement.

"We are having a 'wedden' in the family in two weeks." All eyes went to Catherin. She looked at Jane surprised and blushed, dropping her fork.

"It's to be Will," Jane went on. "He will wed Catherin Sutton at her father's home over on the river a week from Sunday. He will bring his new wife here. I want you to all make her welcome and be good to her."

Catherin turned to her brother, "Oh, Will! What's she like? I'm so glad for you and hope you will be very happy."

Now Will was ill-at-ease. "She is something like you, sis, only not as fancy. She has sorta reddish hair in the sun, tall, a little skinny, sweet and pretty and laughs a lot. She is a good worker," Will finished his description in a fluster.

"I'm glad too, Will," Lizzie spoke up. "Now we will have two sweet Catherins."

274

"I hope she knows how to wash clothes," Trude said. "If she don't Mammy Jane can learn her quick enough."

Jane smiled and let her get by with her sass. The exciting talk went on around the table about the wedding. Guessing what she would wear by the girls. Jane and Tom smiled at Will and was happy seeing him happy.

Will's Wedding Plans

The days sped by in the excitement. Jane insisted that Will have new clothes for his wedding. He and Tom went off to buy a suit. Catherin got busy making him a nice white linen shirt.

Jane decided they could have the company room for the first few days. She was remembering her own marriage bed. The girls cleaned every inch of the room airing the bedding and putting the nicest sheets on. Cleaned out the bureau for clothes and belongings.

Jane and Tom talked together and thought someone in the family should go along. They decided to send Catherin to the wedding with Will.

That night when Tom and Will returned with a nice enough blue suit, Catherin had the shirt finished, all but the buttonholes which took some time to do. Will had to try the suit on for all to see. Catherin let him put the shirt on even without buttons. It fit perfectly. She had made more than one shirt for Will and knew it would. The outfit was topped off with a new hat of pale grey.

Trude as always had something to say. "Don't look like Will, I think that girl is getting cheated marrying a stranger."

They all laughed at that. "He looks just fine," Catherin said. "The other Catherin will be real proud." Will, not used to such trappings, was nervous.

At supper Jane made the announcement that someone from the family should be at the wedding. Everyone looked around the table to see who it would be. Will's eyes lit on Catherin. They all looked at Jane to find out who would go.

"Tom and I have decided it would be proper for Catherin to go with her brother to his wedding."

"Oh, Will, do you want me?" Catherin asked, turning a shining face to her nervous brother. "You bet I do, sis," Will said with relief in his voice. "You can help me stand up for the 'I do's'," he said with a grin.

For once Trude didn't come out with anything. After getting by before she decided wisely to keep her mouth shut.

It was again a lively meal with the discussion about the trip. Catherin was preoccupied by the end of supper with what to take, what to wear and all the other things involved with going.

Jane had asked Tom to get a couple of dress lengths when he went with Will for his suit. Catherin would need some new things when Mr. Wentworth came to call. She might as well have them for this trip.

Tom had bought a lovely pale yellow silk and a "spriggly" blue calico for the second. "I would have gotten blue silk, but was afraid the bride might wear blue. So got the yellow for the wedding and the calico to travel in."

"Well!" Jane said, "seems you are quite up on woman's wear."

"There was never a prettier bride than you, Jane, with your 'spriggly' blue calico and bonnet to match. Not to mention that big full flannel nightgown on our weddin' night."

"Hush, Tom," Jane said blushing as she did when a new bride.

After supper Jane brought the new dress lengths and laid them in Catherin's lap. "Your pa got these for you. You had better get busy if you want them ready for the weddin'."

Catherin couldn't resist giving her pa a quick hug. "Oh, thank you," turning to Jane, "thank you, Mammy."

"I'll finish the buttonholes tonight on Will's shirt and get at these tomorrow."

"Get Lizzie busy to help, she needs to learn fine sewing," Jane told her. "You don't need to concern yourself with the house, Trude can take over."

"Me! I can't run the house," Trude said in a loud voice.

"You can learn. It's time you started learning to be a good cook. You will be looking for a husband before you know it," Jane told her.

"Not me. I'm not going to have an old husband," Trude said, her pretty mouth drawn down in a pout.

"Nature seems to see to things like that, Trude. Sometimes you can't help yourself. You are a comely girl and it will happen whether you want it to or not." Jane had to use patience with Trude. At times she tried her sorely. "Tomorrow you will work with me, you will surprise yourself at what you can do," Jane said.

Trude gave her a look and went off to her room.

The lamp burned late that night till Catherin finished Will's shirt for his wedding. She laid it aside to be pressed on the morrow, and went to her bed, her mind going in circles about how to make her new dresses. She felt guilty the other girls not getting any and her going to have not one but two. It was a while before she fell asleep.

The Wedding

Everyone was up early. Catherine had her sewing laid out on the bed in the company room ready to cut out the calico, she would leave the silk for last and take plenty of time on it.

She and Lizzie looked at pictures in a catalog comparing this one and that one. Finally deciding, they used the pink silk to go by and soon had the calico ready for the sewing machine. Lizzie basted while Catherin ran up the seams. They talked and laughed having a great time with their work.

Trude was in the kitchen with Jane, who was showing Trude how to set sourdough for biscuits and how to cook this and that. She had helped little in the kitchen doing cooking, always managing to escape the actual work. Catherin and Lizzie would rather let her go as keep after her every minute.

Jane knew it was time Trude was made aware of housekeeping. And would tend to it herself with a firm hand. She had been guilty too for not doing it sooner. Jane stood over Trude letting her cook the dinner, only taking hold when necessary herself.

Dinner was a little late, the men washed up and ready to eat before it was on the table.

Trude finally called them in. Her hair hung down in her eyes and flour on one cheek gave note to the struggle she had gone through at the stove.

The table didn't look bad as they all sat down. Trude dropped into her chair with a sigh.

"It looks good, Trude," Catherin said as she seated herself. "Look, even sourdough biscuits, my favorite."

Trude said nothing, just glared at her tidy sister who accomplished everything with seemingly little effort.

"How's the sewing coming?" Tom asked, to get the attention turned from the exasperated Trude.

"It's coming along well with Lizzie helping. She is going to be good at cutting and sewing," Catherin told them.

279

The time flew it seemed with everyone busy at their own job. Will had touched up the paint on the buggy and greased the axles. The harness had been washed down with soap and oiled till it looked like new. The leather seats polished and cleaned in readiness.

The day before they were to go, Jane baked one of her famous nut cakes with plenty of black walnuts inside and out. It was a picture as she arranged it on a clean white cloth in the big basket wedging some of the cloth around the cake plate so it wouldn't slide. Then tying another cloth over the top and sides to keep any dust off.

It would be cumbersome to take but Jane wanted to do that much toward the wedding.

The dresses were finished, pressed, and laid out on the bed. Tiny ruffles hemmed by hand were gathered around the neck and at the cuffs of the yellow silk. It looked very stylish even to Jane. She admired the style and the nice sewing job the girls had done.

It would be necessary for the two to spend the night. If the marriage took place around ten in the morning, they could be back home late that same night, which is what Will had planned. Jane had a feeling he wanted his first wedding night spent under his pa's roof.

Everything was readied the night before to get an early start the next day. The morning was clear, a warm breeze came in from the South. While breakfast was cooking, Will harnessed the team, ready to hook up the buggy.

Jane had been up early to make extra food to pack a basket lunch for the two. Lizzie came to help.

Will loaded everything into the back seat of the buggy. His and Catherin's new clothes for the wedding wrapped in a sheet on the seat. The baskets underneath and Catherin's carpetbag holding all their underthings and toilet articles.

A big heavy plaid throw was on the seat to wrap around the girls in case they were cold.

A hurried breakfast with Jane urging them to eat well. "It's a long time till dinner time," she told them.

The young people were both too excited to take time for a proper breakfast. Catherin was pretty in her new made calico dress. It enhanced all the lovely curves of her young body. They were ready. A heavy shawl for Catherin, and Will wore a mackinaw.

The roads, Will said, were in good shape for that time of the year. The rain hadn't started yet to churn up the dust to mud.

It was warm enough that the wraps would keep them comfortable.

"You put in another shawl, Catherin, you will be in the back seat coming home and may need it," Jane told her.

A few tools were packed under the seat too, just in case of trouble. Will always wanted to be prepared.

John, the quiet one, slapped his big brother Will on the back. "Don't break a leg, brother, as you jump the broomstick," he laughed loud at his joshing his brother.

"I won't, John, when I come back, we will start looking for you a girl as nice as my Catherin."

"Don't bother. I'm not ready yet," John called as the buggy started off down the drive, everyone waving and calling, "Good luck, hurry home."

Jane turned to Tom by her side, "That's the first one. There will be a steady stream from now on."

Returning inside, they all got busy at chores.

Trude came upstairs after the kitchen was put to rights. Finding Mammy Jane pounding and fluffing the feather tick on her bed, she asked, "You want I should start the wash, Mammy Jane?"

Jane looked up in surprise. "It looks like a fine day," she said. "If you've a mind to go ahead, there are always plenty to wash. We won't want to put the kettle on as soon as Will brings his wife home. We will want to do some visiting, I recon."

Trude went noisily down the stairs. She is learning, Jane said to herself with a smile.

Jane was heavy with child and it was an effort to smooth the feathers across the bed. Thank heavens she didn't have to bend over the washtub now.

The girls worked hard all that day getting ready for the company to come. The washhouse was scrubbed till it smelled sweet and clean after the wash was on the line.

Everyone slept well that night after the hard day of work. Will's wedding day dawned bright and clear. Jane stepped out on the upstairs portico as she usually did, checking the day before going to the kitchen.

The willows by the creek had a faint look of green as the tiny leaves struggled to free themselves. They will green up today if

281

the sun comes out, Jane thought to herself. The apple orchard was full of buds soon to open in a cloud of fragrant blossoms. Jane allowed herself a few moments of idleness to survey the farm and the new day before going to the kitchen.

Lizzie was already in the kitchen, the coffee on and flour to her elbows making biscuits for breakfast. Trude came and set the table. There wasn't much left for Jane to do. Everyone was anxious for the day to be over.

Every time the girls passed a window they looked off down the road hoping against hope to see the buggy.

"They aren't even married yet," Jane told them. "It will be after dark by the time they get here."

"This is the longest day I ever saw," Trude said, around noon.

Lizzie smiled at her, "It does seem longer than usual."

The men were getting things ready to start the plowing. All the machinery was gone over and oiled, axles greased in readiness.

The windows were opened to the sunshine and soft breeze. "Leave them open an hour," Jane told the girls. "The house needs a good airing."

Jane had Harn kill a couple of chickens for the girls to clean up late in the afternoon. We will fry the best parts and leave them in the warming closet for Will and the girls. Put the rest to cook, we will have a big pot of chicken and dumplings for our supper.

Suppertime came and went, everyone enjoying the good meal of chicken and dumplings and hot biscuits with honey and butter.

The girls quickly cleaned up the supper things, polished the big cookstove till it looked new. Put things aside for a cold supper for Catherin, Will and his new wife.

Trude walked out into the yard several times looking off down the road wanting to be the first to see the buggy. She got more frustrated each trip as there were no sign of anyone on the road.

Tom had built up the fire, the evening turning cool as the sun went down.

Lizzie sat with her knitting close to the lamp where she could see. The last youngun had been put to bed. Little Florence wanting Catherin as usual. She was getting to be a handful. Jane would be glad when there was another baby to take the attention from her.

Dark had settled down soft as a woolly blanket, Jane had started getting uneasy. They should be home if there had been no trouble. Just as she was getting as restless as Trude, they heard the buggy.

The lamps had been lit upstairs and down to make a welcome sight as the buggy came up the drive to the big house with a flourish. Will brought the buggy to a halt at the front gate. They all went out to the piazza to meet the travelers.

Will came up the flagstone walk with his arm around his new wife, Catherin following close behind. He brought her to Jane. "This is my wife, Catherin, Mammy Jane, and this is pa, Trude, Lizzie. You will meet the rest later."

"How nice your house looks all lit up. It's a picture to see from the road and I'm glad to meet you all," Will's bride said.

"Will has told me so much about everyone of you and it was so sweet having his sister at the wedding."

"Come on in by the fire. You must be frozen," Jane invited.

Catherin ushered them inside. Taking her wraps off and hanging them on a chair in the hallway to take to her room. Will went to bring in the things from the buggy, Trude went to help. "You are to sleep in the company room for now," Trude told him.

They carried in the many parcels and bags from the buggy and deposited them in the hall for sorting out.

"Don't clutter up the room before your Catherin even sees it," Trude told him. Leaving his mackinaw in the hall closet he joined the others in the sittin' room. John came to put away the buggy and team.

"There's stuff in the warming closet, Catherin, for your supper. The table is set." The fire had been built up when the buggy had been heard so the coffee would be hot. Lizzie went with them to sit while they ate.

"Thank you, Mrs. Jarvis, for the lovely cake you sent. Everyone said they had never tasted better," Will's wife said.

Trude sat with them too while they ate. Tom and Jane waited by the fire.

"She seems a fine girl," Tom commented. "I used to know her pa before he went over on the river, that was before he married. He came from a good family."

"She seems all right," Jane answered. "I'm glad Will finally has someone of his own."

Trude and Lizzie cleaned up the late supper things telling Catherin to get the new bride settled in their room.

"Come along, Catherin, we will get your things sorted out and

283

I'll show you to your room. You must be as tired as I am." Will's sister took her in hand.

"Oh, what a nice room, your home is lovely, Catherin. I'm so glad to have married into such a nice family."

"I'm afraid I'll be leaving soon. I have a suitor who is coming for a visit this spring. I'll tell you all about it later," Catherin said. "There is water in the wash pitcher, clean towels and soap on the washstand. The bureau is empty for your things. You can put them away tomorrow. Just make yourself comfortable." Catherin turned down the big bed, smoothing back the "comforts" to show the snowy sheets and big puffy feather pillows.

"Good night, new sister, I'm glad to have you here." Catherin kissed Will's bride on the cheek.

Will looked up expectantly as his sister entered the room. "Give her a few minutes, Will. I'm going to bed. I'll sleep this night through." Going to Will she kissed him on the cheek. "Thank you, little brother, for such a nice new sister. Good night everyone."

After awhile, Jane got up to go upstairs to bed. Lizzie and Trude had already gone. Tom got up and shook hands with his oldest son.

"Good luck, Will. She is a fine girl. Make her happy and you will be too."

Will banked the fire and fiddled around awhile before going across the hall to his marriage bed. He knew that Catherin must be nervous for he surely was.

Robert

Will and Catherin were given a few days to be together. They took walks around the farm, Will showing her everything. On Sunday they took the buggy and drove up to look at the Hall farm and see the house there.

Nothing had been said about where they would live or if they wanted to stay at the homeplace.

Monday morning early everyone was up and out, the spring plowing started. Two teams were hitched and the work began in earnest.

John and Will took the plows first, turning the black soil in the garden to the sun. The gardens were always plowed first. They had to be planted early for food. Tom was taking care to see everything was done right and on time.

Harn was at the sheep barn, the ewes were lambing now and had to be watched over. They would have a hundred lambs this year or close to it. It had become Harn's job to take care of them.

Will's wife helped around the house, Catherin, Lizzie, and Trude were always busy with the many things to see to.

Little Nathan and Minerva had been put to raking the yard. The rain ditches along the eaves had to be cleaned out. Big spoons were used to scoop out the loose soil. The grass covered the deep little ditches and they weren't seen but served to carry off the water when it rained.

Another garden was being plowed this year, at the end of the yard down by the privy. Just small vegetables for the kitchen table would be planted there.

Trude was in charge of the yard work and kept the younguns busy at it.

Jane sat on the upstairs portico, she held a rug in her lap that she had been working on. The miseries had been on her since morning. She would send for Florence soon. The baby would be born sometime tonight. It was another chore to get through for Jane. She was always glad to have it done with.

She could hear the girls below the stairs. Catherin was sewing. Will's wife and Lizzie were chattering while they basted or done fancy work in between.

The new girl would have to have a different name, they couldn't always call her Will's Catherin.

Jane watched Trude directing the dumping of the sled full of dirt from the ditches and called to her, "Trude, tell Catherin to come here."

"Which Catherin?" Trude wanted to know.

"Your sister, of course, and right away," Jane said with impatience.

Catherin came quickly up the stairs, surprised that Jane didn't come for her. "Is something wrong, Mammy Jane?" One look at Jane's face and she knew. "It's time. Come, I'll get you in bed and send Trude to fetch Florence." She took Jane's work from her and laid it inside the hall. Taking her arm, she led her into her room. Turned down the bed and brought the padding from the hall cupboard, quickly spread it over the feather tick, brought a clean gown.

Jane started to undress. Catherin held the gown and got her into it and then to bed.

"I'll be back directly, you rest. Everything will be alright." Catherin raced down the stairs to call Trude and send her on her errand. It never failed to frighten Catherin to see how helpless Jane became at this time. She never had an easy time, but never a sound, only a small moan, passed her lips.

"What is it?" the other two girls came into the hall as Catherin sent Trude off.

"It's Mammy Jane. It's her time. Build up the fire in the kitchen, Lizzie, and put plenty of water on." Catherin raced through the house to the kitchen throwing orders over her shoulder. She made the tonic as usual as soon as water was hot and took hot irons to put at Jane's feet.

Trude saddled a horse and was off in a cloud of dust to fetch Florence.

By the time Florence arrived, Jane's tonic had taken effect. Jane seemed to doze a little between pains and there was more color in her face. Catherin sat by her side, she had been by with the last two.

286

Florence went to her friend. "How do you feel, Jane?" She placed her hands on Jane's protruding belly.

"They're pretty hard now. A couple of hours maybe. She gasped as a severe pain hit.

"I would say so too. The baby has moved way down. Shouldn't take long. We should be used to this by now," Florence said with a laugh.

"Never—get—use-to-it—," Jane said trying to get her breath. Catherin went to fetch pan and water from the kitchen. "Can I help?" Will's Catherin asked.

"Have you ever been around a birthin'?" her sister-in-law asked. "If not, I think it's time, come along. Bring the teakettle."

The pains racked and wrenched Jane's poor body. Each one worse than before.

"Open the windows, can't breathe," she told Catherin.

The three women worked over her all afternoon. Around five o'clock a baby boy's cry sounded through the house. "It's a fine boy," Florence said as she handed it to one of the girls to clean and dress while she tended Jane.

It had been a hard few hours. Jane was exhausted. As soon as she had been cleaned up and the bed changed, she fell asleep. They all tiptoed out of the room. Catherin took the new baby all wrapped, only a little pink nose showing for the younguns to see.

The men were working at Yellow Jacket today, they would have a surprise when they came home tonight.

Tom had seen Trude's wild ride to Florence's so knew what to expect.

Jane slept till supper was over. Catherin had taken the new baby back and placed it at Jane's side. She didn't move as Catherin tiptoed out again.

"I never realized they were so cute and sweet right away. It's not easy to birth them, I can see." Will's wife had gone through an experience this afternoon that she had never been through before, and one that she would probably go through soon herself. It would make it easier knowing what to expect and she told her new sister so.

"I thought it might help you if you never saw a birth before," Catherin told her. "It's the unknown that frightens us so, although I have to admit that it scares me to see Mammy Jane pale and helpless. She is such a strong person."

Tom went up to see Jane after he had washed up and ate. "It's

287

a fine boy, 'little princess,' " he told her as he kissed her cheek. "Are you all right?"

"Yes, just tired, I guess. How would you like Robert for this one?"

"Robert Jarvis. That sounds fine to me. I've always liked Bob for a name."

"He sleeps all the time. Hasn't even wanted to eat yet," Jane told him.

"I'll have the cradle brought up from beside the fire for him tonight," Tom said. "You rest now, I'll be up to bed soon." He kissed her again as he left.

The younguns were all excited about the new baby. All but little Florence. All she would do was cry and yell, "I want Mammy," until they were all ready to wallop her little bottom.

Catherin rocked her in Jane's chair till she fell asleep.

Lizzie and Will's Catherin cleaned up the kitchen. Everyone was ready for bed, knowing daybreak came early and a new day of work.

Letter From Charles

The plowing continued. The three girls were in the garden planting peas, beets, lettuce, radishes, and such.

They heard a horse and Catherin went to the house to see who it was. One of Florence's boys had been to the post office and brought a letter for Catherin.

Her heart beat pitter-patter as she opened the envelope.

My dearest,

The time seems endless as I await your answer.

When will it be convenient for me to meet your family? I pray it will be soon. My heart grows weary with the waiting for a glimpse of your sweet face.

My work goes well here at the Capitol. There has been some talk that I may be promoted to a higher position.

I know my work is well done and think I deserve this consideration.

My home and heart is empty without you, my sweet Catherin.

Tell me that you will return with me as my wife. Waiting most anxiously for your answer.

I remain your most devoted servant,
Charles Wentworth

Catherin had dropped into a chair as she read, her shaking limbs unable to hold her weight. A rosy flush covered her face and there were stars in her eyes as she read the letter again.

"I must send him an answer," she said to herself. "He wants me to go back as his wife. Oh, I don't know," she wildly looked around her at the familiar things she loved. "I want to go with him. I don't see how I can. Mammy Jane needs me."

Tears came to her eyes as she bowed her head. Knowing that Jane had plenty of help and could do nicely without her. She had to say one way or another, a *yes* would take her off to a wonderful life with Charles, *no* would tie her to her family forever. There would never be another chance like this. She loved Charles, of that she was sure.

Going slowly up the stairs, the letter still in her hand, to the mother she had known so long. Surely Jane with her strength and farsightedness would know what she should do.

Jane sat in the rocker by the window nursing the baby. Looking around she saw the distressed look on Catherin's face. "What is it, girl? What news have you got that upsets you so?"

Catherin pulled a chair close and read the intimate letter to Jane.

Jane listened to every word rocking the baby. She remained quiet. Catherin looked up from the letter, "What am I to do, Mammy?"

Jane carefully thought over what she was going to say. "That is a fine man who wrote such a letter. Do you love him, Catherin?"

"Oh, yes!" came out in a rush. She dropped her head to hide the blush flooding her face.

"That's all I need to hear," Jane told her. "You write to that young man and let him come for you. You don't throw away a chance like that. It may never come again," Jane said as she saw the relief on Catherin's face.

"We will start getting ready for a wedding. The first one in the house. This house has been saddened by a death. A happy 'wedden' will cleanse it of sorrow. I will be up and about in a few days to help. We will get everything ready by the time your beau comes."

The apple trees were in full bloom now. The redbud and dogwood made the hills glorious with their color.

The planting would be laid by in a couple of weeks, then she could let Charles come for her. Mammy Jane was right, of course. She had been wishy-washy about it. After all, she was past twenty and should have some sense. She suddenly decided on June 10 for her wedding day. Charles could come a few days before and get to know the family. It would be a long while before they could come back to the farm again. As Catherin went back to the garden the girls looked at her with concern.

"You were gone so long. What is it, Catherin?" they asked.

"A letter from Charles," it was the first time she hadn't called him Mr. Wentworth, her sister noted.

"I talked it over with Mammy Jane. I'm to be married June 10."

"A wedding!" Lizzie half crying, half laughing, hugging her sister. "Oh, I'm so glad for you. I just know you will be happy. The city is where you belong."

They all hugged and chattered. Laughter rang out as they finished their planting. The kitchen was busy with happy cooks that evening.

As usual the news was told at the supper table, with joshing from her brothers which she had expected.

Tom looked long and hard at his eldest daughter and could see the happiness bubbling over in her dear face. "I think you have made a wise decision, Catherin. It will sadden your Mammy and me to see you go. We want happiness and a home of your own for you. You will come back for visits, the capital isn't that far away."

"Can I come visit you?" Trude wanted to know. "Maybe you can find me a man with a big house. I want a young one though."

"Of course, you can all come. It will be a place to stay when you go to market in the city," Catherin answered, looking at them all.

The talk went on. Questions asked that Catherin couldn't answer. Catherin took a plate to Jane and told her all about the table conversation.

Jane ate and watched the excitement play across Catherin's lovely face and was glad for her.

That night Catherin and Lizzie talked and talked in their room, planning what to wear and what had to be sewed for her trip.

They finally fell asleep close to ten o'clock which was half the night to girls raised on a farm and used to going to bed early and rising early.

It had been an exciting day for all and morning would come soon.

The Wedding Chest

Jane and Tom had talked in the night about the wedding. It was decided he would take them to the county seat for the materials they would want for dresses.

Jane wanted Catherin to have a "Wedden Chest." She had longed for one when she was married but didn't have one. She would give her the one that had belonged to Catherin's mother. And fill it with things for her.

She called Will in to write a list of things she wanted from the town store. "Put down one blue wool blanket, two of the finest linen sheets, and four pillowcases." She had the new blue "comfort" they had made for the company room. That could go in and a pair of new white feather pillows, "and put down something foolish for a bride."

"You want me to write it like that, Mammy Jane," Will asked.

"Yes, I don't know what they have. If I could go myself I'd find something."

"No doubt you would," Will mumbled as he wrote. Handing the list to Jane he left her.

Jane gave the list to Tom, "Now mind you get this while the girls are not around. I want Catherin to be surprised and bring me a roll of fancy wallpaper with roses in it."

The girls were all going, Trude at last got to take a trip, and the two Catherin's and Lizzie.

"Are you sure you can manage, Mammy Jane?"

"I'll manage, you go on along." The four young women and Tom left around three in the morning. They wanted to come back the same day. It would be a long trip but could be done with the fine team to draw the buggy.

It was a strange house left to Jane. She couldn't believe the difference the girls made in the household.

Jane had Will and John carry the big wedding chest to the shop house to be repainted. The inside would be done with the paper

292

that Tom would get. Jane would have John reline the big chest for her. He was so good at things. The chest would look like new when it was finished.

Jane ran up two pillows and went to the granary loft where the new feathers were stored and filled them till they were plump and soft.

Everything could be finished without any of the girls knowing. It would be a real surprise, especially to Catherin.

Nothing had been given to Will yet. They were waiting to see what he wanted to do. It had been decided that he and his wife would sleep in the washhouse so the company room could be readied for Mr. Wentworth.

It was late in the night when Tom returned with the bunch of tired girls. Everyone had gone off to bed except Jane who waited up for them.

They came in each carrying packages, left them in the hall until the next morning and went off to bed.

Jane waited for Tom to put the team away in case he wanted to eat something before going to bed. "I'm more tired than if I plowed all day," he told her. "All I want is to go to bed. What a day," he moaned as one after the other his shoes hit the floor. He was asleep almost as soon as his head hit the pillow.

Jane was up early and had breakfast ready for the men. They ate and were off to their plowing. Jane let Tom and the girls sleep knowing they were tired out from their trip.

It was eight o'clock before Tom came downstairs. The girls came soon after.

"It's not easy to travel," Trude informed them. "I liked the town but it's too much trouble to get there. I think I would just as leave stay home."

"I'm glad you finally got it out of your system," Jane told her.

The girls brought all the packages in for Jane to see. Catherin had decided on a white silk with tiny blue forget-me-nots and blue satin for a sash. Lace for trim around the ruffles she planned. That was to be her wedding dress.

"Oh, I selected a lovely dress length for you, Mammy Jane. It's darker blue. I know just how I'll make it for you. You shall look elegant. You wait and see." They talked and compared.

Will's Catherin had selected a green silk, Lizzie pink and Trude an old rose for their dresses.

"You had better get busy, there's only four weeks left. You don't

293

want to be at the sewing machine when Mr. Wentworth arrives," Jane said.

"I'm not gonna have all this fuss when I marry, if I ever do," Trude informed them.

"We'll just make you a sack dress," Lizzie told her. "You would like that just fine." They all got the giggles over that remark.

"I put the things you ordered in your room, Jane," Tom said as he came through the sitting room where all the women were.

They were soon all busy flying around starting their dresses. Jane went upstairs to see what Tom had bought.

The blanket was the softest and nicest she had ever felt. The sheets had lovely stitching along the hems. The paper was just what she wanted for the inside of the big trunk. The present was the prettiest clock imaginable, milky-white with tiny painted rosebuds on the pedestal. Must have cost plenty, Jane thought as she turned it this way and that. It was just right for Catherin. She cared more about pretties than all the other girls put together. Jane carefully put it back into the straw in the box until the wedding day. She would give John the paper to line the trunk tonight when the girls went to their room. She wanted it to be a surprise to all.

Tom took Nathan and Trude to help plant a garden patch at the Hall farm. He suspected Will and his wife would want to move there when it was big enough to eat.

The household was humming with activities going on for the big day. The date was set for Catherin's beau to arrive June 7. That would give him three days to get acquainted.

"And change his mind," John told his sister, to tease her.

They made Trude's dress first. It looked lovely on her. Mammy Jane's was the second one. It was made with dozens of little tucks running up the front of the waist to a tiny collar with the tiniest ruffles around it. Jane wondered how the girls ever got it sewed. It fit snugly around Jane's high bosom and small waistline to flare out in a full skirt with tucks running around in eight rows above the hem. Long sleeves with cuffs and the tiny ruffles. It was a picture when done and Jane looked tall and distinguished in it.

"It makes me want to marry you all over again, Jane," Tom told her with a twinkle in his eye as he watched the trying on.

It took the girls two weeks to get all the dresses made. And of course Catherin had to make a nightgown and underthings trimmed in ribbons and bows.

Jane was glad she could afford the things for her. She wouldn't be ashamed in front of her new husband.

The sewing was finished down to the last thread. The dresses were pressed and laid between sheets to keep fresh till the big day. The house was cleaned from top to bottom. Everyone from far and near was invited to the wedding feast. Everything was done for Catherin's beau to arrive.

Then the cooking and baking would start. The big wedding chest set finished and packed in Jane's room. All the nice things with the surprise clock on top filled the big empty space.

Jane had a comforter over the chest to hide it from view. It was new looking with the paint job John had done on it. He was proud of it, as was Jane.

The work and the plans went on. Tomorrow Mr. Wentworth would arrive. Catherin was in a dither but had never looked lovelier.

Mr. Wentworth

Charles had planned to spend three nights on the road, which made for a good day of driving. He had decided to drive his own team and buggy for Catherin's return with him.

The house was sparkling. All the younguns had been washed late in the afternoon and clean clothes put on them.

Lizzie had baked apple and pumpkin pies. She had planned a big supper for when Charles arrived.

The men all came in from the fields early. They had orders to wash and change clothes for supper.

Catherin and Jane wanted everyone to look their best for Charles at supper and for his first impression. Catherin spent quite a while in her room that afternoon readying herself. There had been casual looks down the road all afternoon. It was after three o'clock before the watch started in earnest.

The men were at the barn doing whatever they do when hiding out from the womenfolk. The sun was over the highest hill to the West. Only an hour remained till it would suddenly disappear in a rosy cloud and be seen no more that day.

"Someone's coming! Someone is coming!" the younguns called from the front piazza.

Catherin flew to the front to look. The team and conveyance was far away in the distance but she was sure it would be Charles.

She raced up the stairs to put another pin in the already perfect hair and take another hurried look in her bureau looking glass.

She stood at the portico upstairs. There was a good view from there and she suddenly couldn't remember what Charles's face looked like. Panic struck her, she was shaking from head to foot. What's wrong with me? Surely I'm not going to swoon. Oh, no. I don't want Charles to find me in a dead faint on the floor when he arrives.

Calming herself she went slowly back down the stairs. Little heads peeked from around every door and window. In fact there were several big heads as well watching Charles's approach.

Little Nathan waited to swing the big red gate wide for him to enter.

"Everyone in the sittin' room," Jane ordered. "Let Catherin greet her beau in peace."

The fancy buggy with its drop curtains and matched blacks came at a sharp clip to the front yard gate. A tall man in a suit and hat emerged tying the reins to the hitching post in front.

Catherin stood on the piazza. One look and she couldn't contain herself any longer. She flew down the flagstone path to Charles who took her into his arms, turning her face to his, kissed her on her glowing cheek. After a few words they turned toward the house.

Jane let everyone go to the piazza to welcome Catherin's beau, she leading the procession.

"This is Mammy Jane, you remember Lizzie, this is Trude," as more poured through the door and Catherin continued to call names. Poor Charles looked frustrated. "Oh, my, is this all your family?"

"Not quite all, some are hiding out in the barn," Catherin giggled.

Everyone asked questions, "How are the roads?" "How fast can your team travel?" till poor Charles turned this way and that not knowing who to answer.

Jane finally took hold, "Mind your manners. Let Mr. Wentworth get his breath."

The men came to take his team and were duly introduced. His carpetbags were brought into the company room. After he refreshed himself, Catherin took him around the farmyard to show him everything until supper was ready and so they could have some time together.

"He's not 'too old,' " Trude said. "I think he is nice."

"He cut a fine figure even if a little fancy," Jane spoke out.

The supper was plentiful and the talk lively. Mr. Wentworth sat next to his future father-in-law where they discussed the political issues of the capital and the market prices which Charles had a good knowledge of.

"You have a fine farm here, Mr. Jarvis, well-run, well-organized," Charles informed them.

"I have to give Jane credit for the organizing. She planned all

297

the buildings. I don't know when she will maybe decide to put in a railroad." They all laughed.

Catherin wanted to help with the dishes, but the girls pushed her out of the kitchen. "You don't want your hands all red for your weddin'. Get going and entertain your beau," they told her.

"Looks like pa's took over that job," Catherin laughed. "I'm so glad they like each other."

"He's not too bad," Trude told her.

"I'm glad you all like him. He is quite taken with all the family. He is an only child and can't understand such a big family," Catherin said.

"Are you going to have babies?" Trude asked.

Catherin's face turned so red she looked on fire. "I expect I will," she finally answered and left the room before Trude could come up with more questions.

The lamps were lit, Tom and Mr. Wentworth continued their talk. Jane and Catherin sat and listened. The younguns were sent off to bed. All the others went one at a time. Tom finally said, "I suspect you are tired from your trip, Charles. We go to bed early on the farm and are up at cock's crow."

Charles got to his feet and came to Jane, "That was a fine repass," he told her, shaking her hand.

Jane never batted an eye, she had never heard a meal called a "re-pass" before. "Thank ye and good night, Mr. Wentworth."

Catherin and Charles said good night in the hall, each going off to their separate rooms. Tom shut up the house and he and Jane went to their room where they talked for a long while.

"I went to the newspaper and announced Catherin's wedding and invited whoever wants to come," Tom told her.

"I'm glad you did, I wondered how people would know," Jane said.

"It's set for two o'clock on the tenth. That will give people time to come and get home before dark," Tom told her.

"They will have time to visit before we feed them. I want a nice fat sheep butchered. We have a big ham I've put aside and we will have about four or five hens killed to fry. No telling how many will come," Jane said, telling Tom of her plans.

"I'm satisfied with Mr. Wentworth for Catherin's husband," Jane said.

"He's a good man and has a bright future at the capitol, he will take good care of our Catherin, she will be happy I'm sure," Tom answered.

They talked on of the plans for the next few days, finally falling asleep holding hands.

The girls talked and giggled till one by one they fell asleep.

Mr. Wentworth lay soberly thinking over the magnitude of their big healthy, happy family, wondering what it would be like to live in a family like this one. His thoughts turned to the one nearest his heart. Catherin was more precious than he remembered, her quick wit and her sweetness and her beauty. Some had tried to tell him that a farm girl wouldn't fit into his way of life. There was no doubt that Catherin was from a fine old family and would fit in anywhere. She was charming and graceful. His love for her left him weak when he thought about her. It would be a glorious day when they wed. Sleep came fast and swift blotting out the image of his lovely Catherin.

Catherin's Wedding

Catherin and Charles hooked up his buggy and went for a ride around the countryside. They took Nathan and Minerva along with them. Catherin showed Charles all the farms, took along a lunch that they ate on the front porch of the Hall house. They talked and laughed and became better acquainted. "I'll miss all this," Catherin said as her eyes swept the mountains around her.

"Not too much, I hope," Charles told her. "You will be much too busy giving teas and helping me in my business life."

"Oh, my! that sounds grand. I'll have to learn a lot I'm afraid."

"It will come natural to you, my love. You are a born hostess, look how you are entertaining me," Charles smiled at her. "And your Mammy Jane, she is a lady if I ever saw one. She walks like a queen with ease and grace. You have the same walk, my Catherin."

While Catherin and her beau talked and rode about the farm, the big house was filled with activity. The butchering of the sheep and chickens was done by the men. The sheep cut up and quartered, left in cool salted water overnight in the cellar. The chickens were put in water too. The cooking would be done very early in the morning of the day of the wedding. The days flew by, everyone having a job to do. It was to bed early for everyone that night. The women would be up by four o'clock with the meats in the oven to bake or on the stove to cook.

Lizzie baked bread the day before, the pies and cakes were all made, enough to feed half the county. They were in the big Cliff Cellar out of the way.

Jane coated and spiced the ham to bake. Lizzie's job was frying chicken, a quarter of the lamb would also be baked and some of it boiled.

Catherin awoke on her wedding day when the first cock crowed. The other girls were up already and in the kitchen helping Jane. She lay thinking of the day before her, the first faint rays of light

300

coming through the white lace curtains. Getting out of bed she walked out on the upstairs portico. "It's going to be a glorious day," she said out loud. "Thank you, God, for all the blessings." Getting dressed, she rushed downstairs to help all she could.

The kitchen was overrun with women at every table, pounding, patting, flouring and turning. It looked like an army kitchen with all the things being done.

Boards had been laid from shelf to shelf in the cellar to hold all the cold dishes of beets, pickles, kraut, pickled pig's feet, cole slaw, peaches, every bowl and dish they had would be put in use.

The men were putting wide boards on sawhorses in the yard. Another on blocks of wood for seating. Tablecloths would be put on for eating outside.

By early afternoon people had started to drive in, by wagon, buggies, and some on horseback, some brought bundles wrapped for Catherin.

Catherin had gone to her room to rest before the ceremony. She wouldn't be down till time for the wedding.

Jane was dressed with a big white apron covering her new dress. The others were coming in one at a time in their new outfits. The younguns were all at the washhouse playing.

Florence came with her brood. Trude saw that they went across the bridge to the washhouse. She had made a big pan of popcorn balls to keep them busy and out of the way.

Jane went to the front piazza where she and Tom sat or stood to meet each newcomer. Charles was made acquainted with everyone who came.

He was amazed at all the people. "So many children," he remarked.

Jane was surprised too at the turnout, and started to worry about the food if there would be enough.

The time flew with everyone talking and visiting. The Reverend Mr. Cottrell came with his wife and little boy.

It was almost time for the ceremony. Florence took Mrs. Cottrell aside. They were going to sing together just before the ceremony.

Easing inside, the wedding would take place before the fireplace in the sitting room. Lizzie went to see if Catherin was ready. The girls positioned themselves in a "V" leading out from the fireplace mantel on one side and the boys, Will, John, and Nathan on the other side.

301

The women started their song, a hymn. Charles stood between the two lines waiting.

Tom went to the stairs and met Catherin as she came down and brought her to Charles's side. The ceremony began.

"We meet here this day of our Lord to wed together this man and woman in Holy Matrimony," the minister went on amid the scraping of feet and giggles from some of the younguns.

"I now pronounce you man and wife," the minister finished.

Charles turned to Catherin and for the first time, touched his lips to hers.

Slapping of backs and shaking of hands, the men and boys rushed Charles outside where they had a jug waiting.

Jane had made sure it was weakened down by pouring half out and adding water.

All the women and girls gathered around Catherin to feel her dress and see the gold wedding band Charles had placed on her finger.

While Catherin had been upstairs, Jane had Will and John fetch the big wedding chest. It sat by the window, the other bundles lay on top. They all waited. Catherin was steered toward her presents by her sisters. Tears came to her eyes. Florence had tatted lace doilies for her. Another had done fancy work on a cushion. The storekeeper, Mr. Cheniweth, had brought a set of lovely glasses with rosebuds painted on them.

When Catherin got to the trunk, she stood, her hands together as though in prayer. "Mother's trunk! it can't be. It's so new and pretty," Catherin's eyes found Jane's.

"I thought you might like it as a remembrance," Jane told her.

Catherin slowly lifted the lid, taking out each item. Every woman in the room gathered around to admire and touch. There was so much noise and confusion no one heard what the other said.

"It's lovely, Mammy Jane." Catherin came to her and kissed her cheek. "Thank you for being so good to me. I'll cherish it always."

Jane couldn't get over how many had come, even to Mr. Cheniweth and his wife, the Witts who had bought the Jarvis homestead, and so many she hadn't expected.

Thank heavens they had made a lot of food. It was a beautiful day, they could all go outside in the yard and eat out there. There were lots of comments on Jane's house and her family. She suspected some came just to see it and come inside.

Jane sent the girls to spread the tablecloths and start carrying out the food. Better feed the men before they drank themselves senseless. They would think it funny to get Charles drunk on his wedding night, Jane didn't intend to allow that.

Several of the women helped to carry out dishes, soon they were all filling plates and eating and talking, enjoying themselves like never before.

Catherin and Charles stood on the piazza talking to this one and that one as they passed by.

"What's in that jug they passed around?" Charles asked Catherin.

"That's moonshine and it has wicked effects sometimes," she told him.

"I don't know how anyone could drink enough of that. My throat still burns from just a little swallow."

The celebration went on and on, the vittles disappeared like magic. There were still lots of food as the first wagon started to leave. All had come to wish the newlywed couple happiness.

Florence and her family were the last to leave. She hugged Catherin to her. Tears ran down her face. "I'll miss you," she told her. "I hope you will be back again soon. I know you will be very happy. You looked so beautiful today."

She shook hands with Charles. "Take care of our girl," she told him. Florence's cheerful nature couldn't be kept down long. "I'll have a long way to come if you call in the night," she said, her laughter following her out to their wagon.

Everyone started gathering up dishes to take back to the kitchen.

"I've never seen so many dirty dishes in my life, every dish in the house is dirty," Trude wailed.

"For once I think you are right," Jane answered as the dishwashing started.

"I'm going to take off my good dress." Each one followed Lizzie upstairs. They wouldn't have another silk dress soon, and knew they would have to take care of it.

Catherin and Charles went for a walk through the orchard at sunset. They made a fine-looking couple strolling arm in arm through Jane's prize trees. They would be leaving the farm the next day. Catherin would be sorely missed.

Jane watching them, wondered if she would ever have the girl home again. Thank God she was going to a good home and wouldn't have to work so hard the rest of her life.

The couple finally came in. Catherin went to her room to finish gathering her things together. Her books Charles had given her were in a box in the hall. There were several boxes and bundles. Everything had to be ready for an early morning loading in the buggy.

Her night things and the dress she would wear the next day were put in the company room. She and Charles would spend their first night as Will had done under their parent's roof.

Dishwashing went on for what seemed hours, the pan emptied of dirty water and a clean sudsy one replaced it. Jane helped put away the uneaten food, seeing it was stored in the cellar where it would be cool.

Charles and Catherin had gone to their room. The house soon quieted down. Trude, glad to do anything away from dish washing, saw to putting the younguns to bed. They had had such an exciting day that there wasn't much trouble, they were half asleep already.

Jane was tired but pleased by the day. She doubted there would ever be a bigger wedding in the house again.

Jane and Tom talked before going to sleep. They decided to give Catherin a hundred dollars in money for her wedding present. She would have something of her own. "She couldn't take a cow to the capital," Tom said with a laugh.

"What do they do for milk?" Jane wanted to know.

"There's a man comes every morning with a wagonload. He leaves what you need in a jug on your front step. I've seen him going from one house to the other," Tom explained.

"Harrumph," Jane said as she made herself comfortable. After the big day, the house slept.

Catherin Goes Home

Everyone was up early. The day promised to be a perfect one. A glow showed over the Eastern hilltops. The sun would soon be up. The men were at the barn readying Charles's horses and buggy for the departure. They would leave right after breakfast. Everyone was helping with the cooking. Lizzie saw that the younguns were dressed and ready for breakfast.

The buggy was brought to the front gate. The boys helped load the wedding chest. Catherin went with an old rug to tuck around it. "Don't scar it," she told them. "I want to keep it pretty." Her good dresses were wrapped in an old sheet and put on top of the chest. With Charles's and her things, the buggy was full. A big dinner had been packed for them to take along.

The younguns kissed Catherin good-bye, telling her, "Come back for Christmas."

Tears ran down her face. She loved each one so. "I'll miss you," she told them hardly able to talk.

The buggy was ready including the dinner basket. Catherin hugged each sister, then her sister-in-law. Will came last for a long hug and kiss. "Come see me," she told him. Tom got a long hug and kiss.

She went to Jane. "Take care of yourself, Mammy Jane, and thank you for making this the happiest day of my life. I'll write," she said, as Charles helped her into the buggy.

"Sure you don't want to take a jug along, Charles?" Will asked with a laugh, they all joined in as Charles answered.

"No, thank you. I believe I had enough at the wedding." "Good-bye all, good-bye," Harn waited to see them through the gate at the road. The buggy with the beautiful team was soon out of sight taking their Catherin away to what was to be her home.

The big house had seen weeks of preparation and two weddings in that many months. Jane had said to Tom that there would be a steady stream from now on.

305

The men went off to the fields, they were plowing and planting the last of the corn.

Lizzie soon had the wash kettle on, there were dirty clothes everywhere. The company room had to be made up again, this was the time of the year when people were coming through and needed a place to stay.

Will's Catherin hurried from the dishwashing out the door to the privy. She was gone a long while. When she came back she was pale with a white ring around her mouth.

Jane gave her one look and knew what the problem was. Quietly she mixed the apple cider and honey, handing it to her. "Drink this, you will feel better soon," she told her.

"I don't know what got into me. I feel so queer. I ate too much at the wedding," Catherin said as she drank Jane's tonic.

"I doubt that's the cause," Jane told her. "Mix yourself a teaspoon of vinegar and one of honey in water, drink it when you get up in the mornings. You will feel better in a few weeks."

Catherin looked at Jane, her eyes got big and a smile lit up her face. "Is that why I'm sick?" she asked.

"I suspect so, it's about time for you to catch," Jane answered.

They went about their work, Catherin feeling better and helping with the wash. The lines were full of flapping clothes by nine o'clock. The house had begun to take on its orderly appearance. Jane already missed Catherin. The work didn't go as smoothly or quickly. She could turn out more work than any of them.

The day seemed to fly, Jane put the younguns to cleaning up the yard. Carrying the boards to the shed and rolling the blocks of wood back to the woodyard.

By the time the men came in from the field, things were back to normal. There was still food left. It was reheated and set for supper. The women were thankful for it after the long day they had put in with washing and cleaning. They were dead tired.

On Sunday Catherin and Will took a walk to the Hall farm to look at the garden.

Jane and Tom sat on the piazza watching what traffic went by and talking off and on, mostly just sitting silently.

"I think Will and Catherin may want to move to the Hall farm," Jane said to Tom. "She is in the family way. They will want to have a home of their own now."

"I'll offer it to him," Tom said, "He can do what he wants. We can all still work together."

"They can do on what furniture there is there mostly. Some things can be added. The stove will need some stovepipe. I've had the girls keep the place swept out and it's in pretty good shape," Jane told Tom.

That night at supper Will brought it up. "Pa, Catherin and me want to start our own home. That is, if you will let us have the Hall farm to work. I can give you part of the crops for living there."

Jane spoke up, "Will, you know you are welcome to live there as long as you want. There will be no talk of crop sharing in this family," she said firmly.

"That's right, Will. Jane and me talked about it this afternoon. We can still work the farms together, helping each other out," Tom told his son. "When did you have a mind to move?" Tom asked.

"Soon as we can get things together some. We can eat from the garden now. We need bedding and a few things to do on. Catherin thinks her family will give her some things. We plan to go see them before we move if we can take one of the wagons," Will said.

"The planting is finished. We have a little time before haying and hoeing corn. We can all pitch in to get things ready," Tom told him.

The next day the girls, John, Tom, and Will took tubs, soap, brooms, and rags to clean with. The men took tools, put extra boards on the wagon and all went to see what had to be done to the house.

It was a nice little house, two rooms downstairs with a lean-to kitchen and an attic room up a narrow flight of stairs.

John found the stairs needed a few nails here and there. He had them fixed in no time. Boards were over the windows, they were all unbroken except one that was cracked in the kitchen. It would hold awhile.

The cooking stove and heating stove was in good shape, just needing a cleaning and polishing. The pipe above the roof would have to be replaced. The wooden bedstead was solid, a good scrub would fix that. Jane had taken one to the cabin at one time but one was left. The table in the kitchen would do, needed a new bench since Harn had taken it to the cabin too.

Everyone worked all day, washing, scrubbing, and nailing. Stopping long enough at noon to sit on the porch and eat the dinner the girls had brought.

307

The spring had been kept cleaned out, it was running free with plenty of sweet water.

Will and Catherin decided to leave the following day to visit her folks.

They told Jane at supper all that had been done. She nodded as she listened. "There's plenty of straw and feathers for pillows, we will get that ready while you are gone. You can go to town for whatever else you may need after you know what Catherin's folks will give her to bring back." They all agreed that would be the best plan. The two planned to leave early the next morning. Catherin hurried around after supper getting together the things they would need on the trip.

Will Moves

Tom and Jane talked that night after going to their room.

"I'll give them ten hens and a rooster and set a couple more for them," Jane said. "They will need a cow. One with a new calf for plenty of milk."

"How about that old Brindle cow? Her calf is about a month old, she gives lots of milk," Tom said.

"That will be fine. She has a heifer calf that will give Will a start," Jane answered. "We can give them two pigs from that last sow's litter. They are ready to wean."

"That will set them up better than we were. Too bad we can't give them five younguns to start out with like you had." Tom laughed and laughed over that one.

"I don't think Catherin could manage all of that. She will have a houseful soon enough," Jane told him.

"She won't be the manager you have been, Jane," Tom told her tenderly.

The next day Jane showed the girls how to take a fleece of wool and open it out in the basket at the run, swoosh it back and forth to wash it, then spread it on a sheet to dry in the sun. It would then be used to make a warm comforter. Jane had flannel and calico she had sent for to make one for Will and Catherin. She and the girls would make it while they were gone. While the wool was drying in the sun, Jane started the girls on making the straw tick and ticks for the pillows, how to measure and sew them leaving an opening for filling. When they were finished Jane went with them to see they were filled right and the opening sewed securely.

The next day the wool was ready for the "comfort" making. The lining was spread on the bed, the wool carefully pulled and spread evenly to cover it all with a thick layer. Then the top was put on. Jane took the knotting thread, running it along the side a long stitch, a very short one, a long, and a short. The thread was cut in the long stitch and the ends tied across the short stitch.

309

Jane did the sewing, even rows all over while the girls cut and tied. They had it finished by early afternoon, all but hemming it. Little Minerva helped and was quick to catch on how it was done. Lizzie would hem it by hand and it would be finished.

"Oh! It's so soft and light as a feather," they said as it was lifted off the bed.

Jane felt it. It is nice. I think I'll have to make one for my bed. I only have a cotton filled one. This will be truly warm."

"It's pretty too," little Minerva said.

Jane had sent for material when Tom went to town, knowing Will's wife liked green. It was a green calico flowered and plain green flannel lining and as Minerva said, it was pretty.

"There are lots of flour sacks," Jane said. "We will make a sheet and pillowcases for them. That will finish the bed."

"It will all be ready when they come back," Lizzie said.

The men took the wagon back to the farm. They wanted to fix a place for the pigs and chickens. Lizzie and Trude took the bed and went along. John took boards and tools. He was going to build a corner cupboard in the kitchen and put up some shelves over the work table that he had made the first day there.

The girls made up the bed with the big puffy straw tick and fat pillows. The green "comfort" over it looked real nice. The stove was polished and looked almost new. Lizzie had taken a rag rug she had made from old clothes and put that by the bed.

"With a rocking chair, a bureau, and some curtains this room would look nice," Trude said, looking around her. "I like a room without too much stuff in it. You can sweep easier."

Lizzie smiled at her standing in the middle of the almost empty room. Lizzie remembered how they had lived and said to herself. They can get along on what's here with some dishes and cook things.

It was a week before Will and Catherin came back. Having to pass the house before reaching home, they stopped. They were both surprised when they opened the door.

"Oh, a bed. It looks nice," Catherin said, "and my favorite color." They were even more surprised to find the kitchen ready to cook in, only needing dishes and food. John had made benches for both sides of the table. They didn't need chairs and the shelves were just right with a new work table below. "And a new corner cupboard. It is nice, Will. I'm so pleased. We will have a real home here." Catherin held a kitten in her arms all this while. Her sister had given it to her.

Will started bringing in the things that had been given to them. Catherin's mother had given her two quilts, some dishes, and an iron pot, an old rocking chair that needed a new rocker. Will had said, "I can fix it" and loaded it on the wagon. There were two straight chairs and a fairly good bureau and a looking glass. Her married sister had given her a sewing basket and some towels and dishrags, a new sheet and pillowcases. Her dad had rolled up a length of wire for her a clothes line. He had slipped her a ten-dollar gold piece too. He had given Will two or three extra tools he had and gave him ten dollars too.

Will unloaded everything but the rocking chair. He would take it to the shop and see if John could fix it.

They were glad to be back. The big white house was a different world to how most lived. It stood tall and inviting behind the orchard. Catherin's family lived well but nothing like Will's family.

Everyone ran outside to meet them. "We're glad you are back," Tom said. "How's the road?"

"It's fine. Everyone is too busy working to travel it enough to churn it up," Will told his pa. "We got a nice surprise at the house. I felt like going right to bed, would have, but didn't want to have to eat raw onions for breakfast." Will laughed, glad to be home.

"Our house is starting to look like a home, with all you done while we were gone," Catherin said with a smile. "I'm afraid we didn't get much to bring back. We have plenty to do on, a good new bed and enough in the kitchen, and a good house that will be warm in winter. Even a rug to put my feet on when it's cold," she smiled at Lizzie. "Thank you. Thank you all."

"You are welcome," Lizzie said.

They talked about their trip and Catherin's family. Her sister was going to have another baby. Her brother might marry this summer.

"Pa, if I can use the team, I'll go fetch pipe for the stove and a few things from the store and we will move this week," Will looked at his pa for an answer.

"Will, you don't have to ask, you know that," his pa said.

"I'll go, too," Catherin said. "Lizzie, can you come? I want to get some material to make curtains and would like your help."

Lizzie looked at Jane.

311

"Go ahead and help her," Jane answered. "Trude is getting good enough till she could run the house by herself."

Trude looked quickly at Jane, "Who, me?" She looked very pleased nevertheless.

While Will hooked up the team, the girls got ready. They would have to do some measuring for their curtains.

"You'r' not going into debt for things, are you?" Jane asked.

"Oh, no. My pa gave me some money for things. I don't intend to spend all of it. We will have to have some to pay the mid-wife when the time comes," Catherin said with a blush.

"There are flour sacks you can use for kitchen curtains, if you've a mind to," Jane told her.

"Then I'll only have to buy enough for the sittin' room. I want to get some flannel to start on too. I may not be back again," she said.

They were soon off. They returned late in the day only having to go to the store at Minnora.

They had gotten the stovepipe and the things Catherin needed. She had to have a washtub, water bucket, washboard, clothes-pins, and had quite a load when finished. They unloaded it at the Hall farm before coming on home.

The men went the next day to install the stovepipe. They would do some work on the little cellar that was dug into the hill. Every-thing would be ready for them to move in the next day. While the others worked at the repairs, Will brought in several dead trees for stove wood. He managed to chop quite a pile for the kitchen stove that afternoon.

The girls worked all day on the curtains. Catherin wanted them tied back with ruffles, there was a lot of sewing on them. Thank heavens for the machine.

Jane remembered the hours she had spent hemming ruffles by hand when she made curtains for the cabin. It was worth it though, she thought to herself.

The girls had gotten white material with a green vine running through it. They would look nice when done.

"Your house will look nice," Jane told Catherin.

"I'm so excited," Catherin said. "And Will is so proud."

The curtains got finished just at dark. They were pressed and laid on the bed. "Tomorrow is the big day," Catherin said as she looked at Will's smiling face as they went off to the washhouse to sleep.

312

John brought in the chair he had fixed in the shop house. It was oiled and shining like a new one. You couldn't tell which rocker had been broken. Harn and Tom were busy getting the animals together. They brought the big Brindle cow and calf and tied her to the wagon. Then a crate with the chickens was loaded. The pigs were in a big wooden box.

Catherin and Will stood looking when they came to board the wagon. "What's all this?" they asked, surprised looks on their faces.

"I'm giving you the cow and calf. She is all yours. Jane is giving Catherin chickens and two pigs, a male and a female," Tom said.

Will shook his pa's hand hard. "You have been more than good to us, pa."

Catherin had tears in her eyes, as Jane came out to see that everything was being loaded. Catherin ran to her and kissed her cheek. "Thank you, Mammy Jane." Will's eyes met hers, "Me too, Mammy Jane. I'm much obliged."

"There is a jug of molasses and flour and meal, a few other things we can spare. Get one of our tubs and load them in it, send the tub back." Jane had given them enough food to last a month. She remembered what it was like the first little while.

Lizzie went along to help hang the curtains, everyone stood in the yard waving good-bye.

"Come see us real soon," Catherin called.

"There goes the second one," Jane said to Tom as the wagon went off down the road, pulling the mooing cow and piled with the odd assortment of things.

That night at supper Lizzie told them all how nice the house looked, the curtains were so pretty and Catherin had bought green checked oilcloth for the table and shelves. She had helped her cut and fit it.

"They are both so happy with all the things Mammy Jane and pa gave them. They were starting off good. Catherin says she has a nicer house than her sister now."

The chatter went on and on till Tom called, "Bedtime, everyone."

313

Will Is a Father

First they had two Catherin's, now none. They were both missed but nothing like their own Catherin.

Will and his wife settled in and was happy and well-off according to some standards.

Summer came with the younguns out of school and everyone busy. The haying started early. Will, John, and Anis hired out for the haying after finishing at home. Jane and the girls worked hard putting by all the fruit and things for winter. Will's Catherin was busy filling their little cellar for winter.

The first snow fell at Thanksgiving time, John went in the sled to fetch Will and Catherin for the Thanksgiving feast. All the younguns piled in the sled for the ride there and back.

Catherin was heavy on her feet being in her seventh month. Jane's little Rob was crawling, getting into everything.

Winter set in in earnest. There was lots of snow from Thanksgiving on. Anis set his trapline early and was catching prime fur. Will had run a line on his place too. He didn't have as much luck but did catch some. The furs meant cash money in their pockets.

Christmas came and went with the usual commotion. They had their second letter from their Catherin. She and Charles were well and caught up in the social life at the capital. She gave teas for the ladies and such. A lot was written about their house, the clothes she wore and that she missed them all and the farm. Her letters sounded so hurried as though she had little time to write.

Catherin's and Will's baby was born early in January. Will had come for Jane and then gone to fetch old Doc Dye. It was a long birth at the end of a day and night. They had a fine boy. They called him Caleb, after Will's uncle.

Jane was in the family way again. She was glad to be rid of the monthlies but dreaded the last month of carrying a baby and birthing it.

There had been a revival meeting at the schoolhouse that win-

314

ter. John had taken Lizzie and Trude a few times to hear the preacher. Trude had somehow met a boy from Roane County by the name of Kennen. She seemed to be taken with him.

Mammy Jane couldn't believe that Trude could be in love. Looked like that was what it was. She was sixteen now. Things quieted down after the revival broke up and nothing much was said through the rest of the winter.

Trude would walk to the Hall farm to see Catherin and the baby when the snow wasn't too deep.

Tom came down with a fever and had to stay in bed for a week. Jane doused him with all kinds of remedies and he was up sitting, wrapped in a quilt by the fire after a week. There were the usual snotty noses all winter to doctor and keep under control.

One of Florence's and Jed's boys got real sick. They were scared to death it was diphtheria. It turned out to be a bad sore throat and cold. Jane went to help sit with the boy and do all she could.

Florence would have another baby about the same time as Jane would.

Everyone had just about given up that spring would ever come. A few days of sunny weather and the first sign was the willows along the creek showing signs of yellow. Armloads of them were gathered to make baskets. John formed hickory splints into frames and a whittled down bail to which the willows were woven to form the baskets. The willows formed patterns and made good sturdy baskets that would last for years to hold eggs, or vegetables.

Lizzie and Trude made a small one for egg gathering and a larger one to take them to the store in for Catherin. It took them several days to get them to their liking.

Little Minerva and Etta made a small one for play. It wasn't too bad a job. "The next one will be better," Jane told them. "The more you try, the better you will get. Anything worthwhile is worth working for." Their little fingers were nimble but didn't have the know-how yet.

Their winter projects had to be put aside now. Plowing time was here. Everyone was needed for the planting. All but the littlest younguns had work assigned to them.

Another farm had been added at the head of Bear Run, almost two hundred acres. The men had done some clearing through the winter. Harn went with the men a few times. Finally Tom told him to do the barn chores and stay around where he could come to the fire often. He was getting crippled in his hands now. In cold weather he could hardly get around.

Jane still gave him tonic at bedtime so he could sleep. She could tell he was in considerable pain.

The spring and summer flew by and it was harvesttime again. Jane gave birth to a girl in late fall. She was called Milissa, a pretty little thing with golden fuzz on her head. Florence came, with Lizzie's help at the birth it was done. Florence was due anytime now herself. She and Jane were running neck and neck having babies. It had been over two years now since Catherin wed. No word came from her about a child. Catherin who loved babies so and still with empty arms.

Jane was up and around again after the birthing, her old self again. Harn came into the kitchen where she was starting supper. He leaned on a chair, "Jane!" he got out. Turning to see what he wanted, Jane saw he was holding on with both hands to the chair back. His face almost purple, sweat stood in big drops on his face. "Harn, what is it? Sit down." Jane got him on the chair. His head leaned against her bosom.

"Lizzie, get my tonic quick." She held the cup to Harn's lips. The sweat poured down his face. "Drink it slow," she told him.

"Lizzie, turn down his bed in the cellar house and then come help me get him there." By the time Lizzie got back, Harn was some better and had gotten some of his strength back. They half carried and half dragged him into bed. They propped his head up with two pillows. Harn's eyes were closed and his breath shallow. "How do you feel, Harn?" Jane asked.

"Better, I had such a pain." He placed his knobby hands over his heart.

The rheumatism was taking its toll. "You lay still and try to sleep. I'll make you some hot broth. You'll feel better soon." Jane went back to the kitchen.

Harn stayed in bed several days. He was too weak to raise up alone. With all the care Jane gave him, he didn't seem to get any better.

John went for old Doc Dye. He took one look at Harn, then at Jane. "His heart," he told her. "He has rheumatism in the muscles around his heart. There is nothing that can be done. He may come out of it and he may not."

Jane told the doctor what she had been doing. "Keep it up.

316

Here is some pills for the pain if it gets bad." He gave her a small packet of twelve pills. "Just keep him quiet and warm, that's about all that can be done."

Jane thought about Harn that night, how he came to her when she needed him. He had worked so hard and seemed happy enough. He never seemed to miss not marrying, happy with her and her family. It was hard for her to get to sleep thinking of him. She had told the boys to call her in the night if Harn wanted anything.

Days went into weeks as Jane watched over him as he grew weaker and more helpless, doing what she could to ease his days.

Harn

The first winter snow was falling, the big flakes drifting to the ground lazily to cover everything in sight. Jane stood at the window in the cellar house looking out. She had been up early tending Harn, trying to get some nourishment down him.

"Jane, Jane," he called weakly from the bed.

She went to him taking his gnarled, work-worn hand in hers. She sat on a chair by his bed.

"You've been good to me, sis. I've had me a good home here. Your younguns has been like my own. I love them every one." His eyes closed with the effort to talk.

Jane sat waiting, holding on to him.

He aroused again, "Is it snowing?"

Jane nodded.

"I like snow," he continued, "I'll be going away soon," his voice got weaker. "You don't need me anymore, little sister. You done good, got a good family and plenty. Tell the younguns old uncle Harn loves them. You have been my life, sis, remember that when you hurt, I hurt; when you was happy, I was happy." His eyes were closed, each word an effort.

Jane sat looking at her brother. His eyes suddenly opened. He looked at Jane then at the window where the snow fell so softly. A smile lit his face. He gave a slight squeeze to Jane's fingers and closed his eyes with a sigh, he breathed his last.

Jane sat a moment longer looking at her brother's peaceful face. Tears ran silently down her cheeks. They would all miss old Harn. She most of all.

She went back to the main house. Preparations had to be made for the burying. John came in as she reached the kitchen, he and Lizzie turned seeing the tears on Jane's face.

"Harn's gone," she told them. John turned quickly going back out into the snow. He had been very close to his uncle. Tears came to Lizzie's eyes.

318

"That dear old man. He has suffered so much. He will be at peace now," she said, going on with the work she was doing.

Jane went through to the sitting room to tell Tom. Will had come for the team to haul wood, he and his pa sat talking. She could tell them both. He could go get Catherin and stay at home till the funeral was over.

John had gone to the shop house where he would soon be working on the coffin. Nathan was there helping him. He was learning to be a fair carpenter too.

Jane helped hurry dinner, there were things to be done. She would wash and dress Harn for his laying out. They would have the funeral the next afternoon in case the weather worsened.

When dinner was over Jane went to her sad job. The tears ran down her face as she washed and dressed the worn deformed body for the last time.

Trude was sent to tell Florence and Jed. The grave had to be started. Tom and Anis trudged up the hill to the cemetery, their tools on their backs. Tom did the measuring off and selecting the site for Harn's last resting place. He chose a place under an apple tree a couple of rows from the family graves. Harn had said many times he didn't want a tombstone, just a fieldstone to mark his grave.

Jed came back with Trude to help, he and his oldest boy. The hammering and sawing went on in the shop, the man and the boy building the burying box that was called a coffin. By late evening the box was finished, ready for the lining and covering that Will brought. Lizzie and Trude would do that job.

Will had brought Catherin and the baby to spend the night till after the burying tomorrow.

Jane, with John's help, lifted Harn into his casket when it was finished. They put it in the hall for the night on chairs where it was cool.

The night passed slowly, some going to bed to sleep awhile, then getting up to keep watch while the others slept. As soon as it was light, the men went to finish the grave.

The snow had stopped in the night, leaving everything covered in a soft white blanket.

John was finishing the rough box, everything would be ready for the funeral at two o'clock.

The preacher and his wife came in a sled. They were early so as to spend time with the family.

The time came for the last journey to the burying hole for Harn. His coffin, made with loving care, was placed on a sled. The team stood restless, stomping the snow till the "getta up" came that started them on the slow way up the hill to the cemetery. The family formed behind the sled. Slowly climbed the hill where they had made the journey before in sorrow.

The fresh dirt of the grave lay on the snow-covered ground like a sore wound.

The coffin was opened, Harn's body was adjusted from the uphill journey. As they stepped back for the preacher to take his place at the head of the grave, the snow started to fall softly. Some of it clung to Harn's hair and eyebrows. John stepped forward to close the lid—"No," Jane said, "almost the last thing he said was 'I like the snow.' Let it touch him." John stepped back as the preacher read from the Bible.

"A man is born of woman"—his voice droned on in the cold air. He finished the sermon, the women sang a hymn, the prayer was given, the coffin lowered into the ground.

"There's a good man gone to rest," Jed said as the first shovelful of dirt echoed on the boards atop the coffin. The adults stayed till the grave was mounded up into a raw mound in a field of snow. The lowly fieldstone with the letters H. M. cut into it by John was placed at the head. With a sigh and a wipe of her eyes, Jane turned and started down the hill to the big house and the living that needed tending to.

There was hot coffee and cake for the mourners. Lizzie and Trude had taken the small younguns back to the house and had everything set out when they all came back.

"We must write and tell Catherin, she thought a lot of Harn and orta know about it. You do it, Lizzie," Jane told her.

They all said their good-byes and left. Will and Catherin were the last. "We might as well get home. We have chores to do. The snow was still falling as they left the warm kitchen. The baby in Catherin's arms, a bundle of blankets not resembling a baby at all.

Jane went slowly up the stairs to stand at the portico watching the sled out of sight. Going into her room, she sat in the rocking chair by the window, watching the snow blot out the doings of the afternoon, remembering Harn and all he had done to make the family what it was today. She sat on rocking and remembering.

Lizzie called her several times before she roused herself, "I'm coming, Lizzie," she said as she went down to supper.

320

Trude

After Christmas another "revival" was held in the school-house. John took the three older girls and Nathan in the sled to the meeting.

Trude was in a daze for days after. If she wasn't sulking, she was in tears. She would get in one of what Mammy Jane called "muley" moods and go off to visit Catherin.

Lizzie was glad to see her go. She and the other girls did her work to be rid of her stubbornness.

Spring came with the apple orchard a picture to behold. Jane would stand on the upstairs portico, the fragrance filling the air. Those still moments she treasured more than anything else.

The plowing had started early with everyone busy. Trude went to Will's and Catherin's with something she wanted Catherin to show her how to do. She seemed always to have a bundle under her arm. The day was warm and sunny.

The girls got the wash out early in the day. The men took their dinner with them. They were working at the head of Bear Run and wouldn't be home before dark.

Trude announced she was taking her silk dress to have Catherin help let it out. Lizzie offered to help but Trude wouldn't let her. "Catherin will do it and we can talk. Is it alright if I stay the night?" Jane looked at the pretty willful girl. "It will be alright," Jane told her.

Catherin was in the family way again. "See how Catherin is." "She has green sickness," Trude answered. "She don't feel good at all."

"Maybe you can help her some then," Jane said doubtfully.

"Sure," Trude said as she went gaily out the door and down the road.

"She sure is in a good mood today," Minerva said.

"Thank the Lord," Lizzie seconded.

321

"Wonder what she's up to?" Minerva asked no one in particular as she watched Trude hurrying down the road out of sight.

Will didn't come in when the men came from work, he went on home. It would be dark by the time he got there.

Trude didn't come home all the next day. Towards evening, Jane looked off down the road. "I wonder what that girl is up to?" she said to herself. Not knowing she was echoing Minerva's question of the day before.

As the men came in, Jane walked out to the woodyard. "Oh, Will," she called. "Send that girl home, we need her here," she said.

"Who?" Will asked.

"That Trude girl," Jane answered. Knowing it would be dark, Jane didn't expect her that night. She would likely come with Will the next morning.

It was scarcely daybreak when Will came to join the men for work.

"Where's Trude?" Jane asked.

"I don't know," Will said. "Catherin said she only stayed a little while day before yesterday. Said she had to come back to help with the wash. That you sent her to see how Catherin was."

Jane's heart started to pound. It had been years since she had thought of the time she was trapped in the barn. There's no soldiers now, she told herself, as her mind raced here and there, trying to figure out where Trude was.

"Lizzie, you and Nathan saddle one of the riding horses and go to Florence's and see if she is there."

"Tom, you'd better stay home today till we find that girl," Jane was giving orders right and left.

"That girl will get the strapping of her life for this," Jane said. She was scared half to death thinking of the things that could happen to a young girl out alone.

Lizzie and Nathan were soon back. No one had seen Trude down that way.

Minerva piped up, "I'll bet she run off with that Jim Kennen. I don't like him a bit. I'll go see if she took her clothes." She came running down the stairs, "All her clothes are gone, except the ragged wash dress she wears for doing the wash."

Jane's eyes flew to Tom. His face was a thundercloud.

"All you younguns get to your chores, no more about this,"

Jane told them. "I need to talk to your pa." The others went quickly from the room knowing there was a storm in the making.

"She's been gone two nights, Tom. If she is with that man, best they marry if he will have her. And right away," Jane said.

"He will have her alright," Tom said as he took his rifle from the rack.

"There is no need for that yet," Jane told him. "They must have gone over White Oak. You ride to Billy Conley's and see if they have seen them."

Tom left the rifle and went to the horse tied at the "stile block," mounted, putting heels to its ribs, went at a trot down the road. He didn't stop at Will's, urging the horse on at a fast clip. He soon was over at White Oak at the Conley farm. Billy was working on the fence by the road. Tom stopped and asked his shameful question, "Have you seen my girl Trude come this way?"

Billy looked at him, a grin on his face. "Yep. Saw her go past two days ago. She was riding behind that Kennen boy from over Roane County way. I wondered about that. What did they do? Run off to marry?" Billy asked. "They sure enough looked in good spirits going past here."

"We thought she was at Will's house overnight," Tom said. "I'm obliged to you, Billy, for telling me." Tom rode on toward Cheniweth's store to see what he could learn from him.

"Howdy, Tom, what can I do for you?" the merchant asked.

"I'm lookin' for my girl Trude, has she been by here?"

"Two days ago. Young Jim Kennen was here asking for the justice of the peace. I sent him on over to Tom Knotts's place. Your girl was with him," Mr. Cheniweth said.

"I thank you," Tom said as he started out again to the home of the justice. He knocked on a side door where Knotts had a small office.

Knotts opened the door. "Tom, come in," he invited. "What can I help you with?"

"I've come about my girl. Has she been here?"

Knotts looked surprised. "Why, yes! I married her and young Kennen two days ago. Here is the note you sent giving your permission since she is under age. I thought you knew all about it. It's signed with your mark and Will as witness."

"None of us ever seen that note," Tom told him. "Do you know where they went from here?"

"I recon back toward Linden where he lives. They seemed

323

happy enough. I wondered about them marrying like that with none of the family about. I remember what a 'Koo-Doo' you had for Catherin's weddin'." Knotts went on, "I hope you don't blame me. It's all legal as far as I'm concerned."

"I'm obliged," Tom said. "Do I owe you anything?" Tom asked.

"No, young Kennen paid. Seemed to really like your girl," the justice answered.

Tom mounted his horse without saying anything else, ready to go back to tell Jane and the rest. That foolish girl, only seventeen. Well, she had made her bed, she would have to lay in it. When Tom arrived back at the big house everyone stayed out of his way till he talked to Jane.

When he told her, she just nodded her head. "She's done what she wanted, foolhardy as it is. Best to leave her be. She has always been headstrong."

Tom nodded, "I recon you'r' right, Jane. I hate to see a girl of mine go off like that to no tellin' what. As you say, it's done. Best forget it."

cA Letter From Trude

There was no word from Trude as the spring wore on into summer. Finally toward fall a note in Trude's childish writing came for Lizzie.

Dear Liz

I'm all right. I'm sorry for the way I done. I run off with Jim. We are going to have a baby. We are all right. We live in a cabin by his folks. We don't have much but we don't want much.

Hope Mammy Jane and pa's not still mad at me. I like it here. Tell pa I'm all right.

Your sis
Trude.

Thank God she is alright, Jane thought, as Lizzie read the letter to her and Tom. Neither one made any comment as Lizzie finished.

"I'll write to her tonight," Lizzie said as she left the room. She sent off a long letter telling all the news and that they missed her. There was no return answer. Trude had her own life now. She wasn't one to hang on to things, even family.

That fall Tom took lambs, calves, and pigs to Charleston driving them down. He let Lizzie and Minerva take the buggy to visit their sister Catherin while he and Nathan drove the animals. It took well over a week to go down and back.

Jane now had a fine herd of horses, more than thirty. She wanted a market for them. Tom's pa would know where they could be sold. She was sure. She sent a fine team of geldings tied on behind the buggy.

The girls came home full of the news of Catherin's house and fine clothes. Charles liked the team of young horses and insisted on buying them himself at a good price.

Tom proudly brought the money back to Jane—three hundred dollars for the team. The market for the lambs was good. Pigs were down but fifteen still brought a tidy sum. He had gotten twenty dollars a head for the eight yearlings.

Jane was glad for the money that came so easily to her now. It was hoarded and "made to count" as it was when she was making pies and selling them to the soldiers.

Next year, Will would have pigs to sell. He and Catherin were doing well and expecting their second baby.

All the years their Catherin had been married, she still didn't have any babies. Her life was full of social things now, her family all but forgotten.

Will and John loaded wagons with flour and drove two full wagonloads to the "Farmer's Market" in Spencer, thirty miles away.

John made friends with the owners. He liked the smell of the big feed store and walked around examining everything, asking questions about prices, sales, and such.

"Are you interested in this kind of work?" Mr. McKade, the owner, asked John.

"I like your store. I like the smell of the newly ground grain," John answered.

"How would you like to work for me, young man? You're Tom Jarvis's boy, aren't you?"

"My pa's Tom Jarvis. If he can do without me, I would sure like to try my hand at it," John said, with a smile.

"We could start you off at five dollars a week. There's a roomin' house around the corner where you can stay and get your meals."

"I'll see what I can do," John told him, "and let you know next week when we bring in another load."

They shook hands, "You think about it, young feller," McKade told him.

John's heart was singing. He didn't like farm work like Will and his pa. This was a job he would like. Everything smelled clean and new. He hated the smell of manure that he had to shovel from the barns. The mud—now that was something else. The town was to his liking where you could walk down the sidewalk and not get stuck in mud. In the town there would be something happening all the time. His mind raced this way and that, driving the team back over the long road home. I hate to leave pa, he thought. He won't want me to leave. Nathan is big enough to do a man's job now. I have to take this chance. I may

326

never get another, he told himself. Building up in his mind what he would say when the argument started with Mammy Jane and his pa.

It took John several days to catch his pa alone and time was passing. It had to be done.

"Pa, I have something I want to talk over with you," John said.

"Now, who do you want to marry?" his pa asked, his eyes sparkling.

"I don't want to marry. I want to take a job in town. Mr. McKade offered me a job in the feed store. It's good pay to start and I would really like to try it. I like the town."

Tom looked at John's earnest face. He was twenty now and had a right to his life. He never had taken to farming like the other boys. He knew it was what John wanted and that he would be good at it. "All right, John, looks as how you have made your mind up. You go ahead and give it a try. Mind you do a good job. This is a proud family. I don't want any failures on my hands."

"I'll do good, pa, you wait and see. Do I have to ask Mammy Jane?" John asked shyly.

"No. I'll talk to her. When you plannin' to go?"

"Next week when the wagons leave. I'll stay. Someone can go along to drive back. If you ever need me real bad, I'll come home," he promised.

Tom told Jane that night. She was silent for a long time. "We will miss him," she said. "He never has liked farming. I thought he might be a carpenter. We can't keep him. He is old enough to do what he wants. He has been a big help since he growed. I'll miss him," she said with a sigh.

John's face was full of smiles the morning he was to leave. A new adventure awaited him.

Lizzie had washed and ironed all his clothes and had them ready. She had been busy this past week making him some handkerchiefs. They were all done and folded lovingly with his things. "You will probably end up with a big house like Catherin's and never come home again," Lizzie teased.

"I'll be living in a roomin' house. I guess it will be much like living in a big family only no babies," John told her.

There were hugs and good wishes as John climbed in the wagon, Nathan beside him. He would drive the team home, following the one Will drove.

327

Tears were in Lizzie's eyes as she told her brother good-bye.

Jane's heart was sad as he left, another one. He, the quiet little boy she had raised, held a special spot in her heart. She raised her hand in farewell as the wagons pulled out.

The Loom

There was sickness up and down the valley all winter. There had been talk of a little boy dying down on Beech. They weren't sure if it was diphtheria or what.

It was decided that Catherin and her little boy would be brought home to stay for the birth of her second baby.

Jane kept a careful eye on all the younguns. The slightest sore throat saw them put to bed and kept there while she doused them with her remedies.

Tom had his usual two week bout with fever and a bad cold. It was a good month before he felt like leaving the house for any length of time.

It rained for days, dark clouds hanging low over the hilltops sending gloom into every valley and household. Some thought the rain and lack of snow brought so much sickness.

The girls did fancy work and made quilts during the long dreary days.

Jane had decided to make use of all the wool they now grew. Store made cloth was going up in price especially the woolens and linens. She had sent for a Mr. Weatherbee who installed looms. They had spent some time going over all the ifs and ands. Where the best place would be for the loom, finally deciding to put it in the company room between two windows for light. It would be close to the fireplace for warmth too. The loom would take up much of the big spacious room. There would still be plenty of room for one bed and a bureau, table and chairs. Jane wanted a big loom. She had in mind not only to make the cloth they needed but carpet for her house.

Anis and Mr. Weatherbee got busy first selecting dry chestnut for the framework and the shuttles and such. There was always a plentiful stack of lumber in the workshop ready for use. The measuring and figuring had to be exact for the loom to work prop-

329

erly. Each piece had to be smoothed with a drawknife till it was slick as the palm of your hand.

Mr. Weatherbee's maiden sister would come to show the girls how to thread the loom and use it.

Everyone was excited about making their own blankets and clothes. And to think of loomed carpet on the floors was more than they could imagine.

The work went slow as Mr. Weatherbee would go home and sometimes have a problem there and not come back for days.

Christmas came and Catherin's time grew near. The usual baking and fixing for the big feast they would have was in progress.

A package came from the capital from Catherin and Charles. There were lockets for all the girls and pen knives for the boys. A fancy bound book of poems for Lizzie. Gloves for her pa and the men. Jane received a piece of taffeta for a skirt. It was always an exciting time, especially for the younguns.

This year there wouldn't be sledding since there was no snow for Christmas. In fact the weather was so warm Anis and Will and a couple of the boys went off up Bear Run hunting.

The seventh of January Catherin woke in the night with pains. She managed not to awake the household till they were up at dawn. Will got up and saddled the horses and went to get Florence. She and Jane would tend Catherin through the birthing.

It was going on to ten o'clock that night before it was over. A little girl wrapped from head to toe in Catherin's arms. She and Will were pleased, they had wanted a girl.

Florence had eight now herself but hadn't had any for three years. Jane was with child again. They sat talking about Florence getting behind.

Florence's laughter rang through the house. You always knew when she was about. "I doubt I will have any more, Jane. I am some older than you. With the last one I wasn't quite right. It was a good three months before I got back to myself."

This was about the only time the two women found time to talk. At a birthin' or sickness.

Florence's older daughter Lenna would marry in the spring. She was eighteen now. The women talked on enjoying their visit till Florence had to leave.

It was spring before the big clumsy-looking loom was finished to the builder's satisfaction.

330

It was plowing and planting time and the working of the loom would have to be put by till fall.

There was another note from Trude saying she now had two babies. Not much more was in the note. She had never been home since she had run off.

Everyone was glad to see the sun and the trees in leaf again. Up and down the valley men labored planting crops.

Jane and Tom's farm prospered. More stock was added each year as the animals were culled and the best kept for breeding. Jane gave thanks each day for the bountiful plenty.

The birth of her child came just before harvest. There was little trouble with her "laying-in" after so many. She was up in plenty of time to help with the cooking for the men of her family and hired help they had now during harvesting.

Autumn came early with the hilltops crowned in gold and red. An early snow fell in October to hang heavy on the still full leafed trees, the crack of breaking limbs sounded like gunshot through the day and night, damaging the timber beyond belief. After two days the sun came out hot enough to melt the heavy snow sending every stream over its banks.

In early November winter set in in earnest. Overnight the temperature dropped to near zero with a cold wind blowing from the North. Thank heavens with their management and planning there was plenty of wood cut and stacked in the woodhouse and feed for the livestock.

One snow fell on top of another. Hardly a traveler was seen on the roads. The winter was long and as the old men said, a bad one.

Anis and Will caught more fur that winter than ever before. Heavy and full—good grade pelts.

Miss Weatherbee came right after the first snow to start up the loom. Everyone gathered around as she threaded it, explaining as she worked.

The girls had been making "carpet rags" for months. Every shirt tail or dress tail that wasn't completely worn out was cut into inch strips and sewed end to end. The colors were mixed every which way. Big balls of string overflowed a big split basket. The smallest girl was set down with needle to tack carpet strings. The first weaving would be the rag rugs for the girls to learn on. Before winter was over there would be a woven rug by every bedside.

The clatter of the loom shuttle could be heard from morning to night. The first rug was finished, with carpet-warp fringe on the ends. Lizzie and the older girls brought it to Jane. She was to have the first one. Together they all ohed and ahed over the finished rug, deciding it was quite a marvel to be able to make them themselves.

Miss Weatherbee had brought along flax and some washed wool to teach them how to spin and combine the two for weaving linsey-woolsey.

Next year wool would be washed and dried, carded ready for use and they would grow flax for the weaving too.

Miss Weatherbee would come for September and October to do most of the weaving and in the process teach the girls.

The loom became a gathering place in the evening to watch whoever had the honor of sitting at the big shuttle that day.

Trude Comes Home

Spring came slowly with rain and wind. Hardly a week went by that the creeks didn't overflow.

Elizabeth had decided to go see her sister Trude. She hadn't come home since running off to marry. There had been a few letters but that was all.

Elizabeth had her trip and stayed about ten days. She returned to tell about Trude. That she was expecting her third baby in the fall.

Lizzie had met a man who would be coming to call sometime that summer. She blushed and stuttered as she told the girls about him.

This was the worst summer anyone could remember. It rained so much that plowing had to be done when the ground was still too wet. Some never got crops in at all. There was sickness up and down the valley.

Jane kept a watchful eye on them all. If she heard a sneeze, she had her remedies ready. The slightest scratch seemed to fester and become sore. There were always one of the younguns with a piece of fatback tied on a finger to draw out the pus.

Tom had bought twenty-five gallons of sheep dip from town. This was mixed in water to "soak" any injury in.

Jane had some of the mixture poured in the privy to keep the flies down.

Elizabeth's beau came sooner than expected. He brought word that Trude was sick and wanted to come home.

Tom readied the wagon, putting a full straw tick in with quilts and went after her. Lizzie went along riding horseback with her beau following Tom in the wagon.

Trude was very ill by the time they reached the cabin where they lived. Her two babies had been taken to her in-laws.

Elizabeth couldn't believe how terrible her sister looked and

333

how terribly sick she had become. They settled her in the wagon leaving as quickly as they could.

"Mammy Jane will get me well," Trude said, with a feeble smile.

When they arrived Trude was settled in the company room with a fire going to take the dampness out. Jane hovered over her trying to decide what was best to do. She doused Trude with her tonic sitting by her side till she fell into a restless sleep. Tossing and turning all night her head became hot and dry.

Jane decided to send for the doctor. What she had been doing didn't seem to be doing any good. It was late afternoon by the time the doctor arrived. He shook his head the minute he opened the door and again after he had examined her.

"Has anyone been in the room, Jane?" he asked.

"No. I've tended her since Tom and Elizabeth brought her home," Jane answered.

"It's typhoid, Jane. She is very weak and with child. It will be a miracle if she pulls through and if none of the others catch it. There is lots of the fever around this rainy weather. Makes it worse," the doctor explained. "The creeks overflowing spread it mostly from privies."

"I've been having sheep dip poured in ours to keep the flies away," Jane told him.

"That's good, keep it up and boil everything that's used in this room. There's not much I can do. I'll leave some medicine for the fever. Try to get some broth down her to keep up her strength. She is at a disadvantage being with child and so far along."

"I'll be back to see her in a couple of days. You know what to do as much as I do, Jane," the old doctor told her as he took his leave.

Jane sat by Trude. One minute she would fling off the covers, the next her teeth would be chattering with a chill. Bathing her face and keeping her warm was all that could be done.

All through the night Trude tossed and turned calling for her man. Once she called, "Mammy Jane, help me."

Jane's heart went out to her as she did what she could. Nothing seemed to help. The broth Jane spooned into her came back up almost as fast as it went down, leaving the girl weaker it seemed.

It was three days before the doctor made another visit. Examining Trude, he shook his head.

334

Jane watched him not expecting much encouragement. She knew how really sick Trude was and expected little.

Trude kept asking for her husband all through the night. "I want to see my babies," she mumbled.

Jane quieted her, "They will be here soon. You get better so you can see them."

Jane had spread a pallet by the fire where she stretched out for cat naps while Trude slept.

It had been ten days with Jane fighting every minute to keep the girl's strength up. It had begun to be a losing battle, that morning as she tried to brush Trude's hair noticing that it came out in handfuls. Every bone in Trude's body stood out like a skeleton with skin stretched over it. Her poor protruding stomach was a horrible thing to see. Jane placed her hand on her to see if the baby still lived. There was a small flutterin' telling her that it did.

That afternoon Trude's husband came with the two younguns. He stood outside the window to look in at his wife. Jane lifted Trude and placed an extra pillow under her head. "Trude, Trude, Jim is here with your babies," Jane told her.

Trude's eyelids fluttered as she tried to look where Jane pointed. A slight smile lit her face, "Jim," she whispered weakly, trying to reach a hand toward him.

He held each of the younguns up to look at their mother, both were crying as he lowered them to the ground.

Jane laid Trude back and she fell into a quiet sleep, her face at last peaceful. Lizzie wanted to relieve Jane in the sick room.

"No!" Jane said, "no one is to enter here. I'll do what I can. The Lord knows it's not much that can be done."

Trude wouldn't even swallow the broth Jane tried to feed her. All day and the following night Jane tried to get her to eat. She seemed in a stupor, not even knowing Jane.

The doctor came again. "It's just a matter of time, Jane. We can't save her. You had better tell her husband."

That night Trude died. Jane washed her poor body and laid her out in one of Lizzie's nightgowns with a dust cap to cover her head where her hair was all gone.

A casket was made hurriedly and a grave dug by the side of her little baby sister. She was lowered in the ground while Lizzie read the psalms. No one came to the quick funeral for fear of the fever. Even the younguns were kept away.

Trude's husband wept, long broken sobs that tore deep inside him as his young wife was buried.

A few days later he took his younguns and returned home.

There were quick funerals up and down the valley, where young and old alike dropped from the fever. Little children were left orphaned in a matter of hours. Expectant mothers and strong men, it made little difference, the fever took its toll.

Little Angel Gone

Coming back to the house after the funeral, Jane went upstairs to her room. Exhausted, she sank into her rocking chair by the window where she sat with tears streaming down her face.

Poor Trude, her life had been so short. She was only twenty years old and it was over. To Jane it was like losing one of her own. She had raised Trude from a baby as her own.

Weariness overtook Jane. Her tired eyes closed and she sat dozing in her chair. Lizzie calling her to supper awoke her, bringing her back to reality.

It was a sober group around the supper table that night. Each lost in their own thoughts as they quickly ate and went off to bed. Jane had searched each face wondering if the fever would be satisfied with one or would there be more.

With the coming of morning she knew. Little Ida, the apple of her pa's eye and the very picture of Jane, had chills. She was put to bed in the company room where sulphur candles had burned overnight, everything washed down and aired out.

Jane's heart turned over. Oh, God, not her, she prayed. She was the sweetest of the lot, with her golden hair and face of an angel.

From the time she was born her pa would whisper in her ear, "My littlest angel." He loved them all but it would break his heart if anything happened to her. She had just turned fourteen and crossed from being a child to being a woman. Jane thought at first maybe that was what was causing the chills.

She had hardly gotten her in bed with hot irons at her feet when the vomiting started. Jane knew it was typhoid and sent for the doctor.

He came as soon as he could, exhausted from tending the sick. "It's the fever, Jane. I can't tell you anything different. It's in God's hands. Do what you can, I'm no help."

Jane sat watching the golden head on the pillow tossing and

337

turning. She held the little hand and prayed, doing what she could as the little girl grew weaker and weaker.

It took two weeks for the life to seep away leaving the cold life-less form of the once happy little girl. Jane knelt by the bed no longer able to pray, hoarse sobs shook her as she kissed the sweet face of her daughter.

Another long walk up the hill behind a little white coffin. Jane and Tom leaning on one another, trying to find comfort when there was none, as the coffin was lowered into the ground.

The big house that Jane loved so was full of sorrow. In a month's time, they had lost two daughters. Tom wouldn't be con-soled and took long walks alone in the woods.

The fever was satisfied with its victims. None of the others came down with it as the days passed.

A month went by and Jane could breathe easier. It was done but what a waste and what a price they had to pay.

Lizzie

That fall Lizzie decided to marry Ed Boothe. He had been coming to see her for several months.

Jane hated to see her leave, the last of Tom's children she had raised. It had taken Elizabeth some time to make up her mind, she was now twenty-six.

Ed himself was thirty-six. He was the oldest of a big family in the next county.

They were married quietly on a Sunday afternoon with only the family present. After dinner they started out in Ed's buggy. He had brought it to take Lizzie's things back to where they would live with his people.

"We are going to give you money, Lizzie," Jane told her. "I don't think you would want a cow, pigs, and chickens," she said with a smile.

"We don't need much," Lizzie said. "We will be living with Ed's family for awhile."

Jane handed her an envelope with two hundred dollars in it. "With this you can buy your own home," Jane told her.

Lizzie kissed Jane's cheek, "I'll miss you, Mammy." Hugging her pa and all the others she climbed into the buggy to go to her new home.

The hurt hadn't gone from losing Ida and Trude. Jane missed Lizzie most of all. She had been her right hand for so long.

Jane's girls were young ladies now but Lizzie had been another woman in the house.

Jane had birthed ten of her own babies in this time. Work went on as usual, everyone had a job to do.

The railroad had come within thirty miles of the farm, making sale of the livestock easier. Buyers would come from the big cities to look over the pens full of sheep, cattle, and hogs.

Logging had become a big thing with the great stands of timber in the areas.

More beds were added in the washhouse as men asked for bed and board. The accommodations for stabling of horses and the plentiful table made the farm a desirable place for the hard-working loggers.

Will now had his own team and was in the thick of things. He liked logging above all other work.

There was hardly a day that the long family table wasn't full of big hearty men, the womenfolk eating after the men were fed and on their way.

Jane charged a dollar a day for a man and team. Sometimes there would be ten a day. Big money coming in. She wouldn't allow drinking or card playing and kept a clean strict place where they all felt welcome.

If one happened to fall sick, she doctored and cared for him as one of the family till he was on his feet again.

Tom enjoyed talking to the men who came from far and near. The "comers and goers" still stopped over at the big house, the judge who rode circuit, men from the state capital, ministers, who happened to come through. The company room was usually full.

Jane kept adding farms to her growing empire. The judge kept her informed as to hardship sales or those being sold for taxes. On his advice she bought up more and more land. Having a ready dollar put by made it possible.

The once penniless girl was a big landowner known far and wide as was the big white house for its hospitality and friendliness.

Accident

After the terrible summer, winter didn't seem in any hurry to start. The autumn days hung on with sunshine, every day warm and lazy.

Timbering was in full swing. Crosscut saws could be heard pulled by big husky men as they cut through the virgin timber.

Nathan was now eighteen and a tall quiet lad. He had a job trimming limbs. He wasn't much for teaming and didn't like pulling the big six-foot crosscut but took his turn as need be.

The first snowfall came the week after Thanksgiving, just enough to cover the ground.

The big wagons with logs piled high, sometimes three teams hooked up to pull them, were an everyday sight as they passed the house. The younguns ran to the windows to watch the slow process of the heavy loaded wagons, as they came in sight, stood watching as they made their way through the mud down the road and out of sight around the turn.

Will worked his team steadily with the others. His Catherin was with child again. It would be born in the late spring.

Winter had really come by Christmas. Snow fell on frozen ground to lay a few days and start a thaw that made logging and hauling a tough and hazardous job.

Jane cautioned the boys to be careful. Some of the men had been hurt already. One was brought to Jane with a big cut on his leg, shooting blood out a foot when the crude bandage made from his shirt was removed.

There was nothing to do but sew it up, getting out a big needle and strong thread she dipped them in "sheep dip," gave the man a big slug of whiskey and sewed. She bandaged it with a pad wet in turpentine and it healed in a few days' time.

There were always skinned knuckles, scratches, and bruises to get Jane's attention. She kept her salves and poultices handy.

341

The men decided to shut down a week at Christmas so they could all go home to be with their families.

John came home for the first time since moving to Spencer.

The day before Christmas they were all surprised when Lizzie and Ed rode in for the holidays. All the family would be together except their Catherin. They rarely heard from her anymore.

Will and his family came and stayed several days. The excitement of preparing the usual big Christmas feast filled the big house.

Jane didn't know when there had been so much laughter and talk. Every room seemed full of happy people.

Tom sat by the fire taking first one youngun then another on his lap to rock them for awhile and told them "tales."

At night big dishpans of corn was popped and chestnuts roasted in the fire to munch on. The younguns sang Christmas songs they had learned at school, with Lizzie leading them in one song after another. Will would join in with a ho, ho, ho, that made the small younguns howl with laughter and roll on the floor in glee.

They all said, "This is the best Christmas ever." Jane and Tom nodded in agreement. Thinking of the sorrow they had such a few short months ago and of the snow-covered mounds on the hill that their hearts still ached over.

John had two weeks he could spend with the family. Ed and Lizzie decided to stay for awhile. Ed wanted to go out with the loggin' crew to see how he would like it, and maybe work for awhile with them. They were still living with his folks and didn't have a home to look after.

Jane and the girls were glad to have Lizzie around again. She worked along with them and was pleasant company besides.

Will and Catherin had gone back to their home after Christmas.

In the long winter afternoons Lizzie, Minerva, Etta, and Florence set in the company room working on "fancy work" or learning to use the loom under Lizzie's watchful eyes.

John and his pa had long talks as they sat by the fire. Sometimes walking to the barns and shed to look at the stock or just for something to do.

The sun came out and melted some of the snow. In the night it got colder and by morning a snow was falling on the frozen ground.

Tom asked the loggers at breakfast if they shouldn't "lay-off" a few days. Makes good skidding weather, they informed him, and off they went.

Will stopped in that morning to see John, "Little brother, want to come try your hand with a team?" Will asked, with a laugh.

"No, thanks, Will, I think I'll just sit and talk with pa. Have to be going back soon," John answered.

Jane went to the door as Will left. "You be careful now," she told him.

"I will, Mammy Jane," he called back, his frosty breath floated around his head like a cloud.

Will had a fine team of dappled Belgian horses and treated them like one of his babies.

As Will got to the loggin' road some of the men had already started to load their wagons. "Hey! Leave some for me," he called with a laugh.

"You're late," they called back. "Get the lead out, you won't get loaded today." The loggers all liked Will and looked to him when there were problems of any sort.

The first wagon rolled off on the frozen ground. The driver riding the brake till he was down on the main road.

Will was next with his wagon, he had another team hooked with his own. His wagon piled high with big logs. He stood on the tongue holding on to the brake as he guided the four powerful horses down the hill.

The wagon behind was almost ready to go. The last log being rolled up the log ramp to the top of the heap. The loggers misjudged, rolling it over the top. It went crashing down the hill through the trees making a "god awful" noise.

The first team of Will's jerked to the side of the road. The big Belgians had to follow putting a strain on the wagon tongue. Will jumped down to control the team. As he jumped the frozen wagon tongue snapped like a rifle shot twisting the wagon toward where he was. Not having good footing on the snowy ground he slipped.

The men from the other wagons ran to help him. The heavy loaded wagon lurched toward the fallen man as he tried to scramble out of the way. A rear wheel rolled over his body about midway with a sickening crunch of flesh and bone. A second wheel went over him as the wagon tippled and rolled over with the top heavy load sending logs crashing through the underbrush as they loosened from the wagon.

343

"Oh! My God!" Nathan said as he ran to his brother and knelt on the frozen ground beside the mangled body.

Men rushed to the team that was still hitched to the broken wagon tongue and floundering through the trees in flight.

Nathan lifted Will's head. Blood slowly ran from the corners of his mouth. Men gathered around not knowing what to do.

Will's body was crushed from the neck to his legs, no spark of life left. It had all happened so fast not even a yell had left Will's lips as he tried to control his teams.

Nathan sat on the ground, his brother's limp body in his arms. Tears ran down his face. "Get a wagon ready, we will take Will home," he ordered.

The smallest wagon was soon brought down the hill. A couple of horse blankets folded in the bottom. They gently lifted Will and laid him on the blankets.

"This will kill Mammy Jane," Nathan said to no one in particular. Nathan and Ed climbed up in the wagon to take Will back to the big white house.

"How will we ever explain this to Mammy and Catherin?" Nathan asked Ed as they drove along the slippery road.

"It was a 'freak' accident. Might never happen again in a lifetime," Ed answered.

Nathan drove slowly not wanting to face the family with the tragic news.

Jane saw the wagon at the big red gate come through and slowly make its way toward the house. "Something has happened, Tom," she said as she turned to him in her chair by the fire.

Tom rose from his chair and followed Jane as she grabbed a shawl tying it over her head as she went toward the yard where the wagon was headed. The wagon came to a halt as she reached it.

Looking at the two men drivers she guessed. "Will?" she asked as she took hold of the wagon for support. She looked at the broken body it held.

"Oh, God! Not another one," she said. Jane had never fainted in her life. It took all her willpower to hang on to her senses now.

Lizzie came running from the house, took one look, screamed, and sank to the ground. Ed jumped down from the wagon, gathered his wife in his arms, and took her toward the house.

Tom stood beside Jane shaking, his teeth chattering, every drop of blood gone from his face. Jane pulled herself together see-

344

ing Tom was in shock, put her arms around him, "Come, Tom, there's nothing we can do here." John helped get Tom back inside, tears streaming down his face.

Setting Tom in his chair by the fire she threw a blanket to John, "Wrap him," she said as she hurried from the room. She was back soon with a strong tonic. She held it to Tom's lips. His head rested against the back of the chair, his eyes closed. The chills still shook his body. "We will have to get him in bed and warm," Jane said as she hurried to turn down one of the beds. Bring his nightshirt, Minerva. Get hot irons, Etta," Jane shot orders to the girls.

John helped get his pa to the bed. They sat him on the side of it removing his clothes and getting him into the flannel nightshirt. Jane tucked the blankets to his chin and put the hot irons at his feet.

The tonic had begun to take effect, the color coming back to his face. "He will be alright soon," Jane said. "Minerva, stay with your pa. Don't let him throw the covers off."

Jane went to the other bed where they had put Lizzie. She was coming to, her eyelids fluttered open. Seeing Jane she tried to raise herself. "Lay still a few minutes, Lizzie," Jane told her.

"Oh, God!" Lizzie said as she started to sob, her husband held her close as she cried.

Jane went back to the yard. Nathan stood by the wagon where his dead brother lay now covered with a blanket.

"We will have to get him inside," Jane said. "Put him in the company room, John will help in a minute." Going back to the house she went to the company room, spread a couple of sheets over the bed to lay Will on.

As soon as Lizzie got control of herself, Ed went with John to help bring in the dead man. They had trouble trying to carry him. All the bones were broken in his body. Seeing the problem, Jane sent John to fetch a wide board while she and Nathan removed Will's clothing. "We will have to lay him out straight," she told her son. "Go fetch water and a rag, I'll wash him and get him ready."

With Nathan's help to shave Will, Jane washed the battered body. Folded a sheet on the wide board that had been put on the backs of two kitchen chairs. The men gently lifted Will to the board where Jane covered him with another sheet.

Someone had to let Catherin know and fetch clothes to dress Will.

345

Ed and Nathan took the wagon to the barn and hooked up the sled, filling a generous amount of hay in the bottom for Catherin and the younguns to sit on.

Jane decided she had better go with Nathan to fetch Will's family. Leaving instructions with Minerva as how Tom should be looked after while she was gone, Jane didn't dare give way. There were living to take care of now and Will's wife had to be told. Jane had to be strong to face what lay ahead of her in the next hours.

As Nathan guided the horses and sled across the run up to the house, Jane saw Catherin and the younguns at the window. They knew something was wrong. Mammy Jane didn't come calling in such weather otherwise.

Catherin opened the kitchen door for Jane. One look at her face and Catherin sank down on a chair by the table.

"What is it, Jane? What's happened to Will?" Catherin asked in a low voice.

Jane looked at Catherin big with child. Knowing that there was no easy way she could break the news. "Will's had an accident, Catherin. The wagon ran over him with a load of logs on it. It happened so quick nothing could be done."

"Oh! God! He's dead," Catherin said as she slumped in the chair.

Jane grabbed her, easing her to the floor. The younguns started crying as they saw their mother stretched out on the kitchen floor. Jane wet a rag in cold water, washed Catherin's face till she started to moan and come to life again.

Jane lay a hand on her shoulder to keep her still a moment longer. "Think of your baby, Catherin, you'll have to be strong now." She helped her to sit up, then to her feet, walked with an arm around her to the other room. "You lay down for a spell. I'll get the younguns ready and find what I need for Will."

Catherin's eyes were dry as she lay looking at the ceiling above her and Will's bed.

Jane took Will's weddin' suit from the cupboard, found clean underwear, socks, and a shirt and the string tie he had worn to be married. Laying them on the kitchen table she found outer clothing for the younguns.

"Catherin, what clothes do you want to take?" Jane asked.

Catherin slowly got up from the bed and began gathering together what she would need.

346

Jane went through to tell Nathan to see everything was alright at the outer buildings.

Jane bundled the younguns in a quilt in the hay as Catherin closed the doors and joined them for the ride back to the homeplace.

Farewell to Will

Lizzie came to the yard to help with the younguns as the sled drew up. Going to Catherin she gave her sister-in-law a hug holding her for several minutes, then taking the children inside.

Tom was still asleep as they entered. Jane took Lizzie aside telling her about Catherin. "There were no tears, that's a bad sign," Jane said. "You keep an eye on her. She is in danger herself being as far along as she is. I'll have to get clothes on Will while I can."

Jane took the clothing to the company room to clothe the poor crushed body of Will. She couldn't stay the bitter tears that made rivulets down her cheeks. As she worked she heard nailing and sawing in the shed and knew that John was at his grim task of making Will's coffin. Jane was so thankful that John and Lizzie were here at this time. How she would have gotten through the days ahead without them she didn't want to think about.

Tom had never been strong since the war and was little help now.

By the time Jane had finished with Will, her good friend Florence had come. News traveled fast and soon there were several men gathered in the shed helping John.

Jane and Nathan walked with Jed and another man to the cemetery to decide where Will's grave would be. Jane decided to bury him next to his mother.

The grave had to be started. This was the first one Tom hadn't measured off for the men who came to dig.

Jane let Nathan measure the grave and mark it off, "It's time you learned," she told him. The grave was started as Jane went back down the hill.

Jane finished making Will ready, he looked so peaceful. Such a strong young man. What a waste, she thought to herself as she stood looking at him.

"Mammy Jane? can I see Will now?" Catherin asked.

"You will have to remember your baby, Catherin," Jane said as

348

she went to her. "Come along now," Jane took Catherin's arm and walked her across the hall to her husband. Jane nodded for Lizzie to come too. Jane silently drew the sheet from Will's face.

"Oh, God! It's Will!" Catherin said as she slid to the floor in a heap.

Jane and Lizzie were on either side of her and grabbed her as she started to fall, easing her gently to the floor. "Stay with her, Lizzie, till I get some tonic."

Jane was soon back holding a glass to Catherin's lips. They got some of the liquid down her. When she was able to walk, they took her back to the sittin' room placing her in a rocking chair where she sat and stared out the window, never a tear had been shed, keeping the hurt bottled up inside her.

Work went on in the big house. A roaring fire was built in the big fireplace in the washhouse where the men came taking turns at the grave, some warming themselves while others dug. More men came to help as the word spread about Will.

Just before dark Catherin's mother and father came in a big buggy. Jane had never met them before. When they arrived, she brought them in to Catherin. Saw that they had hot coffee and chairs by the fire. It had been a long cold trip for them.

The Cooks came bringing a big cake and other cooked foods. The big house was filling up with Will's friends. He was well liked.

Jane saw that seats were put in the company room for the wake. As Jane worked, she remembered how many times she had sent Will for covering and padding for coffins. The last time she had him buy a bolt of white and one of black and extra hardware, padding and such to have on hand in the house. He didn't realize he had bought things for his own coffin.

Jane fixed a small basin of soda water, found white cloths to use, wet them in the solution and put them on Will's face and hands. They would have to be changed all through the night to keep his flesh from turning black before the funeral. There was no fire in the room where he was laid out for the same reason.

People came and sat awhile in their wraps and when they got cold went across the hall to the fire in the other room to warm themselves.

John had the coffin done, ready for the lining and covering. It was taken to the washhouse where the women could finish it by the fire.

Lizzie and Florence went to work on it. Minerva helped holding the tacks and such.

Jane saw that food was being prepared for everyone, managing to meet people as they came. The big house was lit up in every room as night fell. People were still coming and going.

The minister came at dark to stay part of the night for the wake.

It was late by the time the coffin was finished. The minister had everyone go to the other room where they all knelt in prayer, he leading them while Will was placed in his coffin.

They all went back filing by the coffin to look on Will's face before sitting on the long boards to sing hymns. Jane was so thankful that Will's face had not been damaged in the accident.

The preacher left at midnight. He would come the next day to hold the funeral at two o'clock as was the custom.

The men working on the grave had gone home to rest at dark. They would be back at daybreak to finish it.

All through the night people went from one room to another. Hymns were sung off and on all night in the room where Will lay.

Jane had taken Catherin and her parents to an upstairs room to rest.

Morning came clear and cold. Tom was up feeling better. He went to see that the chores were done at the barns and outbuildings.

The sun came out around noon. Jane saw Tom going slowly up the hill to check on the grave that was being finished up.

By afternoon people had started to gather, the women coming inside to warm themselves. The men had started a fire outside the graveyard so they could warm themselves without walking off the hill. They gathered around the big bonfire stomping their feet, hands buried deep in pockets, telling over and over again about the accident that had taken Will's life, trying to figure out what he could have done to save himself.

The big kitchen stove was a busy place as food was prepared for everyone.

Anis and Ed went to Will's to milk and feed his animals. The minister and his wife arrived by one o'clock. He took notes to write up the obituary for the service.

By two o'clock the orchard was standing full of horses tied to the trees. The big yard was full of wagons and buggies. Most went on the hill to await the family, standing around the fire or walking in the cemetery to look at the graves there, some to stand silent by Old Harn's grave.

At two o'clock the minister led the procession up the hill in front of the long black coffin that held Will's body.

Catherin insisted on going to the grave and she and her parents walked slowly behind the coffin.

The service lasted most of an hour with the talk from the preacher and the singing of more hymns.

The last good-bye was said as Will was lowered to his last resting place. The sobbing women and the clearing of men's throats sounded on the cold winter air. It was over.

Catherin's folks were going to stay over the night. They wanted to take Catherin and the younguns home with them for awhile.

Lizzie and Ed would stay in her house if Catherin decided to go.

Journey for Catherin

The next morning Catherin's folks wanted to start home. Catherin had decided in the night that she couldn't stay in the house that had been Will's and her home. She would leave with her parents, and wait till spring to come back for her things.

Lizzie and Ed would stay in the house and take care of things until she returned. They went along with Catherin to help her pack the things she could take in the buggy.

Jane didn't think Catherin should make such a long trip in the cold and on such icy roads. There was nothing she could say and had to let her do as she and her family decided.

The big house seemed empty when they were all gone. Ed and Lizzie would now be staying at the other house.

The raw mound of earth could be seen from the kitchen window. Jane would look at it and in her heart call, Oh, Will! Will! and tears would course down her cheeks as she remembered the little boy who had been such a help when she arrived as his new ma.

Jane was grateful that John stayed another couple of days and spent more time with his pa. Tom looked as though he had aged through the ordeal. "I must take better care of my Tom," Jane said to herself.

Ed came with Will's team, he and Nathan went back to the timbering. It was a sober group that worked that day, the men missed good-hearted Will more than they cared to admit.

The weather changed and a thaw came. The road became a quagmire with the horses struggling through the mud pulling the big heavily loaded wagons splashing mud on the drivers and themselves till you couldn't tell who they were.

Some of the horses fell in the deep mud and would get tangled in the traces, one had a broken leg when they were untangled from the muddy mess. The brute had to be destroyed. The death of man or beast made little difference. The logging continued.

All through the winter loggers came to the big house for food

352

and lodging. The first hint of the end of the long winter was the yellowing of the willows by the creek and the spicewood sending out its little yellow flowerets telling Jane it was time to gather for the spring tea. The younguns were sent to gather armloads of the tender branches. Jane carefully washed and broke the branches seeping them in big kettles on the stove. Everyone got a cup with sugar mixed in it. This was to clear one's blood in the spring.

Ed and Nathan quit their logging job as plowing time came. The menfolk were in the fields from sunup to sundown.

It was a beautiful spring and the apple orchard white with blooms. Coming on the house from the road, it was a picture to behold.

Will's Catherin came back in late May. She had lost her baby soon after Will's death being six months along. Her life had almost been lost with the too soon birth of the child.

Her father and brother came bringing a wagon to take her household plunder back. They intended to take Will's big Belgian team and the other wagon.

Catherin brought a young cedar tree from her home. Taking it on the hill to the cemetery she planted it at the head of Will's grave sobbing, saying a final good-bye to Will.

Saying good-bye to Catherin was hard knowing they would never see her or Will's children again. They were losing all of Will's family now.

The house was empty after Catherin's things were removed. Ed and Lizzie came back to the homeplace again.

Jane was glad to have Lizzie home again, as were the girls.

Some of the household management could be turned over to Lizzie. Jane had the morning "miseries" again which meant another child in late winter. She could do with all the help she could get. Lizzie was so good training the girls to sew and cook. Things Jane didn't have time or energy for.

The School

The years flew by. The big household was a busy place filled with Tom's and Jane's family and their many friends who came to visit.

There were more and more "Comers and Goers" who would stop over to spend the night in the company room, bringing news from far and wide.

More families were moving into the area filling up the "hollers" with shack homes and plenty of younguns.

The county had decided to build a school in the valley. There were lots of the younguns who didn't attend the school on White Oak, it was so far to go.

Everyone was excited about having their own school close at hand. Assessments were asked for from those able to give to help build it.

Tom and Jane sent a hundred dollars. It would be worth having a school close where even the youngest could attend.

Minerva was a young woman, she and the older girls had given up going to school, Jane had hoped one of them might go on to teach. However, her hopes were never realized.

Anis and Nathan helped on the building. The school was finished by January. It stood painted white with blue smoke curling from the stovepipe extending from the tall roof. The floors had been oiled to keep down the dust from so many muddy feet.

A young man by the name of Haverty was brought in to teach. He walked up every "holler" to enroll each child old enough, talking to the parents about the importance of education.

When the school opened, the "hollers" spewed out youngun after youngun till there were thirty-five eager faces before the teacher.

A big blackboard had been installed across the front of the room behind the teacher's desk. Most of the teaching was done there. The books were few and pencil and paper nonexistent. The

354

"scholars" came nevertheless with their tattered clothes and tin dinner pails. Most learned to read and write and to count to some degree.

The new teacher "stayed over" at times when the creeks were up till he couldn't walk the ten miles or so down on Beech where he lived.

He was always welcomed by Jane and Tom and could have stayed the winter without charge. Tom enjoyed the learned way he spoke. There were long conversations by the warm fire during the long winter evenings.

Jane watched as "teacher's" eyes lingered on Minerva whenever she was around. She could do worse. He came from a good family and had been to "Normal School," this fact alone carried lots of sway with Jane.

Minerva was a lovely young woman past twenty now. She had taken over most of the management of the household since Lizzie and Ed had gone back to live with his folks.

Florence was an unmanageable sixteen with mischievous eyes and a head of curly brown hair, and a continuous giggle. She thought herself grown and "made sheep eyes" at the teacher, when she thought no one was looking. She had been sent to school with the rest, learning very little. She was too busy teasing and having fun to learn and at this point couldn't read or write. She had been spoiled from the start by them all.

Jane had given her a few smacks on the behind at times. There was such a hurt look on her face and in her eyes for days afterwards that Jane couldn't abide and usually left her to go her own way.

Rob was a strong boy for his age. He worked alongside the men, loved driving a team as well as Will did when he lived. Rob had a hankerin' for dogs and fox hunting and would disappear into the woods regularly during the summer months.

Tom had gotten some of his strength back and helped with all the work on the farms.

Jane never let her girls work at farm work only in the garden and around the yard and house, even though some of the work had to have hired help to get done.

There was talk of a store going in up the creek from them and a federal post office. It was to be called Oka.

After crops were in, the foundations were laid. It would be on two levels, the living quarters below the level of the road with the store on the second story, its front porch level with the road.

Everyone was excited about having things so close. The family putting in the store was from Roane County where their family had been in mercantile business for years.

A Village Grows

The store was in. The shelves filled with everything imaginable
There had been a small log church built close by which jokingly
was named the "Frog Pond Church" since there was a swampy
place where the frogs tried to make more noise than the hymn
singing in the church.

A "gristmill" had been built on the creek where families could
bring a grist of corn or wheat and have it ground for the family
bread.

Oka was becoming a village now. On Saturday afternoon the
men and young boys gathered at the store to sit and smoke and
talk. A game of "Horse Shoes" or "mumblety-peg" almost always in progress.

This was the time the womenfolk did their baking for the Sab-
bath or visited a close friend.

Their trips to the store was usually done through the week
when they took their baskets of eggs to trade for the things they
couldn't grow or make themselves.

Walking into the cool dark of the big store savoring the smells
of new cloth, leather, and coffee was a treat for them all. They
didn't share it with the men on Saturday letting them enjoy the
company of each other that day undisturbed.

Tom took his turn at the store where his advice was asked on
animal breeding and farming. His farm was the biggest and most
prosperous in the area, therefore, his opinions were listened to
and repeated among the other farmers.

Jane's last child, a boy named after the doctor who delivered
him, was called Spencer. They had to send for old Doc Spencer to
come all the way from the town that was named after his family.

This was the first time Jane had a long delivery or any problems. Of course she was older now and had birthed fourteen so
far.

357

The girls didn't like the name of Spencer and started calling the baby Little Dock.

He was two years old now and Jane hadn't started her monthlies. She began to think that they were over with and that Little Dock would be the last of the children to be born.

Jane's Tom still called her his angel and there would be babies as long as she could bear them, she knew.

More and more people were still at home yet. Jane knew that soon some of them would be marrying and leaving.

Nathan was twenty-eight and was going on Sunday over on Sandy to see a Smith girl. They were to be wed soon, she felt sure.

Jane and Tom hated to lose any of their large family. Their big house was full of coming and going. Jane knew once it started there would be a steady stream of weddings like it was with Tom's first family until they were all gone.

Minerva and the Haverty man who still taught the school were "sparking." There would be a weddin' there soon. There were always young men around her girls every Sunday, the house filled with them. Sunday dinner was an occasion with the big table sometimes being filled three times before they were all fed.

Jane kept a sharp eye on them all. There would be nothing ever said about her girls.

She knew they were talked of being the prettiest girls in the county. The large farm and big white house was spoken of with envy and was a choice gathering place for young and old alike.

The day arrived when Nathan told his parents that he was going to marry in two weeks. The Smith girl and he would be married at her home on a Sunday.

Jane wanted to empty the house at the Hall farm for the couple.

"You can live there and stock the farm as you want," Jane said.

"No, Mammy, we will live with her folks for awhile. We want a farm of our own. I've saved some money," Nathan told her.

Jane knew better than to say more, Nathan was a man and knew his own mind.

The day arrived for the weddin'. Nathan owned his own team and buggy which he had ready.

Tom and Jane called him into the company room and closed the door. "We hate to see you leave, son, and want to wish you well," Tom said. Jane had three hundred dollars ready to give for their weddin' gift. "Nathan, your pa and me, we want you to have this, put it to good use when you get your own place. Come back, we want to give you a cow and a pig," Jane told her son.

Nathan shook hands with his pa and left for the big day.

Only a short time passed till Nathan had bought a small farm down on Big Sandy where he was working on a house for his new wife.

Tom, Anis, and Rob loaded a big wagon with lumber and drove it over to help a few days. Jane and the girls sent foodstuff along for them.

A couple of months passed before Nathan brought his wife for a visit to the homeplace. She was a pretty little thing and a sensible girl from a good family. Her family were helping them get "set up."

They stayed a week and went back with the buggy full of plunder, crates of chickens, pigs, and a cow tied on behind the buggy by a rope.

Their little farm was well set up. Nathan's pa and ma knew he would soon have a flourishing farm.

School started in September with the same teacher back. He had been back a couple of times through the summer to "spark" with Minerva.

October came and Minerva and young Haverty had a talk with her parents asking permission to marry. Minerva was now twenty-three and they readily gave their consent. A simple wedding was performed on a Saturday afternoon by the Rev. Mr. Cottrell. The couple would remain at the homeplace.

Minerva's sisters teased her, telling her the teacher only married her so he wouldn't have to walk the ten miles home.

She took it all in stride and things went on as before in the household.

They hadn't been married long till Minerva would hurry toward the privy as soon as she was out of bed in the mornings. She would return pale and shaky after those bouts.

Nothing escaped the sharp eyes of Jane. Meeting her at the door as she returned from her trip down the path to the privy, Jane said, "You stay in bed tomorrow, young lady. I want you to go now and lay down, I'll fetch a tonic for you."

Minerva went meekly to her room glad to stretch out on the soft bed and be taken care of.

Entering the room Jane held a hot cup of tonic for her to drink. "This will make you feel better, stay in bed tomorrow till I bring you a cup. The sickness won't last long, just till the baby lodges itself proper." Jane turned and left the room.

The morning miseries didn't go away as they should have. Jane became worried about her daughter. Meeting "teacher" in the yard after two months had gone by and the nausea continued, Jane said, "I think Minerva needs to be taken to a doctor."

"What is wrong? Is she sick?" a look of bewilderment on his face.

"She is with child and her miseries are lasting too long. I don't seem to be able to do much," Jane told the young husband.

Minerva was bundled up and taken to see old Doc Dye. All he could tell her was "rest and wait and see."

Jane wouldn't let her do any heavy work and made her rest in the afternoons and remain in bed late each morning.

Minerva's body thickened with the child going into the fifth month still with morning sickness. Jane knew something was wrong and wasn't surprised that in the sixth month Minerva went into hard labor. Jane sent for her friend Florence. Together they wrapped the tiny little baby in a blanket.

A box was made and a small grave dug in a corner of the cemetery where a little unmarked mound held what would have been Minerva's first son.

Days went by with Minerva weak and helpless, mourning her lost baby. Jane sat by her bed talking, "Girl, you have to snap out of this. There is the living to see after, there will be more babies. Your husband needs a wife not a sniveling, weeping, clinging vine. No more feeling sorry for yourself. It takes a strong backbone to deal with life," Jane continued, "I want you out of bed in a chair this afternoon, and walking tomorrow. You hear me, girl?" Jane asked as she closed the door on her way out. Her heart ached for her oldest girl. Someone had to get her up and strong again.

Minerva regained her health slowly. The time came when the tears had stopped and life for her became worth living again.

Jane watching the young couple knew that things were right with them again and heaved a sigh of relief.

Normal School

Times were changing, Jane and Tom's children all grown. Little Dock had been sent away to Normal School.

Milissa and Etta had married young brothers of Lizzie's husband. They were both living close by and each expecting their first child.

Florence was still at home, still too busy flirting and having fun to settle on one man to marry. Prushia, they all said, was stuck-up with her high tone talking and fancy clothes. Jane would look at her seeing Catherin's way about her. Her talking was something to hear. Out of them all, Prushia and Dock had the best education.

Dock had been away at school six months when word came for his parents to come to the school.

Mammy Jane and Tom readied themselves and went in their fine buggy to see what was wanted. Arriving at the main office they went in.

"This is my husband, Tom, I'm Jane Jarvis. We are here about our son Spencer," Jane informed the dean in a no-nonsense voice.

"Oh, yes! Mr. and Mrs. Jarvis. Won't you sit down please?" the dean asked.

"About your son, we here at the school think he will be better off sent somewhere else. We have strict rules here and it seems he has broken most of them. We have had him in for talks which I might add has had little effect. He is a bright student and has good possibilities if he would apply himself." The dean stopped to see how his talk was affecting the boy's parents.

"Just what has Dock—Spencer—done?" Jane asked.

"He teases the girls—," the dean paused, "let's just say he has conducted himself as no gentleman would," the dean coughed behind his hand and looked embarrassed.

"If you would care to leave the room, Mrs. Jarvis, I would discuss this further with your husband," the dean informed her.

Jane looked him straight in the eye, got up without a word and left the two men together.

She didn't wait long until Tom joined her with a grin on his face. "Don't look so woebegone Jane, it's not that bad. We will take him to Glenville and enroll him there so he won't miss any of the school year," Tom told her.

"I want to know what he did. I'll tan his hide if he has done something to shame his family," Jane told her husband.

"Seems he was setting next to a young lady," Tom couldn't keep from grinning at this stage, "he could see the print of her garter through her dress and reached over and flipped it."

Jane looked shocked, "I hope the young lady slapped his face."

"She and the rest of the class seemed to think it funny. The school is expelling her too," Tom answered.

"Where is Dock?" Jane asked.

"He is in his room at the boardinghouse they call a 'dorm,'" Tom answered her.

Little Dock came to the door at the first knock, startled at seeing his mother, he backed into the room. "Come in," he said, pulling out the only chair for his mother to sit on.

Without preliminaries, Jane said, "I suppose you know you have shamed this family, and caused a young girl to be thrown out of school?"

Dock was "cockey" and proud and stood straight as his mother "raked him over." "I didn't mean to shame you, mother. It was just a silly thing to do. I'm sorry I've caused you trouble."

"Young man, you've run your ma and me over here for your foolishness. We have to find another school for you. You will get your hide tanned if anything like this happens again." Tom couldn't keep the grin from the corners of his mouth. "Get your things together, we are taking you to Glenville," his pa told him.

"I'm ready, all packed," with that Little Dock went to a corner where his things were behind a curtain and started carrying them out to the buggy.

The trip to the new school was made mostly in silence. Tom and Jane stayed over in the hotel after getting Dock settled in school and the dorm.

"No more 'shenanigans' or I'll use my blacksnake on you," his mother promised in parting.

"I'll behave, mother," Dock told her.

The two-year course was completed without any further troubles

362

and Little Dock came home educated, his mother bursting with pride, never showing it to him in any way.

His pa would sit talking to Dock feeling him out to see what he had learned in the fancy school they had sent him to, both enjoying the sparing talks together.

Lizzie Comes Home

The spring Dock graduated and came back to the homeplace was busy. Jane's three boys, Rob, Newton, and Dock, were all busy on the farm. With hired help, more and more planting was done.

Newton had a pair of matched steers that was his pride and joy. He kept them slick and well fed and was never far away from them at any time. They obeyed his every command and he used them for any work he had on the farm.

Rob still liked his foxhounds and Little Dock the ladies.

Tom was proud of his boys and the farm they worked together. Anis, once so strong and so much help, had been regulated to looking after the barns and yards. He had gotten old and showed it. His walk slow, stopping after the least exercise to "catch his breath."

During the hottest part of the summer, sweet Lizzie was brought home to her last resting place to lay on the hill with her mother, brother, and sister. Lizzie's many miscarriages had taken their toll of her health. She had caught the flu in the spring which had gone on and on till the young life was over. There were no children left to mourn her. She was thirty-six and had a longer life than sister Trude who died at twenty.

Jane was saddened, she had loved Lizzie. Tom looked like an old man as he and Jane followed the coffin up the hill. How many times they had made the slow walk to the burying place, their hearts broken with the loss of a loved one.

My Tom, I never noticed his once golden brown beard is now almost white, his step has slowed, My Tom. Jane's mind was on Tom while the hymns were sung and the coffin lowered in the ground.

All through the summer and fall Dock readied his team of matched bays and his new buggy and went "sparking." First one young lady and then another caught his eye for a time.

364

Robert was seeing an Ellison girl and had announced they would marry by Christmas.

Jane and Tom had bought more farms through the years. One over the hill from Bear Run would be given to Rob when he married. There would be a barn-raising the first of September. Trips were made with his pa to lay out where the house and barn would be built. Measured and staked out with trees marked to be cut. Preparations were in progress for the big day.

The girls excitedly talked as they baked and cooked for the dinner that would be taken to the farm for the "raisin'."

The day arrived bright and sunny, the wagons and buggies came from each direction pulling into the fields under the trees where tables would be made from boards for the noontime meal.

The sound of saws and axes, the laughter of the men telling tales could be heard from the hillsides. The women visited and talked, showing off their newest babies.

Jane came to the raisin' meeting her daughter-in-law for the first time. Noting that her pretty mouth with its rows of pearly teeth was usually spread in laughter. She seemed to get along with everyone, this one and that one calling, "Oh, Delila, will your house be here? Will your garden be there?" Young Delila went from group to group answering first one and then another of her soon to be new sister-in-laws.

Jane decided she would be lively enough to keep young Rob busy and away from his hound dogs.

It was a small barn and the men soon had it up with the roof being put in place.

The foundation for the two-room house was laid ready for it to be built from cut lumber.

The young people all gathered as soon as the last roof shingle was put in place to play games in the new barn. "Old Dusty Miller" was a favorite since the boys and girls held hands with their arms around each other.

Lots of joshing and laughter was heard as they chose partners for the game.

As soon as the sun went down everyone was called from the barn to ready themselves for the trip home. Tired younguns were loaded into wagons and buggies among the leftover mess of the dinner.

Good-bye and advice was called till they were out of sight of those left around the new barn.

The family would help on the new house the next day.

365

Newt

In three years' time Rob, Florence, and Metta had all married. Jane was beginning to forget just how many grandchildren she and her Tom had.

The girls remained at home for the first year after marrying till their husbands furnished them a house to live in, usually with their first younguns.

Minerva and teacher were talking of moving to town. Prushia wanted to go also, she didn't like living on the farm and wanted something better.

Jane felt she was losing control of her large family. Dock and Newt had started running together. Going off each Saturday to chase the pleasures they wanted like hound dogs after a rabbit.

Jane had smelled whiskey a few times on Newt. She would have to watch him closer.

The farm still prospered with more and more businessmen making it a stopover to the capital.

Keeping an eye on things Jane noticed her whiskey jug going down. Then one day the bottle she had poured out to make tonic disappeared altogether.

The next day Newt didn't appear for breakfast.

"Where is Newt?" Jane asked. No one seemed to know.

"Off with his yoke of oxen, no doubt," Tom told her.

Nothing more was said. Around ten o'clock Jane was upstairs and discovered Newt still in bed.

"Are you sick?" she asked in alarm, pulling the covers from around his head. The smell almost knocked her off her feet. "You no good worthless boy, laying drunk in my house," Jane spoke softly as she proceeded to tie the corners of the sheets together around Newt. Leaving him tied in the bedding, "I'll fix you," she said as she hurriedly left for the downstairs.

Newt squirmed and worked himself from the bedding. He knew Mammy Jane was in a rage and would be back soon.

Slipping down the stairs he saw their big collie dog on the piazza. Half carrying and half dragging the animal, he hurried back up the stairs. He lifted the dog onto the bed, tying it as he had been tied. Hearing Mammy Jane on her way up the stairs he ran to the portico climbing down to the ground by way of a trellis full of vines. He headed for other places fast.

Jane had gone for her "blacksnake" whip. She would teach that boy about getting drunk and on her whiskey she kept for medicine. Her thoughts were going around and around as she reached the top of the stairs.

The bundle she had tied up before going for her whip still lay as she left it.

Pulling back her arm she flicked the whip toward the mound of bedding, remembering another time when she cut two men to ribbons. She couldn't do much damage through the covers. It would let Newt know she meant business however.

As the whip landed a loud howl came from the pile, scaring Jane half to death at the suddenness of it. Her arm was raised for the next lick, down it came, the bundle of bed clothing bouncing all over the bed.

That ornery boy! he has put old collie in his bed. Jane gathered the bundle, carried it to the portico and dropped it to the grass below. Old collie yelling every breath escaped to the shed.

"Newt, where are you? I'll whip the hide off you," Mammy Jane yelled. Old Newt was long gone. He knew better than show his face for several days till Mammy Jane quieted down.

Tom sat on the piazza watching the whole thing. Doubling up with laughter when Mammy Jane threw the collie over the upstairs banister.

Newt had been drunk but he could still use his imagination.

Mammy Jane stomped through the house all day looking for Newt.

"Jane, come sit a spell and stop frettin'," Tom called when he heard her come through the hallway.

Jane did as he asked, lowering herself into a comfortable rocker. "I get so mad letting a youngun outsmart me," Jane told Tom.

"Boys will be boys," Tom said with a chuckle that turned into a laugh as he looked over at Jane.

Jane laughed low, "That was some trick he pulled, I couldn't have thought of a better one myself."

It was a treat having Jane by his side, Tom tried to think of something to keep her sitting talking.

"Did I ever tell you about the time I was plowing over at the Duffield farm when I was a boy?" Tom asked Jane.

"No, I don't think so, what happened?" Jane asked.

"I was plowing in a cove, going from one hill to the other, the longest rows of corn I ever did see. I was using an old Dun mule called Ben. I remember it was hot and the dust blowing, settling on me and that old Dun mule. It got hotter and hotter. I was working a field of popcorn that day. All of a sudden that corn got so hot it started to pop. There we were, old Ben and me, with popcorn flying all around us coming down on old Ben's back. He started to shake, his teeth chattering like nothing you ever heard. All of a sudden old Ben fell over plum froze to death. He thought it was snow all along."

Jane looked over at her Tom. His eyes sparkling, he looked almost young. She could hold it in no longer, her laughter rang out like she had heard Florence's do so many times.

They both sat laughing bringing the girls to the door to see what was going on. Seeing their pa and ma so happy they quietly left them to be alone together.

"That was quite a story, Tom," Jane told him as she began to chuckle again. "I'm not forgetting that boy, he is going to get himself in serious trouble," Jane continued.

"He is a man, Jane, you can't treat him like a youngun anymore. He will be alright soon as he finds a good woman."

They sat together lost in their own thoughts watching the shadows creep up the mountains till the sun tipped the tallest peak and was lost to sight.

368

Annie of the Flowers

Sometimes in the night Newt had "snook" back to the house taking food and his hound dogs. A small tarp and blanket were missing from the shed as was his gun.

Tom told Jane, "My guess is he has gone off fox chasing till you get over your mad."

"That boy! He'll be the death of me yet. I hope he didn't take whiskey with him. He'll shoot his fool self," Jane answered.

Newt had brothers and sisters living up and down Beech where he could go if need be.

The house was quiet as Newt opened the kitchen door. Going to the "warming closet" he got meat and biscuits, took some ground coffee and salt, put them in a tin bucket with lid adding that to the sack he carried.

The moon was coming up over the hill as he started off up Bear Run. Old Bozer and old Blu trotted along by his side, their tails wagging in joy. Newt blew out his lantern. He didn't need light to travel as the moon got higher lighting up the road. He didn't want to use the oil up. He only had what was in the lantern.

The dogs wove in and out through the trees along the way. Coming back to get a smell of their beloved owner then trotting off again.

It was well after midnight as Newt followed ridge after ridge going into Roane County. He could hear old Blu strike a trail. He could tell it was a cold one from the bellowing bark he let out. Striking a low gap, he headed up another point to the ridge that circled around the village of Tarriff. When he hit the ridge, the timber was thick and tall, his legs were beginning to tire, must be on to three o'clock. Whistling for his dogs he decided to make camp. Found a big oak tree, spread his tarp on the ground and lay down pulling the blanket over him.

The quiet sent his mind back over the past few days. To the girl he had been seeing, she was a sweet thing from a good family. He

369

knew his mother would like her. Somehow he just couldn't decide to marry her. His thoughts trailed off in a jumble as sleep overtook him.

The morning song birds with their noisy chatter in the branches over his head awoke Newt. He opened his eyes to see the sun high overhead. Lying still, listening to the birds he suddenly felt as though something or someone was watching him. Sensing his dogs were off and gone, he slowly raised himself on one elbow. On a rock about thirty feet away sat what he thought at first was a child. Watching, she raised her arms above her head stretching and yawning. Throwing her head back her golden hair tumbled around her shoulders falling almost to her waist. The sun shining on it glittered like gold. A lazy smile touched her lips.

"Howdy! You sure do sleep late," she said as she turned toward him.

Newt was so surprised he hardly knew what to say. "Howdy yourself, little girl," he answered her.

"I'm no little girl. I'm sixteen," she shot back at him in a saucy voice, tossing her hair over her shoulder with a dainty hand. "I live over yonder in the 'holler.' My ma don't know I'm here."

Newt sat looking at the young girl before him. He couldn't believe the pounding of his heart. She was the prettiest little thing he had ever laid eyes on.

The girl got gracefully to her dainty feet and tiptoed through the patch of oxeye daisies over to where Newt still sat on the tarp. She sat down Indian fashion beside him looking into his eyes, "I like you," she told him.

"What is your name, little girl?" Newt asked.

"I told you I'm not a little girl," she pouted for a minute sticking out her lips to form a rosebud. "My name is Annie, with an 'E', my ma says."

Newt sat watching her, the light filtering through the oak leaves playing over her peaches and cream skin.

"What's your name?" she asked, her blue eyes with long golden lashes turned up to him.

"Newt, little Annie of the Flowers," he answered.

A child-like gurgle of laughter came from the baby mouth. "I like you. I like little Annie of the Flowers for a name," she said with another laugh.

The child-like figure suddenly jumped to her feet, "I have to go now. Annie of the Flowers will see you tomorrow," she went on

370

tiptoes, arms waving, her hair streaming out behind as she ran through the field of daisies out of sight down the hill toward the "holler."

Newt laid down, his face turned up to the leaves above him, "She don't seem real," he said out loud. "She is like one of the 'dancing fairies' Lizzie used to read to us about."

Old Blu came in, flopped down beside him trying to lick his face with his tongue hanging out a mile.

Newt reached over, rubbed the old dog's head, "Good boy, good old Blu," Newt said as he built up a fire, went to a stream nearby, filled the bucket half full of water and added coffee. He sat waiting for the coffee thinking over what had happened. Maybe I was dreaming, he thought to himself. The coffee finished boiling, he sat eating meat and biscuits and drinking coffee strong and black at peace with all around him. It does a man good to get away by himself. Guess I'll stay another night or two.

Stowing his bedding and food on a high limb of the tree he and his dogs roamed the woods all day. Late in the afternoon, he shot a rabbit. Bringing it back to camp, he skinned and gutted it by the stream giving the cast off parts to the dogs, built up a fire and put it on a splint to cook.

The moon came up and he could hear the whooo-ooo of an owl and other night sounds as he and the dogs settled down for the night.

The sun was high when Newt opened his eyes. He sure liked to sleep late. Old Blu was lodged tight against his back. "You old fool dog, move, I can't turn over." If anything he moved closer. "Move, I say." There was a delighted giggle. "Don't call me a fool dog. I'm Annie of the Flowers."

Newt turned over, their faces inches apart.

Raising the blanket, she slid over against him putting both arms around his neck, she kissed him on his mouth. Newt's arms came around her, holding her to him, the sweet little face nestled in the curve of his neck. His hands were in her hair as he kissed her eyes, her little nose, finally the sweet rosebud mouth. Fondling her she snuggled closer and closer, her gurgling laughter beneath the blanket sent quivering pleasure through every vein of his body.

"Little Annie of the Flowers, I love you, love you, love you," he said as he kissed her again and again.

"I love you, love you, love you," she answered, with more

371

tinkling laughter as she untangled herself from his arms. "I have to go now," she got up to her feet and away she danced down the hill. Newt watched her out of sight, again his body weak with his love for her.

Newt had trouble falling asleep that night, his thoughts on Annie. Again he slept late. Annie was nestled close to him. He turned taking her into his arms covering her face with kisses. His hands fondling the sweet curves of her body, their love complete.

"I have to leave today, Annie. I'll come back on a horse and take you with me over the hill to live in another county."

A silent tear rolled down her cheek, "Annie of the Flowers is sad," she said. "Annie have to say good-bye." Her laughter rang out as she raised a little hand waving, "Good-bye, good-bye," she sang.

Jumping to her feet, "Annie have to go now, good-bye, good-bye," the echo followed her as she disappeared over the hill from sight.

Newt sat looking after her. What a strange girl, he thought. And oh, how I love her. I'll marry her, he decided as he gathered his things for the trek through the hills home.

Newt arrived back at the homeplace near dark just in time to set down to supper with the family. No one questioned his absence. Jane said nothing, thinking it better left alone.

Sleep came fast to Newt that night, bringing dreams of dancing fairies.

A Mr. Noe rode in the next morning looking for Newt, offering him a job only a man with a yoke of steers could get to. Newt yoked his team of cattle and went off to be gone for almost a week. The end of the week when Newt returned he borrowed a riding horse and set off to see Annie.

Whistling as he rode along, deciding in his mind what he would tell her pa. He intended to bring Annie home with him as his wife.

Having a general idea where the house would be, he soon rode up to a small neat cottage with a picket fence, both were weather beaten but in good repair. A man worked at an outer shed hammering away at something or other making more noise than he did headway.

"Hello, the shed," Newt called as he rode over toward the man.

"Howdy, stranger, what can I do fer you?" the man answered.

"My name is Newt Jarvis from over at Oka, in Calhoun Coun-

ty. I'm looking for a girl named Annie, could you be helping me,"
Newt asked.

The old man looked him over from head to toe. "What you be wanting Annie fer," he asked.

"I've come to ask her pa and ma to marry Annie, I want to take her back to my folks, as my wife," Newt answered.

There was a long pause—"Recon I better get ma. You wait," the old man went toward the back door. Soon he and a neat-looking older woman walked toward him.

"This is ma. You better tell her what you just told me, young man."

"Howdy, mam, I'm here about Annie, I want to marry her and take her back to my folks," Newt stood first on one foot and then another, he could feel the sweat trickling down under his arms. This was worse than he had imagined on his way here.

The old lady pulled her apron up to hide her face as sobs shook her.

"What is it? What's wrong with Annie?" Newt asked in alarm.

"Young man, don't you know? Our little Annie girl—" the old lady broke down again in sobs, the apron covering her face.

"Our Annie, she han't right. The doctor tells us she never grow up in the head, always be a little girl," the old man finished. "You can't marry Annie."

Newt's heart died in that instant, he knew Annie was different but not this. Turning, he rode away not looking back.

Three weeks later he married Stella the girl he had been going to see and brought her back to the homeplace where she was accepted as one of the family.

Anis

The big house was full to overflowing, Minerva and "teacher," Metta and her man, Newt and his new wife besides the younguns and the unmarried.

Jane and Tom liked their big family around them. Everyone had a job to do and the work went on day after day planting, harvesting, building, and repairs.

The moon was coming up over schoolhouse hill as Mammy Jane stepped out onto the piazza. She could hear Newt's hound dogs in the distance. Standing with her hands on her hips, she listened. Looking toward the orchard she saw someone walking beneath the apple trees. Wondering who it could be Jane walked out the path toward the front gate. "Who is there?" she called.

The figure started toward her slowly taking his time. "It's me, Anis."

Jane waited till he came to her. He had gotten old the last few years. As she watched he seemed almost feeble. He leaned on the gate when he reached her. "The moonlight is so bright I just thought I would like to walk in the orchard one last time. I always loved that orchard," he raised his eyes to her face. "Almost as much as you do, Jane. I don't know if I ever told you or not—" his voice slowed, she could hardly hear the last words. "I have liked it here working on the farm seeing it and the younguns grow. You've all been good to me. I'm not much help now but I want you to know I appreciate it. You've done good, Jane, real good."

"You better get back in the house, you will catch your 'death'," Jane said, turning to go back herself. She watched as Anis turned toward the kitchen door to go to the cellar house where he had slept all through the years.

As the family sat down to breakfast the next morning, Jane looked around the table, "Where is Anis? He is never late. Dock, go see if he is sick."

Dock got up from the table and went through to the cellar house, "Anis? you lazy this morning?" he asked as he went over to the bed and shook the old man's shoulder. The covers fell back and he could see at a glance that Anis wouldn't be coming to breakfast. "Oh, Lord!" he said to himself as he hurried back to the family. "I think you had better come, Mother."

Jane got up and followed Dock back to the bedroom feeling in her bones what she would find. She stood looking down on the peaceful face of the old man.

"Go back to your breakfast, boy, no need to say anything till they eat," his mother told him. Jane started getting clothes together to dress the body. She would bring water and have Dock shave him as soon as breakfast was over.

As Jane returned to the kitchen, chairs were being pushed back. The family had finished breakfast. Only Tom sat with a last cup of coffee.

"I have something to tell you," Jane said as everyone turned toward her. "Anis is gone, he went peacefully in the night. Dock, you and Newt start on the coffin; Tom, you get someone at the grave. We will put him beside Harn. That's where he always said he wanted to lay." Jane was getting water and soap ready. "Dock, you can shave him for me first so I can lay him out." Everyone went to the jobs she had given them.

One of the younguns was sent to the store to put up a notice of the death and when the funeral would be.

By noontime there were fifteen or twenty men and boys at the graveyard, taking turns digging.

Anis now lay on a board in the company room waiting for the coffin to be finished.

Another trip up the hill behind a coffin. It wasn't as bad as when it was someone young. A fieldstone with an "A" cut into it was put at the head of the grave. Anis had told them many times that was what he wanted.

Jane said a last good-bye to a good friend, remembering their talk of a couple of nights ago. Somehow she thought he knew then that he would be going soon. They would all miss Anis, he had been around so long.

Dock's Jeannett

Jane didn't want to lose her last and favored son. At least not to a grasping little "twitt" without a brain in her head. Jane had worked for the girl's grandfather when young. This generation she didn't know. She made up her mind to see for herself. Dock had informed her he meant to marry the girl and soon.

The matched team of bays and the new buggy he took her riding in might have influenced her in making up her mind.

Jane wanted the best for Dock. He was the youngest and last to go, the very picture of her Tom and smart as they come. He had had every advantage in schooling, better than they could offer some of the others as they grew up.

Tom and Jane hoped he would pick the daughter of one of the big landowners who would match them in a wedding gift to the couple. This didn't seem the case. This girl's family or so she heard had little besides a lot of younguns and if her mother hadn't changed, a lot of pride.

As she saddled her riding mare, all this went through her head. She intended to have a talk and a good one with this little Miss Jeannett. Usually a few words to the point and a stare would make anyone Jane came up against quake a little and soon lose interest. It had worked with some of the girls that had set their caps for her boys.

It was a good long ride and on a day that didn't look too promising. Clouds were gathering in the West and a sharp breeze turning the leaves every which way, looked like rain by nightfall.

Dressed in her most severe black, Jane led old Nell to the stile block and mounted sidesaddle. Jane wanted to look every inch the Lady of the Manor. She found through the years that black would make the weak and unlearned quake and become unsure. She wore it to advantage whenever necessary.

Old Nell stood quietly while she mounted and at a leisurely pace they passed through the big red gate out to the main road.

376

As Jane rode along she enjoyed seeing the fat cattle grazing against the hillside and knowing they all belonged to the Jarvis family. The well-tended fences and fields gave proof of good management and a farseeing eye to the future.

Jane waved to her daughter who came out on her front porch with a youngun holding on to her skirt. The farm Tom and she had given to her daughter and husband for their weddin' didn't show much improvement. With a critical eye, Jane saw a gate to the pasture field hanging by one hinge. Metta would be the next one to get a talking to. "Never mind that now, I have other things to think on," Jane said to Nell as they rode along, up past the Frog Pond Church, gristmill, and store, soon to the hill she must cross that separated the counties.

A nod and a wave of the hand to neighbors along the way. They would all be talking and snickering knowing full well where Jane was headed and for what. She had never let their opinions bother her before and they wouldn't bother her now. She was determined to see this through and to "best" it if she could.

Finally in sight of the house which she had never seen before. It certainly was not to be classed with her house, but did have a well-kept appearance. A long L-shaped structure with a wide porch around the front "L." Whitewashed with catawba trees and silver maple in the yard. No down fences here or hanging gates. Neat picket fence enclosed the yard and that had a fresh coat of whitewash. A row of hanging buckets of Wandering Jew lined the porch along above the hand railing.

Jane saw a couple of young boys running toward the house to alert the family. Never having seen her, she was sure they knew who she was.

Jane went riding straight up to the gate in the white picket fence, with no smile of greeting.

Ora came out as Jane reached the gate. "Mornin', Jane, get down and come on in."

Jane hadn't seen her for years but she hadn't changed a lot, still had the arrogance she had as a girl. A house full of younguns and a husband hadn't changed that.

Jane knew she sat her horse well and that in her black she made a striking figure. They were on even footing now.

"I've come to talk to your girl," she said.

"Won't you come in then?" Ora asked.

"Have her come here, please," Jane answered.

377

Ora returned to the house. A minute or two passed and a young girl came out toward Jane. She opened the gate and came through within an arm's reach.

"Good morning, Mrs. Jarvis," she said as she held up a small hand toward her.

Looking her up and down she was amazed at her beauty, having taken her unaware, hoping to put her at a disadvantage. She was neatly dressed, sleeves rolled up to her elbow, her hair pulled back in a bun on her neck. A smudge of flour on one peaches and cream cheek gave evidence of being busy in the kitchen.

Ignoring her small gesture of friendliness, Jane stared at her upturned face.

"I want you to know that fancy rig my boy drives you around with don't belong to him. I hear you want to marry him because you think he has money."

Jeannett stepped back so as not to have to look up at Jane quite so much. "Is that what you think? You are wrong. I want to be friends with you and Dock's family. I love him and hope to make him a good wife, with or without your approval."

Jane was amazed that this slip of a girl would stand up to her in such a straightforward way.

"We will see about that. If it's money you want, I'll pay you two hundred dollars to leave my boy alone," Jane told her.

The girl's head snapped as though Jane slapped her, color flooded her neck and face.

Jane looked into her eyes and saw them change from baby doll blue to orange sparks and slant like a cat's eyes.

Suddenly Nell lunged, almost unseating Jane, something she had never had done. Pulling on the reins to quiet her, Jane could feel her trembling beneath her.

The girl walked over, put her hand on Nell's nose. She shivered and stood still.

"I think we should tolerate each other if we can't be friends," she said and with a smile opened the gate and closed it behind her as she went back to the unfinished work she had left.

Turning Nell quickly, Jane urged her to a fast trot down the road and out of sight. The strange incident of the look the girl gave her and the change in her eyes to say nothing of the way Old Nell carried on. Jane had never been up against anything quite like that before. She felt a shiver go down her spine. There wasn't

378

much that could give her such a feeling and she couldn't understand it.

Pondering on this, Jane looked up in surprise she was at her own gate not realizing she had traveled all that distance going over in her mind what had happened when she confronted the girl.

Dock came out and took Nell as Jane dismounted. With a smile at the corners of his mouth he asked, "Well, how did you make out?" not waiting for an answer he chuckled as he walked the mare toward the barn.

As Jane mounted the steps to the piazza, the rain started to patter on the roof. She had just returned in time it seemed.

Ora, watching out the window, saw Jane's horse almost throw her. She certainly cut a nice figure on her fat mare, all dressed in black and her back ramrod straight. She controlled the mare with ease and the help of Jeannett.

She dreaded to think what might have happened. That girl had strange ways. I will be glad to see her married into a strong family. She had watched Dock and her together and he was so bedazzled with her that she imagined she would be the strong one and have the whip hand, not him. His mother Mammy Jane was something else.

One had to admire Jane starting out with questionable parentage and on the road as a hired girl so young, and with no schooling, she had done well for herself.

They had the finest house in the county and the biggest and best stocked farms. Jeannett would be lucky to settle in a family like that. Ora had heard they gave each child a farm when they wed. Lord knows they couldn't give much.

Thinking back on some of the strange things that had happened, like the time Clark threw a rock and hit Jeannett on the forehead leaving a mark she carried still. It scared him when he saw the blood and he looked at his sister (he said she turned into a cat when she looked at him). He started to run, fell, and broke his arm.

Clark could tell tales that stood your hair on end, yet they were inseparable. Jeannett kept telling him she was sorry. Which thinking of it now didn't make sense. He was the one who threw the rock that marred her beautiful skin.

She would soon be married and that would settle quite a few things. Her work would be cut out for her, a few younguns and

379

the "spells" that Ora tried to ignore would be squelched like a bug.

It would be someone else's worry. Lord knows she had enough of her own. Jeannett was one of her prettiest girls and sweet tempered most of the time. In fact you could almost say she was her favorite even though she tried not to show one better than the other.

Dock Weds

The day was going to be hot, the haze hung low over the hill-tops with no breeze to stir it.

The big house awoke as day broke, the people within beginning to dress and start about their chores.

Dock hated getting up in the mornings and lay with one eye peeking out of his nest in the covers. Today was a big day in his life, his "weddin' day." Mammy Jane didn't want him to marry. It wasn't the girl he was planning to marry, it was just marrying she objected to. He lay thinking on the day ahead, a smile lit his face as he thought of his mother's trip to see Jeannett. They were a pair those two. They would get along alright, Jeannett could hold her own with his mother.

Dock finally sat on the side of the bed and put his shoes on getting ready for breakfast. There would be a fuss if he was late.

"Good morning, mother, Dad," Dock said as he sat down to breakfast. Jane looked at her youngest wondering if he had changed his mind about the girl. Deciding that he hadn't she said, "Dock, your pa and me have decided to give you Bear Run to run sheep on. That is, if you stay here with us, you can do whatever you want with what you make."

Dock looked at Jane knowing how she felt and that she was too stubborn to give in. "Dock, you and your wife come home when you are ready. I'm sure your mother will want you to. You are twenty-one and your own man now. You've been doing business on your own for some time and should know your mind. I hear she is a fine girl."

"Thank you, Dad, I know you will both like her. In fact she is a lot like mother," he ducked his head and looked at his mother from his lowered eyebrows.

Dock soon had his buggy and team ready in the yard and finished getting ready himself. He came through the house all dressed in his blue suit with his hat at a jaunty angle, his brown curly hair falling over his forehead beneath.

No wonder the girl wanted him. He is a fine looking man, favors my Tom, Jane said to herself as she watched him leave the house.

The family saw him off with joshing and teasing about his weddin' night.

Jane would have liked his weddin' in the big house. The girl's family wouldn't have allowed that. They would see her married at home before letting her go off with a man.

Jane thought of her own weddin' years ago in Jeannett's grandparents' big house, how nice Mrs. Cook had been giving her dress goods for her weddin' dress and making the big dinner. It had been a long time, she hadn't forgotten the sweetness of it and her heart melted somewhat toward the girl Dock was marrying.

Three days later Dock came home bringing his new wife. Bringing her into the sittin' room he named the family to her. "Dad, this is my wife Jeannett." The girl went over to Tom holding out her hand with a smile on her pretty lips, "I'm glad to make your acquaintance," she said. "Mother, I think you two have met," Jeannett didn't offer Jane her hand remembering the other time that she had, Jane was sure. The girl just nodded turning to the others as Dock called their names.

They were put in the company room to have some privacy for a few days.

The girl fitted in, going to the kitchen early to help with breakfast.

Metta was starting the biscuits, "How I hate making biscuits," she said to make conversation with her new sister-in-law.

"Let me make them, I always did at home, I don't mind," Jeannett said, taking the flour sieve from Metta.

As Tom took a biscuit from the big platter he remarked, "There has been a light hand to these this morning, our Metta does have a heavy hand with biscuits." They all laughed.

"Jeannett can have the job I hate it," Metta said. "If she likes she can come to my house and make biscuits every day." Metta looked over at Jeannett, "Now if she likes to do the wash I'll be glad to be rid of that too.

"Oh, I love clean clothes to hang on the line," Jeannett said.

Jane's ears perked up, that was one of the things she liked best, that and her animals and garden.

The newly weds settled in. When Jane had a problem with anything it seemed Jeannett knew and would be there to help solve it without fuss.

Jane still didn't like Dock being married but she had respect for the girl. She was pretty as a doll and could turn her hand to anything.

Jane had to admit she couldn't hold a light to Jeannett when it came to making biscuits.

Chains

The building of Newt's house was almost finished. Tom and Jane were giving him the sixty-five acres down Beech from the Yellow Jacket farm. They were putting the final touches to the little "Jinney Lynn" house. It would be finished in time for a party on Saturday night for the couple.

Everyone was excited getting ready. It would be a "pound party." Everyone invited was expected to bring a pound of something, butter, sugar, coffee, salt, or whatever they had.

Tom and Jane had planned to drive down in their buggy taking a pig and some chickens as their gift.

At the last minute Jeannett couldn't go. She had one of her blinding headaches, throwing up every few minutes. "I'll stay in bed," she told her husband. "You go."

Jane decided she would stay home with Jeannett. "You go along, Tom, you and Dock, you can take the things. I would just as soon be here."

Everyone was off laughing and joking, taking all the younguns with them to the party.

Jeannett went to the cellar house where she and Dock now had as their bedroom and laid down on the bed. She left the lamp burning on the bureau.

Jane sat in her rocking chair by the window looking off down the road at the lights bobbing in the distance as people went to the party as dark fell.

The house had never been so quiet since being built. The big rambling rooms with only the two women at opposite sides of the big house.

Jane sat thinking of all the things that had happened here, musing on her life how it had turned out. Jane sat on—the room in darkness. A small chamber lamp burned in the hall sending weak rays through the open doorway. The big clock on the sittin' room mantel struck nine, Jane could hear the echo in the hall.

384

There was a noise downstairs, Jane listened, there it was again. Bang! Clatter! she got up and walked into the hall and called down the stairwell, "Girl, is that you?" she listened, there was no answer. Swarp! Swarp! sounded as though someone was hitting the side of the house with a chain. It would be just like Dock and Newt to sneak back to scare them.

Picking up the chamber lamp Jane went downstairs and started across the cellar hall to see if Jeannett was alright. As she reached the door it opened. Jeannett stood in the doorway. "Is there something wrong, Mrs. Jarvis?" she asked.

"Did you hear anything?" Jane asked in return.

"Yes! Sounded like someone slung a chain against a building. I can't tell where it came from," the girl told her.

"Come, we will see what is going on," Jane said as she led the way from one room to the other all through the upstairs and downstairs. They searched to end up standing in the middle of the sittin' room floor. "That beats all," Jane said in bewilderment.

"Swarp! Bang!" came the sound again and again.

"There is a chain on the washhouse door, maybe that could be it," Jane said, lighting a lantern. They headed across the bridge to the washhouse. The chains were hooked over a nail tight and couldn't possibly swing against the building.

They both stood listening, the night was pitch dark around them. The lantern sent out a small pool of light for them to walk by.

"It must have been one of them ornery boys trying to scare us," Jane said. "Come on back to the house, girl, I'll set with you till they come home."

Nothing more was heard till the sound of the buggy driving in the yard. And the others coming home on foot.

Jane met Dock and looked him in the eye, "Did you try to scare us?" she asked.

"What are you talking about?" he asked.

Jane knew if it had been him, he wouldn't have kept the grin off his face. "Your wife will tell you about it," Jane said as she went back to her room and to bed.

Tom came home from the store a few days later to tell at the supper table of an old man falling down a well.

"The old codger was close to eighty and wandered around at night. They found him down the well next morning. He didn't have the strength to pull himself out. There was a chain down in the well. He had banged it back and forth against the casing trying to be heard. Knocked big chunks out of the well casing. It happened the night of the 'Pound Party' at Newt's house. The well was too far away from the house and no one heard the old man."

Jane looked over at Jeannett, chills going down her spine. The girl quietly left the table.

Nothing was ever said between them again about that night. Some very strange things had taken place since that girl had lived there and Jane couldn't understand the why of it.

She remembered another time. Prushia had ordered a new bonnet. All the way from New York and had waited weeks for it to come. Finally it arrived. She wanted her sisters to see it and was getting ready to go to visit. The bonnet lying on the bureau while she fixed her hair. Jeannett had walked over and picked it up to try it on herself. Prushia grabbed it back. "Don't do that, it's mine and wouldn't be becoming on you, besides your hair is dirty," Prushia said sharply.

Jeannett had walked away watching Prushia fix her hair and don the bonnet. It was fetching on her and she wore it with "style." She pinned it securely. The horse waited at the stile block, they all followed to watch her mount and ride away. Prushia was a fine horsewoman and rode straight and tall as her Mammy did.

She mounted gracefully, starting to turn her mount toward the road, the new bonnet went flying to land under the horse's dancing feet. A squeal came from Prushia as she grabbed for her hair that was tumbling around her face. By the time she quieted the horse, the bonnet was tromped to pieces.

Jane glanced at Jeannett, there was a small smile on her face and her eyes glittered golden.

Prushia cried for days over her bonnet. "Strange, strange!" Jane said to herself. There wasn't a breath of wind that day to blow the bonnet off and besides she had watched Prushia pin it securely.

Annie Two

Newt and Stella had been in their little house over three years now. Newt still got drunk now and then, when he did he tossed and turned in the night, "Annie, where are you? Annie of the Flowers, come back, come back, come back," and tears would roll down his face.

His young wife didn't know what to do. She would hold him tight till he would fall asleep. Their lovemaking at these times was something special and Stella never asked him who Annie was.

The autumn sun was high in the sky on an afternoon in October. It was a day when everyone went lazily at their duties enjoying the last of summer.

An old man riding a big workhorse came through the gate from the main road toward the house. He was dressed in patched clothes, the gear on his horse was old and worn. In front of him on the saddle horn on a pillow sat a beautiful little girl of about two years.

"Now who can that be?" the girls who spotted him wondered. Two of the girls were in the backyard as he rode up.

"Howdy, misses, I'm looking for a Newt Jarvis who lives hereabout, I'm told," the old man said. "Do you be knowing where?"

Going toward him the girls answered, "This is his parent's home, he lives down Beech not too far. Won't you get down?" Metta reached for the little girl as the old man nodded that he would.

"My! she is a pretty little thing," Metta said looking the child over, she turned to Jeannett—"She looks just like Mammy Jane," she whispered in amazement.

Glancing at the old man busy tying his nag to the hitching post, "I wonder who he is? and what he wants?"

Mammy Jane came out to see what the commotion was.

"Mammy, this man is looking for Newt," Metta told her

mother. The old man came toward where the woman stood. "This is Newt's mother, sir, I'm afraid I don't know your name," Metta said.

Removing his tattered hat, the old man bowed slightly, "I'm from over Roane County way, my name is Ben Parsons and I'm looking for your boy Newt, have business to talk with him."

Jane eyed the little girl, she knew at a glance that there was Jarvis blood there. Taking the child from Metta she said, "You girls get back to whatever you were doing."

"Come this way, sir," Jane took him to the company room and closed the door.

"Can you tell me what this is all about, Mr. Parsons?" Jane asked in a business-like way.

The old man twisted his hat around and around in his hands. "I would rather talk to your boy about it."

"I see—who is the mother of the youngun?" Jane asked.

A tear rolled down the old man's weathered face. "My little girl, she died and ma is sick and can't care for the tyke. We love her, she is the only thing we have left of our Annie." Sobs shook the old man as he tried to get control of himself.

"Annie!" Jane had heard Stella asking the girls if they knew who Annie was.

"Are you saying that this baby belongs to your Annie and my Newt?" Jane asked.

The old man nodded, "We didn't know till most time for the baby to be born. Your Newt come, wanted to marry Annie, he said he loved her. Our Annie was so sweet, such a pretty little thing—" his voice trailed off. "She wasn't right, our Annie, the doctor said after the fever when she was a little girl that she would never grow up in the mind. She got sick again after the baby and our Annie died. Ma and me figured we would keep little Annie, now ma is sick and the doctor don't want her to do anything much. We talked about it and decided her pa should have little Annie." He looked at the child as though he was parting with a treasure of pure gold.

"What makes you think the child belongs to Newt?" Jane asked, knowing from the moment she had seen the blond hair and blue eyes that she did.

"Our Annie was a good girl, she went for walks in the woods; she loved flowers and wild things. She told us she had met Newt and his dogs in the woods several times. Our Annie didn't know how to lie." The old man hung his head as he told the sad story. "Your boy tried to do right by our Annie, ma and me couldn't let him marry her and her not right."

"We will take the youngun and see that she is cared for. I think Newt's wife will want her, if not she can live here. She will know her rightful family," Jane said.

The little girl had fallen asleep in Jane's arms. She gently placed her on the bed and pulled the covers over her.

"Come and have some coffee and a bite to eat. I'll have your horse fed and watered," Jane said.

The old man sat eating a piece of bread and meat, a cup of steaming coffee before him.

"You tell little Annie we love her and sometime she come to see us again," the old man said as he mounted his horse to leave.

Jane took some money from her apron pocket. "My boy wronged you. I want you to have this to help pay your wife's doctor bills," she lifted the flap on his saddlebags and dropped the roll of bills in, knowing he was proud and wouldn't take it otherwise.

"Don't say the boy did wrong, little Annie now lives on," with that the old man rode away, the tears silently falling from his eyes.

Newt and Stella came that evening to spend the night. Stella wanted to stay the following day and do some sewing on the machine.

Little Annie was playing in the sittin' room as they entered.

"Whose child is that? Why she looks just like Newt!" Stella said in amazement.

"That's little Annie," Jane answered. Stella's eyes flew to Newt. A look of bewilderment crossed his face as he stooped to pick the little girl up. He looked into the face of the smiling little girl. "Oh, Annie! Annie!" he whispered as he buried his face against the child.

Jane told the story to them both as Stella sat holding the little girl, leaving out the part where Newt wanted to marry Annie.

When Newt came for Stella the following day after work, there were no questions as Stella carried the little girl away in her arms as though she belonged there.

The Peddler

It had rained for days and the mud churned into a mire stuck to one's feet till they were weights pulling you down.

It was still drizzling and dreary. The younguns played between the corncribs out of the wet.

One ran in with the news, "A peddler is coming up the road."

Jane went to the piazza to look. A man bent under his heavy load, a tarp over his shoulders, struggled through the mud. As he neared she could see he carried a trunk in a harness-like contraption on his back. Another smaller case hung on his chest.

At first she had thought him an old man. As he came closer she could see he was middle age and had a large gangly build.

Starting to come to the front gate, Jane called out—"Go to the back, man! and get some of the road mire off you." She didn't want the carpets tromped full of mud. Jane was mightly proud of her carpets and saw to it they were not abused.

She could hear him at the "boot scrape" on the back porch. Stomping and scraping to get the caked mud loose. Jane went through the long hall to the back to see how he was doing and to offer him a cup of hot coffee.

"Be gollies, that's a hog waller if I ever seen one," he said in his funny way of talking. He had removed the dripping tarp and loosening the harness, knelt on the floor to ease the trunk from his back. His sandy hair stood on end in a tangle of curls.

When he raised from the floor, he turned toward Jane, a giant of a man, somewhere toward forty years she guessed.

"Come to the kitchen and have a cup of coffee, man, and get the dampness out of your bones," she told him as she led the way.

"I be thanking you, Misses," he said, following her into the cheery kitchen. "My name is Timothy, I'm bound through these hills that remind me of the Green Isle selling a tad of this and a tad of that."

"You talk peculiar. Where are you from?" Jane asked.

390

"From Old Ireland, Misses. I'm a peddler with me wares going from door to door through this wide country of yours," he answered.

The younguns had started to gather around to hear the strange talk of the peddler and to stare at his big frame and cheerful face.

"It's a fine farm you have here. Aye, a fine farm. Would you be having a place a man could lay his head the night? I'm most worn out walking the bog the road has become," he said.

"We never turn strangers away. My man will want to talk to you. His family came from across the sea many years ago," Jane told him.

Tom came in, took Timothy in to the sittin' room where a small fire was lit to take the chill and dampness out.

Supper was cooking and the family started gathering for the evening meal. When the meal was over they all gathered in front of the fireplace for the opening of the peddler's big box and hear him talk.

The girls were all gathered around anxious to see the laces and ribbons from Ireland that Timothy had promised.

Jane had watched with a cautious eye as the big Irishman's eyes traveled over the girls, lingering longest on the lovely figure of Dock's Jeannett.

The peddler jumped from one side of the box to the other, bringing out this and that to hand to one of the admiring females around him.

Jane watched as he managed to get close to Jeannett brushing the back of his hand against her full firm bosom as he showed her a length of silk.

In its folds he slid his hand down her thigh. Jeannett jumped back as though his hand had been a redhot poker from the fire.

No one noticed in the confusion around the trunk of trinkets. Jane watched it all, saw Jeannett's blue eyes slant, the color changing as Timothy tottered and fell on the hearth stone, his big hairy hands clutching his chest.

"Stand back, everyone," Jane gave the order as she saw the girl slip from the room unnoticed.

Tom jumped up from his chair, "What happened to the man?"

The younguns stood back to give room to stretch the big man out on the floor. Jane went off to the kitchen to fix a tonic for him.

Jeannett stood calmly looking out a kitchen window.

"The peddler has had some kind of a spell," Jane said as she mixed the tonic to take back to the sittin' room.

Jeannett looked up at Mammy Jane, their eyes met but she said nothing as Jane hurried from the room.

They soon had the peddler sitting up in a chair.

Jane told the girls to put the things back into the trunk and close the lid. Then had the boys move it into the hall. "We won't be buying anything," she told them.

"I wouldn't put a sick man on the road in the dark," Jane said looking at the peddler as he started to feel better. "You may sleep in the shed tonight. You will find a bunk there. You had better leave at break of day."

Tom looked at Jane, a question in his eyes. He showed surprise but didn't question her on the orders she had just given.

She sent the younguns off to bed, their mothers' herding them off wondering what had come over Mammy Jane. None dared to cross her as they quietly and quickly left the room.

Big Timothy sat still staring into the fire, turning with fear in his eyes he looked first at Jane and then at Tom.

"What's in this house?" he asked. "I swear by all the Saints the Devil had his arms around me, squeezing till my breath had left me body, and I fell to the floor." The big man's hands shook as he held the cup drinking the last of the tonic.

"Your trappin's will be in the hall where you will find a lantern to light you to the shed. It's best you go now," Jane told him.

Looking all around him his eyes bulging with fright he grabbed the lantern and went toward the shed they pointed out to him.

When he was gone, Tom turned to Jane, "What did he do, Jane? What come over the man?"

"He done enough, the fear of the Devil is on him. Let's say no more about it." Jane picked up their chamber lamp to light the way to their room.

As Jane descended the stairs the next morning, she noticed the peddler's trappin's still in the lower hall. Going on into the kitchen thinking the big Irishman might stay to eat breakfast before leaving started to help with the meal.

When everything was ready she sent one of the boys to tell him to eat and be on his way.

"He's not there, Mammy Jane. The lantern sits, still lit, don't look like he slept there. The bunk is still made. No sight of the man," the boy she sent said.

"Likely he is walking around somewhere. He will be in for food," she answered.

All day the big man didn't show up. Jane would go into the hall to see if the boxes were still there. Seeing them where they had been stacked the night before she would walk through to the front piazza to look up and down the road.

Late in the afternoon when the man still hadn't shown up, Jane called Jeannett into the company room and closed the door.

"Girl, I saw what went on last night. The man was a scoundrel and I sent him packing. Now I want to know what has happened to him? Why would he leave without his packets? Do you know where he is?"

Jeannett looked Jane straight in the eye as she answered, "No, I don't know."

"Did you tell Dock what happened?" Jane asked again.

Again Jeannett answered, "He doesn't know, no one noticed but you. It's done with, I don't want to talk about it," she said as she left the room.

Several days went by. The boxes of the peddler still in the hallway. No one saw or heard of him. Finally Jane had the boxes brought into the company room. She sent for Dock and waited by the boxes for him.

"Close the door," she told him as he came into the room.

"What is it?" he asked.

"Do you know what happened to the peddler?" she asked her son.

"I never saw him after he left the fire to go to bed in the shed," Dock answered, looking at his mother.

"Open the trunk, we will see if he has anything to tell us where he has gone." Jane motioned him to open it.

Dock lifted the lid, looked through the contents replacing them when he found nothing. Turning to the smaller box he opened it. There were racks of small things, thread, shoe laces, and such. In one of the corners under the notions was a tin box. He lifted it from the case. "If there is anything it must be in here," he said.

Leaning forward Jane watched as he found the latch and opened the box. It was filled with gold coins and paper money. Jane straightened up in amazement.

"There's a fortune here," Dock told her. "At least ten thousand dollars." He counted out several fifty dollar gold coins, held them out for his mother to see.

393

Jane sat thinking for awhile.

"Go get a crowbar and close the door. Don't let anyone know what you are about. And hurry."

Soon Dock was back. Together they raised the hearth stone, took out some of the crushed stone base underneath and set the box of money into the hole, carefully replaced the hearth stone. "We could be accused of murder," Jane said. "What could have happened to the man? He didn't go off and leave all that money." Jane and Dock looked at each other trying to solve the mystery.

"Tonight after everyone is in bed carry the trunk and case to my room. Behind the bureau there is a door we will put it in the attic under the eaves so no one will find it. Don't mention this to a soul," Jane told him as they left the room and she turned a key in the lock.

No one asked questions about the boxes when they disappeared from the hall.

The big Irishman never came back and was never mentioned in the big house again. The box of money and his trappings forever hidden, with only Dock and his mother knowing the secret.

At times Jane would say to herself, what did happen to the man? There had been strange things happening around the place since Dock had brought Jeannett there to live.

Tom's New Home

She could hear the hacking cough of Tom. He grew progressively worse.

I'll move his bed tomorrow to the washhouse across the run where he will be isolated from the children. It will be said I've done it to be rid of Tom. It is clear to me that he has consumption, the coughing grows into longer spasms and soon the hemorrhaging. There was a slight trace of blood on his handkerchief today. His days are numbered, then the full burden will fall on my shoulders. I've carried the load most of my life but with the knowledge that a man was by my side.

The last days I can have him to myself again. Our time alone has been almost nonexistent. I love him still with a yearning no one ever dreamt of. My Tom of the smiling eyes.

Jane stood in their room looking out at the orchard, thinking of the days ahead. The girls had been sent to prepare the washhouse.

The big kettle filled with water soon came to a boil, the fire was let die down under the big copper bottom.

As soon as the sun was up, two of the girls took brooms, buckets, and plenty of lye soap and headed for the washhouse. It was to be spotless when Jane moved Tom in.

The feather ticks were carried out, beat and puffed and laid in the sun to air. All the doors and windows thrown open to let the spring breeze and sun in. The old straw ticks were thrown out into the yard where the boys took them and emptied them in the chicken house for the hens to scratch in.

They were to be washed and dried in the sun and refilled to put on the beds again.

Jane could hear the commotion as the furniture was being moved about and washed. There wouldn't be a speck of dirt when it came time for her to inspect the job. Her girls had learned early that Mammy didn't condone any nonsense.

Plenty of hot water, lye soap, and elbow grease cured lots of ills, she had learned, and they were learning it too.

Another girl took the emptied straw ticks when the boys returned them, shook out to the last straw.

Filling a tub from the big copper kettle and grabbing a washboard she set to work with the lye soap. Soon they would be hanging fresh smelling in the sun on the clothesline. As soon as they were dry they would be taken to the cowbarn where the straw was stored in the loft and filled with new straw.

Carefully lifted down from the loft so as not to touch the ground and carried back and placed on the beds. The freshly aired feathers put on top. A newly filled straw tick was looked forward to with zeal. It was a puffed up soft sweet smelling mountain of a bed.

Picking up the wash pan, Jane filled it from the teakettle on the stove, got a clean nightshirt and towel and went up to Tom.

His blue eyes followed her as she put the pan down. With her back to him, she lathered soap on the washcloth while she controlled the tears that came, seeing him so frail and helpless.

Lifting him she placed another pillow behind his head to wash him. Taking one of his hands in hers, she could feel the fever and dryness of his skin and her heart ached.

"You are going on a trip," Jane told him.

His eyes looked into hers and a smile flitted about his lips.

"A long one?" he asked. "You're not sending me back to the war?"

Jane had to smile. "No, not that. I'm going with you. It will be across water," she told him.

"Oh! Land and sea travel. I'm looking forward to the trip. Just as long as you are with me," he said softly.

They had so little time for nonsense or to be alone for that matter, always younguns around and sharing their room. The house was always full of others.

She quickly washed him and changed his nightshirt, combed his hair and his long white beard. It was full and luxuriant and she wondered if it maybe sapped his fading strength. He looked so distinguished with it. He grew it when he came back from the war to cover the ugly scars of the minie ball that hit his jaw breaking it and knocking out several teeth.

Jane puffed his pillows and put another behind his head so he could sit and look out the window for awhile.

"The clouds are falling," he said as he looked out the window.

Not knowing what he meant, she looked up the "holler" toward the cowbarn and there came a big puffed white cloud with feet walking toward them. The boys had filled the straw ticks and were walking them back on their heads. It did look like a walking cloud at that.

He gave a chuckle as she left the room.

To have something catch his fancy did her heart good as poorly as he had gotten.

After his afternoon nap, Jane meant to have the boys help him out onto the portico for awhile.

She knew in her heart it would be the last time he would ever sit there. The move to the washhouse would be the last trip for him until they carried him up on the hill. With that thought, her eyes lifted to the bright sun on the white tombstones and her heart gave a lurch.

She had lost so many but still had her Tom. How could she ever go through that. Losing him to the war so long was bad but she always knew he would come back to her. This time it would be permanent.

Standing in the kitchen door, Jane could see the girls were finished. They were putting things back together.

She walked to the bridge across the run and went to inspect the finished job.

As she stepped up to the front door, the fresh washed smell told her that every corner had been reached. As she looked around she said, "Good, good, we will make the beds tomorrow with fresh linen. Have the boys lay a fire in the fireplace and fill the woodbox. The evenings are cool and Tom will need the warmth. You have done a good job. Leave the windows open tonight and close the doors. You can get to your other chores now."

Tom's Trip

The day was sunny. A small pillar of blue smoke curled from the washhouse chimney. The bed had been made and the cabin was being warmed for Tom.

Since yesterday Jane could see he had gotten weaker. Dock and Newt came to carry their pa, making a chair by crossing their hands together. Jane helped to get Tom's arms around each of his son's shoulders. He was so frail, either one could have picked him up like a child and carried him. They made a big "Koo-Doo" about carrying him, not wanting Tom to know how bad he was.

Jane settled him in the nice fresh bed that had been warmed with the warming pan. The sun streamed through the windows making the room bright and cheery.

"This is nice, Jane," Tom told her and closed his eyes.

"You take a nap now. I'll go make you some chicken and dumplings for your supper. Jeannett will set with you," Jane said. He smiled. He seemed to like the girl and she seemed to like Tom.

Bringing some fancy work Jeannett sat in the rocker by Tom's bed as Jane went off to the kitchen.

Dock and Newt were in the sittin' room as she entered. "Your pa's real bad, boys. I doubt he will live a month," Jane told them.

They both looked startled, "Is he that bad, mother?" Dock asked.

"Yes! Your pa's going to die and soon," a sigh escaped Jane's lips. "He has the consumption. There is nothing can be done. I've watched him get worse each day. Spend as much time as you can with him. We won't have him through the summer." Jane left the room, her back straight to those who looked. What they couldn't see was her breaking heart. She would have to be strong. There was no one who could help.

Jane spent most of her time with Tom doing what she could. The doctor came just to make her feel better, there was nothing he could do.

"Tom, you get yourself up and out of there, the farm needs you," the doctor would tell him knowing he would never be up again.

"Jane will take care of things. She always has. They will get along just fine, Doc, without me. You know I won't be here long," Tom said weakly.

June came and Tom could no longer lift his head from the pillow when the coughing spells hit him. Jane had to raise him up to keep him from choking on his spittle.

She was up most of the night with him, at first she sat crying till her strength was gone. There were no more tears to shed now. She herself was thin and haggard looking.

Tom would manage to whisper, "Go, little angel, and rest, don't make yourself sick."

Jane didn't want to leave him, she didn't want to miss one word that he might say to her.

The first of July, Tom seemed to rally and get stronger as he told Jane, "It's no use. I'm just pulling you down with me. I'll be going soon. I love you, Jane, and have from the first time I saw you. You've made me a very happy man—" his eyes closed for several minutes. "You will be alright with the younguns around you. I don't want to leave you, Jane, but I'm doing more harm than good—I'll go soon, kiss me good-bye."

Jane bent over the bed and kissed the white face, "Oh, Tom, don't talk like that. I can't do without you, I love you so."

"That's all I wanted to hear, goodnight, Jane," he said very low.

Jane sat through the night dry-eyed, dozing once in a while to come suddenly awake to make sure that Tom still breathed. She could tell he was much weaker. Around three o'clock she felt a slight squeeze of her fingers as she sat holding Tom's cold hand.

Tom wasn't breathing. Oh, Tom! Tom! She buried her face against his. My Tom. He was gone. Jane sat trying to think what she should do. She went to the fireplace, punched up the fire. The kettle was on full of water. Going to the house, she went to the bureau in the downstairs hall where she had Tom's suit and clothes ready. The house was quiet, everyone still asleep.

Jane tenderly washed and dressed her Tom for the last time laying him out on the bed with a sheet over him. She sat waiting for the household to awaken.

Jeannett came to her before daybreak sensing something was wrong.

"Tom's gone," Jane said as Jeannett opened the door. "Go tell the rest, send word to the family. Dock and Newt can go to Spencer. I want a store bought coffin for Tom. Someone will have to ride to Nathan's and tell them," Jane knew that all her orders would be carried out.

Dock came to his mother immediately and stood looking at the sheet-draped figure of his father, tears streaming down his face. "I'll take care of everything, mother, you get some rest."

Soon the household was bustling with activity as the family started to gather. The weather was so hot and the funeral had to be hurried.

Tom was buried on July the Fourth. It was the biggest funeral anyone had seen in the area, people coming from miles. There were two judges and one attorney present, even the old doctor came.

Jane stood dressed in black to welcome the friends of her Tom as she knew he would want her to.

Several days passed before the family all left the homeplace and the household got back to normal.

Jane couldn't keep her eyes from going to the new mound on the hill as she wandered through the house listless and lost.

"I can't go on this way," she told herself. "There is the living to see to."

Anyone passing in the night could have seen a figure of a woman all dressed in black walking in the orchard. During that sad time she walked miles in the night when there was no one to see, walking away the hurt of losing her Tom.

Bear Run

Tom and Jane had given the Bear Run farm to Dock before Tom died.

Dock had built a small house and moved a few weeks after the funeral. Jeannett was expecting their first child.

Minerva and teacher had moved to town, not before leaving another baby in an unmarked grave. There were now five little mounds in the corner of the graveyard. Two of Minerva's, two Etta's, and one of Milissa's.

Prushia had gone away too. She still hadn't married. Too choosy, they all said about her, and too stuck-up.

The big house was almost empty. Metta and her man still lived on the farm Jane and Tom had given her. She came often with her younguns. The younguns were destructive and Metta was always wanting something, never satisfied.

The work had to go on around the place. Jane hired a man to help. Old Andy wasn't too bright but had a strong back and did what he was told.

Jane had decided to go back to breeding her horses and had every mare on the place in foal. Every day she was up keeping busy. Dock came down the "holler" most every day working at this and that.

Jane would saddle old Kate and ride miles if she heard of anyone having a sickness or of a birthing she could help with. You could see her go tearing up a "holler" all in black.

The months turned into years. The "comers and goers" had dwindled to a stop bypassing the big empty house.

The girls would come in the spring bringing a passel of younguns to run and scream, breaking things, leaving finally. Jane would just get things put to rights and another bunch would descend on her. It was no pleasure having them. They were so destructive. They none liked to work or for that matter, seemed to know what it was.

Dock and Jeannett had lived in Bear Run eight years now and had three younguns.

Suddenly or so it seemed to his mother, he decided to buy out the store at Oka. The man who owned it had been killed in an accident, and his wife didn't want to keep it.

Dock and his family moved from the "holler." The younguns didn't come by going to school now and it seemed lonelier than before.

Dock kept hired help working the farm and Jane would stop them on their way home to ask for news.

One by one Jane closed off the rooms of the big house. Stretching wires for lines she put all the feather ticks and blankets over the lines to keep them aired and so mice couldn't get to them. Laying leaves of tobacco among them to keep out moths and bugs.

Jane had been milking six or eight cows carrying in the milk then carrying it out and pouring it on the ground. "What's the use?" she asked herself as she turned the cows and calves together to roam where they would.

It was hard to get help, everyone had more than they could do at home.

Old Andy finally took off where there was more life. Jane couldn't blame him when he did.

Jane's big house needed whitewashing. The fields were growing up in brush and the fences falling down.

Every spring she would hire some youngun to whitewash the big tall gravestone at Martha's grave. While that was done, Jane walked around visiting each grave, kneeling here and there to pull weeds. Tom was the last to be buried. It was now fifteen years since that time.

Minerva had died and been buried somewhere in Ohio. She had come home a couple of years ago, an old woman. Her husband long gone and her younguns all with younguns of their own.

After these days Jane would go back to the house and have a big drink of tonic and go to bed to blot out all the memories.

Her beloved apple orchard was almost all gone now. As each tree showed the last few leaves on a long twig she walked beneath them talking "Good-bye, old friend."

The old woman sat looking up the "holler," a plate of cold meat and bread on her lap. Her eyes would raise to the graveyard on the hill as her thoughts traveled over the past. "They're all gone now, My Tom, and the children. Let's see, now, there is Will, and Lizzie, Calvin, and Little Ida—her mind would wander off to something else as she sat looking into the past. This July would be twenty-one long years without her Tom. "I've lived my time and beyond," she told herself. "I'm tired now."

She would take a drink of tonic not bothering with mixing honey and water anymore and go to bed to a dreamless sleep.

Dock and Jeannett had built a big house and closed the store. All their younguns were gone and they lived alone.

"We will have to do something about mother," Dock said.

"Yes. She is too old to be living alone. I doubt she eats half the time," Jeannett answered.

They went to see Jane finding her feverish and weak and in bed.

Jeannett cleaned up the kitchen and had Dock kill a chicken. She soon had a big pot of chicken and gravy and hot biscuits.

"Mrs. Jarvis, I've fixed your dinner," she told the old woman as she helped her to sit up in bed. The bedroom needed cleaning and airing. First they would have to get Jane up and feeling better.

Jane ate as though she was starving. "You are a good cook, girl, you've always done better by me than my own, I want you to know that." She laid back on her pillow and was soon asleep.

"I've never known your mother to be sick," Jeannett told Dock.

"She was always strong," Dock answered. "I sometimes wonder how she ever done all this, all the work and now it's falling down around her head."

"Someone has to be with her now. She seems to have given up," Jeannett answered.

Months passed, Jane got stronger and roamed around the place again examining this and looking at that. It wasn't long till she lost interest when she knew all her planning would come to naught. There was no one to do the many things that needed doing. She would turn away with a sigh, go for her "toddy" and sleep the afternoon away.

"Let her do what she wants, she has earned a rest," Jeannett told her husband.

Jane would awaken and call out "Girl! are you there? Girl! are you there?"

"I'm here, Mrs. Jarvis," Jeannett would answer, going to her.

Jane would pat her hand, "You are a good girl, go about your work. I'm alright."

The doctor was called in when after several days Jane didn't get out of bed. After checking her over, the doctor announced, "There is nothing wrong with your mother, Dock. Only old age. After all, she will be ninety-five," the doctor told him.

Word was sent to the family. Metta came right away.

"Here is someone to see you, Mrs. Jarvis," Jeannett said, going to her.

"Who is here?" Jane asked, "I didn't think anyone would come to bury a body if they died. Oh! It's you!" she said, looking up at Metta as she went to the bed. Turning away she said, "Don't let your younguns destroy the place."

"She is the same old Mammy Jane," Metta said with a laugh. She stayed several days. The last couple of days they couldn't get Jane to eat or drink anything. In the afternoon Jeannett leaned over the bed to straighten the covers around Jane's weathered face. Opening her eyes she half smiled, "It's you, girl," she said, closing her eyes again.

Metta and Jeannett sat talking. Jeannett got up from where she sat, "It's time I started supper" and went toward the kitchen. Metta bent over her mother, looking at her face, there was no movement. She put her hand against the wrinkled skin, it was cold to her touch. "Jeannett! Jeannett! Call Dock, I think Mammy is gone," Metta called.

Jeannett came rushing from the kitchen drying her hands as she came. She went to the bed, laid a hand on Jane's brow—"Yes, she is gone, I'll fetch Dock."

The undertaker was called to come for Jane. She would be embalmed in town and brought back home for the wake and funeral.

A lovely orchid colored casket was selected. Jane was dressed in black, which she had worn since losing her Tom. Her beautiful hair now snowy white and still curly framed her face. When she was brought home she didn't look quite right with her dust cap missing. A granddaughter found a black lace one among her things that Minerva had crocheted for her. It was placed on her hair with the ruffle framing her face. The dress was too low necked and the sleeves not quite long enough. There were yards and yards of black lace bought long ago to trim the coffins. The granddaughter ruffled some, added it to the sleeves to come well over the worn hands. A stand-up ruffle was inserted around the neck. Now she looked like "The Lady of the Manor," that she had become.

All the furniture was removed from the sittin room and folding chairs brought by the funeral home. A large folding screen with a sunset framed in maroon draperies stood behind the coffin. Candles burned in tall glass containers at each end of the casket.

At the funeral the house was full and only standing room as the front yard was filled. Loudspeakers were put out on the piazza for those on the outside to hear the hymns sung and the service.

Mammy Jane took her last trip up the hill to the cemetery. Flowers were sent in from everywhere. Twenty lovely granddaughters carried bouquets and preceded the casket, which was carried by the grandsons of Jane and her Tom. They would have been so proud.

The birds sang in the trees and a sweet breeze blew as Mammy Jane was laid beside her Tom.

The Legend of Mammy Jane lives on.

About the Author

Sibyl Jean (Jarvis) Pischke was born at Oka, Calhoun County, West Virginia. She spent many happy hours through her childhood on family land that had been patented by the Jarvis family before the civil war.

She attended the one-room school where her father had also gone to school. Sibyl graduated from the Calhoun County High School, in Grantsville, West Virginia. The school paper, *The Calhoun County Clarion*, published numerous poems of hers.

She attended the Capitol Academy of Cosmetology, a branch of Marshall College, Charleston, West Virginia, graduating as an outstanding cosmetologist. She moved to Ohio where she was owner of Beauty and Slenderizing Salons, and wrote a column called "Charm Chats," for a local paper. Attending the Community College in Cleveland she majored in the arts.

After retiring from cosmetology, Sibyl went into the florist business where she became a well-known and accomplished designer, with shops in West Virginia and in Ft. Lauderdale, Florida.

Sibyl is an avid gardener, belonging to several garden clubs, and winning numerous ribbons as a designer.

As a promise to herself and as a third career she has turned her thoughts to writing, choosing her paternal grandmother's life and her beloved West Virginia hills to write about.